D0975675

MEGAN MORRISON

TRANSFORMED

The Perils of the Frog Prince

Tyme #3

ARTHUR A. LEVINE BOOKS

An Imprint of Scholastic Inc.

Text and maps copyright © 2019 by Megan Morrison
Maps by Kristin Brown
The world of Tyme is co-created by Megan Morrison and Ruth Virkus.

All rights reserved. Published by Arthur A. Levine Books, an imprint of
Scholastic Inc., *Publishers since 1920.* SCHOLASTIC and the LANTERN LOGO
are trademarks and/or registered trademarks of Scholastic Inc.

The publisher does not have any control over and does not assume any
responsibility for author or third-party websites or their content.

No part of this publication may be reproduced, stored in a retrieval
system, or transmitted in any form or by any means, electronic,
mechanical, photocopying, recording, or otherwise, without written
permission of the publisher. For information regarding permission, write
to Scholastic Inc., Attention: Permissions Department, 557 Broadway,
New York, NY 10012.

This book is a work of fiction. Names, characters, places, and incidents
are either the product of the author's imagination or are used fictitiously,
and any resemblance to actual persons, living or dead, business
establishments, events, or locales is entirely coincidental.

Library of Congress Cataloging-in-Publication Data available

ISBN 978-1-338-11392-1

10 9 8 7 6 5 4 3 2 1   19 20 21 22 23
Printed in the U.S.A.   23
First edition, April 2019
Book design by Baily Crawford

*For my parents, Gerry and Mike, who never
let me get away with anything.
Thank you.*

TYME

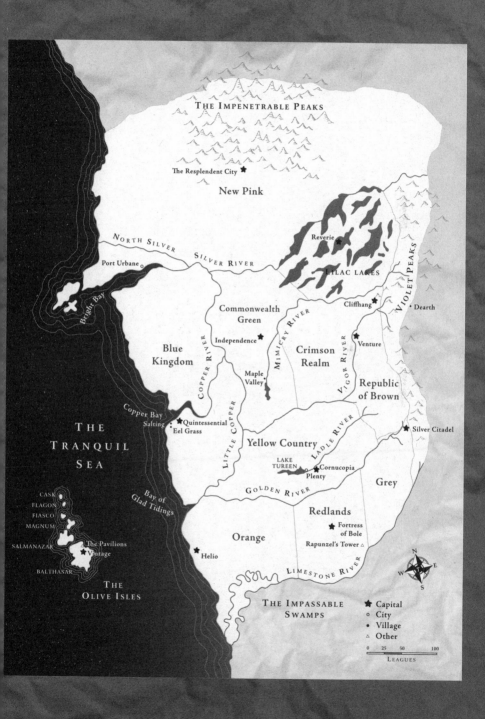

PLENTY

All-Tyme Championships (ATC)

LAKE
TUREEN

North Handle

PLENTY

Royal Governor's Inn

Copper Door Confectionary

TOWN
SQUARE

Lid Lane

Practical
Elegance

LADLE RIVER

South Handle

0 .25
LEAGUE

CORNUCOPIA

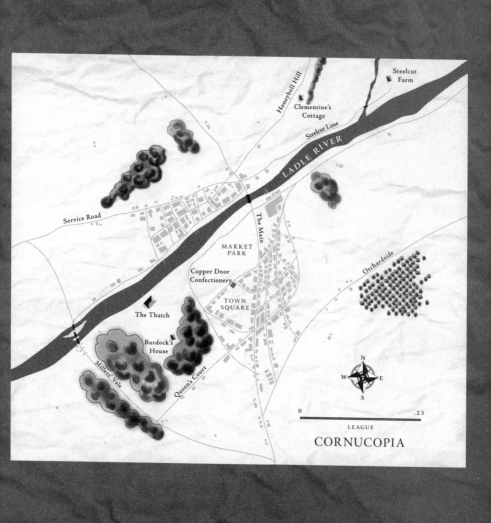

PROLOGUE

Fifteen months ago

UNDER a bright, hot sky, on a flat rock that jutted like a tiny island from a turquoise lagoon, the youngest prince of the Olive Isles lay laughing.

"Nice try," crowed Syrah as the so-called best launchball players in the country butchered their practice exercises. "That the best you can do?"

One by one, team Olive's human players were launched from the sea by their muscular, strong-tailed mer-partners. One by one, tucked tight like cannonballs, they flew into the air, trying to get high enough to clear the polished wooden bar that glinted twenty-five feet overhead, held aloft by two poles that were anchored to floating platforms. And one by one, as the players attempted to unfurl and gracefully arc over the bar, they smacked into it, knocked it into the sea, and plummeted after it. Syrah laughed harder at every smack, until he had rolled onto his back and was whooping with unfettered glee.

"Amazing," he gasped. "Best show on Balthasar."

"The bar's set higher than regulation on purpose, you know," snapped the only player on the team who did not have to call him Highness, because she was his youngest older sister. Marsala treaded water and scowled at him. "We're aiming higher than we actually have to," she said. "It's called training?"

"It's called comedy."

"It's harder than it looks, Syrah."

"It doesn't look hard at all." He'd played launchball a million times. He never lost. He would have been a significant asset to the national team — Nana Cava told him so all the time. She wanted him to play. Said it would be good for him to belong to a team, to work hard and accomplish something. Once or twice, he had almost agreed — he wouldn't have minded making his nana proud. But in the end, they practiced too much. Hours and hours of effort, every single day. He didn't need any practice.

"I could clear that bar no problem," he said, "*and* hit the center target on my way down."

Marsala snorted her disbelief.

Syrah sat up. "Give me the ball."

His sister threw the heavy golden orb at his head, and her aim was good, but his reflexes were better. He caught it and twirled it up onto the tip of his finger, where it spun for several seconds before tipping into his palm.

"Show-off," Marsala muttered.

Syrah leapt to his feet on the rock. He stretched his lithe brown body and untied his sarong, enjoying the admiring looks he got from a group of mermaids who were watching the scene from a nearby jetty. Still holding the golden ball, he dove backward off the rock, sliced into the warm water, and surfaced again beside his sister.

"Who'll launch me?" he demanded. Araxie, a muscular mermaid with skin the color of lilacs and arms as thick as tree trunks, put up her hand.

"Ready?" she asked.

Syrah grinned. "Always."

Araxie dove under, and the rest of the team swam away to give them room. Syrah treaded water until the current surged beneath him, signaling that Araxie was now hurtling upward and toward him. Instantly, Syrah tucked his knees under his chin, flattened his feet, and wrapped one arm tight around his legs. His left arm he kept tucked hard against his side, like a wing. In his left hand, he gripped the golden ball.

Araxie's hands struck the soles of Syrah's feet and pushed, launching him out of the sea and into the air, a compact ball of muscle. Tight and perfect he soared, keeping his head tucked until the moment he reached the apex of his flight. He raised his head. The bar was right before him. He unfurled his body and arced. The flat of his stomach just scraped the polished wood — for one frightening moment, he feared he might fail — but the bar did not dislodge. He had cleared it.

Of course he had.

Triumphant, he took aim at the target — a system of concentric circles made of rope, which floated atop the waves thanks to buoys. He hurled the golden ball at the center circle and dove again toward the surface of the sea, cutting into the waves. When he surfaced, he whipped back his long, dark curls, turned to his sister — and laughed at the scowl on her face. He had definitely hit the center.

"Here come the Gourds," shouted Araxie.

Syrah looked over his shoulder in the direction Araxie was pointing. The lagoon was fringed nearly all the way around with palms and flowers that grew wild on thin strips of white beach, but there was a break where this secluded place met the Tranquil Sea. Framed there between clusters of enormous purple hyacinth blooms, a great ship had come into view, flying bright yellow sails.

"I hear Delicata Gourd's a real contender for next year's ATC," said Marsala. "Maybe she'll practice with us tomorrow. I'd like to see her moves."

"Deli doesn't have *moves,*" said Syrah. "I always beat her."

"Last year, maybe," said Araxie. "But I hear she's been training eight hours every day, even when she's in a place where there's no water."

"Right," Syrah scoffed. "She launches without water?"

"She runs," said Marsala. "She lifts and practices positions — she'll be tough to beat."

"Gourd women always are," said a merboy who had just swum up to the group. His green curls gleamed wetly against his pale forehead. "Araxie," he said, and his bright green fins emerged from the water before him. "How's the water?"

Araxie put up her enormous black tail fins. "Kai," she returned, and the two slapped tails. "Clear and cool. You swam here with the Gourds?"

"So we can keep training. Deli wouldn't let up till I agreed. She's swimming here now."

"She jumped off the ship?" asked Marsala.

"She couldn't wait to practice, and then she saw you all through the spyglass, so she figured she'd join in," said Kai. "She wants to train for a couple of hours before dinner."

Syrah snorted. Deli Gourd was insane. He had never met anyone as dutiful and fun-free as she was. It was most of why he didn't like her.

But Deli liked *him* plenty.

He swam back to his warm rock, half-annoyed and half-curious. Deli was in love with him — she'd written him a long letter about it last summer. *Syrah, I can't take it anymore. I have to tell you something.*

He couldn't remember most of it, but a couple of parts had stuck in his head.

You think of us as friends, I know. I've stopped myself from writing this letter so many times because I don't want to ruin our friendship. . . .

Like they had a friendship. They spent time together twice a year, but that was only because their families were intertwined: The Huanuis and the Gourds had history. Big history. There was no getting away from that.

Last week under the waterfall, when you kissed me, I cried. You couldn't see it, but I did. . . .

He had definitely seen the crying, which was why he'd swum away as fast as he could. That kiss had been a joke — a complete joke. It wasn't any fun if she was going to be so serious about it.

And then, the day before leaving the islands, she had handed him that letter and asked him how he felt about her. He didn't feel anything, and he told her so. She was overreacting. If she wanted to pretend that one stupid kiss meant love, then that was her problem. Not his.

Now, here she was, swimming toward him with powerful strokes. When she reached Kai, she surfaced, glittering all over with water, her tight black curls tied severely back in a knot. She was leaner and more muscled than he remembered, but her face and shoulders were still covered in little moles that were black against the deep, dark brown of her skin. Those moles, thought Syrah, were part of the problem. Maybe without those things all over her, she would've been attractive.

He stretched out on his stomach with his arms folded under his chin, and he waited for her to notice him.

"Marsala," Deli said, breathless from her long swim. "Hi. Hope you don't mind if I get a few launches in."

"Spying on our team secrets?" Araxie teased.

Deli didn't seem to hear. She was looking up at the bar, shielding her eyes with a hand. "Looks high," she said.

"It's above regulation," said Marsala.

"Good," said Deli. "It'll be a challenge."

"The only one here who's cleared it so far is Syrah," said Araxie, nodding toward the rock where Syrah lay. Deli glanced toward him. Syrah cocked an eyebrow and gave her half a smile.

"Hey there," he said. "Miss me?"

Deli looked at Marsala. "*He* cleared the bar? Did he hit center?"

Araxie nodded.

"Ball."

Marsala looked only too glad to hand it over. Deli leaned toward Kai and whispered something to him, and he raised a green eyebrow.

"You sure you want them to see that?" he said, and Deli nodded. Kai shrugged and dove under, and Deli treaded water, her face grim.

"Think you can beat me?" shouted Syrah. "Let's see those moves, Delicata Aurantia."

She didn't acknowledge him. Moments later, she curled into a tight ball and — to Syrah's surprise — she sucked a breath, tucked her head, and sank beneath the surface.

One second. Two. Then — *slam* — she burst from the sea with speed and lift so intense that Syrah whooped with delight and pushed himself up to sit so that he could follow her flight. Her curled body flew up — up — over the top of the bar. She cleared it with a foot to spare.

Marsala whistled. "We're stealing that technique," she said, and Araxie nodded, staring up.

Deli arced. She stretched. She hurled the golden ball, smacked the center target, and dove into the waves again with such grace that she might have been a water fairy. Syrah sprang to his feet.

"*Very* nice," he said, when Deli finally came up for air. He dove into the water and frog-stroked quickly toward her. He surfaced so close to her that when he treaded water, his toes touched hers. She flinched at the contact. "Let's have a contest," he said. "One-on-one. You and me."

Deli submerged. She didn't surface again for nearly a full minute, and when she did, she had swum a startling distance toward the shore and was not slowing down.

"Guess she's not a fan, little brother," said Marsala, grinning. "*Interesting.*"

Syrah silently agreed. Deli Gourd had never been so interesting.

He swam back to the beach and jogged toward the Pavilions. It only took about twenty minutes to get there from the lagoon if the runner was fast, which Syrah certainly was. He sprinted, dodging palms and leaping over the gnarled roots of twisting olive trees. Sure-footed as a bezel, he raced atop the jagged rocks that lined the bottom of the high cliffs, only stopping when he came to a curtain of thin waterfalls that spilled in shining ribbons from a hundred feet overhead. As he always did, Syrah plucked a fragrant white flower from the plumeria tree that bloomed near the foot of these falls, and then he ducked behind them, enjoying the cool, delicious mist on his skin as he sidled along the slippery stones and onto the grounds of his family's palace.

The Pavilions were massive, covering much of Balthasar's northwestern shore with lofty columns and open halls, all startlingly white against the dazzling blue sea and sky. The buildings stretched high, connected by walkways and bridges, with many winding stairways leading up and up to airy apartments with domed roofs. There were enough of these to house many dozens of Huanuis, which was good, because the last time Syrah had tried to count how many of his family members were living here, he had gotten to sixty-five before calling it quits.

Before heading up to his room, he stopped by Nana Cava's apartments, where he found her sitting at the mirror, looking into it with her half-blind, hundred-and-three-year-old eyes. Syrah's second-oldest brother, Concord, stood behind their great-grandmother, braiding what remained of her hair in a wispy gray circle around the top of her head.

"All done," said Concord. He kissed her head. "See you at the feast." He passed Syrah on his way out. "You're dripping on the floor," he said. "You better not leave it for Nana to slip on."

"I *won't*. Skies." Syrah went to Nana Cava and tucked the plumeria bloom into her hair. "Nice braid," he said, grinning at her in the mirror. "You look ninety again."

"And you look wet." Her milky gaze penetrated him. "You're out there every day, Syrah. Why not just join them?"

"Because they're terrible. Deli's going to crush them next year."

Nana Cava's cloudy eyes narrowed. "You should pay attention to Delicata Gourd. You might learn something."

Syrah nodded. Paying attention to Deli was definitely on his agenda, though not for the reasons his nana hoped.

"What about next year?" his nana demanded. "Have you given your answer?"

"About what?"

"The apprenticeship in Cornucopia."

Syrah hesitated. He didn't want the apprenticeship. Following Exalted Nexus Burdock around during Yellow Country's election season sounded like the world's dullest way to spend a summer. But he knew better than to say so.

"I'm still thinking about it," he lied. "Weighing the pros and cons."

"The only *con*," his nana said, her voice creaking with the emphasis, "is that you would have to work."

"I already spent two weeks with Burdock last year," he protested. "It's not like I'll learn anything new."

"This is a rare opportunity. One that thousands of students in Tyme would fight for. You might even surprise yourself by finding it interesting. To bear witness to history — I tell you, it changes you. Are you so foolish that you would throw away that chance?"

"*Okay*, Nana."

"Don't take that tone."

Syrah sighed. "Sorry," he muttered. "Look — I'll really think about it. I will, I swear." He gave his nana a kiss, dried her floor, and left.

He dressed for dinner in a white sarong with olive embroidery that showed off his dark islander tan, and he tousled his long, damp curls into what he thought was seriously attractive condition. Then he ransacked his room, looking for the letter that Deli had given him — he was sure he still had it. Pretty sure. It had been full of compliments, and those were always worth reading again. It had also come with a necklace, which she had given him as a gift. He had never worn it, but if he could find it, then maybe tonight was a good time to try it on.

He found the necklace at the bottom of a basket of old schoolbooks, and he held it up, admiring its gleam. Mother-of-pearl, carved in the shape of a leaping frog, strung on a fine leather thong. He tied it around his neck and the cool shell rested against the skin of his chest. He checked the mirror and flashed himself a smile before heading downstairs to supper.

The Huanuis, hundreds strong, had gathered from all across the Olive Isles for the wedding of Princess Marsanne of the Olive Isles and Christophen Gourd of Yellow Country. Now that the Gourds had arrived, the Pavilions would be nothing but one big party for days — feasting and dancing by torchlight beside the sea. And this was only wedding number one: They'd all go across to the mainland next week for the second half of the celebration.

Syrah jogged down the white stone steps that led from his royal apartment to the grand terrace that overhung the sea. He ducked behind the wide green palm ferns that flanked one of the many columns, staying out of his family's sight. He could hear one of his sisters complaining — Bianca, who was massively pregnant and always in some pain or other — and he heard his mother reassuring her. Uncles and aunts chattered among themselves, cousins played their four-strings, babies babbled and wailed. The smell of sizzling fish hung in the moist air. Syrah moved along the back of the terrace, staying behind the big painted vases and stepping barefoot and noiseless along the mosaic floor until he spied Deli standing on her own at a corner of the wide white railing, staring away from the Tranquil Sea and into the west, where the Huanui vineyards stretched for leagues, all the way to Mount Olopua. She wore a yellow sarong that showed off her shoulders and collarbone, but her face, as usual, looked tense and worried. She had a crease between her brows like she'd just heard something she didn't like.

She seriously needed to relax. He had some ideas on how he could help her with that.

"Uncle Syrah?" His twelve-year-old niece, Asti, peered at him through the leaves of the fern he was hiding behind. "What are you doing?"

Syrah held a finger to his lips. "Playing a game," he whispered. "Want to help me win?"

Asti looked intrigued. "How?"

"Go get Deli Gourd. Tell her she needs to hurry down to the bottom of those steps there — the ones that go down to the vine-yards. *Don't* tell her I told you to."

"What if she asks why?"

"Tell her that you think somebody might be hurt."

Asti shrugged and headed off toward Deli, while Syrah moved quickly toward a set of steps that led down from the terrace to where the vineyards met the beach. He hopped up onto the sloping white wall that served as a railing, jogged lightly to the bottom of it, and stood there for a moment to bask in the sunset.

The Tranquil Sea was breathtaking here. Nowhere else in Tyme did it reveal its full glory. Syrah had been to the mainland many times; he'd seen plenty of its coastline and its beaches. It didn't com-pare. The sea that met the mainland was dark and moody; the waves were cold and rough, the surface sharp and hard. Not like home.

Here the sea kissed the white shores, calm and soft, warm and inviting. Here the water was clear all the way to the bottom, every silver fish and pink shell visible beneath its surface. Here the waves made rhythmic music as they moved, lulling everyone into serenity.

He heard quick footsteps approaching, and he leapt down from his perch and hurried in between two long rows of grapevines, crouching to stay hidden.

"Hello?" he heard Deli call. "Do you need help? Where are you?"

Syrah grabbed a vine and shook it a little. The moment Deli slipped in between the long rows of vines, he stood up fast, bringing them nose-to-nose. She shouted and backed right into the corded vines. Syrah couldn't help laughing.

"What's the matter with you?" she demanded angrily. "I thought someone was really hurt!"

"I *am* hurt. You wouldn't even talk to me earlier."

Deli turned away and tried to leave, but Syrah grabbed her hand and held it fast.

"Stop it," she said through her teeth.

"Stop what?"

"Bothering me." She yanked her hand out of his grip and ran back to the narrow steps that led up to the Pavilions.

Syrah ran faster, sidestepped her on the stairway, then turned around and blocked her path. "That sarong suits you," he said. "You should dress like that more often."

"Get *out* of my *way*."

"Notice anything?" he replied, and he tapped the necklace. "Remember this?"

Deli looked away and said nothing.

"I kept your letter, you know."

"Just move!" She sounded almost tearful.

"You don't want to be around me anymore?"

She met his gaze, and in her eyes was the same devastating seriousness that had made him swim away from her last year. Tonight, though, he was glad to see it. She *did* still like him. She was just trying really hard to hide it. If he said the right things, he was pretty sure that he could make her kiss him again within the hour.

"Okay. I get it," he said quietly. He slouched a little to affect sadness, and stepped aside. "I just hoped we could hang out and talk."

It was a risk — she might really leave — but he didn't think so. She glared at him, fists clenched. "Fine," she said. "Talk."

Syrah one. Deli zero.

"Is your dad running for reelection next year?" he asked.

She looked surprised by his choice of subject. "It's . . . not public knowledge yet," she said slowly. "But actually, he might not."

"He'd give up being governor? Why?"

"My grandmother doesn't want him to run. She knows he'll just keep winning, and she wants somebody else to have a chance. And nobody says no to Grandmother Luffa."

That was because Grandmother Luffa was terrifying. She was also, in Syrah's opinion, very wrong. "She still thinks democracy is the way to go, huh?" he asked.

"It's better than staying stuck in a monarchy."

Syrah clapped a hand to his heart as though wounded. His family had been monarchs of Olive for a thousand years.

"No offense," Deli added, smirking a little.

Syrah shook his head and sat down on the stone steps. "If you want to mess up your whole country, be my guest."

"Democracy doesn't 'mess up' the country," Deli answered, her tone quick and warm. "It gives people a voice!"

"An uneducated, inexperienced voice," said Syrah, folding his arms and leaning back. He had studied this topic last spring, during his two-week internship with Nexus Burdock of Yellow Country. He always had to spend time with diplomats when his family traveled — it was supposed to improve his ambassadorial skills for later in life. Usually it was a deadly bore, but with Burdock it hadn't been as bad. The Nexus liked to debate, and he didn't dumb things down like some teachers; he made it hard for Syrah to beat him. Deli didn't know what she was in for.

"The people of Yellow Country aren't uneducated!" she said hotly.

"Your citizens know how to read and write," Syrah agreed. "But we're talking about running a country. A monarchy ensures that future rulers are raised from birth with a complete understanding of international history, law, and policy. They're schooled in the delicate arts of negotiation and intercultural customs, not to mention martial strategy in case there's a need for war. Is that what your people learn in school?"

"Well — no. But they could learn it later, if they decided to train for leadership."

"A few years of training can't make up for a lifetime of learning," said Syrah. "A monarch is raised in the heart of government and understands the nuances of rule."

"But what if that monarch turns out to be a tyrant? Look at the Pink Empire."

"They're the exception. No other monarchy in Tyme has been violent."

"Crimson."

"They're run by fairies." Syrah waved a dismissive hand. "They don't count. But as long as we're looking at countries, how about Orange? The most enlightened, most educated country in Tyme, so people say. And they're a monarchy."

"An *elected* monarchy."

Syrah shrugged. "They understand the power of tradition," he said. "They didn't scrap their whole system like Yellow is trying to."

"You think tradition is more important than freedom?"

"Our people in Olive are perfectly free."

"Except they don't get to choose their leaders or their laws."

"And your people do? What if forty percent of your people vote for a candidate that doesn't get elected? Don't those forty percent have to live with whatever leader the other people picked?"

Deli looked at a loss. "If it's what the majority wants . . ."

"Then the rest of your people don't matter, because there are less of them?"

Her eyebrows flew up. "I did *not* say that."

"*Now* forty percent of your populace is dissatisfied," said Syrah. "These dissidents will band together to undermine the elected leader. They might even bring about a civil war."

"Dissidents?" Deli repeated, frowning. "Did you read a history book to impress me or something?"

"So you're impressed," said Syrah, grinning. "Good. Now admit you're wrong."

"You made good points," said Deli. "But I'm still right."

"Then let's agree to disagree." He put out his hand.

She hesitated, eyeing him, and then she shook his hand and dropped down to sit on the step beside him. "I didn't realize you cared this much about government."

"I'm supposed to be in Yellow to observe the election next year. It's part of my ambassadorial training. Nexus Burdock offered me an apprenticeship."

"*You're* going to apprentice with the Nexus?"

"Why so surprised?"

"Uh, because it sounds like *work*."

"Maybe I'm starting to like a little work."

It was a good lie, and it had the desired effect. Deli's eyes changed. She considered him with real interest. "This is a new side of you," she said.

"Do you like this side of me?"

She glanced away from him. "I should get back," she said, but she didn't get up.

He nudged her bare shoulder with his. "Want to take a walk?"

She looked pained. "Syrah . . ."

"Come on," he said quietly, and took her hand. When he pulled her to her feet, she dropped his hand — but she walked away beside him. It was almost dark now, and torchlight danced along the shore. Deli shivered, and Syrah put his arm around her.

"Cold?" he asked.

She stopped walking. "You're being way too nice," she said. "I know you don't mean it."

"Why would I do it if I didn't mean it?"

"Good question," she said, drawing back. She crossed her arms. "What do you want?"

Syrah smiled. "Nothing. I just like you."

"Name one thing you like about me."

He shrugged. "That was a pretty cool launchball trick earlier."

"I was good at launchball last year. You didn't like me then."

"How can you say that? I kissed you, remember?"

This was clearly the wrong answer. She gave a low laugh and stepped all the way out of his reach. "Yeah, I haven't forgotten," she said. "See you around, Syrah."

She went back to the party. Syrah stayed where he was, watching her go, but he did not pursue her. Not yet. If this was how she wanted to play it, then he would gladly play. Hard to get was fun to get.

✦   ✦   ✦

As it turned out, however, Deli was frustratingly good at staying ungotten. The next day, during the wedding preparations, Syrah couldn't find her anywhere. The day after that, during the actual wedding, he had too many ceremonial duties to uphold to do practically anything else. He tried to wriggle out of them, but no luck; Nana Cava was half-blind, but she still saw everything. There was one moment, right after the ceremony and before the feast began, when he almost caught up with Deli on the beach, but Nana Cava grabbed him by the back of his tunic. For such an old woman, she had a surprisingly good grip.

"You didn't braid your wreaths."

"Yes I did," he lied. "All twenty. Maybe somebody else didn't do theirs."

"Come with me and do your job," she said. She leaned on his arm. "Now."

Reluctantly, he supported his nana back into the arching halls of the Pavilions. They walked among the columns, until they reached the small room where all the wreaths had been assembled. A pile of palm leaves and twine sat waiting for him.

"Sit."

Syrah sat. He picked up leaves and started quickly braiding them together. Nana Cava slapped them out of his hand.

"Like I taught you," she said. "Use the peg."

"Who cares how good they are? People are just going to make stupid wishes on them and throw them in the fire."

Nana Cava didn't answer. She slowly settled onto a stool and fixed her eyes on him.

Syrah scowled and started braiding. It was ten full minutes before his nana spoke.

"Delicata Gourd has your attention."

Syrah glanced at her. "So?"

"So why should any girl of substance bother with you, the way you behave?"

Syrah tossed his hair. "Have you *seen* me, Nana?"

Nana Cava snorted. "One day, you will look like *this*," she said, pointing a gnarled finger at her wrinkled face. "What else are you made of?"

"Money? A royal title? I'm told my sense of humor is amazing —"

"Be serious." Her voice was hoarse. "Every day, whether you mean to or not, you are becoming the man you will *be* —"

She stopped and coughed. The sound was so cracked and rough that it made Syrah feel cold, and he looked up from his wreaths, trying not to be afraid. She sounded older all the time, but he couldn't let himself think about it. Nana Cava was going to live forever.

When he had assembled twenty proper wreaths, he carried them to the upper dining hall, which overlooked the sea. It had no walls except for the columns that held up the roof, so Syrah had a perfect view of the torchlit beach, though he barely appreciated the beauty of it. He stood at the top of the steps, handing each guest a braided palm circle and wishing he could just go and talk to Deli, who was standing at the head of his family's table, listening intently to something his mother was saying.

When he was finally done, he sidled up to Deli, who didn't notice he was there.

"We won't need an army." Syrah's eldest brother, Crown Prince Taurasi the Perfect, was speaking. Their mother, Queen Claret, was listening intently to him, as she always did, her hands clasped in front of her mouth.

"We don't know that," she replied. "Force may be necessary."

"Better to have it and not need it," Syrah's eldest sister, Barbera, put in.

"You're suggesting we should send our army across the sea, march them to the Resplendent City, and then turn them around and bring them home, just as an exercise?" said Taurasi. "That's an extraordinary and unnecessary expense."

"Perhaps," said his mother. "But the Pink Empire cannot be trusted."

Syrah was surprised into speech. "Pink Empire?" he echoed. "Why bother with them? They've been asleep a hundred years."

His siblings looked at him, some with pity and tolerance, but most wearing expressions of annoyance. They never wanted his opinion. Syrah glared back at them all.

"How are your studies going, Syrah?" asked his father, chuckling.

"Not well, apparently," said Barbera. "Ever heard of the Hundred-Year Day, baby brother?"

"Obviously," Syrah shot back. "But that's almost two years away."

Their mother spoke — but not to him. She hadn't so much as glanced in his direction. Her focus was still on Taurasi. "Everyone who has ever underestimated the Pink Empire has paid in blood," she said to her eldest child and heir. "They may be asleep, but I will not disregard history — and neither should you."

So they weren't going to answer his question. But he was used to that. He turned to talk to Deli instead — and realized that he had missed his chance. She had returned to her family's table and wedged herself in between her mother and her brothers, too snugly for Syrah to sit near her.

Frustrated, he went down to the shore. He waited by the great fire until the guests gathered on the beach to toss their wreaths into the flames, shouting their good wishes for the happy couple. Syrah prowled the crowd in search of Deli — this was a perfect moment to kiss her, if only he could find her — but either she was expertly avoiding him, or she had already gone to bed.

By the end of the week, he still hadn't managed to speak two words to her. They boarded separate family ships to the mainland, and for a few days, he could only stew. He brought her old letter with him onto the ship and read it several times, slowly, noticing things he'd skipped over before. *I'm not your friend. I'm so much more than that — or at least I could be, if you'd let me. I'd do anything for you. Whenever you walk into a room, I can't breathe. . . .*

It was deadly flattering stuff. Cold as she might be acting, this was how she felt, and he had no doubt that he could get her to admit it.

"What's this?" Marsala demanded. She had sneaked up to the railing where he stood, and now she snatched the letter out of his hand. "'I love you,'" she read aloud. "'I don't know how to stop. I've tried to for so long. . . .'" She made a face like she'd eaten bad fish. "What crazy person would write this to a spoiled brat like you?" She flipped the letter over, and her eyebrows flew up. "Not Deli Gourd," she said. "She never."

"She's in love with me."

"I doubt it," said his sister. "She couldn't get away from you fast enough all week long." She eyed the letter. "When did she write this?"

"None of your business," said Syrah, snatching the letter back.

"So it's old," said Marsala. A delighted look crossed her face. "You're standing here in the sunset reading an old letter? Sounds like *you're* the lovesick one. Too bad you'll never get her."

"Want to bet?"

"You're disgusting," said his sister, turning on her heel. "No, I don't want to *bet*."

Syrah stuffed the letter into his pocket and gripped the ship's railing. He *could* get Deli Gourd — and when they reached Cornucopia, he intended to prove it.

The second wedding feast was held after sunset in the grand back gardens of the governor's mansion, which everyone called the Thatch. It had a sprawling, sun-bright, straw-thatched roof, and dozens of big picture windows that looked out on the surrounding farmland and the Ladle River. The night was clear and full of stars, and early spring warmth touched the air. Magic flames thrashed in small crystalline lanterns that floated in rows, forming a pathway through the empty pumpkin field and casting soft lights over the yellow starflowers that had been scattered like a carpet over the grass.

The smell of hyacinth mingled with the scents of fresh-baked bread and grilled beef that wafted across the grounds. Mingled sounds of laughter and feasting and music filled the garden, making the atmosphere complete.

It was nice enough, Syrah thought, squinting critically at the lanterns. But the wedding on the beach had looked better. Nowhere was more romantic than the sea. His eyes traveled the party, searching for Deli, who as usual was difficult to locate.

He finally found her standing near an enormous kettle of stew, wearing the official colors of her country — a dress the color of a sheaf of wheat, and butter-yellow starflowers in her curls. She was talking to a young man whose dark skin glinted as he moved, as though his flesh were studded with gold flecks. Syrah was momentarily distracted. He had seen Blue fairies with skin the color of sapphires and merboys with tails as orange as flame, but he had never seen anyone whose skin appeared to be laced with metal. It had to be magic, to shine like that. The young man took Deli's hand and kissed the back of it, then tipped his big country-boy hat and headed back to his own table.

She was alone.

Quickly, Syrah slipped away from his family. He headed toward Deli, taking a roundabout path so she wouldn't see him coming and try another dodge.

The *ting* of silver striking crystal rose above the din of conversation. The guests fell silent. At the head table, Grandmother Luffa stood. Like Nana Cava, Luffa was 103 years old, but because she was fairy-born she looked and sounded no more than 50.

"Ninety-eight years ago," she said, her voice ringing out across the feast, "the Pink Empire seized these gardens where we stand. My parents and siblings were slaughtered in the house behind me, and my country was conquered for the second time."

Silence ruled the garden. Not a bite was eaten, not a single bird called. Syrah stopped dead in his tracks, just behind Deli's shoulder.

"I do not wish the terrible events of that night to bring grief to this beautiful union," Grandmother Luffa went on. "But history must be remembered if joy is to be appreciated fully. I alone escaped the brutal events that deprived me of my family. I alone was smuggled away to a place where I gained a second family. A family to whom I owe not only my life, but the life of my country."

Syrah heard Deli sniffle.

"The Huanuis did more than take me in. They raised me as a sister to their own children — to Cava, dearest to my heart. When I grew old enough, the Huanuis gave me their army, and Cava herself rode with me across the waves and into battle. Together, with the might of the Olive Isles behind us, we defeated the Pink usurpers and reclaimed this country's independence. The Huanuis spilled their blood with ours. Because of them, we live free."

Deli sniffled again and reached into her pocket. She withdrew a handkerchief and dabbed at her eyes.

"For many decades since, a wish in both Cava's heart and mine has been to see our blood joined for happier reasons. The joy this marriage brings to us cannot be described." She placed one hand on Marsanne's shoulder, the other on Christophen's. "Ancestors, bless them," she said. "Ancestors, guide their union. Give them peace and bounty. Let them turn with the years as the soil turns, ever renewed, ever fruitful."

"As the soil turns," replied the congregation in one voice as

Marsanne and Christophen kissed. The guests cheered and threw salt toward the happy couple.

Syrah leaned forward until his mouth nearly brushed Deli's ear. "Hi there," he said.

Deli yelped and nearly jumped out of her skin. She whirled to look at him.

"I'm trying to pay attention!" she hissed. "Have some respect."

Syrah gestured toward the married couple. "Hope that'll be us someday?"

"Us?" Deli repeated in disbelief.

"So that you can be more than my friend," he said, grinning. "And do anything for me."

Deli's eyes hardened. "Stop quoting that stupid letter," she whispered. "Didn't I already pay enough for writing it?"

"Pay how?"

"Don't you even remember what you said?"

Syrah frowned. What had he said? His memory was vague.

Deli gave a rich snort and stalked away, out toward the dark meadow beyond the gardens.

He pursued her. "Remind me," he said, when they were far enough from the party that no one could possibly hear them.

"You called me pathetic," said Deli, rounding on him. "You said kissing me was a joke, and I couldn't expect you to like me when you could get a million prettier girls on Balthasar. You told me to come back here and find some farmer boyfriend who wouldn't care that I have all these *moles*."

Syrah cringed. Now he remembered. "I'm sorry," he said, and he meant it. "I shouldn't have said that. Your letter just surprised me — I didn't know how to react."

"You were cruel."

"And I'm *sorry*," Syrah repeated, impatient. "What else do you want me to say?"

"Nothing. You did me a favor. I didn't think I could ever get over you."

"But now you *are* over me?" He gazed straight into her eyes. "Are you sure?" He leaned in, but she shoved him back.

"Don't you dare kiss me again and pretend like it's nothing."

Syrah couldn't help rolling his eyes a little. "Why does every little thing have to be such a big deal with you?" he said. "It's just a kiss."

"I don't do *just* a kiss. I *mean* the things I do." She wheeled around and headed back toward the party with quick steps.

He dogged her. "Deli, come on. I apologized. You're being unreasonable."

"Go away."

"Let me make it up to you."

"*Go away.*"

"You couldn't breathe when I walked into the room. You wrote that, remember?"

They had reached the outskirts of the party again. People stopped and turned to see what was happening, Syrah's sister Marsala among them. She stood by the stew kettle with a group of her launch-ball mates, all of them watching.

"Okay, fine," Deli said. "Let's say I kiss you — then what? Do you want a serious relationship with me?"

He hesitated. "Serious?" he repeated.

"Didn't think so." Deli put her hands on her hips. "You just want to see if you can win, and then you want to walk away. Well guess what?" She stepped up and got right in his face. "This challenge is closed to amateurs. Qualified competitors only, thanks."

Marsala whistled approvingly. A couple of her friends hooted in support.

The young man with the glinting gold in his flesh was also watching them. The one who had kissed Deli's hand earlier. He was sitting alone at one of the tables, leaning back in his chair, and his eyes were trained on Syrah like he was measuring him.

"Who's that?" Syrah demanded suddenly, pointing toward the young man. "Your boyfriend?"

"His name is Harrow Steelcut," said Deli. "And it's none of your business."

"I think it is," said Syrah. "I think you can do better."

"You mean *you?*" Deli laughed. "Harrow's worth a hundred of you. Though that's not saying much, is it? Anything multiplied by zero is still zero."

She pivoted and strode away into the thick of the party, leaving Syrah behind. Marsala and her friends burst out laughing, while other nearby groups of wedding guests whispered furiously, some laughing like his sister, others glancing pityingly at Syrah. He was hot with shame and fury.

"Burn," crowed his sister. "She cut you *down.*"

"Shut up!"

"*Grow* up," Marsala replied. Her friends enveloped her, and the group of them moved toward the dance floor, still laughing. Too angry for words, Syrah swiped a small rock from the dirt and was preparing to chuck it at the back of his sister's head when a firm hand grasped his elbow. It belonged to Exalted Nexus Burdock of Yellow Country.

"Don't," he said.

"Why?" Syrah shot, furious.

"For one thing, it's generally considered bad manners to throw rocks at parties." The Nexus smiled, and the lines in his face deepened. He had a lot of them for someone just barely over forty. "For another, that scribe over there is watching you."

Syrah glanced in the direction that Burdock was looking and saw a short middle-aged man whose quill was poised over parchment, ready to strike. Syrah lowered his hand and dropped the rock. Out of the corner of his eye, he saw that Harrow Steelcut was also still watching him. Syrah wheeled toward the young man and gave him a narrow glare, which Harrow met with a courteous nod. He tipped his hat. The gold in his face glittered.

"I accidentally overheard your, ah — interaction with Delicata," said the Nexus, pushing a hand through his sandy hair.

"You and half the party," Syrah said bitterly. He wished Deli would drop dead. Marsala too. "You think the scribe heard?" he demanded.

The Nexus was noncommittal. He fingered the gleaming amulet that rested against the front of his official robes. "I think we should take a walk," he said.

"So the scribe *did* hear?" It was bad enough that his sister and a bunch of wedding guests knew he'd been rejected. If that stupid scribe wrote up a story about it, then tomorrow, every single person in Tyme would know.

Delicata Gourd was going to *pay.*

"Syrah." The Nexus's voice was patient. "You have a good mind. Don't waste it worrying about girls and scribes — *use* it. You still haven't told me whether you plan to accept my offer."

"Offer?" Syrah repeated, unhearing. His eyes were on Harrow, who was making his way to Deli on the dance floor.

"To work with me next year, during the election. I can arrange a seat for you in some of the council meetings and you can observe the transition — there's no finer education."

Syrah barely understood what the Nexus was saying. Deli was leaning close to Harrow now, listening to him. When she drew back and nodded, Harrow glanced in Syrah's direction, caught his eye, and shook his head. Then he turned his back and put a protective arm around Deli's shoulders. Syrah had an urge to pick up the rock again.

"Syrah. Are you listening to me?"

Deli's triplet brothers chose that moment to come barreling up. They were twelve, inseparable, and troublesome enough to make the adults in both families despair. One of them — Tommy — seized Burdock's sleeve.

"We did something," Tommy gasped. "It was supposed to be a joke, but —"

"It's Tommy's fault," said Bradley. "He put it in the dough."

"The dough?" Burdock frowned, and then his eyebrows shot up. "Boys. Tell me you didn't tamper with the wedding loaves."

"I didn't," Bradley insisted.

"Tommy sneaked a Ubiquitous acorn into the dough," said Walter calmly. Walter was always calm. "Bradley dared him to sneak up to the kitchen windows and throw it in while the cooks were mixing. He said if Tommy didn't do it he was going to tell Roxbury Russet that Tommy likes her."

"And I *don't*!" Tommy cried, distraught.

"What kind of acorn?" Burdock demanded. Tommy cringed and said nothing.

"Ubiquitous Instant Fireworks," Walter replied.

Burdock looked at the feast tables. Hundreds of traditional Yellow Country wedding loaves, one for each guest to carry away as a blessing for their health and bounty, were being paraded out from the kitchens now and arranged in high piles on a long banquet table. "You don't even know which one it's in, do you?" said Burdock in despair. *"Boys . . ."*

"Can't you figure it out?" Tommy pleaded. "You're Exalted."

"It doesn't work like that —"

"It's that one," Syrah said, pointing. He had been scanning the loaves throughout the conversation. At the bottom of one of the piles, one shining loaf of braided bread looked just a little too shiny. Like maybe it was going to explode.

Burdock squinted. "I don't —"

"The glowing one," said Walter. "I see it."

"Look out!" Tommy shouted. "It's gonna blow!"

The boys raced toward the loaf table with Burdock close behind them.

"You're welcome," Syrah called after them.

"Your Highness."

Syrah jerked in surprise and turned to find that the scribe had sneaked up on him. He usually enjoyed the attention he got from being written up in the *Criers*, but not tonight. He bristled and edged away.

The scribe tossed back his long fringe of graying hair and looked over at the loaf table, where the triplets were now trying to pull the glowing wedding loaf out from the bottom of its pile without toppling the entire thing. One of the cooks tried to slap Tommy's hands away until Burdock spoke to her. Then her eyes widened and she began to lift loaves off the pile with incredible speed, until she had freed the one with the acorn inside. It was sparking now. Tommy tried to grab it, but Burdock snatched it from the cook himself, and held it between his hands. His amulet gave off faint light, and his hands did too, but the loaf did not stop sparking. Instead, it began to fizz loudly, giving off gold and green sparkles that danced up Burdock's arms. Looking panicked, Burdock flung the loaf high into the air — and not a moment too soon. It burst apart in a dazzling display of fireworks that lit the party and made the guests cry out with delight. They applauded.

Burdock wiped his brow, grabbed Tommy and Bradley each by an arm, and dragged them toward their parents. "You don't have to tell!" Syrah heard Tommy cry.

"That looks like a story," said the scribe, jotting down a few notes. "Troublesome triplets strike again, eh?"

"They're just kids," said Syrah.

"Unlike you and Delicata Gourd." The scribe smiled slyly.

Syrah took the bait. "What are you going to write?" he demanded.

The scribe consulted his notes. "'This challenge is closed to amateurs,'" he quoted. "'Anything multiplied by zero is still zero.'" He grimaced in sympathy. "Rejection can be painful," he said. "How do you feel, Your Highness?"

"Get lost," said Syrah, through gritted teeth. "You have your story."

"There are two sides to every tale," said the scribe. "Surely there's more to your history with Ms. Gourd. Something about how she 'couldn't breathe when you walked into the room.' When did she say that?"

Syrah stared at the scribe as an idea slowly occurred to him. Deli's letter. He'd been carrying it around with him since he'd left the Olive Isles. He dug into his pocket now and found it there, still folded. Waiting.

He gestured for the scribe to follow him away from the party and a little farther into the fields, until they were harder to hear and see.

"You want the truth?" he asked.

The scribe lifted his quill. "Always."

"Delicata Gourd didn't reject me. It's the other way around." He withdrew Deli's folded letter from his pocket. The scribe reached for it, but Syrah held it back. "It's a love letter," he said. "From her to me. But I didn't give it to you. You found it on the ground, you understand?"

"You have my word."

The scribe reached for the letter again, and Syrah hesitated — but only for a moment. So what if this was going to embarrass her? If he was going to be a joke in the *Criers* tomorrow, then she could be one too. It was only fair.

He let the scribe pluck the letter from his fingers.

"Remember," he said. "You found it —"

"On the ground," the scribe replied, unfolding the letter with interest. "Many thanks."

Syrah returned to the party, where Deli was now dancing with Harrow Steelcut, looking perfectly at ease. Happy, even. The usual crease between her brows was gone. He watched her, satisfied. Tomorrow, she was going to get what she deserved.

✦ ✦ ✦

He felt equally smug the next morning, sitting up in his bed in the grand guest wing of the Thatch, eating his eggs and fruit, imagining just how Deli would react when she saw the *Crier*. He hoped he got to see her face.

There was a rap at his door, and then it opened before he could answer. Nana Cava stood there, gripping a *Town Crier* in her hand.

"Downstairs," she said. "Now."

She had never used that tone with him. There was a cold look in her milky eyes that he had not seen there before.

She dropped the *Crier* on the floor and shut his door without another word. Syrah's heart did a nauseating shuffle in his chest. He hadn't thought about Nana Cava when he'd slipped that letter to the scribe.

As he dressed, he told himself that it was fine. He could convince her that it wasn't his fault. He swiped the *Crier* from the floor and made his way to the stairs, where he stopped, unpleasantly surprised. His entire family was waiting for him at the bottom of the steps, right there in the front hall of the governor's mansion. His parents, his seven siblings, and even some of their spouses stood packed behind Nana Cava like a furious choir. Behind them all stood Deli's grandmother Luffa, erect and motionless, her face devoid of expression. Armed guards waited on either side of her.

An immediate apology was his best move. Syrah made his expression contrite and went quickly down the steps. "I'm so sorry," he said quietly when he reached Nana Cava. He held out the *Crier*. "I had Deli's letter in my pocket last night, and it must have fallen out by accident. I never —"

Nana Cava reached forward with a lurch, snatched the paper from his hand, and struck him across the face with it.

"Liar."

Syrah stood shocked. She had never hit him. "But, Nana, I didn't —"

His brother Carnelian gave a low laugh. Syrah flushed.

"All of Tyme has read the letter Deli wrote to you in private," Nana Cava said. "All of Tyme is laughing now, at her expense. Her humiliation is your doing. Admit it."

Syrah made his face as plaintive as he could. "But I didn't mean it, Nana. I told you, it probably fell out of my pocket —"

"No." Nana Cava's voice was hoarse with fury. She searched his eyes. "Delicata rejected you. Marsala told us how it happened. She saw you hand a folded paper to that scribe."

Syrah cast a glowering look at Marsala, who stood with her arms crossed, glaring right back at him.

"How could you do it?" Nana Cava pressed. "Don't you understand what you've betrayed? The Gourds are our people — have you no loyalty to your own people?"

"I told you, I didn't do anything!"

His nana studied his face, and as she did, the anger left her expression. Tears rose in her eyes instead, swift and terrible, worse than any slap across the face. Syrah's breath caught.

"I was wrong about you," she said, her voice a quiet rasp. "I thought you were more than you pretend to be. But you are not pretending."

"Nana," he began, uncertain.

"Leave this house." She pointed to the door. "You are no longer welcome."

Syrah blanched. She couldn't mean that. The *Criers* were a joke, just a joke — and Deli had completely deserved it. Why was he the only one getting in trouble?

"Where am I supposed to go?" he demanded.

"Back to the ship. You will stay there until we leave for Balthasar."

Cooped up on the ship for a whole week, while everyone else feasted and partied? While Deli got petted and comforted, and the rest of them laughed at him behind his back? No.

Above him, at the corner of the balcony, barely visible from the hallway beyond it, Syrah caught sight of Deli, who stayed pressed to the wall, hugging herself and watching him.

Fury shot through him. "This isn't *your* house," he said to Nana Cava. "*You* can't ban me."

Only now did Grandmother Luffa move. She motioned to her guards, who stepped forward, seized Syrah by his arms, and marched him to the front doors of the Thatch. He was too shocked to fight them — he only twisted his head to look over his shoulder. His family watched him like a many-headed serpent, cold and pitiless.

"This *is* Cava's house," said Grandmother Luffa. Both her voice and her eyes were like stone. "As she raised her sword to liberate it, so may she cast you from it."

"But —"

The door slammed shut. The guards marched Syrah to a carriage that waited in front of the Thatch. People stopped to watch the spectacle. Gardeners. Passersby. Children with their parents, groups of whispering friends, and a scribe. The very same scribe to whom he had given Deli's letter. Syrah tried to jerk his arms away from the guards, but no luck. They held fast.

"What happened?" the scribe called out, jogging up to the guards. His floppy, graying hair jogged with him. "Did they blame you for the letter?"

"You can't write about *this*," Syrah hissed, hot-faced.

The scribe grinned and knocked his hair back. "'Traitor Prince Tossed From the Thatch' — that'll sell some *Criers*." The scribe jogged away again and climbed up into a carriage. "Follow the prince," he said to the driver.

The guards escorted Syrah into the carriage and shut the door, and the horses picked up at once. Syrah sat there, miserable and furious. It had not occurred to him — not for a second — that they would all turn on him like this.

He'd teach them.

The horses stopped. Syrah stuck his head out of the carriage window and saw that they were at a crossing, waiting for several wagons to pass by.

He tested the door. The guards hadn't tied him up or locked him in — they'd been told to escort him, apparently, not to arrest him. The moment the horses started moving again, he threw open the door, leapt into the road, and pelted with all his speed away from the carriage.

"Halt!" he heard the guards shout. "Catch him!" cried the scribe. Syrah heard heavy footfalls behind him, but he was young and swift and more than capable of putting half a league between himself and his pursuers before he was even winded. By the time he glanced back to check where they were, they were too distant to be seen.

Determined, he kept running until he approached the wooded acreage that lay just beyond the governor's grounds, past the pumpkin patches and the rolling farmland that belonged to the Gourd family. He wasn't quite sure where he was going. Where should he go? Far enough away to hide and scare his family into thinking he was really gone, that was for sure. When they regretted their decision and came looking for him, he didn't want them to find him right away — he'd give them a good scare. He could find enough to eat, probably. There were farms all around, after all.

The woods at the far edge of the governor's vast property were cool and shadowy. When Syrah hurtled into them, he was dazzled by the bright, impossible greenness of the world around him. Soft emerald moss grew in a thick, rolling carpet over the forest floor, littered with leaves and dappled with sunlight. Everything was blanketed with moss here — the rocks, the fallen logs, the trunks of the trees. It was like a fairy glade — or what he thought one must be like. It *felt* like a magic place. He'd played here as a boy, with Deli. They'd played imps and fairies, hiding under leaves and inside hollow logs and way up high in the trees, happy to have a playmate of the same age who was equally physically fearless.

His fists clenched. Deli was the traitor, not him. She was the one who had started this thing between them — he would never have bothered with her if she hadn't thrown herself at him first. If she hadn't been so crazy and pathetic about him, Nana Cava wouldn't hate him, and his whole family wouldn't be against him, and a scribe wouldn't be writing lies about him. It was her fault, and now *he* had to pay.

Syrah stumbled hard and dropped to his knees. He swore in irritation, then looked behind him and realized he'd been lucky. If he'd gone just one step to the left, he would have fallen into a near-hidden sinkhole, camouflaged by moss, that dropped suddenly away into the ground. Since childhood, he'd been warned about that hole. Its mouth was wide enough for a couple of grown people to fall right in, and it was darker and deeper than anything Syrah had ever seen. Many times, the hole had been covered for the sake of safety, and just as many times, those carefully constructed covers had simply vanished. Imps were doing it, some people said. Fairies were doing it, said others. Brownies, elves, and mortal mischief-makers were blamed in turn, but no culprit was ever caught, and no covering was ever allowed to close the hole for long. Once, the Gourds had even attempted to fill the hole with dirt, but the story went that no matter how much dirt they'd poured into it, the soil had only fallen into darkness.

Syrah crawled to the edge of the sinkhole and peered down into it. Its depths were as dark and unfathomable as he remembered from childhood. Involuntarily, he shivered. Once, when they'd been five or six years old and playing hide-and-seek, he'd heard Deli scream, and he'd found her huddled and shaking right here, tears streaming down her face. She swore that she'd fallen into the hole. She said she'd been falling and falling forever, and then she felt hands lift her — and then she was out on the moss again, like nothing ever happened. It was magic, she'd insisted. A magic hole in the ground.

Syrah had scoffed at her. There were no such things as magic holes in the ground — except wishing wells, but those were only legend. Everyone in Tyme knew that.

Still, just now, he could have used a wishing well. A wishing well would have been perfect. He could've wished for Nana Cava to regret kicking him out. He could've wished for his whole family to turn into the snakes they were.

Rain began to fall, dripping through the trees and onto his back, and Syrah scowled. With nowhere else to go, he was going to get soaked. He was going to have to stay out here for hours — even days, probably. He'd be wet and hungry, and nobody cared — and he hadn't even *done* anything.

He lay on his stomach, still staring down into that endless darkness.

"Deli should be the one in trouble, not me," he whispered into the sinkhole. "I wish people like that, who think they're so special, would get what they deserve."

His whisper vanished into the darkness. He thought he heard a faint *plink*, like the echo of a distant coin dropping into water. And then he heard a watery roar from deep in the soil, as though the ocean itself were rushing toward him from beneath the ground. Instinct told him to get back — he pushed himself up, but too late —

A geyser erupted from the sinkhole. It connected with his face like a fist and threw him back with such force that he was lifted off the ground. He scrabbled at the air as the water pushed against him, holding him hostage.

Your wish is granted.

He didn't hear the words; he felt them. Like they were rushing into him through his skin, borne by the water itself.

The geyser vanished. Syrah plummeted to the mossy forest floor. At the same time, an explosion of violet light lit the woods, throwing every plant and tree into relief. He tried to cry out in alarm but found that he had no voice. He was mute, and the world was changing — everything raced past him in a blur, all streaks of color and light. Abruptly, the movement stopped, and he sat there, panting, not certain where he was or why he felt so strange and sick.

Everything was still green, but the landscape had changed; ringed around him were giant bushes made of tangled moss and massive toadstools, tall as trees. Beside him was a blade of grass as tall as the white columns of the sea pavilions at home. Syrah stared up at it, aghast. He opened his mouth again and tried to speak —

"Ribbit."

He heard himself. He tried to scream.

"Croak."

Syrah reeled. He tried to move. He felt himself bounce, higher than he ever had, as though it were nothing to him. He bounced again, in his panic, and flew into the blade of tall grass. It showered him with dew, and he bounced again to shake the water out of his eyes. He tried to look down at himself but found that his neck did not bend. Or he had no neck. He could only roll his eyes downward, and when he did, he caught sight of his hands — and nearly fainted. Blood rushed to his head. For a moment, he stopped breathing.

His fingers were green. There were only four of them on each hand, and they were green. They were also webbed, with gelatinous bulbs at their ends — he knew hands like this. He'd seen them many times. Just not on human beings.

These were frog's hands.

Something enormous and wet struck him like a cold ocean wave, and he tumbled away, disoriented. No sooner had he found his feet again than he was struck by another wall of water, and he landed at the foot of another blade of endless grass. He must be really tiny, he realized, to be so much smaller than grass. He must be one of those minuscule frogs he had sometimes discovered in the vineyards back home. The kind so small it could sit comfortably on a grape. So small that even raindrops had the power to upend him.

So small that no one would help him, because no one would see him there.

But someone *would* help him, he thought frantically, even as the rain batted him into a rushing brook that bore him away. Somehow, his family would figure out where he'd gone. They'd get dogs and follow his tracks, and then they'd search for him, and they'd find him — and they'd fix him. They *had* to fix him. He couldn't stay like this forever.

He couldn't.

Chapter One

*F*IFTEEN months.

Fifteen months, one week, three days, and about two hours. Syrah had felt every minute. Every minute that he hadn't spent hibernating, anyway.

He sat on a large, wet leaf, staring up at the rain and regretting, as he often did, the night that had brought him to this pass. It was Deli's fault, he thought bitterly for the hundred thousandth time. If Deli hadn't been such a witch, then he never would have ended up like this. He would never have been thrown out by his family or tricked by that rotten well — he would've stayed human, like he was supposed to.

He sighed, just barely, as he thought of being human. He had never appreciated how wonderful it was. He'd had hands. A voice. He'd worn clothes and eaten cooked food.

Out of the corner of his bulging eye, Syrah noticed the scuttle of a shiny red bug. Instinctively, he turned his head and unrolled his tongue. It still surprised him how efficient this method of hunting was. The bug was in his mouth in an instant, and Syrah swallowed. His eyes retreated into his skull and pressed the food down into his throat. He settled his belly and the undersides of his thighs into the rainwater that had collected in the leaf he was sitting in, and he absorbed a long cool drink through his skin.

It was strange, what a person could get used to. He could never have imagined drinking through his skin, and the idea of swallowing live bugs would have once made him gag, but he did it all the time now, and it wasn't anything, really. He preferred catching those tiny fish he sometimes managed to grub in a stream, but bugs were easier to find, definitely more appetizing than snails — and one did what one had to do to survive.

Fifteen months as a frog had taught Syrah plenty.

"Come here, Prince Frog."

Syrah hopped in a circle and looked up at the blond teenager who had been his protector for the past eight months.

"Ribbit," he said fondly, and Rapunzel smiled down at him.

She was a good kid. Not perfect — she'd nearly let him freeze to death, once — but she cared about him, and in her possession, Syrah felt safe. Much safer than he'd been without her — and much safer too, now that he was normal-size. During his first few months as a frog, he had remained as tiny as the wishing well had made him, so minuscule that even minnows could have eaten him. Certainly enough of them had tried. Fish, birds, kittens — these were now the creatures of his nightmares. During the first months of his ordeal, mouths had lunged for him, claws had swiped at him, beaks had swooped to pierce him — and worst of all, enormous spiders had pursued him, their crazed, clustered eyes shining, their pincers raised like monstrous daggers. Syrah had never been afraid of spiders, but being the size of a thumbnail had altered his perspective. When he was human again, he would crush every spider he encountered. He would be the mad spider crusher of Tyme, exacting his revenge on every eight-legged creature. His sister Bianca would give him one of her speeches about how all creatures exist in balance. He would eat a bowl of live spiders in front of her face to shut her up.

Several strokes of good fortune had finally landed him in Rapunzel's pocket — though they hadn't felt like good fortune at the time. He hadn't felt lucky at all when a brook had washed him into a line of irrigation, which had carried him to a river, where he'd nearly been dinner for the fish. He hadn't felt lucky when he'd finally washed up on shore and overheard a pair of hunters discussing the best game in the Redlands, which meant that he was a terrible distance now from Cornucopia.

On the other hand, it *had* seemed like luck when he had accidentally found his way into the glade of the Red fairies. Surely, he'd thought, they would notice him. They would recognize that he was human, and they would help him. But the Red fairies had been consumed in their war against the witch Envearia. They had been haggard with fear, their magic had been weak, and they had paid no mind to the spellbound frog in their midst.

And then Rapunzel had come to the fairy glade — and so had Jack, who noticed Syrah, and scooped him off the ground, and gave him to Rapunzel as a birthday present. The best moment of his frog life so far had come when the Red fairies restored Rapunzel to her human size. Inside her pocket, Syrah had grown into a frog the size of a fist, and his relief at the change was still fantastic. He was big. He was visible. He could crush most spiders with a single, vicious hop. Still, even as a normal-size frog, the world was too treacherous for him to risk traveling alone. He'd been biding his time all these months, and now he was close. *So* close.

Rapunzel crouched before him now and extended her hand.

Syrah hopped into it, and when his belly touched her palm, he felt and heard the thoughts inside her mind. *I wish Witch could see me at the ATC, I miss her and it hurts, it hurts — Why can't I work this stupid ring? I don't want to miss the tournament.*

This too was something Syrah had gotten used to — or almost. It was still strange, absorbing people's inner lives just like he absorbed water to drink. He doubted it was something all frogs could do — magic had made him a frog, after all, and so magic had also made him a little bit magical. It was a handy gift. It had allowed him, the first time Rapunzel ever touched him, to discern that he would probably be safe in her care.

Now he stayed near her wrist and carefully avoided touching the fairy ring that flowed around one of her fingers. More than once, he had scraped his belly against the ring by mistake, and it had overwhelmed his mind with visions he could hardly bear. The birth of the Olive Isles as they burst from the sea. The first stars, flung violently into the night sky. And a great blackness — a living, breathing, unknowable blackness, hidden beneath a hill. Tyme's oldest secrets were in that ring, and he wanted no part of them.

"Are you ready to go?" Rapunzel asked.

Syrah replied with his most affirmative croak, and Rapunzel set him on her shoulder, where he settled comfortably and surveyed the world from a proper human height. He was more than ready to go. He could scarcely wait another moment. Rapunzel and Jack were on their way to the All-Tyme Championships in Yellow Country. There, Syrah would finally find people who remembered him as a man. People who would help him.

"You're still using that ring wrong," said Jack. "Let me see it." He shoved his black hair to no avail. It fell down again immediately, shiny and straight, half obscuring his black eyes.

"The Woodmother gave it to me," said Rapunzel, rubbing the ring. "And Glyph said the trees would teach me where to go. If I just keep trying —"

"Come on, you've had a thousand chances," said Jack. "Let me try."

Syrah clung to the last scraps of his patience. He had never been long on patience, but his time with Rapunzel and Jack had forced him to build some.

"Just wait!" Rapunzel cried, flipping her long braid back over her shoulder and nearly smacking Syrah in the face with it. He pressed closer to her neck and avoided the slap. He was attuned, by now, to her hair-throwing fits; he almost never got hit anymore.

"Here's a map," said Jack, shoving a Ubiquitous one into Rapunzel's face. "Here's where we want to go." He thumped the town of Plenty in Yellow Country, on the shore of Lake Tureen. "And here's where we are now," he said, crumpling the map into a useless wad and shaking it at Rapunzel. "We have no idea! The opening ceremonies are going on right now, and the delegates' feast is *tonight*. I told you we should have taken that carriage when we were in Smoketree. At this rate, you'll miss the whole competition." Jack shoved the map into his rucksack.

Rapunzel held up her hand in front of her eyes and turned it back and forth. The ring glinted. "I don't *want* to miss it," she said. "Purl is traveling all that way to see me play jacks."

"And Tess and my mother."

"But I need to figure this out by myself. Without any help. It's important, Jack."

"Why?"

"Because it *is*." She dropped her ringed hand to her side.

Jack sighed. "Let's just walk until we find a town," he said. "Then we'll take a carriage."

"Wait — where's that book you brought?" Rapunzel asked suddenly. She made an impatient gesture with her fingers. "The one you borrowed from your mother."

"Why?" Jack asked, but he was already digging in his rucksack. He found the tattered little book and handed it to Rapunzel. The lettering was so faded that Syrah could barely make out the title. *Edible Plants ~ An Illustrated Guide.*

"This says where different plants grow," Rapunzel said, flipping through it. "We're in the middle of the woods somewhere, so if we can figure out which plants these are, can't we figure out *where* we are?"

Syrah croaked appreciatively and bounced on Rapunzel's shoulder. Yes. A reasonable idea.

Jack looked impressed. "Sounds good," he said.

Rapunzel had already found a useful page. She put her finger on the picture and peered at the nearest patch of flowers. "Does this look right to you, Prince Frog?" she asked.

Jack rolled his eyes, but Syrah croaked his agreement anyway. The flowers in the woods and the flowers in the book were the same. Marigolds.

"And they grow in . . ." Rapunzel squinted at the page. "Well, in summer, they grow all over the place," she said, disappointed. "Orange, the Redlands, the Crimson Realm, Yellow Country, the Blue Kingdom, the Lilac Lakes, Commonwealth Green . . ." She turned the page. "Never mind, this doesn't help."

"Yes it does." Jack had come to stand next to Rapunzel, and he peered at the book alongside her. "Pick another plant — there are tons around here. We'll keep identifying them until we narrow it down to the place where all of them grow. Like that mushroom there. My mother warned us not to eat those."

"Huh," said Rapunzel. "I'm sure I've eaten mushrooms that look just like that."

"You'd be dead," Jack replied. "Those might look like morels, but they're not." He reached over and flipped pages until he reached a page toward the back of the book. It listed several poisonous plants that were easy to confuse with other, edible plants.

"Bluepeace," Rapunzel murmured, dragging a finger down the page. "Hemlock, juggetsbane, moonseed . . ." She pointed to a drawing of a mushroom. "This one? Slumbercap?"

Jack peered at the drawing. "Yep," he said. "See? The inner lining has a silver cast, it says." He plucked one of the mushrooms from the ground and turned it over. Sure enough, its inner folds shone faintly silver.

"'Crumble the dried mushroom into hot liquid,'" Rapunzel read aloud. "'Slumbercap will dissolve, emitting a silver curl of steam. Even a small amount of slumbercap may cause extreme difficulty breathing. A few mouthfuls of the poison will result in paralysis of the lungs. Death by suffocation will occur within minutes.'" She shuddered. "Well that's not very nice."

"None of these are," said Jack, tossing the mushroom away. Syrah watched it fall and made a mental note not to hop on any of those. He didn't want to go absorbing that stuff. "But the point is, these mushrooms grow in Violet, and then down across the central belt of Tyme." He pointed to the book. "The Republic of Brown, Yellow Country, and southeastern Blue."

"Between that and the marigolds, we're either in southeastern Blue or in Yellow Country," said Rapunzel, looking hopeful. "That's closer to Lake Tureen than we thought." She flipped through the book until she came to a drawing of a tree, and she looked up at the ones that shaded them. "These are birch trees, aren't they?"

Syrah hopped. They definitely were.

Rapunzel laid her palm against the peeling white patches of the nearest birch tree trunk. "Birch," she said, consulting her book again briefly. "Now, where do you grow?"

The ring on Rapunzel's finger began to glow.

Syrah's eyes bulged. He hopped repeatedly on Rapunzel's shoulder, but she was too busy reading to pay attention, so he leapt from her shoulder to Jack's. Jack turned his head, caught sight of Rapunzel's ring, and gasped.

"Your ring," Jack said urgently. "Look."

Rapunzel stared at her finger, then lifted her chin and looked up into the slim, leafy branches of the birch they stood beneath. Syrah looked up too in fearful wonder.

"My ring is warm," Rapunzel murmured. "Jack, hold my hand." She leaned toward the tree, keeping her ringed hand pressed to it. "Birch?" she said, almost shyly. "Hello there, Birch."

There was no wind, but the birch leaves rustled musically. The ring glowed brighter.

"We're trying to go to Plenty," said Rapunzel. "Could you show us the way? Please?"

Silvery fog rolled swiftly toward them. It enveloped them, so thick that Syrah could not even see Rapunzel's neck in front of him. The fog coiled into long, dense funnels of silvery whiteness, then burst silently into smoke and dissipated. When the mist cleared, the landscape had changed. They were still beside a cluster of birch trees, but these ones grew along the side of a wide road that descended into a valley. Beautifully tended farms nestled together like a great pastoral quilt on either side of the road, rolling toward a bright blue lake that shimmered in the distance. Syrah began to bounce on Jack's shoulder. He knew this vista. He'd traveled this road. They had reached the ATC. Here, he would find his family. Deli's family. Nexus Burdock. Somebody who knew him.

"These are birches too," said Jack, looking around.

"Is that how it's done?" Rapunzel looked up at the leaves. "I can travel from birches to birches, or maples to maples, or willows to willows?"

"We could make a map," said Jack. "A tree map."

"Yes! And then we really could go everywhere!"

Syrah barely listened. Too ecstatic to stay perched, he bounced into the dry grass and boinged in jubilant circles. His misery was nearly at an end. After fifteen months of grueling patience, somebody was going to make him human again.

Rapunzel touched the nearest tree trunk.

"Thank you, Birch," she said.

The branches overhead gave a satisfied rustle. The ring's glow dimmed.

"We still have to hurry," said Jack. "The invitation says the feast tonight is formal. You need to get changed."

Rapunzel looked down at herself. "I can't wear this?"

"It's an official event. They expect you to get fancy."

"Then you have to get fancy too."

"Fine."

Rapunzel and Jack eyed each other for a brief moment, and then

Rapunzel blushed. She pulled her hand from Jack's and strode off down the hill. Syrah bounced frantically after her, croaking as loudly as he could. If she forgot about him now, if she left him behind and some family of weasels popped up and ate him —

"Come on, Prince Frog."

Jack scooped him up, and Syrah's panic ebbed. For a moment, pressed against Jack's palm, he experienced his mind as well. *She's getting better at all this* — *She didn't need my help at all* — *She held my hand.*

There was a lot of Rapunzel in Jack's mind lately.

Syrah rode on Jack's shoulder until they reached the bustling streets at the center of Plenty, where he gazed delightedly around, beaming as much as his frog face would let him at the wonderful noise of it all. People eating, kids laughing, babies crying, and the *Town Crier* box pealing over the top of it all.

"Hear ye! Hear ye!"

Jack walked up to the box, put a coin in the slot, and pulled out the tightly scrolled *Crier* that dropped into the undertray.

"Uh-oh," he said, frowning as he opened the scroll. "There's some kind of sickness going around the villages east of here. Five people have died of an unknown fever, and there are a dozen others unconscious. . . ." He shook his head. "This *Crier* is all bad news. Listen to this: 'Ubiquitous Productions has refused the Exalted Council's request for a meeting, though several recent deaths have been reported. . . .'" Jack trailed off, shaking his head. "Crop *rot*. This thing says that some kid fell from a rooftop when her Ubiquitous rope crashed ten hours early. And some other family's house burned down because they got an acorn that sparked — just like the one that started that fire in Quintessential."

Rapunzel looked over his shoulder. "'The Exalted Council's official recommendation is to discontinue use of the acorns until a full investigation can be conducted,'" she read, sounding worried. "But Jack, the only other clothes I have are Ubiquitous ones. What will I wear?"

Jack answered by pointing toward a shop called Practical Elegance. Through its windows, Syrah watched enviously as young people held garments against themselves and looked into mirrors to judge their reflections. He had been like them once.

When they entered the shop, many of the customers turned their heads. Their eyes flickered over Jack's tattered traveling clothes and Syrah on his shoulder, and they raised their eyebrows at Rapunzel's muddy boots and unkempt hair. Some of them whispered to each other, smirking. One girl even pointed at them, then dissolved into a fit of quiet giggles with her friend.

Rapunzel was impervious. "I don't see anything fancy," she announced rather loudly as she glanced around the shop. "Let's go somewhere else."

As if by magic, a saleswoman appeared beside Rapunzel.

"This way, sweets," she said, smiling brightly, and she led Rapunzel through the crowd and toward the back of the shop. Jack went toward a rack of men's tunics, and Syrah looked up at the enormous sign that was pasted on the wall between the tall windows. FAIREST OF THE FAIR CERTIFIED it said in fancy letters. *At Practical Elegance, we care for the dignity of our employees. We maintain safe workshop conditions and pay fair wages and benefits.* Beneath this, the royal crest of Blue was seared right into the wall, beside a framed letter signed by Prince Dash Charming, which several customers were reading. A store clerk stood there too, smiling and holding up a small card. "Five percent of all proceeds earned during the ATC will go directly to fund local orphanages," she said. "This charitable outreach is possible in partnership with G. G. Floss of the Copper Door! Make a purchase here, and receive a limited-edition luxury truffle! This offer is exclusively available during the All-Tyme Championships."

Jack lifted a paper tag attached to the collar of a tunic. "'Waterproof, wrinkle-free, stain-resistant, travel-friendly, and crafted according to the highest ethical standards — the Practical Elegance guarantee,'" he read. He flipped the tag over and whistled at the outrageously high price. "I could live for a year on that money."

"But they're *so* worth it," said a tall, young man who stood nearby. He had long, white blond curls, expertly tousled to look like he'd just emerged from the ocean, and his white tunic highlighted his golden tan. The whole picture reminded Syrah powerfully of himself. "They're reversible, and they seriously don't wrinkle."

Jack gave the tanned fellow a dubious glance.

"I wore one practically every day of the ATC last year," said the fellow, "and it's still in good shape this summer, so, you know. Satisfied customer."

Jack turned to him with more interest. "You're an All-Tymer?"

"Cassis Swill. Launchballer for Yellow." Cassis smiled. "You a fan?"

"I'm here with the jacks champion, actually. She's a friend of mine."

Cassis's eyebrows flew up. He lowered his voice and looked both ways. "The witch's kid?" he whispered, leaning slightly toward Jack. "Where is she?"

"Her name is Rapunzel," said Jack, and Syrah heard the edge in his voice.

"Does she still have all the hair?"

Jack's shoulder stiffened under Syrah's belly. "No."

"Too bad," said Cassis, giving Jack a conspiratorial grin. "A hundred feet of hair — something pretty interesting about that, you know?"

"You'd think," said Jack coolly. "Turns out it's just heavy."

Rapunzel burst from the back of the shop like a firework and planted herself in front of Jack. She wore a sapphire gown that made her eyes as blue as an island sky. Syrah couldn't help admiring her.

Neither could Jack. Syrah could feel his pulse racing in his neck. *Go on*, he thought, not for the first time. *Say something. Tell her she's beautiful.*

Jack was silent.

Cassis, on the other hand, spoke. "Looks good," he said, and he took a lazy step toward her. "You're the jacks champion. Rapunzel, right?"

"Yes." Rapunzel jerked her hair away from the saleswoman, who was trying to wind it into an elegant twist. "I like my hair down," she said, and she shook it out. Golden tendrils curled softly to her waist.

"*Nice*," said Cassis, sweeping his eyes over her. He flipped his hair back from his eyes and jerked his chin toward her in a gesture of approval. Syrah recognized the move. He had used it himself. "So, I'm Cassis. Cassis Swill. You know. Launchball."

"No I don't." Rapunzel turned her back on him without ceremony. "I'm getting this dress," she said to Jack. "It's perfect — look, it comes apart at the waist. The top turns into a satchel if you flip it inside out and button up this end, and the skirt is a waterproof sleeve for a sleeping bag."

"That's pretty handy," Jack admitted. "I should find something like that."

"Right this way." The brightly smiling saleswoman was at Jack's elbow.

Rapunzel took Syrah from Jack and set him on her shoulder. "See if you can get some trousers that turn into a boat," she called as the saleswoman pulled Jack away.

Chapter Two

*T*HE Royal Governor's Inn stood just across from Lake Tureen, where most of the All-Tyme Championship events would take place. All around the inn, a temporary but very fashionable marketplace had sprung up. Traveling vendors hawked their wares in elegant tents, while excited tourists, eager to be part of the scene, laid down their money to have their silhouettes cut from paper-thin sheets of wood by Redlands artisans, or to sip expensive wine made by famous vintners from the Olive Isles.

Syrah's gaze lingered on one of the tents belonging to Olive. Its outside was painted to look like the vineyards of Balthasar, and the artist had done exceptional work. Syrah could almost pretend that he was there among the vines. He breathed deeply, imagining that he could smell soil and grape skins mingling with the scent of the sea.

Longing for home swept through him, so sudden and intense that he felt almost ill. He supposed that was why they called it homesickness.

"Copper Door!" Rapunzel said suddenly. She pointed to a large, cylindrical tent that stood across from the carriage house behind the Royal Governor's Inn. A beautifully sculpted CD topped its peak, and its paneled sides alternated between a satiny cream-colored fabric and a bright, shining copper one. Two of these copper panels were pulled back like curtains to admit the customers — and there were hundreds of customers. The line for candy snaked out of the tent and all the way up the street, past dozens of other tents and shops.

"Let's get our luxury truffle," said Rapunzel, pulling out the ticket she'd received at Practical Elegance.

"We don't have time," said Jack. "The line is *way* too — Rapunzel, don't cut! You have to go to the back of the line!"

But as she often did when she met with a rule she didn't like, Rapunzel ignored it. Syrah, who shared this trait, hopped encouragingly on her shoulder, and she strode straight into the tent, with an anxious Jack right behind her.

"This is not okay," he whispered as people shot withering looks at them. "We can't . . ."

He trailed off. Rapunzel had stopped cold in front of a long, thin copper countertop that stood at the center of the tent. On it, a tableau of candy sculptures was arranged in an unmistakable scene. A tall chocolate tower. A marzipan girl at the tower window, her long, spun-sugar braid hanging down the outside of the tower wall. A marzipan witch with hair of dark licorice climbing the golden sugar braid. Really climbing it — the candy witch moved its marzipan hands on the golden sugar braid and ascended toward the girl in the chocolate window.

"Whoa," said Jack under his breath. He sounded both awed and worried, and Syrah understood why. As a boy, he had loved the magic of Copper Door candies — G. G. Floss was famous for her artistry. Her sweets were almost like edible toys; they glittered and moved and sometimes even made music as they told their stories.

But this was Rapunzel's story.

Syrah felt her heartbeat quicken in her neck. Heard the catch in her voice when she quietly managed, "Why?"

". . . However. Though many tales of witchcraft end in tragedy, this one did not."

The voice came from the woman behind the counter, whom Syrah only now noticed. He had been too fascinated by the tower scene before to see that G. G. Floss herself stood before them. She was a very pale woman of medium height, sandy hair, and slight build, without any particular beauty — her most arresting physical feature was her hands. Her fingertips were stained deep reddish-purple with the Kiss of magic, and on her wrists, twin copper bracelets caught the light and gleamed. She held her hands suspended over the candy scene, moving her fingers like a puppeteer. The marzipan witch with the dark hair climbed into the tower, and then the little marzipan girl floated out through the tower window and landed on the copper countertop. The girl withdrew a tiny licorice bag from her sparkling sugar pocket, and from that tiny bag she pulled a minuscule set of gold-dusted candy jacks.

"Rapunzel escaped her tower and set out to see the world," said Miss Floss. "She even became our jacks champion. And when she returned to her tower, she bravely defeated the witch who had kidnapped her in infancy and held her captive all her life."

She flicked her purple fingertips, and the marzipan witch plummeted from the tower window and struck the countertop.

"Stop!" Rapunzel shrieked, and she reached out and seized the candy witch.

G. G. Floss looked up from her tableau, startled.

"Liar!" Rapunzel was breathing hard. "You don't know — you have no right —"

And now every customer in the tent was staring at them.

"Come on, Rapunzel," said Jack quietly. "Let's just go."

"Rapunzel!" The murmur went up through the tent, and Jack winced, realizing his mistake. "The witch's child?" "The jacks champion!" "Her hair's too short."

Miss Floss stared at Rapunzel a moment, then recovered herself. "Marcel," she called out, and a mustached man came almost instantly through a flap at the back of the tent. "See to the customers. Please, follow me," she said to Rapunzel and Jack. "I hoped you'd come. I have a gift for you." She vanished behind the flap through which Marcel had emerged.

Rapunzel looked uncertainly at Jack, still clutching the candy witch.

"Your call," he said.

She squared her shoulders, grabbed the marzipan girl off the table, and marched through the flap at the back of the tent with Jack on her heels.

They emerged in another, connected tent that appeared to be the Copper Door's temporary storeroom. Sensationally beautiful candies filled the bowls and boxes and platters that lined the shelves. Sugar-paste roses with delicate, velvety petals, rainbow jellies that were clear as glass and scattered colored light all around them like little prisms, marshmallow birds that fluttered and chirped, and gingerbread people unlike any Syrah had seen before. Instead of raisins for eyes and bits of licorice for mouths, they had painted candy faces that were unsettlingly real. Everything in the tent was a work of art. Rapunzel, Jack, and Syrah all gazed around for a minute, enchanted by the tiny wonders.

"I'm so sorry I offended you," said G. G. Floss, coming forward. "It was never my intention, Rapunzel. And you must be Jack."

He looked surprised. "How did you —"

"I'm fond of stories." Miss Floss gestured to a worktable where a long cylinder of bright green fondant was being shaped into a twisting stalk with great leaves protruding from it. Beside this, a small marzipan boy with sharp black hair and sharper black eyes stood, gazing up as though into the sky. "I should have the beanstalk finished tomorrow, if you want to come back."

Jack gaped. "You're joking," he said. "That's about me?"

"She doesn't know anything about you," said Rapunzel savagely. "She got *my* life all wrong."

"I was just playing to my audience," said Miss Floss. An embroidered copper oven glinted at the top of her long black apron. "And I wasn't *all* wrong. You did leave the tower. You did become the jacks champion. The only bit I'm not sure of is how you defeated the witch."

Rapunzel opened her hand and looked down at the marzipan girl and witch who were nestled there together.

"I've heard many versions of your tale," said Miss Floss, moving her purple fingertips through the air as though tugging invisible strings. The candy figures stood up in Rapunzel's palm and faced each other. "In one of them, you slew the witch with a dagger." The marzipan girl raised her hand as though to stab the witch, though she held no weapon. "But that seemed a bit far-fetched. Witches are harder than that to kill." The marzipan girl lowered her arm again. "In another, you pushed the witch from the tower — and I won't lie, that's a crowd favorite. Another favorite is the one where Jack climbed your tower and saved you from harm." The marzipan boy floated from his position near the beanstalk to join the figures in Rapunzel's palm. "But I heard a different rumor," said Miss Floss. "One that traveled north with a carpenter from the Redlands. According to his daughter, who works in the Fortress of Bole, Jack was nearly killed by the witch, and he couldn't help you at all."

The marzipan witch struck Jack's candy figure, and he crumpled.

Syrah flinched at the violence of it. He had been deep in hibernation for that part of their journey, and — not for the first time — he was glad he'd slept through it.

"Don't *do* that," said Rapunzel sharply.

"But that part's true," said Jack, his voice quiet. "That happened."

With a gentle gesture, Miss Floss lifted marzipan Jack into the air and sent him soaring back to the worktable to wait beside his beanstalk.

"And of course the story where Prince Dash rescues you is a complete fabrication," said Miss Floss. "I didn't even make scenery for that one, though people simply *love* to tell it."

"He was turned to stone," said Rapunzel. "How could anybody think he saved me?"

Miss Floss laughed. "People don't care about facts," she said. "They believe whatever gives them comfort. And in your case, the truth makes people very, very uncomfortable."

In Rapunzel's palm, the little candy witch changed shape, shrinking until she was nothing but marzipan bones. The candy girl covered her face as though weeping. Then she knelt, snapped the spun sugar braid from her head, and gently wrapped it around the witch's remains.

Rapunzel watched, silent. Her face had slipped into a neutral position that Syrah had come to think of as her I'm-Not-Crying face. She closed her fist around the candy scene.

"True stories have a certain ring to them," said Miss Floss gently. "When I heard *that* rumor, I was certain. Your witch was different from all the rest. She loved you, and you loved her."

Rapunzel's chin jutted out, and Syrah heard her teeth scrape together. She was really working hard to hold it in now. "Then why," she managed, "don't you tell the truth?"

"Because no one wants to hear it," said Miss Floss. "They want to hear that the witch is dead, and that you're a brave hero. And why shouldn't they? Witches are bloodthirsty, White-hatched monsters, and the citizens of Yellow have had to deal with more than their share of them. Like the Mercy Witches, who ate all the children in their village rather than allow the Pink Empire's soldiers to enslave them — you've heard that grisly tale, I'm sure."

Rapunzel shook her head.

"Really? You've never . . . Well, it *was* a hundred years ago." Miss Floss pointed to another worktable, where various shades of blue fondant had been blended and sculpted until they resembled a flowing river. Stuck into this river were little hard-candy children on lollipop sticks who looked like they were bobbing in the water. "What about the River Witch, who lured children into deep waters and then forced them to bargain with her rather than drown?"

Syrah looked away, nauseated. Why, he wondered, had the wishing well ruined his life for doing something as small as giving a letter to a scribe, when there were evil witches in the world who truly *deserved* punishment?

"I've only heard of the Witch of the Woods," said Rapunzel slowly. "I read about her in a book. She ate hundreds of children, it said."

"The most famous of famous. As a matter of fact, I was telling that story just yesterday." Miss Floss rolled up her sleeves, raised her purple fingertips, and flicked them toward the shelves. The little gingerbread children with the painted faces came marching through the air toward her. "The Witch of the Woods. She stole dozens of children from Cornucopia — and dozens more right here, in the woods around Plenty. That was only thirty years ago, so most of them have family who are still alive and grieving." The gingerbread children stopped and turned toward Rapunzel, standing hand-to-hand like a little cookie fence. "Whenever the witch had more children than she needed, she turned them into gingerbread to save them for later. They were still alive, and they knew what was happening, but they could not run away. They starved to death."

Jack looked as queasy as Syrah felt.

"Or so *one* version of the story goes," said Miss Floss. She dismissed the gingerbread children back to their platter. "The Witch of the Woods lived in a house made all of sweets — did you know that?" Miss Floss reached under the table and brought out a stunning gingerbread house, its roof brilliant with sparkling gumdrop shingles and its garden bursting with taffy flowers and trees that blossomed with spearmint leaves and marshmallow fruit, in spite of the white-frosted, snow-covered ground. "Children who approached would break a piece of chocolate from the fence, or pluck a candied apple from the tree, not realizing that in doing so, they entered into a terrible bargain."

"I don't see how that's a bargain," said Jack. "It's theft, sure, but it's not a deal."

"There was a sign on the door," said Miss Floss. "Very small, and written very fine. Children who wanted candy did not bother to read it."

"But that's not fair," said Rapunzel. "Not if they didn't know."

"Since when do bargains have to be fair? You were bargained away at your birth, with no say in the matter. How fair, exactly, was that?"

"How did she die?" Jack demanded. "Did Nexus Keene kill her?"

"The greatest witch slayer in all of Tyme?" One corner of Miss Floss's mouth lifted in a smile. "A good question. After all, who else could manage it? But he denies the deed, and I'm inclined to believe him. Why wouldn't he claim responsibility, after all, for ending such a monster?"

"Maybe he's just humble?" said Jack.

"Maybe." Miss Floss tilted her head. "He is powerful, intelligent, and brave. Why not ascribe every noble quality to him? But no — I think not. This, I think, he would have told the world."

It was true, Syrah thought. Nexus Keene hadn't hidden any of his other great deeds — so why hide this one? No, it must have been somebody else . . . but who?

"Then who did it?" Rapunzel asked, frowning.

Miss Floss snapped her purple fingers, and the door of the candy house opened. Syrah's heart gave a nasty thud. Inside that house was an unnatural darkness — and from the thick gloom emerged two tiny, pasty children, dressed in rags, and hand in hand. They had no faces. Syrah felt suddenly as cold as if he were sitting in a puddle of ice water.

"I heard another rumor," said Miss Floss, "from deep in the Arrowroot Forest, about two wretched children, a brother and sister, who were starving and near dead. They found the house. In desperation, they ate from it, and so became the prisoners of the witch. The boy was caged — the girl, enslaved. But in the end, the boy escaped. He killed the witch and ended her tyranny."

Syrah could not imagine how.

"That's pretty vague," said Jack. "How did he kill her?"

"Who knows? He could have beheaded or strangled her."

"A starving boy in a cage?" Jack frowned. "I doubt it."

Miss Floss shrugged. "All that is known is this: When Nexus Keene found the candy house, the witch's body had already been carried away by the White. But her oven stood open, still ablaze, with one shoe on the floor outside it. Perhaps the boy pushed her in. Perhaps she burned."

Rapunzel opened her mouth in horror.

"But why wouldn't *he* tell the world what he'd done?" asked Jack. "He'd be a hero. Everyone would love him. There's no reason why he wouldn't take credit. . . ." He narrowed his eyes. "Unless he had something to hide."

Miss Floss looked admiringly at him. "You're a born storyteller, aren't you?"

Jack gave a modest shrug. "I don't know," he said. "I used to tell stories to my little sister."

"Ah yes. Tess, isn't it?"

Jack looked astonished. "You really do know about my life."

"I know that you went to great lengths to save your sister from the White —"

Miss Floss stopped. She turned her face away and lifted a hand to flick a tear from the corner of her eye. The copper cuff on her wrist glinted. "Forgive me," she said, almost inaudibly. "Real heroes have that effect on me sometimes. Enough now — let me give you both something. Please." From the pocket of her apron, she withdrew two miniature copper oven charms, designed exactly like the one that was embroidered at the apron's top. "Bring these to any Copper Door Confectionary and you may have anything you like, free of charge, for life."

Jack took his.

Rapunzel did not. "I don't want that," she said. "I want you to stop telling my story."

"There's no stopping stories," Miss Floss replied. "Even if I say yes, it won't matter. The Vox already sing legend songs about you."

Syrah croaked in amazement.

"The *Vox?*" said Jack. "Are you serious?"

"Just take it." Miss Floss gave Jack the second charm, and smiled at him. "The Vox sing about you too, you know."

He grinned.

"Best of luck in the jacks tournament, Rapunzel," Miss Floss called after them as they left the tent. "I'll be cheering for you."

"We'd better run," said Jack, once they got outside. "We're definitely late. Come on."

They hurried past the inn's carriage house and around the back gardens until they reached the grand front doors of the Royal Governor's Inn. A wide, busy road separated it from the shorefront, where a collection of enormous connected tents flew Yellow Country's flag from the highest peak.

Syrah had a mad urge to leap toward that flag — the Gourd family would be there, he was certain. If he sprang away now, he might make it across the busy road. He could be careful, time his progress, make sure that he avoided horses' hooves and carriage wheels. But even if he made it that far, he would still have to brave the sandy shore, where birds would spot him instantly, and he'd have to make his way through tall grasses, where snakes might be waiting.

He had waited too long and come too far to make a mistake now. He clung to Rapunzel's shoulder and rode with her into the inn. A clerk gave Rapunzel and Jack each a room key, and they made their way up the stairs.

"You okay?" Jack asked, setting down the parcels to unlock his door. "All that stuff about witches . . ."

"I'm fine." Her voice was subdued, but Jack asked no more questions. Rapunzel bent down with unexpected swiftness to grab the parcel with her new gown in it, and Syrah lost his balance and had to hop down onto the floor. Rapunzel usually picked him up again when this sort of thing happened, but this time she was distracted. She shut herself in her room.

Syrah followed Jack into his room instead, and he waited on the windowsill while Jack dressed. Dusk had fallen. Across the road, along the shore of Lake Tureen, hundreds of lanterns had been lit, and fashionable people had begun to gather, mingling in the twilight, laughing and eating and being human together.

He distracted himself from painful envy by using his tongue to write the letters of his name in the thin film of humidity inside the window.

S . . . Y . . .

It was an effort to create letters that looked like letters. His tongue was suited to flicking quickly out and in again rather than licking anything at length, so he mostly made small dots close together in a pattern. It took a long time, and he didn't expect it to get results — he couldn't count how many times he had tried to spell things out for Jack and Rapunzel, but they never noticed. Sometimes he hopped out the pattern of his name in the dirt; other times, he painstakingly crafted wet letters on a window or mirror. And then, without fail, something happened to get in the way. Rain fell and washed the letters away, or a carriage came by and trampled them. Or — worst of all — Rapunzel and Jack simply did not see them there. After months of this, Syrah had a terrible suspicion that Rapunzel and Jack *couldn't* notice his efforts.

The wishing well won't let them, said a voice inside him. It was a horrible voice. Syrah tried to block it out, but as the months ticked by, the voice got louder.

Syrah croaked to get Jack's attention, but Jack was busy cracking a Ubiquitous acorn. It fell open to reveal a greasy substance that filled the room with a pungent smell, like body odor and pinesap mixed together. Syrah closed his mouth to keep the smell out. "Ugh," said Jack. "Never mind."

There came a knock at the door.

"Are you ready?" called Rapunzel from the corridor.

"One sec." Jack opened the window without even glancing at the S Y that Syrah had managed to draw, and he chucked the Ubiquitous cologne outside. He finished buttoning his vest, shook out his bloused sleeves, and opened the door.

Rapunzel stood there in her new blue gown, holding a golden badge shaped like two crossed sheaves of wheat. The crest of Yellow Country.

"This was in my room," she said, "with a note that says I'm supposed to wear it whenever I represent Yellow. But I don't know where to put it."

"On your collar."

"I don't have one."

Her gown had no straps either. Syrah saw the lump in Jack's throat bob.

"You have to pin it to the top of your dress, then," Jack said.

"I tried," said Rapunzel, laying the badge against the center of her bodice, like a brooch. "But it keeps going sideways, when I do it." She held the badge out to Jack again. "Would you try?"

Syrah hopped closer to them and sat on a side table, watching in high amusement as Jack grappled with his charge. He took the badge of Yellow Country, uncapped the pin, and tentatively held it near Rapunzel's bodice.

"Hold out the top of the dress, so I can — well, don't hold it out *that* far," Jack said, closing his eyes. "Rapunzel . . ."

"What?"

Syrah longed for the power to snicker. *Go on,* he thought, grinning inwardly. *Do it.*

As if Jack heard him, he opened his eyes. "Don't move," he warned. And then he seized the front of Rapunzel's dress in one hand and attacked it with the pin in the other.

"Done."

The pin shone, straight and golden, at the center of the garment. Rapunzel looked down at it and twisted this way and that to make it pick up the candlelight.

"I wonder if I get to keep it after the games?" she said. "Thanks for making it look nice."

"Sure." Jack gave his hair a casual toss. "Anytime."

"I have something for you to wear too," she said, and she fished a thick bracelet out of one of her Practical Elegance parcels. "Hold out your hand," she said, and Jack did so, looking curious. Rapunzel clasped the bracelet around his wrist. "See, it's made of braided rope," she said. "It feels light, but there's actually a lot, and you can unwind it in an emergency. So you won't have to use Ubiquitous."

"Aw, Ubiquitous is fine. People are just people panicking," said Jack. "I've never had a problem —"

"Don't use them anymore," said Rapunzel. "Promise me."

"But —"

"Please." She met his eyes.

Jack looked away and fingered the bracelet. "Fine," he said, a bit gruffly. "Thanks."

"Come here, Prince Frog," said Rapunzel, dunking a handkerchief into a pitcher of water and placing the wet rag on her shoulder. Water drizzled down her arm and collarbone, staining the gown slightly. "You can sit with me at the feast."

"Leave him here," said Jack. "They won't let you in with a frog, I bet."

Before Syrah could mount a croaking, clammy protest, Rapunzel placed him gently on the wet handkerchief.

"He's staying with me," she said, and she gave him a kiss. "Aren't you, Prince Frog?"

If Syrah had been human, he would have picked up Rapunzel and spun her around just to hear her shriek with joy. She could not conceive of how much he appreciated her. She had no idea he was a person, let alone a prince, yet she treated him with dignity. Usually. And one day, he would reward her. He would take her to the Olive Isles, and he'd show her everything there was to see. Jack too. The three of them would have fine times together, when he could really talk to them. Someday.

Someday soon.

Chapter Three

AT the mouth of the grand tent, Governor Calabaza greeted the delegates. Before Rapunzel approached him, she popped Syrah into her pocket. He wriggled, wanting to stay up on her shoulder so that he could locate Deli, but Rapunzel closed her fist.

"Don't be the way you were the time we went to Cornucopia," she warned.

Syrah went limp. Last time they had traveled to Yellow Country, Rapunzel had spilled a cup of wine. It had puddled around his legs before he could bounce away, so he had absorbed some of it and ended up disoriented. He had still managed to find Deli and get into her pocket, but when she'd taken him out again, he had been too confused to react — and then it was too late. Jack had caught him and buttoned him into a pocket, and he hadn't been able to escape again. That little misadventure had cost him nearly seven months.

He gave a weak, subservient croak to convince Rapunzel that he could be trusted. She petted his head with her thumb. "Good frog," she murmured, and she removed her hand, leaving him surrounded by folds of fabric and tamped down by the wet handkerchief that Rapunzel shoved into her pocket after him.

"There you go," she said, and he felt her hand patting the pocket.

He waited in wet, muffled darkness as Rapunzel climbed the steps to the palace.

"Good evening!" boomed Governor Calabaza. "And you are —"

"Rapunzel."

"Ah," said the governor weakly. "Rapunzel. Of course. The witch *is* dead, yes? Completely? You're certain? Well then, my hat is off to you! Excellent work, excellent — enjoy the feast!"

The level of noise went up as Rapunzel and Jack entered the tent, and Syrah could no longer distinguish their voices over everyone else's. Conversations mingled with the sounds of busy forks and fiddles, and for three-quarters of an hour or so, Syrah remained hidden, pondering his options.

He could jump for it, he supposed, and go hunting for Deli. But there would be quite a forest of shoes to get through without being stampeded. Still, it would be easier to avoid notice now, while everyone was moving. If he tried to sneak out while the delegates were seated at dinner, someone would see him hopping along, and then Rapunzel would catch him, and Jack would put him in a drawstring pouch, and —

"No. I need sleep."

Deli's voice. A thrill coursed through Syrah. He raised the top of his head out of Rapunzel's pocket and saw that she had carried him just outside one of the tent's side doors. Torches threw light upon the sand and grass around them.

"If you could just keep an eye on the boys for another hour —"

"Ma, *please*," said Deli. "Not tonight."

Syrah rolled his eyes toward her voice, and though he expected to see her there, it didn't prepare him for the sight of her. She wore the same dress she'd worn last year at the wedding in Cornucopia.

She even had yellow starflowers in her hair. He stared at her, struck still. It was like time hadn't passed — except that it had, and he'd been miserable. She had *made* him miserable.

Now she was there, right in front of him. He wanted to go to her, to make her understand who he was — but how? Hop up to her? Try to leap to her shoulder? Croak in her face until she paid attention?

Her mother, Roma Gourd, twisted one of the rings that sparkled on her slim fingers. "It's very hard to enjoy a party when the triplets aren't supervised," she said, her pretty face drawn into a frown. "We brought Honey to watch them, but I guess she's sick now, and if somebody doesn't keep an eye on them, they'll set fire to the place, you *know* they will."

Deli shook her head. "I'm competing first thing in the morning, Ma. I've been working toward this for three years."

Syrah croaked his agreement, but nobody noticed; his frog voice blended right in with the nighttime noises of the lakefront.

"Please, sweetheart," said Roma. "Just help me for an hour — one hour, and then I'll take over. And I won't lose track of time this time, I promise."

Deli hesitated.

Say no, thought Syrah. *Tell her to do it herself. They're her kids, not yours.*

"All right, Ma. I'll watch them."

Syrah croaked indignantly, but no one heeded. Deli followed her mother back toward the tent, and Syrah wondered, in sudden alarm, if he should leap for her right now. Maybe, somehow, he could shimmy up the side of her skirt and find a way into her pocket.

He had almost decided to jump for it when a metallic gleam

caught his eye. In the near darkness, several meters beyond the torches, stood a yellow carriage with golden sheaves of wheat crossed on its door.

The governor's carriage. The Gourds' carriage. And one of the windows was open. He could jump into that carriage, wait until the Gourds left the party, and get a ride back to wherever they were staying. It was a much better plan than trying to hitch a ride in Deli's dress. Syrah readied himself to spring.

"Hey, Rapunzel."

Syrah tensed. He knew that voice immediately: Cassis Swill, the launchball player from the clothing shop.

"Want to talk launchball?" asked Cassis lazily. "Or did you come out here to get to know me?"

"It's too loud in there," said Rapunzel, who sounded subdued, just like she had earlier. She was thinking about the witch again, Syrah was certain.

"Right," said Cassis. "Are you courting that guy you're with?"

"Courting?" Rapunzel sounded puzzled. "What are you trying to say?"

"Never mind, I get it," said Cassis, laughing. "It's none of my business."

"What isn't?" said Rapunzel, whom Syrah knew was honestly confused. Courting was not a subject that had come up in her travels. Jack certainly hadn't broached it, though Syrah had often willed him to.

"So," said Cassis. "Want to take a walk with me?"

"Where?"

"Along the shore."

"It's dark."

"Yeah. And it's quiet."

"That's true," said Rapunzel, with a sigh. "All right."

Syrah pressed the long line of his mouth together. This was the moment of escape, and he knew it. Rapunzel wouldn't notice until later.

But there was something about Cassis he didn't trust.

He leapt from Rapunzel's pocket and landed silently on the sand. He shifted himself back into a dark shadow along the outside of the tent, thinking. If he hopped fast enough, he could probably find Jack somewhere in the tent.

And get trampled.

He didn't *have* to find Jack, he told himself. Rapunzel could make her own choices, after all. She wanted to do things by herself — she said so often enough. If she wanted to take a walk in the dark with some glib launchball player who was hoping to take advantage of the fact that she'd been raised in a tower, then that was up to her.

Syrah glanced longingly at the governor's carriage, but he didn't hop toward it. Instead, he bounced toward the open tent flap and rolled his eyes upward, then left and right, scanning the crowd inside the tent. He hopped inside, squeezed behind a sideboard, and wiggled his way between the wood and the tent wall, until his head poked out at the other end. He surveyed this new section of the room, but saw no Jack. And now there were only two choices: stay close to the wall and try to get around the perimeter of the tent without attracting notice, or leap into the crowd and dodge a lot of boots, some of which had spiked heels.

A full skirt swept past the sideboard, and Syrah took advantage of the cover. He hopped alongside the skirt as its wearer made a wide circle around the room, passing another open tent flap. Syrah hopped just outside it, where he could easily watch the guests in the room from a new angle.

No sooner had he taken up his post than Jack emerged from the crowd, deep in conversation with a compact man who wore several medals pinned to a sash around his torso. Syrah recognized him as a glass-mountain grappler who had already had a long career in the sport.

Jack's back was half-turned to the tent flap. He laughed at something the grappler said, then nodded energetically. Syrah leapt back through the doors and made his way directly toward Jack, dodging two pairs of boots and one puddle of spilled wine, and he threw himself against Jack's calf. Jack looked down, startled.

"Prince Frog," he said.

"Prince what?" said the grappler.

"Never mind," said Jack, bending down, but Syrah leapt away before Jack could grab him. He glanced back to see Jack coming toward him, his expression both irritated and determined. Syrah turned and bounced again, leaping away through the open tent flap and bouncing along toward the shore of the lake. He moved rapidly, trusting that Jack was quick enough to stay on his heels.

"Prince Frog," Jack growled. "Come *back*."

Syrah did not. He led Jack onward, all the way to where the lake lapped at the sand — but now Jack was on him, Jack had him by the leg. Syrah wiggled and writhed, but Jack clamped him in both hands and laced his fingers together. Syrah was effectively jailed. He jerked helplessly, but couldn't move much — the pain was too acute. He went still.

"That's it," said Jack. "I'm putting you in a jar and poking holes in the lid —" He stopped short. "Rapunzel?"

Syrah could not see. He had no idea what Jack was witness to. But he could feel, through his belly's close contact with Jack's palm, the thoughts that were suddenly alive in Jack's head.

Can't stand this — I love her — I don't want to ruin us — Skies, what if I ruin —

"What are you *doing?*" Jack said aloud. His tone was incredulous. "Where are your shoes?"

"I wanted to put my feet in."

"Looks like you put half your dress in."

"I didn't mean to. I didn't know it would be so deep right away."

"And get away from those plants, would you? That's juggetsbane. It's toxic."

"I thought it was watercress."

"No, around the edges, there's a light brown . . . Look. I know you want to do things on your own, but this is serious. Until you know how to swim, you shouldn't be in the lake by yourself."

"I wasn't by myself. Cassis was with me."

"Who?"

"That boy from the shop. The launchball player. He went to get me a drink."

Jack was quiet for a minute. When he spoke again, his voice was neutral. "Should I go?"

"Why?"

"So you can talk to Cassis." Jack's tone was heroically noncommittal, but Syrah, who was cradled at his chest, could hear the heavy thudding of his pulse and could also feel, through his belly, Jack's absolute panic and despair. "I don't want to get in your way."

"What do you mean?"

Jack unclenched his laced hands, and Syrah looked out from

between his fingers to see Rapunzel standing knee-deep in the lake, holding her gown up out of the water, her golden hair lit by the moon. If Syrah had been a man, and if Rapunzel hadn't been like a little sister to him, he would have called this a kissing moment.

Jack set Syrah down on a rock. He kicked off his fancy shoes, rolled up his fancy trousers, and waded into the water beside Rapunzel. Syrah knew he ought to head for the carriage now, but he couldn't. Not yet.

"It's nice, isn't it?" Rapunzel said, tilting up her face to catch the moonlight. "So much better than inside. All those people."

"A lot of people will be watching you tomorrow, when you compete."

"That's different. I won't have to talk to them and answer their questions, and —" Her voice caught. "They always want to know how I killed her," she said, so quietly that Syrah almost couldn't hear her. "They want me to describe how she died."

"Who does?"

"Everyone." Rapunzel turned her face and wiped it on her arm. "I came out here to get away from it, but then Cassis asked me questions too. It's just a story to them. Like at the Copper Door. But — to me —" Her breath hitched.

Jack put his arm around her waist, and she rested her cheek against his temple.

"Remember when we went swimming in the Red Glade?" he asked, after a moment.

"*You* went swimming. I almost drowned." But Rapunzel's voice sounded a little stronger.

"Remember when you climbed out of that ravine?"

She nodded. "I think my arms still hurt," she said, and laughed a little. "Remember when you chased those bandits because you liked my hair?" she teased, and elbowed him.

"Yes," said Jack quietly. "Rapunzel, I . . ."

Syrah tensed. *Finish that thought*, he demanded silently. *Do it right now, or I swear I will jump on your head and puke flies all over you.*

But Jack did not finish. He looked like he might do the puking himself. Rapunzel pulled back to look at him, and froze. "What's wrong?" she said. "You look so serious."

"I . . . feel serious."

"About what?"

"You." Jack's voice was low.

"Me?" Rapunzel frowned. "Why?"

Jack hesitated. "You've been out of the tower a long time now," he said. "You're getting pretty used to the world. And that's great — I mean it. I'm glad."

But he didn't sound it, and though Rapunzel was naïve, she was no fool. She eyed him. "Jack, what's this about?"

"You don't need my help anymore," he said. "Not really."

"So?"

"So maybe you won't want me around so much." He paused. "You might want to go separate ways. Spend time with new people for a while. Like Cassis."

"Him?" Rapunzel looked alarmed. "Do you *want* to go separate ways?"

"No, but . . ."

"But what? You're my best friend. I love you. And I *do* need you. You make me happy — don't you know that?"

Jack studied her for a moment. He nodded.

And then he kissed her.

Rapunzel let go of her skirt, and it fell into the water. For a moment, she didn't seem to know what to do; her hands flew up as though she might push Jack away at any second — and then she flung her arms around him.

Syrah cheered silently.

It was time for him to go.

He hopped quickly and quietly up the beach, toward the governor's carriage. He croaked with amusement when he passed Cassis, who stood outside the tent with two drinks in his hands, scowling down at the shoreline. When Syrah reached the carriage, he leapt onto the wheel, hopped up to the windowsill, and rolled his bulging eyes to cast one wistful glance back at the silhouettes on the shore. He felt a momentary twinge of guilt — Rapunzel would be heartbroken when she couldn't find him — but he would make it up to her one day. When he was a man again, he would explain.

Thank you, he thought, and he wished he could say it. *For everything.*

Then he leapt into the governor's carriage, leaving Rapunzel and Jack behind.

Chapter Four

"**W**HY the sudden need for secrecy?"

The deep voice startled Syrah so badly that he gave an involuntary and unfortunately very loud croak. The carriage was no longer empty as it had been before, but he'd been too distracted to notice.

"You lied, Calabaza," came the reply, and Syrah recognized the hard, pitiless voice instantly. Grandmother Luffa. "You promised me. But rumor has it that you've changed your mind."

Syrah, who had landed just inside the window on a leather armrest, had no sooner found purchase with his gelatinous toes than he heard the carriage door open and felt the slap of Royal Governor Calabaza's hand swatting him away. He barely felt the inside of Calabaza's mind — *Never giving this up, don't care what she says* — before he fell back outside.

"I'm running for governor, Mother," said Calabaza as Syrah hit the ground. The carriage door swung shut. "You can't stop me."

Consternated, Syrah hopped under the carriage and across to its other side. He sprang up onto the spokes of the front wheel as conversation drifted out from the carriage windows.

"I will not allow Yellow Country to remain a monarchy," said Luffa. "I did not liberate this nation to see it make the same mistakes as every other fool kingdom in Tyme that values its royal bloodlines over the will of its people."

Syrah heard this with some surprise — and a little flare of anger. His royal family, after all, ruled one of those fool kingdoms. He wondered if Luffa had ever spoken so openly in front of Nana Cava.

He missed Nana Cava. He couldn't wait until tomorrow and the ATC. There, he would find his family — and they would find him. His nana would know him. Somehow, with those half-blind eyes of hers, she would see him. She always had before.

"Oh, calm down," said Calabaza dismissively. "We're not a monarchy. The people elected me, didn't they?"

Syrah leapt from the top of the wheel, up to the armrest of the driver's bench.

"Every time you run for governor, people vote for you out of a sense of duty and tradition," said Luffa. "They even call you Royal Governor — it's a kingship by another name, and you know it. If the position does not pass to someone who is not a Gourd, our democracy will never find its feet."

"If the people don't want me, they can vote for whoever runs against me," said Calabaza cheerfully. "That's the *point* of your little democratic experiment, isn't it?"

Syrah agreed. Luffa had given her people the vote, and now she had to live with whatever they chose. That was what made democracies so stupid. She should have stayed queen — then she could have made up her own laws, disowned Calabaza, and passed her crown to anyone she wanted.

"You pretend not to understand me," said Luffa, "even while you depend upon my being right. You bear my name, and so you are trusted more than you ought to be."

"Why shouldn't I be trusted?" Calabaza snapped. "I've taken care of the country."

"You hold us prisoner to the past."

"I protect our traditions!"

"You have outlawed significant magic that supports agricultural progress —"

"Leave the magic to the magical," said Calabaza. "And the farming to the farmers."

"You are *spineless*."

"Whereas you were a fearless warrior queen," said Calabaza impatiently. "Yes, I know, I know — skies, I'll be *sick* if I have to hear those damned stories again. You want to see a prisoner to the past? Look in the mirror. Everything you are happened a century ago. Your time is done."

Syrah had to hold back a shocked croak. He couldn't believe Calabaza could be so disrespectful to his own mother — especially since she scared the living crops out of everybody else.

"You have never known hardship." Luffa's voice was cold. "Never faced adversity — ancestors forbid this country should face war with you in charge. The nation would crumble."

"Yellow Country isn't in danger of a war."

"But *you* are," said Luffa. "Run for governor, and I will come at you with everything I have."

"Including your old sword?" said Calabaza, who sounded completely unconcerned. "Planning to bring the might of the Olive Isles to bear against me? Going to dig up Cava's old armor and —"

Calabaza stopped short, and Syrah hopped onto the back of the driver's bench, curious to see why. Edging to the corner, he could just see through the window, and he caught sight of Grandmother

Luffa's eyes. The look in them made him prickle all over. She was not a woman who showed emotion — none that Syrah had ever seen — but now she had the eyes of an animal shot through the heart.

"You gave the people a choice," said Royal Governor Calabaza after a minute. "And they're going to choose me. Get used to it."

"I have removed men from power before."

"By beheading them, yes," came Calabaza's callous reply. "Diplomacy was never your strength. Now, if you're finished?"

The *slam!* of his carriage door reverberated through Syrah's body. He heard Calabaza's heavy footfalls as he walked away.

A few minutes later, Luffa followed.

Syrah hopped along the driver's bench until he came to a large picnic basket. It had a leather strap around it, with a brass buckle on top, but the buckle was undone and one wicker flap stood open. He leapt into it and burrowed beneath a napkin. It smelled strongly of mayonnaise, which had always made his stomach turn, but it was a safe place to wait.

Soon, he was jostled awake. He hadn't even realized that he was asleep, but the lurch of the carriage brought him to his senses. He heard the clopping of hooves, and snatches of conversation floating from the open carriage windows.

"— not fair we have to leave early just because of one little joke —"

"— shouldn't have poured it into the punch bowl —"

"— told you Deli would see you."

Syrah knew those voices. The triplets. It was difficult to make out whole sentences over the noise of the carriage, but it sounded like Deli had sent them away for the night. That was good, he thought. It meant that Deli would be able to go and get her sleep before the competition. He still couldn't believe that her mother had asked her to do anything else. He hadn't realized Roma Gourd could be so selfish.

"— crying so hard, I felt bad —"

"— practically tore the place apart. Over a frog!"

They had to be talking about Rapunzel. She had discovered him missing, and she had gone wild looking for him — of course she had. But that couldn't be helped now.

"Bradley, you had a frog down your shirt one time."

"— forgot about that! *It's down my shirt! It's on my back!*" Frenzied laughter followed this high-pitched imitation, and then the sound of a smack and an angry "Ow!"

When the carriage came to a stop, Syrah hopped to shake the napkin off, readying for a jump from the basket. Before he managed it, the wicker flap that had stood open above him fell shut. Syrah heard a brief, scraping noise. He jumped up to test the top of the basket, but though his back struck the wicker, the flap did not budge. Somebody had buckled it. He landed, bruised and frustrated. Maybe this hadn't been the best plan after all.

"Boys!" cried a woman's voice. "Take your lunch basket."

Syrah fell sideways into the wicker as the basket began to shake.

"Boys!" said the woman again, and the shaking worsened. Syrah tried to huddle in one corner to prevent being knocked back and forth. "Basket!"

Syrah was flung swiftly from one side of the basket to the other. His side slapped the wicker with force, and a croaking groan escaped him. "Wait up!" he heard one of the triplets say — he had no idea which one — before the basket began to shake again. Syrah had no teeth to grit, so he pressed his mouth shut hard and hoped very much that the basket was about to be gently deposited somewhere quiet, where he could make his escape.

No such luck.

"You guys," whispered a triplet. "Burdock's not in his room. Let's mess with him."

Syrah pushed himself up against the wicker, trying to see where they were. If he could get into Nexus Burdock's room, maybe he could get his attention. Get him to notice that he was more than just a frog.

"Burdock uses magic on his door." Syrah was almost sure that Walter had spoken; he had a slight lilt in his voice that the other two did not. "If you try to open it, your hand will stick to the knob and you'll get caught and Grandmother Luffa will *not* be pleased."

Syrah strained to see through the minuscule slats in the wicker, but it was woven too tightly for him to get any sense of where they were.

"Tommy, sneak around back," said the triplet who had to be Bradley. "Climb up the garden wall, go through the window, and open the door from inside."

"There are guards out there!"

"Don't be such a minnow."

"Then *you* do it!"

"You're the best climber," said Bradley. "Way faster than me."

His flattery worked. "That's true," said Tommy. "Walter, hold this." Syrah gripped the wicker at the bottom of the basket as best he could with his toes to keep from being flung sideways again as the basket changed hands. He heard Tommy's fading footsteps.

"I'm hungry," Walter announced eventually.

Syrah heard the scrape of the lunch basket's buckle being undone. He shrank back, flattening himself against the far side of the basket as Walter lifted one of the flaps and stuck his hand into it.

"Just shut up about food for two seconds," said Bradley. "Drop that basket and get ready."

Walter placed the wicker container on the floor with the flap still standing open. Syrah remained out of sight, readying himself to jump.

"We shouldn't prank Burdock," said Walter.

"Listen," said Bradley. "Hear that? Tommy's already in there."

"He should use a handkerchief to touch the inside door handle with," said Walter sagely. "So his fingers don't stick to the magic."

"Why didn't you say that before he left?" Bradley demanded.

"I did," said Walter.

"Tommy!" said Bradley in a stage whisper. "Tom, use a handkerchief to touch the door!"

"What?" came Tommy's muffled reply.

"USE A HANDKERCHIEF TO TOUCH THE DOOR," shouted Walter.

Syrah couldn't help a very quiet *rawp* of laughter.

"Shhhh!" Bradley hissed, and then Syrah heard the sound of a door swinging open.

"Skies," said Tommy. "The handkerchief stuck right to it. Good thing you warned me!"

"Now Burdock will know we were here," said Walter.

"So?" said Bradley scornfully. "Come on."

The boys' voices became more distant as they went about their pranking inside Nexus Burdock's inn chamber. He heard the muffled *crack!* of a Ubiquitous acorn, and then a second *crack!* and then a third, followed by a shriek of laughter. When Syrah was reasonably certain that no one was near the basket, he wriggled to the open side, climbed partway up the wicker, and raised himself high enough to scan the corridor.

It was the exact same corridor he'd been in earlier tonight with Rapunzel. His amazing plan had brought him right back to the Royal Governor's Inn. No sooner had he thought this than he heard a very familiar, very unhappy voice.

"What if he got run over by a carriage? What if he drowned?"

The tearful questions were unmistakably Rapunzel's. Syrah dropped down into the basket like he'd been shot and hid under the napkin again.

"He didn't drown," came Jack's steady reply. "Maybe he met another frog down by the lake and decided to stay and hang out."

"You think he left me on *purpose?*" Rapunzel's agonized voice was now right outside the basket, and Syrah knew from the shadow that had fallen over the napkin that she and Jack were standing right beside him.

"We'll keep looking tomorrow," said Jack. "Try to get some sleep, all right?"

Their words became indistinct, and Syrah heard the sounds of doors closing. As soon as he was certain there was no way that Rapunzel could see him, he poised to spring. If he jumped for it now, he could probably hide in Burdock's room while the triplets were distracted.

"Okay, shut the door!" Bradley's sudden whisper was fierce. "Don't use your hand, it'll stick. Use your head!"

"Your head would stick too," said Walter calmly.

"I didn't mean it *literally*," said Bradley in a hush. "Use the napkin in the basket. Skies, Tommy, do I have to think of everything?"

A moment later, the napkin was whisked away, revealing Syrah. He rolled his eyeballs upward to see Tommy looking delightedly down at him.

"Hey look! A frog!"

Syrah leapt for his freedom, but not fast enough. Tommy slapped the basket shut, smacking Syrah in the head and sending him thudding back down into his wicker cage. He tried to moan.

"Stick it under Burdock's pillow," said Bradley. "Quick!"

"It belongs to that girl," said Walter. "Rapunzel. We should try to give it back to her."

Syrah croaked his despair.

"You seriously think that's the exact same frog?" Bradley gave a derisive snort. "Do you even know how many frogs live around the lake?"

"How many?" asked Walter.

"A lot," Bradley replied. "Stick it in Burdock's bed, and let's get out of here."

"You do it," said Tommy. "Unless you're too scared. *It's down my back!*" he mimicked again. "*It's in my hair! Ahhhhh!*"

The basket was thrown open again, and Syrah was seized in a determined fist. He felt only a few brief thoughts — *Stupid Tommy. Next frog I find is going down his pants* — and then Bradley released Syrah and covered him with a pillow. Syrah heard a door slam, followed by the fading sound of raucous, boyish laughter.

Then silence. Merciful silence.

Syrah wiggled halfway out from underneath the pillow to view his surroundings, but for a moment, he could see nothing but a glare of sparkles. Sparkles everywhere. Even in near darkness, the Nexus's room dazzled his eyes. The triplets and their Ubiquitous acorns had left the whole place coated in a film of bright yellow glitter. It was all over the bedcovers too. Syrah couldn't move from his position, or he'd end up hopping right into it, and he had no idea whether he would absorb it or how it would affect him.

He stayed halfway under the pillow and scanned the room, rolling his eyes to take in everything. The space was extremely narrow, small and spare, with scarcely any sign that a person was staying in it, let alone an Exalted Nexus. There were no spells at work, no ink and parchment, no magical ingredients or tattered manuscripts. Only a bed, a wardrobe, a table, and a chair.

Out of the corner of his eye, he saw movement at the windowsill. A spider. Syrah turned toward it, hungry, but stayed where he was. He couldn't get to the windowsill until all this glitter was cleared away.

And the bedcovers were moving.

It took Syrah a moment to realize that his eyes were not tricking him. The bedcovers were moving as though there were dozens of toes wiggling beneath them. The undulations were traveling too, moving rapidly toward the head of the bed. Whatever was under the blanket, it was coming right for him.

Syrah backed up underneath the pillow, his heart fluttering madly. What had the triplets done? What had they left here? Was it a cat? It didn't move like a cat. Should he jump for it, into the glitter?

A shiny black creature emerged from beneath the sheets, and Syrah croaked in terror — then wilted in relief.

A beetle. Just a beetle. The triplets must have used a Ubiquitous Bait Bomb. Syrah's tongue flashed out, and he snatched the beetle into his mouth. He thought it tasted a little like burned toast. He missed toast.

He had barely swallowed when he saw a thin rectangle of light surround the chamber door. The boys' handkerchief fell away from the knob. The door swung open.

Exalted Nexus Burdock peered into the room, a smile tugging at his lips. In one hand, he held the checkered napkin that the triplets had used to shut the door from outside; in the other, an orb of amber light the size of a fist, bright enough to light the chamber. He looked much the same as Syrah remembered him — sandy-haired and kind-faced, though older than his years. Against his official Yellow Country vestments, his Exalted amulet gleamed.

Syrah gazed at the amulet, hope swelling in his amphibian breast. The Exalted were the most powerful mortals in Tyme. If anyone could make him a man again, it was Nexus Burdock.

But how could he communicate with him?

You can't. The wishing well will never let you.

Syrah pressed down this thought, determined not to heed it. He *would* make somebody understand. He had to. The alternative was too horrible to allow.

Nexus Burdock picked up the handkerchief, stepped into his narrow chamber, and gave the orb of amber light a gentle toss. It floated up toward the ceiling, where it hovered, casting a firelight glow over everything within. Then he closed the door and dragged a fingertip through the glitter on the wall. "Ubiquitous," he muttered, dusting his glittery fingers together. "It's everywhere. . . ."

His fingertips glowed suddenly with the light of magic. He flicked this light toward the wall, and it danced rapidly along the glitter, moving like sunlight on a lake, erasing the sparkles as it traveled. In a minute, every last sparkle was gone. Burdock dropped his satchel beside his bed, and his eyes moved to the undulating bedcovers.

He pulled the coverlet back, and recoiled. The bed was full of bugs, a writhing pile of them — Syrah was torn between human loathing at the sight of so many insects, and froggish hunger at the idea of pouncing into the middle of that pile and feasting.

"Boys, boys," murmured Burdock, tutting. "Is this the best you can do?" He plunged his hand into the pile of insects.

The bugs went motionless. For a moment, the whole pile glowed bright silver-blue. Then the pile shrank, evaporating toward the center, until Burdock held just one glowing silver-blue beetle in his palm. This pretty bit of magic he allowed to crawl over his fingers, turning his hand over and then back again to allow it more room to explore, until finally he raised his hand to his lips and blew out as though extinguishing a candle. The beetle disintegrated and vanished.

Syrah watched him, admiring his calm. Most adults would have been furious to find that a bunch of kids had broken into their room and messed with their stuff, but Burdock really didn't seem to mind. He was a powerful man — as an Exalted Nexus, people owed him respect — but he didn't seem concerned with any of that.

It might have been all right, really, being his apprentice for a summer.

Burdock glanced around the room. He bent and checked under a chair, then lifted a corner of the carpet. Next, he opened his wardrobe, and he let out a groan. Every article of his clothing had been turned a garish shade of yellow.

"Very patriotic," he muttered, shaking his head, but Syrah could tell he was amused. Burdock lifted his hands to his wardrobe and began to try to wash the color away with magic of his own. This prank, however, he found more difficult to undo than the first two. One of his tunics grew slightly less yellow, but nothing else changed. The Nexus made a noise of concentration and lifted his hands again.

While Burdock was distracted, Syrah wriggled out from beneath the pillow and made his way to the windowsill, where he unfurled his tongue and gobbled up the spider that still lingered there. His eyeballs retracted, pushing the whole spider, still alive, down into his stomach. He felt it wriggle for a moment, and then it stopped.

The Nexus finally gave up on his clothing, which was now the color of fresh butter. Syrah watched as he remade the bed and re-arranged the pillows. When he found the moist spot where Syrah had been, he raised an eyebrow, checked under the mattress, then glanced around the room.

His gaze fell on Syrah.

"Poor fellow," said Burdock, coming toward him. "Did they lock you in here?" He opened the window, and the warm night air rushed in. "Go on," he said. "You're free."

Syrah croaked loudly and jumped up and down several times. Burdock chuckled and reached out to pick him up, but Syrah leapt away from his hand and down to the floor, afraid he might be shut outside. Burdock moved toward him again.

"You'll be happier in the garden."

I really won't, though. Syrah shimmied beneath the wardrobe. Now he was out of reach unless the Nexus felt like moving all the furniture — which he apparently didn't. Burdock gave up on him, and Syrah crept to the edge of his hiding spot and watched as the Nexus locked his door. He removed his shoes and stockings and doffed his fancy robe. In short trousers and a sleeveless undertunic, he was thin and sinewy as a vine, with pale, corded arms and legs that were marked all over with old scars. Different kinds. Some looked like cuts, others like burns. Syrah had heard how dangerous it was for the Exalted to learn to control their powerful magic; the Nexus had clearly injured himself badly a number of times during his training.

Nexus Burdock raised his hands toward the wall that stood behind his bed. He closed his eyes and bowed his head, and in a moment the wall began to glow. It shimmered, dancing like a curtain of light, and then the entire wall fell away, revealing, to Syrah's utter delight, an extension of the chamber. He hopped quickly from beneath the wardrobe to hide under the bed instead, where he could see straight into the newly revealed space. In truth, it was only a small alcove with a desk in it, but the small space was lit by many floating orbs of different sizes and colors, which floated lazily at various heights, transforming the little study space into something beautiful and mysterious. Burdock sat at the desk, the top of which Syrah could not see from his angle on the floor. He stared down at something in front of him, and he shook his head.

"Seven more *years*," he muttered.

He slumped and rested his forehead against the desk, and he stayed like that for a while. Then, with sudden energy, he got up and wrapped himself in a dressing gown. He plucked one of the drifting magic orbs — a large, shining yellow one — from midair, and he carried it with him out into the corridor, shutting the door behind him. Syrah heard the key turn in the lock, and then, too curious to resist, he hopped up onto Burdock's empty chair. He leapt from the chair to the top of the desk to see what Burdock had been looking at.

It was that day's *Town Crier*. Syrah noticed one of the articles that Jack had mentioned earlier about an unknown sickness that was killing people in eastern Yellow. Burdock had circled the names of the afflicted villages in red, and had scrawled some notes in the margins.

Passed through touch? Two victims relatives, all trade at same central marketplace.

Poison? Vomiting, unconsciousness — juggetsbane? Bluepeace? Color of vomit? Send messenger.

Beside these notes was another article with a headline that read *Royal Governor Runs Again!* Beneath it was an illustration of Calabaza Gourd, with his big hat and his many chins and his welcoming grin. *Governor Gourd rumored to run for fourth consecutive term,* said the caption. Burdock had slashed a huge *X* through the whole thing, and red ink cut across Calabaza's grinning face like a gaping wound.

So Burdock didn't want to see Calabaza run for governor again either.

Syrah abandoned the *Crier* and eyed the inkpot on the table. If only he could dip his toes into that ink, he could write his name. He could make it big, red, and unmistakable, so that nobody could possibly ignore it. But he had tried that once before, a few months ago at Rapunzel's grandmother's house, and it had been disastrous. He hadn't even managed to write the letter *S* before enough ink had seeped through his skin to poison him nearly to death.

But if he could hold the quill in his mouth, and somehow maneuver it . . .

Burdock had left his quill abandoned beside the *Town Crier*. Syrah hopped up to it and considered. Its nib was covered in dried ink, but there was a large clean spot along the shaft — probably where Burdock had held it in his fingers. Syrah tested the spot with his tongue. He tasted no poison. Carefully he took aim, and, as though hunting for a fly, he unfurled his tongue and snatched the quill. His tongue wrapped around the shaft of the feather, and the quill came flat against his face with a wet *snap*. Syrah held it there for a moment, victorious. He had a quill. Given enough time, he could probably write something with it. It would barely be legible, but that was good enough.

The only thing he had to figure out now was how to get ink on the nib without also getting it onto his skin. Maybe if he knocked over the bottle at just the right angle —

The sound of the key in the door made Syrah's heart jump — and he almost jumped with it. Every instinct told him to scramble for cover. But if he stayed where he was, and if Burdock saw him holding a quill in his mouth and trying to write, then surely, *surely* he would understand that Syrah was no ordinary frog.

Burdock entered. He came a few steps into the room, and stopped still when his gaze fell upon the frog in the middle of his desk. Syrah stared at him, willing him to see what was happening. Willing him to come closer. Carefully, he tapped the quill against the side of the ink bottle to make it very clear that he wanted to write something.

Frowning, Burdock crossed to Syrah and crouched down to look at him. Syrah held his breath, waiting. The Nexus plucked the quill from Syrah's mouth. He looked from the frog to the quill in some confusion, and opened his mouth as if to speak.

Yes, Syrah thought frantically. *Yes, you see me. You understand.* He jumped to the ink bottle and got behind it. Using his head, he pushed the bottle forward a little bit. *See? I want to write. I have something to say. I'm a person — I'm Syrah —*

Burdock's eyes glazed over, and he stood up. His curious frown relaxed. He cast the quill aside, picked up the *Town Crier*, and slid it underneath Syrah's body.

"Let's get you outside," he said.

Syrah leapt to the floor, furious. Burdock had definitely noticed him — he *knew* that something was strange — why hadn't he investigated further? Why had he lost interest in Syrah so quickly? Why didn't anybody ever see that he was more than just a frog?

Because the wishing well won't let them. You're stuck like this. Accept it.

No. No, he wouldn't accept it.

Burdock crouched down to grab him again, but Syrah leapt underneath the bed and hid himself in the deepest darkness he could find. He was here at the ATC, he had waited all this time, and someone was going to help him break this spell.

Maybe it can't be broken.

He refused to accept that too. All spells could be broken. That was how magic worked, wasn't it?

Or did some curses last forever?

Burdock did not pursue him. Syrah waited beneath the bed for another hour, until the lights in the room were out. When he could hear the Nexus's measured breathing and felt certain that he was asleep, Syrah hopped quickly to the satchel that Burdock had earlier left on the floor. Fast as he could, he wriggled into it and found an inner pouch, where he burrowed down. If he stayed in here, he could hitch a ride right to the ATC — and his family's box was always right next to the Gourds'. He could find his way to his nana. If anybody was going to understand who he was, it was her. She would see that he wasn't a frog, and she would understand what to do. Wouldn't she?

Syrah silenced the terrible voice within him before it could reply, and he closed his eyes to wait out one more night.

CHAPTER FIVE

*B*Y morning, Syrah was thirsty and wished for a puddle or a damp rag. He missed Rapunzel, who had rarely failed to provide these things for him.

He stayed huddled where he was in Burdock's bag and waited to be carried to the games. Burdock picked up his satchel without even opening it first, and he had only carried it a few steps when Syrah heard the furious sounds of a frantic search. The triplets were shouting.

"*You* had them last," he heard Bradley say. "I saw you looking at them last night before we went to sleep!"

"I put them on the table!" said Tommy angrily. "Walter must've moved them."

"No," said Walter stoutly.

"Burdock!" shouted Bradley, and Syrah heard footsteps pound toward him. "We can't find our passes to the games," Bradley panted. "We've looked everywhere. They'll let us in anyway, though, right? I mean, we're the governor's sons."

"I doubt it," said Burdock. "I don't think they'd let even your father himself in without a ticket. I have mine right here." Syrah felt him pat the satchel and was grateful that he did so gently. "Well, I'm off. Good luck, boys."

"Wait," said Tommy anxiously. "Can't you help us?"

"I'm sure you haven't looked everywhere," was Burdock's reply.

"What? Yes we have!"

Burdock chuckled. "By the way," he said. "Here. You forgot your napkin in my room."

The triplets were silent a moment, and then:

"*You* hid our passes!" cried Bradley, triumphant. "You did, I know it! Okay, okay, you got us back, ha-ha-ha, good one. Now where are they?"

"Shift your perspective," Burdock replied.

Curious, Syrah shimmied partway out of the inner pouch of the satchel and pushed his way up to the top, which was covered over with a leather flap. There was a small gap at the corner of this, which he peered through, rolling his eyes upward. He saw the tickets almost instantly. They were inside the boys' room, trapped in a shining yellow bubble overhead, near the ceiling. Syrah almost croaked his approval, but kept quiet.

"Shift our what?" said Tommy.

Meanwhile, Walter had taken Burdock's direction seriously. First he bent over double and looked at the room upside down. Then he dropped to the floor and rolled onto his back. When he caught sight of the tickets, he grinned.

"I found them," he said.

"Where?" Bradley demanded, and then he followed Walter's gaze, and he whooped. "Now how do we get them down?"

"I'm sure you can figure it out," said Burdock. "Good-bye, boys."

"Wait!" Bradley was standing on the bed now, jumping to reach the orb. "Don't take the carriage, or we won't have a ride! Just give me — one second — I almost — have it —"

Bradley gave a mighty bounce. His fingertips scraped the bottom of the bubble. The explosion that followed was loud, like the *crack!* of a Ubiquitous acorn amplified tenfold. Bradley screamed and dropped on the bed, curling up in terror as bright yellow confetti burst above him and fluttered down onto his hair and onto his clothing. Tommy and Walter shouted with laughter.

"Aaaaahh!" Walter cried, mimicking Bradley's scream. He flung his hands into the air, and Tommy collapsed upon the floor in gleeful convulsions. Bradley uncurled and looked down at himself. When he saw the confetti, he tried to brush it off, but it would not budge. He tried to pick an individual piece of yellow paper from his sleeve. It was stuck fast.

"Oh, come on," he said angrily to Burdock. "Make it come off."

"I don't think so," said Burdock, gesturing to his own outfit, which was a lovely lemony shade from head to foot.

"Tommy did your clothes!" said Bradley. "I just did the glitter!"

"There's a lot of confetti in your hair, Bradley," said Walter, grinning. "A *lot*."

"Anyway, boys, you shouldn't be using Ubiquitous," Burdock warned, plucking the ATC passes from the floor and handing them to Walter. "You know what happened in Quintessential. That fire killed a lot of people — some of them your age."

"If Ubiquitous is so dangerous, why isn't it outlawed?" Tommy asked.

"It will be," said Burdock grimly.

The boys tramped downstairs, Bradley complaining loudly about his confetti hair all the way, and they piled into the same carriage with the Nexus. The rumble of the carriage wheels made Syrah vibrate.

"— like Asti Huanui," said Tommy, bringing Syrah's attention instantly to him. "Don't even try to deny it."

"Why would I deny it?" said Bradley, sounding smug. "Asti's beautiful. Of course I like her."

Syrah listened now with feelings of mingled protectiveness and irritation. His niece Asti was only twelve. Thirteen now, he realized, but still. Bradley Gourd had no business going after her.

You went after plenty of girls at thirteen.

That was true. Deli herself hadn't been much older than that when he'd kissed her. He remembered the waterfall, and the way she had clutched him. The tears that had fallen on her mole-spotted cheeks, mingling with the water, making him retreat and swim away. Tears were too serious. She had been too eager, too earnest — too everything.

"I'm going to kiss her tonight," Bradley announced.

Tommy made a noise of irritation. "Maybe *I'll* kiss her," he said.

"Why would she bother with you? I have all the *charisma*."

Syrah grimaced. Bradley reminded him irresistibly of himself, long ago in another life, when he'd been a confident, swaggering boy. He could not help realizing, with some discomfort, that Bradley sounded like a royal idiot.

"You mean you have all the *confetti*," said Tommy, snickering.

Once outside the carriage, the noise level rose to cacophonous. People cheering, vendors shouting, referees' voices amplified by magic. Syrah's heart quickened. Finally. *Finally.*

The carriage rolled to a stop. There was a general scuffle and slamming of things, and the triplets were gone. Burdock's satchel bounced lightly against him as he walked, and Syrah shut his eyes, trying not to let the throbbing bother him. Soon he wouldn't have to put up with this kind of thing ever again. Soon he'd be walking, talking, using his hands. Soon.

"Tickets!" he heard someone cry, and then, "May I offer you a complimentary cookie, Exalted Nexus? Courtesy of the Baker's Dozen."

"No, thank you," Syrah heard Burdock reply, and then he was walking again. Syrah peeked out of the satchel to get a sense of the situation. At first, he could see nothing but a dense crowd, packed in around them, but soon Burdock was climbing a long set of wooden stairs, and then he was showing his pass to an official guard, who bowed and said "Exalted Nexus," before stepping aside and opening a low gate that led into a private, tented area. Syrah spied tables full of food, a couple of servants, and Governor Calabaza at the center of it all.

"Exalted Nexus!" Calabaza boomed. "Look at you, all in yellow. Very patriotic of you — not sure it's quite your color, though. Join us! Launchball has already started. New Pink had to drop out — two of their team are ill, I've heard. Shame. Commonwealth Green put forth a tolerable effort. Nothing Delicata can't beat. But the coastal nations have an unfair advantage, don't they? I told Deli to set her sights on something easier, but she's just like my mother, unfortunately. She wants victory or nothing, and when she doesn't get it, she'll be impossible to live with."

"Now, Cal," said a female voice. Syrah rolled his eyes to find its owner and saw Deli's mother, Roma, reclining in a chair. "Be positive. She's worked so hard." She fanned herself. "Such a shame Christophen couldn't come back for this. He'd be so proud of his little sister. Of course, no one could expect him to leave Marsanne in her condition — triplets, the Hipocrath says! Did we tell you, Burdock? Triplets. I certainly know how she feels. . . ." Roma sighed and patted her flat belly. "I'm so glad those days are behind me."

"Burdock, did you take a slice of quiche?" said Calabaza. "Our chefs have truly outdone themselves."

Syrah kept his eyes on the gap in the satchel. When Burdock lowered the bag to the ground and stowed it under his chair, Syrah wriggled out. Here in the box, he could move around fairly freely — they were near a lake, after all, and everyone was busy watching the games. It was unlikely that anyone would care if he hopped around a little.

He sprang up onto the top of a low wall, beside a supporting pole. He stayed tight against the pole, looking around to make sure nobody was watching him. They weren't. Near him on the railing was a ring of water where someone had probably set down a glass earlier. A small fly was struggling in it, too soaked to buzz off. Syrah swallowed the fly, then sidled into the water ring, glad to get a drink. While he moistened his legs and belly, he took stock of the world around him.

The wall he sat on was waist height, giving him an excellent vantage. He rolled his eyes, taking in the brilliant view. They were probably thirty feet up, elevated above the rest of the stadium seats that stretched as far as he could see in either direction. Directly in front of the seats below, a Vox sang grand tales of legendary champions past, the blowhole atop its head sucking air so that it never had to stop for a breath, its exaggerated humanesque features shifting from emotion to emotion while people watched, entranced. Behind the Vox, a flock of trained marveilles fanned their enormous silver feathers and sparkled under the sun, opening their peacock-like throats from time to time to send jets of fireworks into the sky. North of this display, on a long runway of wooden planks, candlestick hurdlers stretched their legs and toed the starting line, awaiting the announcement to begin. Beyond the hurdling planks, a tall glass mountain with a tower at its peak had been magically erected. Climbers wearing metal cleats and throwing special grappling claws raced to scale the mountain and get into the tower while spectators cheered with wild enthusiasm. One climber lost her grip and went careering down the slick surface — there was a collective scream — but the climber plunged a glass-splicing spike into the treacherous surface and broke her fall just in time. The crowd went wild.

Down the shore in the other direction, past a pack of Kisscrafters who were competing to see who could spin the most straw into gold, Syrah could just make out the jacks competition. It appeared to be already underway; he saw the shine of Rapunzel's braid at the center of the ring, and he thought he could distinguish Jack's hoarse cheers. He felt a pang of temptation to go nearer — he would've loved to cheer for Rapunzel with all his croaking might. But he had his own prize to win, so he stayed put.

Lake Tureen was vast — he could not see the other side of it. The morning sunlight was still gentle and hazy, kissing the water and making it seem to ripple. The sight of it reminded him irresistibly of morning light on the Tranquil Sea, and he suffered another sudden wave of homesickness, this one even more intense than the last. How he missed the ocean. The islands. The green mountains and the white sand. He longed for the heat of Balthasar's sun on his skin and the sounds of his family gathered around him, playing their instruments and cooking and laughing and talking over each other at once. Even if they annoyed him, or mostly ignored him, he wouldn't care. He just wanted to go home.

Out on the water, a half circle of massive floating platforms supported the launchball teams as they recovered from their efforts or waited for their turns. Syrah scanned to find Deli, but was arrested by the sight of the team from Olive. There was his sister Marsala, stretching her arms in front of her. Even from this far away, he could see that she looked nervous. Sick even. And, in spite of how much she had angered him the last time he'd seen her, Syrah felt a surge of something like brotherly pride. His sister was really going to compete at the ATC, representing the Olive Isles. He halfway hoped that she would win. Olive hadn't won for years — Blue had beaten them out in the last three games. His family must have been wild with excitement.

Syrah looked around, expecting to find them nearby. The Huanuis had always claimed a box right next to the Gourds at the ATC.

But the closest royal boxes this year belonged to Orange on one side, and the Blue Kingdom on the other. Syrah peered to see if any of his relatives were in either of those groups, but couldn't see a single one. He did see Dash Charming, though, looking golden as usual, his arm around a striking girl with bronze curls. Typical Charming.

Syrah hopped along the railing, frustrated. He had counted on his family being where they always were — close enough that he could safely hop to them. Where were they?

"Morning, Huck," said Nexus Burdock, sitting down nearly as far as he could get from Governor Calabaza. He took a seat beside a large man whose skin was so sun-worn it looked like leather. He wore a farmer's clothes, but they were tailored to him. His big country hat boasted a silver cord around the brim, and a huge silver buckle with an S on it glinted from his belt. Syrah did not recognize him. "How's the oat business?"

"Exalted Nexus," the man replied in a slow drawl. "The oats are fine and dandy, thanks for asking."

"Are you here to watch the games?"

"I thought I was." Huck chuckled. "Turns out I'm here to watch my son and make sure he doesn't fall out of the box. Harrow!" Huck raised his drawling voice to a shout. "Don't lean so far out. You can't cheer for Deli with a broken neck."

Harrow. That boy from the wedding. The one with the gold in his skin. Syrah hopped in a circle until he found him, standing at the front corner of the far side of the box, leaning out over the front wall, his skin glittering under the sun. He glanced back, looking solemn.

"I'm just looking around," he said, his voice low and slow like his father's, but softer. He pulled his hat down lower over his eyes as he turned away again.

Huck sat back and folded his muscular arms, his eyes still on his son. "I sure hate seeing him unhappy," he muttered.

"Something wrong?" Burdock asked.

"Oh, he's still sore," said Huck. "He was getting real close with Deli Gourd, but after that mess at the wedding, she shut him down hard."

Syrah smirked to himself. Deli had broken it off with Harrow after the wedding? Of course she had. She must've felt miserable over Syrah's disappearance. She had probably cried for months, regretting how cruel she had been to him. She was probably still grieving.

"That was over a year ago," said Burdock in surprise.

Fifteen months, thought Syrah. *One week, four days . . .*

"Ever been in love, Nexus?" asked Huck, smiling a little. "A year's not much."

"Feelings change quickly at that age."

"Not Harrow's."

"Are you talking about your son?" The voice belonged to G. G. Floss from the Copper Door. She had just arrived, carrying a large, flat box in her hands — black lacquer with a copper CD engraved in the lid. She paused beside Huck's chair. "What a lovely young man. If he hadn't helped me set up my tents when I arrived, I never would have been ready for customers in time. I tried to pay him, but he wouldn't take it."

"I told him to stay busy," said Huck, looking proud.

"Well, if he won't take coin, I'll pay him in chocolate."

"Yes, you've got a good boy there, Steelcut," said Calabaza loudly, plucking a short rib from the absolutely deadly-looking platter of foods that burdened the small breakfast table before him. He cleaned the bone in three bites. "He could give the triplets a lesson in manners."

"So could a horde of imps," muttered Roma.

"Glad you approve of him, Governor," said Huck. "In fact, I'll tell you truly — I hope that Harrow will make your home his own one of these days soon."

Calabaza, who had been pushing aside a bowl of porridge, stopped and looked up. "Make my home his own?" he said. "He's not still courting my daughter, is he? Even if he was, they're children! Well — not *children* — but marriage isn't —"

Huck laughed. "You've got me all wrong," he said. "I don't want him to move in with your family. I was thinking that he and I might move in to the Thatch together, on our own."

"Together?" Calabaza looked astounded. "On your own?"

Harrow glanced back at his father. He looked uneasy.

"That's right." Huck sat back and crossed one boot over his knee. "See, I've decided to run for governor, and I'm going to do my best to beat you. Hope it doesn't mean we can't still be friends. I appreciate the invitation to share this box with you today. What a view!"

Calabaza let out a thin wheeze of air, like he'd tried to laugh and failed.

"Run for governor!" said Roma mildly, from her husband's side. She fanned herself without stopping. "Well!"

G. G. Floss regarded Huck with new interest. Nexus Burdock said nothing and kept his eyes on the games below, but a flush had risen in his cheeks, and Syrah thought he knew why. That red *X* through Calabaza's picture in the *Town Crier* had made it pretty clear: Burdock didn't want to see Calabaza in office for another seven years.

It seemed like a lot of people didn't.

"My mother recruited you, didn't she?" said Calabaza, when he'd recovered his voice. "She's helping you run."

"Nope," said Huck. "I asked her to endorse me, of course — any sane person would. But she refused. She's got her own candidate in mind, she said. A good one too, I'd reckon."

"Well!" said Roma Gourd again, but this time, there was a tinge of worry in her voice.

"Well," Calabaza repeated. "What an exciting election this is shaping up to be."

"Yes it is," came a clipped, cool reply, and Syrah turned his eyes to see that Grandmother Luffa had entered the box. Most people her age would have struggled to climb those wooden stairs outside, if they'd been able to climb them at all, but thanks to her fairy blood, Luffa wasn't even breathing hard.

Behind Luffa followed a very short woman, no higher than her waist, with short, dyed-purple hair and a rectangular valise in her hand. Syrah recognized the woman from the time he had spent shadowing Nexus Burdock — she was Clementine Pease, Yellow Country's minister of agriculture.

"Ma." Calabaza made no attempt to sound pleased.

"Calabaza." She swept to the front of the box. Miss Floss bowed as Luffa passed her, and Huck and Burdock stood and did the same. Harrow removed his hat.

"Madam Governor," he said. "Minister Pease."

Luffa inclined her head. She wouldn't let the people call her "Your Majesty" anymore but they wouldn't stop calling her Madam Governor, even though Calabaza had been the one in charge for decades. The people of Yellow obviously didn't want a democracy, Syrah thought. They wanted things to stay the way they were supposed to be.

Luffa took her place at the center of the front row. She gave a dignified bow and wave toward Orange's box, and then toward the Blue Kingdom's, and then she sat, perfectly erect, and raised a spyglass to her eye.

"Minister," said Huck Steelcut. "Good to see you."

"Mr. Steelcut," Clementine Pease replied. "Your business is booming as usual, I hear."

"Sure is."

"Terrific." She unlocked her valise with a flick of her thumb. It opened into a large, flat rectangle and locked into place with a click. The handle of the case now stuck out of the center of the rectangle, but Clementine pushed it down into a hidden slot, releasing four long metal legs from the corners of the rectangle. The transformation took about five seconds, and when it was done, she had a tall stool. She set it down beside Luffa's chair, hoisted herself onto it, and sat at a height that allowed her to see the games on the lakeshore just as easily as anybody else.

"How's the competition shaping up?" she asked.

"Excellent," answered Calabaza. "Marvelous event so far." He eyed the black lacquer box that G. G. Floss carried. "I wonder what you have there, Miss Floss."

"Oh these!" said Miss Floss, and she opened the box. "I made them in honor of your daughter." Inside the box were a dozen shining golden balls, miniature versions of the kind used in launchball. They looked exactly like the real thing except that they were only as big as egg yolks.

Calabaza let out a whistle of appreciation. "You've topped yourself again," he said. "They're nearly too beautiful to eat."

She offered him the box.

"Raspberry chocolate truffle!" he said as he bit into one. "My favorite! You do spoil me."

"Madam Governor, can I tempt you?" asked Miss Floss, just as Harrow let out a gasp.

"She's up!" he shouted. "She's up, she's about to launch!"

Everyone in the box stood, and Syrah could no longer see anything. He bounded quickly along the side railing to the front wall to get a clear view of the lake. Deli, her black curls slicked close to her head and her dark figure lither and more muscled than ever, stood on her platform, straight and tense, saluting the judges who floated on their own buoyed platform. Her partner, Kai, saluted with his bright green fins. When the referee whistled, Kai plunged underwater. Deli picked up the golden ball and held it cradled in both hands at her chest, and pivoted to the diving board that extended from Yellow's floating platform. Her chest rose and fell with one deep breath. Then she rose up on the balls of her feet and broke into a swift run, which ended with a controlled bounce at the end of the diving board. She soared up, somersaulted, twisted into a downward position, and then her arms shot over her head like arrows, her hands still gripping the ball. She sliced into the lake with barely a splash. The Yellow team whooped. Syrah saw Cassis Swill pump his fist.

Deli did not surface. One second passed. Then two. And then she shot like a cannonball into the sky, one arm tight around her knees, one arm tucked like a wing, her hand clutching the golden ball. As Kai surfaced beneath her, Deli flew up — up — over the launchball bar. She unfurled with the grace of a Bardwyrm and her whole body arched victoriously, arms flung wide, feet pointed behind her — she looked like she could hang there in the sky forever. Then she took aim and fired the golden ball at the target rings that floated on the lake below. She hit dead center, jackknifed, and dove straight down, penetrating the lake once more without seeming to disturb the water at all.

The stands erupted. Screaming cheers swept along the shore. The judges held up their scores, and every single one was perfect. Artistry, height, and accuracy — she'd nailed them all. Syrah's heart swelled. Unless somebody tied that score and forced her into a second round — and *nobody* was going to beat that launch — she was finished. She had done it. She'd won. She flung her arms around Kai, who hugged her back hard, and then her human teammates hauled her out of the water and enveloped her in a jumping, screaming mob.

Beside Syrah, Harrow Steelcut howled with joy. "YEAH, DEE!" he hollered, and he chucked his hat in the air.

Dee? Syrah eyed him viciously. Nobody called Delicata *Dee*. Harrow thought he could give Deli nicknames even after she'd broken up with him? Pathetic.

"Well, I'll be a mermaid's tail," said Calabaza. He lifted his hat and rubbed his bald head. "A perfect score. Roma, she got a perfect score! Isn't she marvelous! Our daughter!"

She was better than marvelous, Syrah thought. She was spectacular. The next time she kissed him, he definitely wouldn't swim away. He entertained himself for a moment imagining how Deli would react when he became a man again. "*It was all my fault,*" she would say. She would probably be crying too. "*I should never have treated you so terribly. I'm so sorry for all you suffered — can you ever, ever forgive me?*"

The sound of wet, violent retching interrupted Syrah's fantasy. One of the staff — a server at the banquet tables — was vomiting over the back wall. Everyone turned toward the back of the box as another server rushed to his side with a rag in her hand.

"My stomach," managed the young man, when his retching was done. "My — stomach —" He doubled over and braced his hands on his knees. "Can't —" he gasped, and he dropped to the floor and retched again, this time toward the governor's chair. The substance that surged from his mouth was thick and white, like no vomit Syrah had ever seen.

Calabaza sprang up and backed away, quite nimbly for his size. Roma rose beside him.

"Oh dear," she said. "Should we —"

Burdock was beside the servant already, crouched, a hand upon his brow.

"Fever," he muttered. "And it's high. How long have you felt like this?"

"Pa?" the servant gasped, whiteness dripping from his chin. He clutched at Burdock's hand. His pupils were so dilated that Syrah could not see what color his eyes were. "Pa, it's so dark —"

Another retching fit seized him, and he convulsed, gagging. "Carry him," Luffa commanded, and the guard at the door sprang to action. "Find a Hipocrath."

"Yes, ma'am."

The guard had no sooner carried the sick servant down the stairs than the serving girl who had given him a rag clutched her own stomach and vomited thick white sludge all over her feet. She stared down at it for a moment, glassy-eyed, then fainted in a heap.

"Skies," said Huck, now on his feet along with everybody else. "What've we got here? Food poisoning?"

"I've never seen any food poisoning that looked like that," murmured Miss Floss, who looked pale and frightened. "It's unnatural."

Clementine Pease eyed the banquet table, then glanced at Huck and narrowed her eyes. He shook his head in reply. The two of them looked away from each other.

"I'll get this one to the Hipocrath," said Huck, lifting the sick girl in his arms.

"Quiet," said Burdock with sudden sharpness. "Listen." Everyone who was still in the box, including Luffa, fell silent at once. And then Syrah heard it.

More vomiting. A *lot* more. He looked down at the stands below, where at least a dozen people were now doubled over, spewing white sludge. More joined them every minute. Some of them were adults, whose small children were now crying, not knowing what to do. Some were small children, whose terrified parents began to shout.

From the Orange tent, a voice moaned in agony while a dog howled in fear. From the Blue tent, Dash Charming cried, "Tanner!" Out on the lake, on the floating platforms, launchball players began to crumple. Cassis fell to his knees beside Deli and retched into the water.

Marsala swayed suddenly and toppled into the lake, where she floated facedown. Syrah stared at her prone body, horror-struck, until her mer-partner grabbed her, flipped her upright, and swiftly hauled her to the shore.

The crowd dissolved into shrieking chaos. People ran for the exits, pushing each other to get ahead. Miss Floss looked down at it all, rubbing one of her copper bracelets with agitated fingers. "White magic," she whispered. "Witchery. It has to be."

"Do *not* start that rumor," said Luffa. "We have no idea what this is." She turned to Calabaza. "Call off the games," she said. "Now. Get the people's attention, and bring them to order." She looked gravely out at the shore, where scores of people lay unconscious. Scores more were buckling to the ground. "You must take charge before this gets out of hand."

"But, Ma!" Calabaza cried, his voice a shriek. "Look at what's happening! We have to leave!"

Everyone looked at him, openmouthed — Syrah included. Leaders weren't supposed to talk like that. Calabaza sounded like a scared little baby.

"You are despicable." Luffa's voice was a lance. "An embarrassment."

"I'm getting clear of whatever this is!" Calabaza donned his tall hat and pulled down the wide brim. "I'm not about to stay and get sick. Roma, let's go."

"You're *governor*," said Burdock. His eyes were cold.

The door of the box swung open and the triplets tumbled in. Tommy looked terrified, and Bradley didn't look much better, still with bits of confetti clinging to him. Walter only looked glazed. He stood beside the tables of food, gazing emptily down at his father's unfinished breakfast.

"Pa!" cried Bradley, rushing to him. "What's going on?"

"Everybody's so sick," Tommy managed. Roma pulled him close.

"Let's go, boys," said Calabaza.

"What about Deli?" said Roma weakly.

"I'll find her," said Harrow. He sprinted out and Syrah watched him go, scowling as much as his frog face would let him. Harrow probably thought he was some kind of hero.

"Nexus Burdock, come with me," said Calabaza. "You need to stay with me."

But Burdock didn't move. His eyes were on a speaking trumpet near Calabaza's chair.

"Burdock!" Calabaza cried. Beneath the brim of his hat, his frightened face was sweating.

Burdock picked up the speaking trumpet in both hands, closed his eyes, and bowed his head. In a moment, the trumpet glowed gold. With high color in his cheeks, Burdock turned to Clementine Pease. "If the governor cannot or will not serve, the minister of agriculture is required to step into the role of provisional governor," he said.

"True enough," said Clementine. She glanced at Calabaza. "You truly won't speak to the people?" she asked. "You're leaving it up to me?"

"Do it, Clementine," said Luffa quietly. "Now."

"Fine." Clementine picked up her tall stool. With a flick of her wrist and the press of a button, the stool became a short stepladder, which she placed at the front of the box. "Give me the horn," she said.

"Or you could do it yourself, Nexus," said G. G. Floss, her eyes on Burdock. "You could reassure the people — they'll want to hear from someone powerful, someone who has magic that might help them —"

Syrah agreed with Miss Floss, but Burdock clearly did not.

He pushed the golden speaking trumpet into Clementine's hands, and she climbed up to stand on top of the ladder.

"This is Yellow Country's minister of agriculture, Clementine Pease," she said. Her brisk, steady voice filled the air, magnified by the glowing trumpet. "People of Tyme, listen to me now and follow my directions to keep your loved ones safe."

The mingled wails of panic died down somewhat. Many people were still shouting and running, but Clementine's words had calmed a handful of them. Those few were now looking toward her voice.

"We do not know the source or nature of this sickness," said Clementine, "so use your common sense. Eat as little as possible until we can rule out the possibility of food poisoning. Stay out of the lake, as this sickness may be waterborne. I am already working with Exalted Nexus Burdock to determine what caused this. We will be as swift as possible in our search for the answer."

More people on the shore were calm now. Even those who were crying were also looking up, waiting desperately for Clementine's next words.

"If you are a healthy adult," she said, "look around for children. There are sick children who need assistance, and there are healthy children with sick guardians. Assign yourself to the first child you see, and keep them safe. See that families stay together. If you are sick but still able to walk, or if you are healthy and able to carry your sick companions, find a Physic's tent. There are four of these tents set up at equal intervals along the shore. Walk to the closest one, stay there, and remain with your loved ones. If you are unable to move or to carry your companions, wait where you are, and help will find you.

"If you have any healing talent, find the nearest Physic's tent and use your skills. If you are in possession of apothecary's supplies or any other resources that might be helpful, bring them to the nearest Physic's tent. All official employees of the games, whether guards, vendors, or event judges, you will now assist the sick. Work together to bring them to healers. That is an order.

"Athletes and judges who are on the lake, remain on your platforms. Do not attempt to swim to shore. Rescue boats will be organized at once to collect you."

As Clementine continued to direct, more and more people stopped to listen and obey. Syrah watched in amazement as adults who had been shouting belligerently just moments before now hoisted sick children into their arms or ushered weeping ones back to their families. Strong, healthy people picked up the sick to carry them. In large, compliant packs, people drifted toward the healing tents, many of them helping one another.

People needed to be told what to do, he thought, watching them all fall into line. They wanted somebody in charge to keep things orderly and safe. When they were left to govern themselves, as they had been a moment ago, it was absolute chaos.

"Stick together," said Clementine. "Help whoever you can. And know that Yellow Country is making every effort to assist you as quickly as possible. The All-Tyme Championships are temporarily suspended."

The glow of the trumpet dimmed. Clementine looked down at it, then handed it off to Burdock and shoved a hand through her thick crop of purple hair.

"We have to get back to Cornucopia to organize relief," said Burdock. "There aren't enough resources in Plenty to deal with an emergency of this size. Calabaza —" Burdock shot a simmering look over his shoulder at him. "Come with me. You must Relay the capital and mobilize the guard."

"Fine," said Calabaza. "Let's just *go*."

"And if it *is* White magic, Nexus?" Miss Floss demanded. "What will you do about it?"

"I'll contact the Exalted Council," he said.

"Send for Exalted Nexus Keene right away," Miss Floss demanded. "If this *is* witchery, then he's the only one powerful enough to —"

"Thank you," said Burdock impatiently. "But you should see to your candy, Miss Floss. The minister and I will handle this." He turned his back on her.

Miss Floss snatched up the candy box from Calabaza's table and swept away down the stairs with her head held high.

"I will visit the Charmings," said Luffa. "If this does turn out to be a magical issue, we will want the support of the Blue Kingdom and their House of Magic."

"Then we all have our jobs." Clementine picked up her step-ladder, clicked open two locks, folded it in half, and it was a valise again. "Let's go," she said, and walked out with Luffa right behind her. Burdock followed, with Calabaza and Roma on their heels, bringing the triplets with them.

Only then, watching them all vanish, did Syrah come to his senses and remember that he needed to stay *with* them. He leapt after the Gourd triplets, bounding from the wall to the chairs and then toward the food tables. He carefully hopped around the puddles of strange white vomit, taking care not to touch a single drop — it smelled strongly of moths — and he caught up to Walter, who still looked to be in a daze. Syrah took advantage of his glassiness to leap onto the souvenir mer-tail that dangled from his hand. He grabbed hold of the stuffed object and hung on, berating himself. He had to focus, or he was never going to get back to his human form. He had to get someone's attention. He had to *think*.

But his thoughts were all full of Marsala. Where was she now? Had somebody taken her to a Physic's tent? Was she lying there alone, waiting for help that hadn't even been organized yet? And what about the rest of his family? Where were they? Were any of them sick? Was Nana Cava? She was so old — if she got sick like that, it might really kill her. Syrah's stomach turned, and for a moment he thought that *he* might vomit. If Nana Cava died, then she would never know what had happened to him. He'd never be able to speak to her again — he wouldn't have a chance to say good-bye.

In the carriage, he wiggled into Walter's pocket. In that darkness, anxious and overwhelmed, he drifted into a fitful sleep and dreamed of a massive moth with spider's legs, hovering over a lake of white sludge.

CHAPTER SIX

*H*E woke disoriented. *Everything is loud — Tommy's voice, Bradley's voice — have to choose which one to follow, but it's hard. Both of them are interesting. . . . Vomit isn't supposed to be white — something is wrong wrong wrong. . . . Not fair that the games were canceled, I wanted to see the games. . . .*

The frog is so smooth. I like how smooth the frog is.

Syrah realized he was sitting in somebody's palm, being petted gently by a careful hand. He rolled his eyes upward and found that it was Walter cradling him. They were in a room back at the Royal Governor's Inn, which looked like a hundred people's clothes and dishes had exploded in it. The carpet could barely be seen.

Syrah hopped out of Walter's hand and found his way to the windowsill, where he looked out at the back garden of the inn. It was growing dark, but the garden's lanterns were still unlit. Syrah wondered if that was because the people who were supposed to light them had fallen ill.

Suddenly, he caught sight of the swinging light of a single lantern. It came from the other side of the garden, where the inn's long carriage house stood half-hidden by the drooping branches of several willow trees. Someone was inside the carriage house, moving around. Syrah's eyes bulged as he tried to see better. Walter got up and came to the window, but he did not pick Syrah up. He just stood there, watching with him.

Someone knocked at the door. Syrah hopped in a circle to see who was there.

Deli entered wearing traveling clothes, and Syrah's heart gave an extra beat. She glanced around at the extent of the mess in the room.

"You haven't packed?" she said. Her voice was hoarse, as though she needed rest, and when Syrah looked more closely at her, he realized that she was bone-tired. He hadn't noticed at first, because of the way she carried herself — sure and strong, the same way she had stood on that floating platform before her launch. "You were supposed to be done by now."

"But are we *really* leaving?" Tommy asked.

"Don't you think they'll start the games up again tomorrow?" Bradley added. "The games are only suspended —"

Deli shook her head. "The games are officially canceled. Pa just announced it. It's over." The frown line between her eyebrows was deeper than Syrah had ever seen it, and for once, he didn't blame her for being so serious. It would be rough, training every day for a competition like the ATC, and then performing as beautifully as she had, only to have that victory jerked away.

"Pack your stuff," said Deli. "I don't care if it's folded, just get it done."

"But your launch was perfect," said Bradley, his voice heated. "You won! Everybody *knows* you won."

"People are sick," said Deli. "That's all that matters now."

"Can we eat yet, at least?" said Tommy.

"No. Nexus Burdock still doesn't know where all this came

from, so for now it's safer if we wait. This sickness, whatever it is . . . it's not just in Plenty."

"Is it in Cornucopia?" asked Bradley, Tommy, and Walter at once. Walter finally turned away from the window and gave his full attention to the conversation.

"We don't know yet," said Deli. "But there are some villages east of here where people have been getting sick. Nobody realized it was this bad."

Syrah remembered the article from the *Town Crier*, and the notes Burdock had written in the margins. The Nexus thought it might be poison — but how could all those people have been poisoned at the same time? His notes had also mentioned that the sickness might be passed through touch. What could everyone have touched? Their ATC passes? No, the athletes didn't have those . . .

Burdock had also made a note about the color of the vomit. He had wanted to know what color it was. How could he have known that the color would matter? Because it definitely mattered — that weird, white vomit was like nothing Syrah had ever seen.

"I'm hungry," said Walter.

"No eating," said Deli sternly. "We can all go a day without meals if we have to. Longer even."

"You think it'll take longer?" asked Tommy anxiously.

"I doubt it," said Deli. "Exalted Nexus Keene is already here, and he's testing everything."

"Keene the witch slayer?" said Bradley, with great interest. "I always wanted to meet him."

"He's busy," said Deli, and then, to Syrah's delight, she looked right at him. "Who's this?" she asked.

"Rapunzel's frog," said Walter.

Bradley snickered. "He thinks every single frog is Rapunzel's frog," he said.

"I'm right," Walter insisted. "Remember, Deli? You held him in your pocket at the jacks tournament last year." Walter offered up Syrah on the flat of his palm so that Deli could study him. Syrah hopped eagerly.

It's me. It's ME.

"You know, it just might be the same one," said Deli, her dark brown eyes narrowed to study him. "I remember he was real green like that."

Syrah gave a single affirmative hop, and a croak to go with it.

"Funny little guy," said Deli. "Almost seems like he understands me."

I do, Syrah tried to say, but it came out as "Rawp *rawp!*" He jumped again for emphasis.

Deli giggled, and Syrah wondered why he'd ever disliked her moles. They were sort of cute on her nose and her cheeks. Like freckles.

"Well, if he is Rapunzel's frog, he's out of luck," said Deli. "She left here with her family an hour ago. Poor thing — she had the lead in the jacks competition before they canceled it. Anyway, I'll figure out where to send her a letter. Can you take care of the frog in the meantime?"

"Yes," said Walter.

YES, thought Syrah, giving a victorious croak and a series of dizzy hops that made Deli giggle again, and Walter too. It would take at least two weeks for a letter to reach Rapunzel, and then she'd have to travel back to get him. Granted, she had that ring to help her, but it would still give him two weeks to communicate with everyone — and now he had protection. He was going back to the Thatch as Walter's temporary pet. He didn't have to figure out how to sneak into the luggage, and he didn't have to worry about getting tossed out of the governor's mansion once he was there. He could plan now. Really plan. This was finally going to happen. He released a long, sighing croak of ecstasy.

"I think he likes you," said Deli. "You should name him."

"Rapunzel called him Prince Frog."

"Cute," said Deli. "Now let's pack."

The carriage ride back was long, but at least it was on paved road, making things much more comfortable. Calabaza and Roma took their own private carriage, and Syrah rode behind with the triplets and Deli. None of the humans were allowed to eat, but Syrah found a line of tiny black sugar ants crawling up one of the carriage walls. He licked the line clean, enjoying the sweetness of anty pulp. When he was a man again, he might even keep on eating ants. They were really tasty.

They reached the Thatch at midnight. Syrah opened his mouth wide, breathed in, and let the scents of the governor's garden overwhelm him. The last time he'd smelled this place, he had been a man. And he was about to be one again. Tonight, while everyone slept, he would start his work.

He was so close.

Upstairs, in the family's wing, Syrah hopped onto the sill of an open window in Walter's bedroom.

"He'll run away if you don't put him in a jar or something," said Bradley, yawning as he traipsed off to his own room down the hall.

Walter crouched down to the sill and met Syrah's eyes. "Will you run away?" he asked.

Syrah gave a firm *ribbit*, and, to reassure Walter that no jar was necessary, he leapt to Walter's shoulder and pressed against his neck. "Ribbit," he said again, then hopped back to the windowsill and settled down to show that he wasn't going anywhere.

"Good," Walter said. He fell into bed without undressing and went to sleep without putting out his lamp. Moments later, Deli appeared in his doorway. Shaking her head, she came into the room and yanked off Walter's boots. With no one now watching her — or at least, no one that she knew of — she let her exhaustion show. Her shoulders sagged, and she rubbed her temples.

"It's fine," she said to herself quietly. "I'm fine."

She pulled up Walter's covers and tucked him in, even kissing his forehead like a mother. Then she picked up the stuffed mer-tail souvenir he'd brought home. For a moment, she played absently with its silken fins.

All at once, her face crumpled. She buried it in the stuffed tail and stifled a sob. She remained like that for a minute, tense all over, and Syrah thought that he had never wanted to be a man more. He could have gone to her. Put his arms around her.

"Selfish," he heard her mutter, her voice muffled. "*Selfish*. It's just a stupid game."

But it wasn't selfish. And it wasn't a stupid game — it was the All-Tyme Championships. Of course she was disappointed; she'd been killing herself for this. Everyone said she worked harder than anybody else, and now that Syrah had seen her performance, he believed it was true. If he'd been her, he would've done a lot worse than cry for ten seconds. He wished that he could tell her so.

"Delicata Aurantia."

Deli uncovered her face and whirled to the door like she'd been caught committing a crime.

"Grandmother Luffa," she said shakily. "Do you need anything before I go to bed?"

Luffa stood there, straight-backed, her dark eyes taking in every inch of Deli. Her expressionless gaze lingered on the flimsy mer-tail toy that hung from Deli's hand. "People died today," she said, in her cool, pitiless voice. "Children died. Their parents died."

Deli nodded, barely.

"If you are crying, *that* is what you should be crying about. Not a sport."

Deli bowed her head. "Yes, Grandmother."

Luffa turned away and left.

For a moment, Deli stood there, head bent, unmoving. When she finally looked up, her face was as hard and expressionless as her grandmother's — the change almost frightened Syrah. With brisk efficiency, Deli tucked the mer-tail against Walter, put out his lamp, and left.

Syrah sat in the dark, amazed. Luffa had scared him all his life, but on his visits to the Thatch he'd mostly been able to avoid her. Deli, on the other hand, had lived with her since birth. It had to be tough living with a legendary grandmother who had led an army and slain a warlord and reclaimed a country, all by the time she was eighteen. It probably explained why Deli was so . . . *Deli* all the time, with her deadly seriousness about life and her absolute perfectionism, like somebody was watching her every move and she had to prove she was worthy.

Maybe somebody was. And maybe she did.

But he was wasting precious time.

Syrah hopped to Walter's desk. The moon was not particularly bright, but Syrah could see just fine. Since becoming a frog, he had found it much easier to see in the dark. And what he saw now was just what he'd been hoping for: a big mess. This was what he'd been missing, staying at Rapunzel's grandmother's house — that place was so immaculate that he'd had to forage outside for every insect he ate, because none of them dared come in. No pen was ever left lying around; no ink bottle was ever left standing open.

Walter's desk was exactly the opposite. There were quills and fountain pens and broken nibs and old blotting papers, and a little bottle of ink, small enough for a frog to tip over, that had been left uncorked.

Perfect.

Syrah chose the smallest, lightest quill. He grabbed it with his tongue, leapt to the floor, and deposited the quill on the floorboards. He had to get it completely out of the way before he tipped over the ink bottle, since there was no way he would be able to control the spill. If ink got all over the quill, it would be useless to him; he wouldn't be able to pick it up without poisoning himself.

He leapt up onto Walter's chair and back onto the desk. A piece of loose parchment with just a few crossed-out scribbles lay on one side of the table. Syrah hopped around behind it, set his front toes on it, and slid it forward, taking tiny hops with his back legs and keeping his front toes pressed down on the parchment until he had pushed the paper all the way to the front of the desk. It slipped over the edge and drifted to the floor.

The final step in preparing to write was to create an ink puddle. This was by far the most treacherous endeavor. If the ink puddled quickly and spread toward him, and he wasn't able to leap out of its path, he very well might die. He considered the small rectangular glass bottle, and the slight slope of the desk. If he pushed the bottle toward the front of the desk, the ink would run down the slope, away from him. It might drip onto the floor, but that was fine.

Syrah hopped around behind the bottle and prepared himself. If this went wrong, he would have to jump for it, far and fast. He tensed, ready to spring, and he stuck out his face. He gave the little bottle a nudge with his yellow, gut-like chin. The bottle wobbled, but didn't tip. Syrah braced himself and shoved his chin harder against the bottle.

It tipped. Syrah leapt sideways and kept leaping until he was off the desk and back on the windowsill, where no ink could follow. He sucked in air through his nostrils as he turned back to see what had happened.

The desk was clean.

He blinked, sure that the moonlight was playing tricks on him, but from where he sat it appeared that no ink had spilled. Confused, Syrah hopped back to the desktop. Gingerly, he made his way to the knocked-over bottle, which he prodded with a gelatinous toe.

Nothing.

Of course, he realized in frustration. If the bottle had been uncorked since before the family had left for the ATC, then the ink would have all dried out by now.

Luckily, Deli had left the door open, so he could explore other options. He wondered if he could get into the old schoolroom. There was chalk in there, and chalk wouldn't poison him. Probably.

He made his way out of Walter's room and kept close to the wall as he hopped along the corridor. The Thatch was mostly dark, but Syrah had been visiting the place his whole life, and though he'd spent very little time in the Gourd family's personal quarters, it didn't take long before he reached the grand staircase that led straight down into the main foyer. He paused at the top of the steps and gazed down. There, right there, Nana Cava had banished him. There, Grandmother Luffa had ordered her guards to escort him away.

Syrah remembered how Deli had huddled against the wall, close to where he now stood, hugging herself and looking down at him. Suddenly uncomfortable, he began to descend the steps, one hop at a time. Deli had brought it on herself, he told himself for the thousandth time. If she hadn't acted so high and mighty at the party, and if Marsala hadn't tattled on him, then his nana would never have kicked him out.

He felt a pang of anxiety at the thought of Marsala. Was she still unconscious? Where was she now? And where, come to think of it, was his entire family? They should have been sitting near the Yellow tent at the games. The Huanuis and the Gourds were practically blood, especially now that Marsanne had married Christophen. Had something come between them?

It occurred to him that maybe *he* had come between them. He had vanished in the Gourds' backyard. For all his family knew, he was dead. Maybe they blamed Luffa's guards. Maybe they blamed Luffa herself. But no — Nana Cava and Luffa were like sisters. Nothing could separate them.

Unless his nana was dead.

Syrah felt clammier than usual. She wasn't dead — she *wasn't* dead. For one thing, her death would have made the *Criers*, and Jack read the *Criers* all the time. Syrah would have heard him talking about an important headline like that. . . . Unless Nana Cava had died before Syrah had met up with Jack and Rapunzel.

It's possible, said the horrible voice. Nana Cava was really old. And what had Calabaza said? Something about digging up Cava's old armor? Syrah had thought he'd meant digging it up out of storage, but maybe he had meant something much worse. Maybe that was why Grandmother Luffa had looked so wounded.

Syrah bounced toward the old schoolroom more vigorously than necessary, trying to shake his bad feelings away. Focus. That was what he needed. Marsala was going to be fine, and his nana was definitely alive, and right now he needed to concentrate on becoming a man again, so that he could see them both for himself.

He found the old schoolroom door barely ajar. It smelled stale inside, like no one had been using it, which of course they hadn't; Yellow Country didn't do year-round school like Olive did. The triplets were out on holiday. It was something Syrah had long envied about life here in Cornucopia — school that stopped in summer. He had begged his parents to let him have summers off too, but they'd just smiled and ruffled his hair. They hadn't even noticed when he'd started skipping sessions with his tutors for a couple of weeks one summer, just to see if he could get away with it. His whole life, they had never checked to see what he was doing. If Nana Cava hadn't always been watching over his shoulder, he would barely have had an education.

He missed his nana with sudden keenness. No matter how many children and grandchildren and great-grandchildren there were, she had always noticed him. Always spoken to him, held him to his duties, tried to motivate him. She had seen him, even when he didn't want her to see him.

She had seen right through him when he'd lied about Deli's letter.

Troubled, Syrah hopped up onto one of the school desks and swept his gaze around the room. Everything had been tidied up for summer, but he poked into every corner, and peered under the lecture podium. He jumped onto the instructor's desk to see if any of the drawers were open enough for him to jimmy the rest of the way. They weren't, but it didn't matter — he saw what he was looking for: a piece of chalk, abandoned on the windowsill. Syrah leapt toward it with such energy that he fairly flew.

He didn't snatch it right away with his tongue. He was afraid it might dissolve before he could do anything with it. It was small — no larger than a daisy petal. If he could only write a little bit, then what should he write?

And where should he write it? If he wrote something in here, it might not be seen for another two months. He had to get the chalk somewhere that his message would be noticed. He considered. He couldn't push the chalk onto the floor, or it might break and be useless to him. He had to snatch it up with his tongue and jump to the floor. This he did, and then immediately released the chalk again so that it wouldn't get too wet. He tasted his tongue, trying to determine whether chalk was poison, but nothing seemed alarming — it was probably just fine. He pushed it along with his forefeet, out of the classroom and down the hallway toward the foyer, until he reached the bottom of the stairs.

It was a good spot. The floor tiles were dark stone; the white chalk would stand out beautifully against them. If he could write out his name at the bottom of the steps, then it could not fail to catch somebody's attention. But was his name the best option?

He had thought about this quite often. He believed that *SYRAH = FROG* was the shortest way to say what needed to be said. However, he wasn't sure he had enough chalk for all that. *SH = FROG?* He wasn't sure. Would anyone understand that *SH* stood for Syrah Huanui? *SYR = FRG?* No. That was just confusing.

He would write *SYRAH*. It was understandable, and it would startle people. The Gourds would pay attention to it. And he could hop back and forth along the letters, croaking like crazy until somebody understood. It was a shame he couldn't write the letters in *front* of somebody. Then they'd realize right away that he wasn't just a frog. But he'd tried that kind of thing before, and people always just thought that he was playing with whatever object he was trying to write with. The objects got taken away, and he got a pat on the head and a nudge into the garden with a "Go on, Prince Frog, find something to play with outside."

Not this time. He'd do this now, by himself, in the dark. By the time the Gourds woke up, he'd be finished.

He slid the chalk toward the stairs with his foot. As he dragged the chalk, he saw that it was already making faint marks along the stones. Excited, he pressed down a bit harder with his foot and dragged the chalk again. He'd made a brighter mark. This was much simpler than having to carry the chalk in his mouth, and it meant he wouldn't melt it with wetness either. His foot was moist, but not so much as his mouth.

He started writing, dragging the chalk a little bit at a time, carefully shaping the first letter. *S* was tricky — so many curves, so many changes in direction — but he worked diligently, one small mark at a time, being sure to press hard enough to make the marks visible. When he finally had an *S*, he hopped up a couple of steps and looked down to see how it appeared.

It was perfect. Jagged and strange, but most definitely an *S*. His heart pattered, anxious and eager, and he leapt back to the chalk to keep working.

Hours passed. By the time he reached the end of the *A* he was breathing heavily through his nostrils. He was hungry and thirsty, and he knew that dawn was coming soon. But he was close. He'd almost made it. Just an *H* now. He rolled the chalk over to the next blank spot on the floor, pressed down, and made a guttural noise of dismay.

The chalk, which had been growing smaller all along, gave way under the pressure of his foot, leaving him with a pile of dust. Agonized, Syrah stared at it, and then he set his long mouth in a hard line. He was going to make this work. He had come too far to lose this chance now.

Using his foot like a brush, he dipped it in the chalk and then swiped it along the floor. He would make a smaller, less obvious *H* with the dust. It wouldn't be big, but it would be there. They'd see it. They'd know.

He worked as fast as he could, and when he was done, he hopped up the steps and looked down at his creation.

SYRAH

He croaked in exhaustion and triumph together, then tucked himself in between two of the balustrade rails. Pale dawn light broke through the windows. Soon, people would wake. Until they did, he would stay right here, and he would wait for somebody to come.

The voice in his mind told him that it didn't matter if somebody came — that just as every attempt before, this one would be foiled. Syrah shoved this miserable thought down as far as it would go. This time, it would be different. It had to be. He had written his name — how could anybody ignore that? They couldn't, that was all. They'd see. They could not fail to see.

CHAPTER SEVEN

SYRAH had barely been waiting for half an hour when the peaceful stillness of the Thatch was shattered.

Somebody upstairs was screaming. A woman. Screaming and crying like she was under attack.

Syrah bounded up the stairs, toward the family's quarters. The screaming continued until Grandmother Luffa's voice rose up sharply over it. "Quiet, Roma!" she commanded, and Roma's wails became instantly muffled like she'd clapped both hands over her mouth.

"Pa?" he heard one of the triplets say uncertainly. "What's happening?"

"Go back to your room."

Deli's voice. So she wasn't hurt. Syrah wanted to hop all the way upstairs and see her to make sure, but he stopped himself. He had to stay where he was. When somebody noticed his name, he had to get their attention and help them make the connection.

The front door of the Thatch flew open, and guards came rushing in. They were on the stairs in seconds; Syrah had to leap aside to keep from being crushed under heavy boots. The guards jangled their way up into the family quarters. Syrah looked down the stairs again and his heart gave a nasty lurch.

They had stomped right through his name, erasing parts of it.

It was still possible to tell — just — that it said *SYRA*, but the little *H* was nothing but a smear of dust now. If people walked on it once or twice more without noticing, then the whole thing would be illegible.

He couldn't let it happen. If they tried it again, he would make them stop. He bounced down to the bottom step and took up a defensive position right in the middle.

Bells began to ring, muffled but near. Syrah felt their vibrations as though they were coming from under the floor — and then he realized that was exactly where they were coming from. Someone was pulling the bell cords to wake the staff, a handful of whom soon shuffled past the grand staircase and into the parlor, some yawning, some still tying their aprons and buttoning their vests. The cooks emerged from their morning preparations in the kitchens.

"Earlier than usual for a meeting," he heard one say to another. "Do you suppose it's about that sickness in Plenty?"

"Not just Plenty," replied the other cook, shaking his head. "I've got family out east in Threshing. Three days ago, their neighbors lost a little boy to this sickness. Just six years old."

A man wearing dark gray garb and an Exalted amulet strode past, his face intent. The cooks watched him go into the parlor, and their faces showed both curiosity and fear.

"Now why would they bother the Relay for a kitchen staff meeting?" asked the first cook.

"Something's bad wrong," muttered the other.

None of them passed in front of the stairs. None of them saw Syrah's chalked name. A moment later, two of the guards reappeared and hurried back down to the foyer. Syrah stayed where he was on the bottom step, croaking loudly to get their attention so that they would not squash him, but the guards were intent on their goal. They merely sidestepped him, then trod upon his name once more. He let out a furious *raaawwp*, which no one heeded. The guards hurried into the parlor.

"Emergency . . ." Syrah heard. ". . . next door to fetch Physic Feverfew . . ."

The rest was drowned out by the pounding of running feet as a woman flew from the parlor and ran to the back of the house, followed closely by a handful of messengers who were also moving at top speed. Syrah sagged, despairing. They hadn't even glanced at the floor, and his name was in bad shape from having been trampled twice. Somebody had to look *now*. He had to make them look.

He leapt over his name so as not to further smudge it, and he bounded into the parlor, where the staff were listening to the guards and looking fearful. He began to croak as loudly as he could.

"Unconscious . . ." he heard, through the racket he was making. ". . . don't panic . . ." ". . . confidential . . ."

Syrah grimaced. Nobody was looking at him. He leapt onto one of the parlor tables, right beside the guards, and he began to jump up and down, croaking for emphasis each time he landed. One of the staff, a teenaged boy in an apron, whose eyes were still pinned on the guard who was speaking, reached out for the window latch, felt for it, and unlocked it. "Is it the same sickness from Plenty?" he asked as he pulled up the window. "Does this mean it's spreading here too?"

"No idea," the guard replied. "So don't start any rumors."

The aproned boy walked over to Syrah and reached for him, but Syrah was too quick; he leapt out of the way. He wasn't about to get thrown out a window now. "CROAK!" he shouted, and the boy took another step toward him. Syrah leapt for the door and checked back.

The aproned boy was following him and looking annoyed. Overjoyed, Syrah continued to hop back out into the foyer, toward the bottom of the stairs.

The front door opened. The woman who had run from the house just minutes ago now returned with a Hipocrath beside her. It was Physic Feverfew, a stout little Hipocrath with a severe gray topknot and blue palms whom Syrah had encountered in some of his scrapes as a boy. Feverfew stamped on Syrah's name as she raced upstairs, but the other woman stopped at the bottom of the staircase, breathing hard. She looked down, and her eyes locked onto Syrah's chalk marks. She frowned. "What's this, Benny?" she demanded, pulling her thick brown hair off her neck. She twisted it into a knot and started securing it with pins from her apron pocket. "Someone writing on the floor?"

"Looks like it," said Benny, hooking his thumbs into his apron strings, which he had wrapped all the way around his skinny body and knotted in the front. He squinted at Syrah's handiwork. Syrah jumped up three steps and surveyed the damage. *SY — A —* was still vaguely readable. The *R* had smudged nearly out of existence. "Somebody was writing something," he said. "S, Y — is that an A?" He shrugged. "Sya? Doesn't make sense."

Yes it does, thought Syrah angrily. *THINK about it.*

"Probably just the triplets making messes," said the woman.

It's not the triplets! cried Syrah inwardly, and he threw himself at the woman's foot.

"Clean it up quick," said the woman, wiggling her boot to get him off it, "before the ministers get here."

Syrah leapt onto the place where his *R* had been, and he let out a moan of croaking agony. His vocal sac ached with effort.

The woman looked at him with some amusement. "This one's looking for a mate," she said. "Making all that noise. Put him outside, would you?"

"That's not my job," said Benny, seeming to forget that he'd been trying to do just that a moment ago. "Why don't *you* do it?"

"Because I forgot my cap." The woman strode toward the door of the staff quarters, and Benny went back to the parlor.

"Someone take care of the foyer floor," he ordered, before heading back toward the kitchens. A grumble from the parlor followed this.

"Thinks he's the biggest tree in the orchard."

"And all he does is wash the governor's dishes."

Syrah slumped where he was, blood pounding and nostrils flaring. His heart sank heavily into his guts.

It's over, said the awful voice. *You're a frog. Accept it.*

He couldn't. He had to figure this out before Rapunzel heard he was here and came back to collect him. Fond as he was of Rapunzel, he couldn't be her pet any longer. But what more could he do? How was he supposed to break this stupid curse?

One minute and a damp rag later, the floor at the bottom of the steps was wiped clean. Syrah crouched beside the foyer wall and watched it happen in listless defeat. That stupid, miserable wishing well had trapped him like this forever.

And it could *un*trap him.

He had to get back to the well, he realized suddenly. The well would know him — the well could fix this. And it wasn't too far from the Thatch. A league's distance at the very most. As a human, he could've jogged there within half an hour.

As a frog, it was a treacherous journey. There were cats out there, and owls. There were weasels, snakes, and dogs. It would take him hours to reach the wood, if he reached it at all, but he had to try. He was out of options.

Determined, Syrah headed to the enormous back half of the Thatch's ground floor, which had two main sections: the kitchens, and the meeting rooms of state. Syrah wanted no part of the kitchens; they were always alive with movement and energy — and knives. He knew better than to risk it as a frog.

He headed for a narrow hallway that divided the cooking and eating areas from the areas reserved for government. At the end of this hallway, he knew, there was a door used mostly by the messengers who constantly came and went from the Thatch on important business. It stood open now — the messengers had left with such urgent speed that nobody had closed it. Syrah leapt along the hallway toward it, and then he stopped cold.

A cat slinked into the hallway, pushing the door further open with a firm rub of its head. Sunlight lit its orange fur as it dug its claws into the long, narrow carpet, closed its eyes, and stretched, pulling its weight backward and fully extending its front legs.

Syrah willed himself to move. He turned away from the cat and leapt as far and as silently as he could, back down the hallway that led to the government offices, keeping his eyes rolled back to make sure that the cat did not follow. The cat kneaded the carpet, ripping at the fibers with its long, curved claws as it continued its luxurious stretch. It purred deep in its body. The sound made Syrah vibrate. He leapt again, terrified, and because he was not looking where he was going, he hit the wall. Not hard enough to hurt, but hard enough to make the quietest *plap!*

The cat opened its eyes and met Syrah's. For one second, the two of them made absolutely no movement; they merely stared at each other, transfixed. Then both of them exploded into motion at once. The cat leapt for him with frightening efficiency, and Syrah bounced frantically out of its way, trying with all his might to outrun it. He rounded the corner at the end of the hall, moving with all the speed he possessed, but the cat was much bigger and caught up in seconds. He felt a claw nick his back, and croaked at the pain. He dove into the first room that had an open door, leaping for higher ground. He reached a bookshelf, and the cat swiped for him. He sprang for the nearest chair, and the cat sprang too. He bounced up onto a long table and over a series of golden hurdles until he came to the table's end, where he turned and dove sideways, hoping to confuse his predator. It worked. The cat tried to change direction too late and went scrabbling off the table's end with an angry yowl. Syrah sprang from the table, aiming for a higher bookshelf. He stretched out as he flew toward his target, reaching out with his forefeet, and he only just made the jump.

The cat was right behind him, but Syrah used his one-second advantage to wiggle in between some books and hide behind them, where the cat could not reach. Or at least he hoped it couldn't. He pressed himself against the back of the shelf as the cat battered at the books in front of him, shoving them so that they wobbled precariously. A groping paw flashed into view a few times, once piercing his head with a sharp, curved claw and making him cringe again in pain. Blood seeped into one eye, half blinding him.

"You bad old cat!" he heard a woman's voice cry. "Get down from there! You know you're not allowed inside!" A minute later, there was a distant slam as the cat was shut back out.

Syrah wilted. For some time, he could not even contemplate moving; he could only shiver in relief, glad it hadn't turned out worse.

That had been much too close. Maybe he shouldn't travel out to the wishing well after all. He'd die for certain.

A moment later, Syrah heard the woman's voice again, muttering. "Better not have broken anything . . . Oh no . . ." Her voice sounded suddenly frightened. "Oh, I'm —"

This was followed by a thud, like something heavy had dropped — and then there was no sound. Syrah was reluctant to leave the security of his hiding place, but he nosed his way forward between two books so that he could see what had happened.

A woman — the same one who had noticed his writing on the floor this morning — lay on the floor below him, unmoving. She stared up at the ceiling, her dilated eyes frighteningly dark. Before he could even consider what to do, voices approached.

". . . emergency measures. What do we know?" The voice was Luffa Gourd's.

"We know enough." Burdock's voice. He appeared in the doorway, his face looking older than ever. His eyes went instantly to the unconscious woman, and he hurried to her side. "Another one," he said grimly, sliding his arms beneath her body so that he could lift her. "And here in the house. Was the staff not directed to avoid eating until further notice?"

"Roma was to communicate it to the housekeeper."

"Doesn't look like she remembered, does it?" said Burdock sharply. He carried the unconscious woman from the room and Luffa slowly made her way to her place at the table, which was marked by a small golden sign that read *Minister of Foreign Affairs*.

He had hidden himself in the cabinet chamber, Syrah realized. This was where the ministers of Yellow Country met to make governmental decisions. The golden nameplates that marked each member's place at the table were the hurdles he'd jumped over before.

So this was where he would have apprenticed with Burdock, if he were still human. This was where Nana Cava had wanted him to be. Syrah looked around, curious.

A long meeting table filled the bulk of the room. At the far end stood a gallery area lined with benches, for meetings that required more seating. Behind this gallery was an entire wall made of windowed doors, which opened into a sizable atrium, also fitted with benches, for larger meetings when the public was free to attend. All around the atrium's windows grew the trees of the Gourd family orchard, where members of the ruling family had been buried for centuries.

The youngest trees in that orchard belonged to Luffa's parents and six siblings, all of whom had been assassinated on the same bloody night, ninety-nine years ago, when the Pink Empire had seized control of Yellow Country for the second time. The second claiming of Cornucopia was taught in every history class in Tyme — not because it was a brutal invasion; Pink had orchestrated hundreds of those — but because that particular invasion had begun Pink's downfall. By killing Luffa's Blue fairy father, the Pink Empire had finally awakened the full fury of the Blue Kingdom, who had retaliated with a powerful vengeance. It had taken many years to stamp out the Pink Empire's power throughout Tyme, but it had all begun that night.

As the other ministers filed into the room, Syrah eyed Luffa. He wondered what it had been like to survive that deadly night. He knew what it was like to survive bloodthirsty spiders and cats, so he knew about terror, and he had been separated from his family for as long as he'd been a frog — but losing them all at once as they were beheaded by a warlord? He couldn't even fathom it. He was a youngest child of many siblings, just like Luffa. What if, when he'd been just five years old, his mother had hidden him in a laundry basket, and then his parents and all his siblings had been murdered while he listened? What if he'd been smuggled onto a ship all alone to flee his country?

"Where's the Nexus?" said Clementine Pease, flicking open an outer compartment of her valise that revealed a cushioned interior. This cushion folded back, rotated, then locked down into place, creating a seat, which she placed in her chair. She sat. "Don't tell me he's sick too."

"I'm here." Burdock strode back in, his expression hard. "There's been an outbreak of the sickness among the governor's staff," he said. "So far, the victims include two kitchen workers, a parlor maid, and the old gentleman who runs the laundry."

"His name is Cane," said Luffa. "He has been with us since Calabaza was a child."

There was a moment of silence in the chamber.

"I hereby bring this emergency meeting of the cabinet to order," said Clementine. "Let the record show that all are in attendance except for Lane Gosta, minister of finance, who is too ill to participate, and Colby Wesson, minister of defense, who is coordinating efforts with Exalted Nexus Keene to stem the spread of disease. Also not in attendance," Clementine continued, looking grim, "Governor Calabaza, who is unconscious."

Unconscious. Syrah realized he had heard this word earlier, but had been so busy trying to get someone to read his name on the floor that it hadn't sunk in. The governor was unconscious. That was why Roma had been screaming — that was why the house was in an uproar.

That was why nobody had noticed his name. His timing had been terrible. Nobody was going to pay attention to a frog and a bit of chalk dust if the governor's life was in danger. In a few days, when Calabaza was feeling better, Syrah could try again. He might not have to venture out to the wishing well after all.

"Physic Feverfew has been with him for an hour, and it's not looking good," Clementine continued. "Calabaza is completely unresponsive. So this meeting, meant to have one emergency purpose, now has two: We must deal with the source of the plague that is sweeping our country, and we must manage the absence of the governor."

Syrah didn't see how. Those were two massive tasks — how could anyone achieve them in one emergency meeting?

"Let's get the second issue out of the way first," said Clementine. "As stated in our constitution, in the event that the governor cannot govern, the minister of agriculture will assume the role. I accept that duty. If you have a reasonable protest, speak it now."

Nobody spoke.

So just like that, Clementine Pease was in charge. It hadn't even taken a minute. In that way, Syrah supposed, democracies were no worse than monarchies. They had their lines of succession clearly marked out, and everyone agreed upon them, which made transitions simpler to manage. He looked at Luffa, wondering what she felt. Her only child was sick. She had already lost so much family. Yet she regarded Clementine with perfect complacency.

"Fine," said Clementine. "I'll serve until we can hold the election."

Election? Syrah thought, surprised. How could they go forward with something like that while Calabaza was unconscious?

"Election? Now?" asked a large woman with deep frown lines and leather-rimmed spectacles. Her nameplate read *Tara Zu — Minister of Justice.* "Has Calabaza no chance of recovery?"

"I'm not a fortune-teller," said Clementine.

Tara narrowed her eyes. "I suppose *you* plan to run for governor?"

"No," Clementine replied shortly.

Luffa pursed her lips and said nothing, but Syrah had a feeling that Clementine's answer was not the one she wanted.

"We need to discuss the spread of this sickness before it gets worse." Clementine sat forward, resting her forearms on the table. "Nexus Burdock, you've received a Relay from Nexus Keene?"

Burdock nodded. "Oats are the cause of the Purge," he said.

Clementine's expression froze. "Oats," she repeated.

"The Purge?" said Luffa at the same moment. "Is that what the people are calling it?"

A disgusting name, Syrah thought, but a fitting one, given all the vomit.

Burdock nodded.

"And you're certain?" asked Injera Teff, minister of general welfare, who was nursing a baby. She shifted the child in her arms. "Didn't this Purge break out all at once, within the span of an hour? How could that have been brought about by oats?"

Syrah had the same question. He listened carefully to Burdock's answer.

"As people arrived at the games, they were offered complimentary oatmeal cookies from the Baker's Dozen. Many chose to eat them, suspecting nothing wrong."

"Cookies?" Clementine's expression relaxed. "Then the problem might be eggs, or butter —"

"Several victims fell ill early yesterday morning, before the games began," said Burdock. "Launchball athletes from Pink, as well as others. It was determined later that none of them ate the cookies, but all of them had eaten oat porridge. And there are other victims, in villages east of here, where this outbreak started days ago. Oats are absolutely the common denominator."

"This makes no sense," Injera cried. "Oats causing sickness? If they were rotten, the bakers would have noticed!"

"The grain appears healthy." Burdock handed the report to Clementine. "But it is corrupt. Exalted Nexus Keene confirmed it through magical testing."

Tara Zu's eyes were narrow behind her leather-rimmed spectacles. "Corrupt? Exalted Nexus, what do you mean?"

Burdock pursed his lips. "It's hard to say," he said. "The oats aren't poisoned, or rotten, or plagued by pests or foreign substances of any kind. The oats themselves are just . . . wrong."

Clementine Pease stared at him. "You're saying they *grew* wrong?" she demanded. "That's what Keene thinks? That Yellow Country is growing crops that kill people, straight from the soil?"

"We don't know —" Burdock began.

"You're right, you don't know," said Clementine, her eyes flint. "So don't you repeat it. A rumor like that will do more than scare people. It'll undermine the integrity of this nation."

The room was silent; the air, fearful. Syrah understood why. His homeland too was a nation of growers. If their grapes or olives caused a sudden plague, it would be devastating for the Olive Isles. Their economy depended on those crops. Their traditions depended on them. He looked around at the ministers' faces, at Luffa's and Burdock's familiar faces, and saw that, in spite of their fear, their expressions were determined. They meant to solve this problem. It was how his mother would have looked, in the same circumstances. How his brother Prince Taurasi would have looked.

It was strange to be here, in the middle of this. Syrah had never been so close to the heart of important things before. His parents and older siblings dealt with these matters. Whenever he tried to chime in, they laughed him off — and, if he was honest, he had never paid close attention anyway.

Burdock had been right. This was an education.

"Huck Steelcut provided oats to the event," said Luffa. "Three hundred bags of them."

Clementine's mouth was pressed tight. She massaged her purple hairline with anxious fingertips. "He wasn't the only one," she said. "We'll have to call in every oat farmer in Yellow Country who supplied the ATC."

"First we issue an international emergency declaration," said Injera. "People everywhere must stop eating oats at once. I ask the presiding governor's permission to Relay the order immediately."

"I did it," said Burdock. "Just before coming here. As soon as I had the information from Nexus Keene."

Clementine turned to stare at him across Governor Calabaza's empty chair. "You issued an international order?"

Burdock's nostrils flared. "Yes," he said.

"Without permission from this cabinet, and without a plan for controlling the damage this information will do to our economy, you informed every government in Tyme that our oats are *corrupt*?"

"It had to be done," said Burdock, high color in his pale cheeks. "Lives are at stake. So yes, I abandoned protocol — if you don't like it, Provisional Governor, then take action. Dismiss me from my post."

The room was silent for another long minute, and Syrah

wondered which of them was right. On Balthasar, if one of the queen's advisors had taken a major action without her consent, it would have been considered treason. Here, though, in this room, it wasn't like that. These people were peers. Equals. Clementine had only been governor for half an hour. Burdock might have risked the country's financial position — but wasn't that worth it, if he had saved people from dying? Syrah thought it was. If he'd been in Burdock's shoes, he might have made the exact same choice.

Syrah suddenly wished that he could ask his mother what she thought. Or even Taurasi. He had always been distant with Syrah — more like a second father than a brother — but he was intelligent. Experienced. He would have known what was right, here.

"Just how bad is this . . . Purge?" asked Tara Zu, in the quiet.

Burdock looked away from Clementine. "It's bad," he answered. "Particularly for the very old and the very young."

Injera tightened her grip on her child, and Syrah shivered. Nana Cava was very old. Had she eaten one of those cookies? Syrah wished he could see her. He wished he could see Marsala. He wished that someone in this room would say their names and reassure him.

"Most people start with a sudden high fever and a spate of white vomit," said Burdock. "It's almost the consistency of paste. Then their eyes dilate, and about half of them fall unconscious. The others talk nonsense for hours, then seem to shake it off. There've also been a handful of cases where people have skipped the first stage and fallen unconscious without prelude. Those who do fall unconscious seem to have the worst cases. Dozens have died."

Like Marsala, thought Syrah. She hadn't thrown up at all — just tipped right into the lake. Did that mean she was sicker than the others? More likely to die?

"Like Calabaza," said Luffa. "He seemed healthy until he failed to wake this morning."

"He also manifested the illness much later than anyone else," said Burdock. "About eighteen hours later, in fact — but that might be due to his fairy blood."

"White vomit?" said Tara. "Is this White magic we're dealing with? Witches?"

"That's . . . unclear."

"Unclear?" Clementine snapped. "Wouldn't Keene *know*?"

"The magic is unlike anything Keene has encountered. He has seen nothing similar among witches, fairies, Kisscrafters, magic creatures, beasts, or plants. He doesn't believe it's been recorded in the histories kept by the Exalted. It *seems* connected to the White, but its origins are unknown. The Exalted Council has been ordered to search and to study until answers are found. We will know more, and soon."

Syrah did not find this answer comforting. He thought once more of Olive's vineyards and orchards, and he wondered if the Purge would spread. It couldn't cross the ocean — could it? Again he wished he could talk to his mother. If he could warn her about what he had heard here, she might be able to take precautions.

But until he broke this curse, he couldn't tell anybody anything.

Clementine looked as uncomfortable as Syrah felt. "Let's bring in the oat farmers," she said. "They're not going to like this. Meeting adjourned."

CHAPTER EIGHT

*T*HE ministers filed out of the cabinet chamber, and Syrah leapt down from the bookshelf and hopped along after them, still thirsty and shaken from his earlier adventure. Maybe if he went back upstairs, Walter would give him water. It was worth a try.

When he reached Walter's room, it was full. The triplets and their mother were all there. Walter sat at his desk with his back to the room, carefully building something out of miniature wooden blocks. Bradley and Tommy flanked him, facing Roma. Syrah hopped in and made his way to Walter's bedside table.

"We're *not* going," said Bradley.

"Yeah." Tommy crossed his arms. "You can't make us."

"Your father is very ill," said Roma tremulously. "Things are complicated."

Their father. Syrah felt a sinking in his guts. Calabaza unconscious meant a lot more than just a bunch of government stuff — it meant that the triplets would be scared. It meant Deli would be scared. He couldn't believe he hadn't put that together right away.

Roma twisted her ringed fingers. "Your grandmother thinks it would be better —"

"*No*," said Bradley. "We're not going to Quintessential."

"But you love Quintessential," his mother pleaded. "Cousin Sharlyn has plenty of room. You'd get to stay right on the park, and you'd get to see Clover and Linden — you know your new cousin Ella is friendly with the prince, and the family is regularly invited to the palace —"

"We're not leaving Pa," said Tommy.

"I built the ATC," said Walter, pushing his chair back to reveal his extensive miniature block creation. "Look, Ma — oh!" Walter's eyes fell on Syrah. They brightened. "Prince Frog."

Syrah hopped from the bedside table to the desk, sidestepping Walter's extremely detailed reconstruction of the launchball event.

"Look at this," Walter said to him. "See? Those are the launchball rings."

"Oh, Walter." Roma gave a sad little hiccup. "You should be thinking about your father."

Syrah reached Walter, who laid a gentle hand on his back. At once, Syrah ached all through with the boy's anxiety.

Pa is sick. They said deadly. I don't want him to die. I don't want to go to Quintessential. I want to go back to the ATC. I wish we were still at the Royal Governor's Inn. I wish we could go back to before Pa got sick —

"He *is* thinking about Pa," said Tommy angrily. "We all are."

"And we're staying," said Bradley.

"Boys . . ." said their mother, but her resolve was clearly weakening. She looked toward the door and her expression changed. She looked relieved.

Deli was there. Roma reached out to her and beckoned anxiously with her ringed fingers. "Help me," she pleaded.

Deli came forward, her face tight with worry. "What's wrong?"

"The boys won't listen," said Roma tearfully. "They're giving me such a hard time."

Deli turned on them. "Whatever she asks," she said. "Just do it. Don't make this worse —"

"Ma wants to ship us off to Cousin Sharlyn's!" Tommy cried. "She wants us to leave!"

Deli looked alarmed. "No one's going anywhere," she said.

"*Thank* you," said Bradley and Tommy together, and Walter's energy shifted profoundly. Syrah felt his relief, equal to what his anxiety had been.

Deli will fix it. Deli always fixes things.

Syrah gazed at Deli's determined face. She looked just like one of those ministers downstairs. Like she was going to solve this problem, no matter what it took. It was funny, but Syrah got the feeling that although her mother was standing right there, the only actual adult in the room was Delicata.

"Just for the next little while," said Roma. "Just until your father recovers and things get under control here. Everything's going to be so difficult —"

"Doesn't matter," said Deli.

Roma played with one of her bracelets. "Would you mind telling your grandmother?" she ventured. "I'd do it, but I don't want to leave your father —"

"Fine."

"*And* I have to visit the Relay," said Roma, sounding tearful again. "Christophen needs to know. It's going to be awful, telling him that his father is sick, when he's so far away. You know your brother— he's so sensitive, it will just destroy him."

Deli's eyebrows went up. "Then why are you telling him?"

"Because he has to sail home!"

"Come on, Ma. Marsanne is going to give birth to those triplets any day now," said Deli. "What good can it do to —"

"I *need* him here!" Roma insisted. "And he'll want to see his father," she added.

"Then I'll Relay him myself," said Deli, who looked not at all pleased. "Right after I talk to Grandmother. You stay with Pa."

"I don't know what I'd do without you." Roma kissed Deli's cheek and left them.

She really was useless, Syrah thought, annoyed on Deli's behalf. What kind of mother left all the work to a daughter who had just found out that her father was deathly ill?

"Thanks, Deli," said Bradley. "We owe you one."

Tommy sat heavily on Walter's bed. "What are you going to tell Christophen?"

"Nothing," she said. "He's busy enough, and we don't even know what's wrong."

Bradley looked affronted. "But Ma said —"

"You want Ma in charge? Then you better pack your bags for Quintessential."

Bradley fell silent.

"Deli, look," said Walter.

"Hey, it's the ATC," said Deli, coming closer to him to look over his shoulder at the reconstruction he'd made. "The floats and the diving boards and everything. Wow." She touched the miniature version of the platform where she had stood and triumphed, with her teammates hugging her and screaming. "You've got every detail." She put her hands on his shoulders. "Pa's going to be okay," she said.

"Is he?" Bradley demanded. "Or are you just saying that?"

"He's got a quarter fairy blood," said Deli. "Physic Feverfew says that'll help him fight it."

Syrah wished that his own family had a little fairy blood. It would have been nice to know that Nana Cava and Marsala had that protection. But none of the royal Huanuis had mated with a fairy in at least five centuries. Any fairy magic they had once had in their veins was practically nonexistent now.

"Can we eat yet?" asked Tommy.

"Soon." Deli went to the window. "You all should get outside," she said. "Grab your fishing poles. You'll know it's time to eat again when the lunch bell rings."

"But if Pa wakes up —" said Bradley.

"Or gets worse —" said Tommy.

"I'll come and find you. Go on."

Walter put Syrah on his shoulder, which he accepted. Getting outside with the boys would be all right. He needed to eat and drink, and it would be easiest with a protector around.

The boys grabbed their fishing poles, stuffed their feet into boots, and headed just north of the Thatch to where the river ran past, cutting straight through the middle of Cornucopia and defining the northern border of the Gourds' property. Even farther north, fed by the river, there was a small lake, magic-made, where the launchball team of Yellow Country trained. East of here was the thriving downtown area, full of shops and tents and people. Here around the Thatch, though, the Gourds owned leagues of farmland, so the river was quiet and private. The triplets sat on the bank and cast their lines, and Syrah reveled in the wonderful sensation of cool water on his parched skin. He hopped and swam and floated in ecstasy, gobbling juicy minnows until his belly was nearly bursting. A distant bell gonged from the direction of the Thatch, and the boys glanced back. Walter was the first to comprehend.

"Lunch!" he said happily, and he reeled in his line at once.

"They figured out where the poison came from," said Tommy, shutting the flaps of the basket in which they'd stowed the few small fish they'd caught. "Wonder what it was."

"I'm so hungry I could eat a glimmerfish," said Bradley, wiping dirt off his trousers.

"Never eat a glimmerfish," Walter replied as they began the walk back to the house. "Or else you'll never be able to sail again without getting seasick."

"That's just a myth," said Bradley.

"I wouldn't risk it," said Tommy. "No matter how hungry I was. I'd hate if I could never get on a boat again."

"Not like we get on boats anymore anyway," said Bradley. "Ever since Syrah."

Syrah was so startled he forgot to croak. His name. In a panic, he leapt from Walter's shoulder to Bradley's, and pressed himself hard against Bradley's neck. "RIBBIT," he insisted, since it was all he could do. "RIBBIT, RIBBIT, RIBBIT, RIBBIT, RIBBIT —"

Bradley squealed and swiped at him. "Get off me!" he cried.

"It's down my shiiiiiiirt!" crooned Tommy in falsetto. "It's on my baaaaaack!"

Bradley flung Syrah into the dirt and tried to slap Tommy with his fishing pole, but Tommy dodged and hurtled toward the house, laughing crazily. Bradley chased him, and Walter scooped Syrah up. He walked calmly along until he stumbled across his brothers in the grass outside the Thatch, crouched low under a window. Bradley and Tommy grabbed Walter by the shirt and pulled him down with them, gesturing for silence.

"The boys are staying here," he heard Deli saying. "It's the best thing for everyone."

"I already sent a messenger to Sharlyn," came Luffa's cool reply. "The boys leave for Quintessential in the morning."

"They're staying here," said Deli again. "*I'll* send a messenger and explain."

The boys glanced at each other. Syrah hopped from Walter's shoulder up onto the windowsill so that he could see what was happening. Deli and Luffa stood just outside the governor's office, facing each other, and Syrah was struck by how powerfully Deli resembled her grandmother. Luffa's hair was mostly gray, and her dark face was lined, but their erect posture and muscular slenderness were near mirrors of each other, and the expressions on their faces were a close match too. Resolute. The biggest difference between them wasn't even Deli's moles — it was that Deli's eyes were alive with frustration, while Luffa's betrayed no emotion.

"I arranged this with your mother," said Luffa, when Deli held her ground in silence. "She approved their going."

"Well, now she approves of them staying."

"And she sent you to tell me." Luffa's eyes glittered. "Couldn't look into the dragon's mouth herself."

"She's sitting with my father," said Deli.

"Isn't she always," said Luffa dryly.

"He's *sick*."

"Your mother is a coward, Delicata, who sent you to take the skinning for her."

Deli's countenance fluctuated between outrage and — was that satisfaction? Syrah thought it was.

"Good afternoon, Mr. Steelcut," said Luffa.

Deli whirled, fists clenched. Syrah swiveled his eyes. He had not noticed the approach of Huck and Harrow Steelcut, both of whom were in their overalls, hats in their hands, like they'd just come from a morning in the fields. Harrow glittered. Huck put out a dusty hand.

"Afternoon, Madam Governor," he said. "Your messenger said to hurry, so here we are. How can I help you?"

"Provisional Governor Pease is inside with the Nexus," said Luffa. "Go in at once. Delicata, take Harrow elsewhere."

Huck cast a concerned glance back at his son. Luffa followed him into the office and shut the door, leaving Deli and Harrow in the corridor. Deli looked away, obviously uncomfortable. Harrow swallowed hard enough that Syrah saw the lump in his throat bob up and down.

"Dee," he said.

Not her name, Syrah thought acidly.

"Hello."

"I'm real sorry," said Harrow, and his low, slow voice gave Syrah a powerful urge to kick him, for all the good that would have done. "You had a beautiful launch. You should've won."

"People are dying," Deli replied curtly. "Sports don't matter."

Harrow glanced at the office door. "What happened here?" he asked. "Provisional governor? Where's your pa?"

Deli looked up at him. Her chest hitched. "He's sick," she whispered. "He won't wake up."

Harrow's face fell. "Dee," he said, and he reached for her. She grabbed his hand, then seemed to remember herself.

She pulled back.

That's right, Syrah thought viciously. *She doesn't like you anymore.*

Harrow shoved his hands into his pockets, looking anxious. "Can I help with anything?"

No. Get out.

"I don't think so," said Deli. "I've got a message to send to Quintessential, and family letters to write, and all the gear we took to the ATC has to get unloaded and unpacked, plus I need to send a message to Kai —"

"I can unload carriages," he said. "If you want."

Deli hesitated. "I can't put that on you."

"I really don't mind."

A loud sneeze sent Syrah leaping into the air in shock. He landed on the windowsill as Deli and Harrow turned to look at him. Deli looked livid. She flung herself toward Syrah, who was so taken aback that he jumped away, out the window, and into the grass right in front of the triplets, whom he had completely forgotten were there.

Deli leaned halfway out the window, hands clutching the sill, her face as furious as Syrah had ever seen it. "You've been *spying* on me?" she shouted. "I just stuck my neck out for you, and this is what I get?"

"We weren't trying to!" said Bradley, backing away from the window with his fishing gear. "We just —"

"You better get over to those carriages and get every single one of your trunks up the stairs *right now!*"

"I want lunch," said Walter plaintively. "We haven't eaten since breakfast yesterday —"

"Don't you even *touch* lunch until you've unpacked your things — and clear out Pa's carriage too! Go!"

They hustled away so fast that Walter forgot to grab Syrah,

who leapt up onto the windowsill again and sprang into the corridor just as the door of the governor's office opened. Huck Steelcut stalked out, his expression hard. "Son," he said. "Let's go."

"I was going to help —" Harrow began.

"Now," said Huck.

"I'll come back," Harrow promised, and he followed his father out of the Thatch.

Syrah watched him go, satisfied. He hopped his way along the corridor, intending to head upstairs and find Walter, but when he came to the foyer he saw Walter heading toward the kitchens, a large basket in his hands. Syrah croaked to get his attention, and Walter crouched to let him hop onto his shoulder.

"Pa's snacks from the ride home last night," he said, holding up the basket. Syrah hopped acknowledgment. Walter reminded him a little of Rapunzel; both of them understood that Syrah was paying attention to the conversation, even if the well wouldn't let them understand any more than that.

When Walter reached the kitchen door, he didn't go in right away. Instead, he opened one flap of the basket and gazed down into it. There was very little food left within, but plenty of evidence that the basket had once been full. Syrah saw crumbs of chocolate cake, smears of raspberry jam, two apple cores, and the crusts of several sandwiches. One half sandwich still remained, and when Syrah opened his mouth to smell it, he nearly gagged.

"Liver pâté," sighed Walter, who obviously felt differently. "With watercress. My favorite, just like Pa. Ma hates it, though." He lifted the half sandwich to his nose to smell it, then set it back down in the basket. "No," he said dolefully, picking at a bit of the watercress, which had gone very faintly brown around the edges from sitting in the basket. "Deli said no lunch until we're done unpacking. And I don't know what I'm allowed to eat anyway."

Syrah croaked encouragingly. It was oats Walter had to avoid, not liver pâté. But Walter obediently closed the basket, and when one of the kitchen staff came through the door a moment later, he handed it over and went back out to the carriages to keep unpacking. Syrah rode along with him, troubled. Something was bothering him — something was out of place. It took him a moment to realize what.

The food in the basket. Why had Calabaza been eating snacks last night? Everyone had been cautioned not to eat anything until they knew what had caused the Purge — had Calabaza simply been too hungry to care? Was that the real reason why he was sick later than everybody else? Maybe those liver sandwiches had been made with oat bread. Syrah felt a cold thrill of anxiety — Walter had almost eaten that stuff, and it might have killed him.

But if the food in Calabaza's carriage was corrupt, then wouldn't Roma be sick too?

No, Walter had said that his mother hated liver pâté. . . .

Syrah sank down into his thoughts, barely noticing the triplets' hungry complaints as they unpacked their carriage and climbed the steps. Why would anyone have put a basket of snacks in the governor's carriage when nobody was supposed to be eating? Had Calabaza made up his own sandwiches before traveling? It seemed unlikely. He was used to being waited upon by his staff. Had Roma done it? No, she wouldn't have wanted Calabaza eating anything, and she had probably protested when he had. Would the kitchen staff at the Royal Governor's Inn have packed Calabaza a late supper for travel? No, that didn't make sense either — the kitchen staff in

Plenty would have known right away that it was dangerous to eat anything until after the investigation.

When the triplets decided they were finished, they raced down to the kitchen for lunch. Syrah stayed behind in Walter's room and hopped onto the windowsill, still thinking. Back at the Royal Governor's Inn, just before they had all left Plenty, he had seen the light of a lantern out in the carriage house. Maybe whoever had been carrying that lantern had put the food in the governor's carriage. But why would somebody do that? And why would they do it in the dark?

He had a bad, sinking feeling in his frog guts. There were a number of people who didn't want to see Calabaza elected again, that was for sure.

But attacking him with snacks didn't make any sense. Nobody had known yet that the oats were the source of corruption; that hadn't been discovered until this morning. So even if somebody *had* wanted to hurt Calabaza, they wouldn't have known to do it with oats.

It had probably just been an oversight, Syrah decided. The staff at the Royal Governor's Inn had likely put a basket of snacks in the carriage yesterday morning, and then they'd forgotten to take it out later, in all the uproar of the Purge. So it had still been sitting there when they'd all left Plenty, and Calabaza had been unable to resist.

That night, Syrah searched the Thatch again for useful writing implements. He went in every room with an open door and he nosed into every corner and every not-quite-closed drawer he could get himself into, looking for another piece of chalk, or maybe an open ink bottle with some wet ink left in it. He found no chalk at all. He found plenty of ink, but every bottle he came across was tightly corked, and he knew better than to try uncorking them himself. He'd end up with a mouthful of poison, and that would be the end of this miserable adventure. They'd find him dead on a desk, have no idea who he was, and chuck him into the garden to fertilize a flowerbed.

It was nearly three in the morning before Syrah finally gave up on the idea of writing. Maybe he should use small objects to spell out his message. He'd tried this strategy before, but always unsuccessfully. He had pushed leaves into formation only to have them blown away; he had made letter shapes out of pebbles, jacks, and even coins, but either someone had kicked them, or scooped them up, or just walked right past them. Sometimes, he wondered how many other people were out there, cursed to live out their lives as tiny, insignificant creatures, writing messages that nobody ever saw. He swore to himself that when he was a man again, he would pay attention whenever animals wanted him to. He would mind their signals, just in case.

Syrah heard soft footfalls on the stairs. A moment later, Deli tiptoed past him. She checked behind her and adjusted a large pack that she carried on her back. She cut down the back corridor, toward the messengers' door. He followed, curious. Where was she going before dawn? And what was in that pack she carried?

He couldn't follow very far. Deli let herself out and shut the door, cutting him off. Anyway, he wouldn't have wanted to follow her outside, where the owls were still hunting in the darkness.

And since Deli was out, he realized, it meant her bedroom was empty. Maybe she'd even left her door open. He hadn't been in Deli's room since they were little kids, and he hadn't been able to gain access to it last night. Maybe he'd find an ink bottle open in there. It was worth a look.

He made his way upstairs and into the family wing. Deli's door was open a crack, and Syrah bounced toward it and wriggled in through the opening. The room was decorated in graceful antique furniture, scarred by centuries of use — even in the darkness, Syrah's frog vision allowed him to see it clearly enough. The air smelled like sweat. Deli's trunk of belongings from the ATC stood open beside her wardrobe, only half-unpacked. It looked like she'd been sorting through it.

Everything else in the room was characteristically tidy. The bed was already made. Syrah hopped around on her desk and found a tightly shut ink bottle and a stack of several finished letters — including one written and addressed to Rapunzel. He pushed that one with his forefeet until it fell behind the back of the desk, where he hoped it would be forgotten for good, and then he scanned the room, looking at her walls and her bookshelves, her bedside table and her open trunk. Maybe there were objects in here that he could arrange into a message. He probably didn't have enough time for it — wherever she had gone, she couldn't be gone long or her family would miss her — but it was still worth a look.

Several competitive medals hung on her walls, but there was no way for him to get them down. Lots of clothes sat in piles on the floor, but most clothing was too big for him to move. The objects on her desk were heavy; the books on her bedside table and bookshelves too thick for him to budge with any speed. He hopped down to the floor and peered under her bed, but there wasn't any mess there for him to work with. There was, however, a packet of papers tucked under the bookshelves, in the very narrow space between the bottom shelf and the floorboards. Maybe he could spread those around. He reached his forefeet under the bottom shelf, planted his moist toes on the topmost paper, and tried to drag it toward him.

The whole stack moved. He dragged at it again, and it moved more. Working slowly, he managed to pull the papers out from under the bookshelf, until he realized that he had a whole file in front of him. If he opened it up, he could move the papers inside individually. He hopped around to the open side of the file and stuck his forefeet underneath the flap, then moved forward, lifting the file cover. He nosed his way underneath it until he was inside the file, then hopped forward, pushing the cover up until he was able to knock it all the way back. It fell open, and when Syrah saw what was stored within, he goggled.

TRAITOR PRINCE ESCAPES!

It was the *Town Crier* from the day after he'd vanished from the Thatch. He read it, horrified to find that it painted a terrible picture of his behavior. It said he'd betrayed a century of family loyalty, refused to accept his deserved punishment, and then broken away from the guards who were meant to escort him out to the coast. It called him a fugitive, and warned that he was "on the loose," "desperate," and "possibly dangerous." A reward was offered for information on his whereabouts as though he were some kind of criminal.

Was *this* what they all thought? That he had just run away?

Uncomfortable, he recalled that, at first, he *had* run away. He had wanted to punish them all for kicking him out. He had hoped to give them all a scare. But when he had never come back again, surely someone had realized that he was in trouble. They couldn't all think he was still on the run somewhere — could they?

There were other *Town Criers* in the stack. Syrah pushed the top one off the pile, revealing a second story, this one from the morning after the wedding. *SECRET LOVE LETTER REVEALED*, read the headline, and, under that, *DELICATA GOURD PINES FOR PRINCE SYRAH*. Syrah glanced through this article too. He knew what it held — he had handed that love letter to the scribe, after all — but he had never had an opportunity to read the article afterward.

> *Times have changed indeed.*
>
> *Near a hundred years ago, former Governor Luffa Gourd, then Princess Luffa of Yellow Country, lost her entire family to the Pink scourge. In her teens, she returned to Cornucopia with an army and reclaimed the country.*
>
> *She restored independence to Yellow, rebuilt its economy, reinstated its monarchy, and then, always a bold forward thinker, abolished the monarchy and established a new age of democracy. One might expect her only female descendent, Delicata Gourd, to share her grandmother's famous guts.*
>
> *One should lower one's expectations.*
>
> *Delicata's contribution to the modern chapter of Yellow Country history is significantly lesser: She spends her time lost in a paroxysm of pathetic — and decidedly unrequited — adoration for Prince Syrah Huanui. Reading her love letter to him (reprinted below in full), one gets a sense that the current generation has completely lost perspective on the past. Delicata declares herself to be breathless, hurting, and willing to sacrifice. Does she even know what these things really mean?*

Syrah read it over again, shocked. *This* was what the scribe had made of that love letter? This wasn't what he'd wanted. He'd only been trying to embarrass Deli, to pay her back for embarrassing him, but instead the scribe had made Delicata Gourd sound shallow and self-centered and petty — exactly the opposite of what she actually was.

For the first time, it occurred to Syrah that he had gone too far.

His actions had been out of proportion. Deli had embarrassed him in front of a few people; he had embarrassed her in front of the world.

He felt hot and prickly and uncomfortable all over. He tried to ignore it, and instead pushed the *Crier* aside with his feet and sucked in air through his nostrils as he revealed a third *Crier*, and a third headline.

THE VANISHING OF PRINCE SYRAH

The article, dated two weeks after his disappearance, laid everything out. The circumstances of his departure from the Thatch, the chase he'd led through the fields, the way he had vanished into the woods, never to reemerge. Farmers had been questioned. Leads had been investigated. Rivers and lakes had been dragged. Somehow, Prince Syrah was simply gone.

This. *This* was his opportunity.

He heard footsteps approaching. Deli was back. Syrah began to push the *Crier* about his disappearance toward the middle of the bedroom floor. He would sit here, on this paper, and Deli would understand.

She crept through her bedroom door and pushed it quietly shut. Only now, as the early morning light touched Deli's skin and made it seem to glow, did Syrah realize that the sun had risen. She took off her backpack, threw it on the floor, and pushed it under her bed with her foot.

"RAWP!" called Syrah, from his position in the middle of the *Crier*. Deli came toward him, frowning. Her eyes fell, not on him, but on the *Criers* beneath him. "What the . . ." she said, and crouched down.

"RAWP RAWP RAAWWWWWWP!"

Deli gently moved Syrah aside, and as her hand connected with him, he knew where she had been. *I just want to train all day — I know I should give it up, it's just launchball — I'm a monster for sneaking out like this with Pa unconscious — I can't stand it here much longer.*

He wanted to tell her she wasn't a monster at all. He had no idea how she put up with her family's constant demands on her. He wished he could say that she was incredibly dedicated and passionate, and that she ought to give herself a break.

If she would just notice him now, and see who he was, then maybe he *could* tell her.

She reached for one of the *Criers* that Syrah had pushed aside. The one with the love letter in it. Her face tightened when she picked it up. "Who took this out?" she muttered.

"*RAAAAAWWWWWP!*" Syrah bounced right on top of the word *PRINCE* to help Deli make the connection. "*RAWWP RAAAAAWWWWWP!*"

She looked at him. Looked back at the paper. Her eyes narrowed.

Yes, he thought frantically, *I'm begging you, Deli — put it together — know that it's me —*

A knock at the door made Deli gasp. She sprang to her feet, threw the door open — and froze.

Harrow was standing there, his arms piled so high with baskets and bags that Syrah could only see his eyes, but he glowered at them anyway and croaked his venomous fury at being interrupted at this critical moment. He wished he were one of those poisonous frogs that could knock a man dead with one touch.

"What are you *doing* here?" Deli demanded. "You can't just come up to my room."

"I told you I'd come back," he said, his voice muffled behind the pile. "I finished my morning chores, and Pa's going to need me out in the fields this afternoon, so this was the only time I could make it." He paused. "Uh — can I put this stuff down?"

Deli got out of his way, and he staggered in and set everything on the floor next to her open trunk.

"The boys were supposed to bring all that up," she said.

"They got most of it," said Harrow absently. He stood up straight again, but his gaze stayed on the floor. His eyes had found the *Criers* that were spread out behind Deli's feet. He studied them while Syrah continued his desperate hopping. "RAWP!" he cried, bouncing on the word *Syrah* until the bottoms of his feet were sore. "RAWP RAWP RAWP RAWP —"

"That frog ought to be outside," said Harrow. "Must be looking for a mate, making a racket like that." He reached down, but Syrah jumped out of reach and hid himself under Deli's bed.

"I didn't take those *Criers* out," Deli said defensively. "The triplets must've done it."

"Okay," said Harrow.

"I said I *didn't*."

"And I said okay."

"If you think I'm wasting time feeling sorry over Syrah, with everything that's going on —"

Harrow snorted. "I *don't* think that," he said. "He should be horsewhipped for what he did to you. Feel sorry over him? Not a chance. Good riddance." He went for the door. "I'm gonna get the rest of the gear."

Good. Get out. Syrah readied himself to spring out and get Deli's attention on him once more.

"Wait," said Deli suddenly, and Harrow's boot steps stopped. "Thanks. For saying that."

"It's just the truth," said Harrow. "Wherever Prince Syrah disappeared to, I hope he got what was coming to him."

Syrah made a noise of agonized frustration. He hopped out from his hiding place and leapt back onto his name with a *splat*, but Harrow only reached for him again, and he had to jump back under the bed so as not to be thrown outside.

This is what happened to him, he cried out silently. *He's a frog, and he's right here, and you're both SO STUPID.* He let out a long, miserable croak.

"Maybe a fairy got him," said Harrow. "Taught him a lesson. Turned him into a pumpkin."

Syrah gave an agonized cry that came out as a pathetic *ribbit*, but he kept on ribbitting until the ribbits became painful. How much frustration was it possible to endure, he wondered, before the feeling would flat-out kill him?

"Actually," said Deli, "I think . . . but it's pretty strange." She stopped. "You'd never believe it. About what happened to Syrah, I mean."

Syrah shut his mouth and listened hard.

"Well now you've got me curious," said Harrow. "Try me."

Yes, try him, thought Syrah, hopping close enough to the edge of his hiding place that he could roll his eyes upward and see Deli's expression. It was anxious. She searched Harrow's face.

"Want to take a walk with me?" she said, and then she quickly added, "Just as friends."

"I guess I've got time for a walk. Sure."

"Then come on," said Deli, heading for her door. "I'll show you exactly where Syrah went."

Chapter Nine

SYRAH croaked, more in surprise than in an attempt to sway their attention. Where was Deli going? What did she think had happened?

"You mean you know?" asked Harrow, following quickly. "But you never said anything."

"I can't prove it and nobody'll believe me," she replied. "Trust me. When I tell you, you'll think my head's hit the launchball bar one too many times."

Syrah leapt after them, following with all the speed he could manage. He went with them downstairs, through the back door of the Thatch, and into the Gourd family grove. He bounded as fast as he could to keep up as they wandered out into the vast pumpkin, melon, and squash patches that sprawled over the back half of the property. Here, they began to outpace him so that he could not keep up. But he could not fall behind. Panicked, he sprang for the back of Harrow's boot, missed, and sprang again. He landed on the toe of the boot, splayed his legs, and gripped the top with all his might.

Harrow stopped walking. "Is this that same little frog from your room?" he asked. "Has to be. Never saw a frog so green." He crouched to pluck him off, but before he could grab him, Syrah hopped onto

Harrow's sleeve, then sprang up to his shoulder and sat there. "Never saw a frog act like this," said Harrow in surprise.

"He's tame," said Deli. "He's somebody's pet. Walter's taking care of him."

"Huh." Harrow turned his head and lifted his shoulder to frown thoughtfully at Syrah. "Huh," he said again.

Real articulate, Oat Boy.

"I don't mind if you ride along, I guess," Harrow said to him. "Seems to be what you want." Syrah croaked in the affirmative and gave an emphatic hop. Harrow regarded him curiously for another moment, then turned his attention back to Deli. They started walking again. "So, where are we headed?"

"Just wait." She strode toward the edge of the Gourd property, checking back over her shoulder once or twice as though nervous that she might be seen. When Syrah realized where she was going, a thrill of anticipation and terror shot through him. They were headed to the wood where the wishing well lay. Maybe she really *did* know what had happened to him.

They plunged into the cool sanctuary within the wood, and Harrow let out a breath of awe as the light changed. The world around them glowed with secret, green intensity. Every leaf, every vine, every moss-covered stone seemed to *sing* green.

"How have I never seen this place?" Harrow murmured reverently. "Must be a fairy wood."

"We used to say it was, when we were little," said Deli.

"We . . . Syrah and you?" said Harrow, a bit too carefully.

"We all grew up together," she replied. "Syrah and I were the same age, so yeah. We used to play imps and fairies in here and pretend it was magic."

"It *is* magic," said Harrow.

Deli shot him a sideways glance. "You say that like you know," she said.

Harrow chewed the inside of his cheek. "Just show me," he said.

They moved deeper into the wood, and Deli threw out an arm to stop Harrow from walking.

"It's here somewhere," she said. "Careful."

"Of what?"

She cast another look at him. "A hole in the ground," she said. "It's big enough for both of us to fall into, and I promise, you won't see it until you're almost in it."

Keeping their eyes trained on the mossy ground, they continued to walk until Deli stopped. She knelt, and Harrow knelt beside her. Syrah dug his toes into Harrow's shoulder, his frog heart hammering in his little frog chest.

The wishing well was as deep and dark as ever, open like a bottomless throat. A thing of silence and emptiness and waiting. Syrah could feel it now as he never had been able to as a man. It *was* waiting.

For him?

"I've heard stories about this pit," said Harrow. "It's too deep to be filled or fathomed, and whenever your family tries to cover it up, the cover disappears."

"All true. Ready for the part you won't believe?"

Harrow nodded.

"When I was five," Deli began, "we were out here playing, and I fell into this hole. I fell for so long it was like falling forever, and I was so scared to hit the bottom, but I never hit anything. And then —" She paused. Shook her head. "And then these — *hands*," she whispered. "I couldn't see them, but that's what they felt like. Hundreds of hands, soft and warm like — like soil under the sun — they lifted me out of there, passing me upward until I was sitting on the moss like nothing ever happened." She peered down into the darkness. "It's magic," she said. "Even though that's impossible."

"Is it? There are fairies, aren't there? And magic creatures and plants."

"But a *hole?*"

"Why not a hole?"

"It's just dirt."

Harrow opened his mouth as if to say something, then closed it again. "You're the one who fell in," he said eventually. "You think it's just dirt?"

Deli shook her head. "I don't," she said. "I really don't."

"So . . . what? You think Syrah fell in here?"

At the mention of his name, Syrah bounced down from Harrow's shoulder. He positioned himself between the two of them and started to hop, determined.

EXACTLY. Keep talking about me — you'll figure it out —

"They found his clothes and shoes here," said Deli. "Like he vanished right out of them. It had to be magic."

YES. Syrah hopped with more vigor.

"Vanished to where?"

Right HERE — come ON — figure it OUT —

"Just . . . vanished, I guess."

"Everything has to go somewhere." Harrow brushed the soil around the well's opening with his fingertips. "What if he fell in just like you did, except those hands didn't ever lift him back out?"

Syrah hopped onto Deli's leg, jumped over to Harrow's boot, sprang back to Deli again and bounced up and down on her head.

She tilted her head, and he fell off. Then she got to her hands and knees and leaned forward, staring down into the well.

"It'd serve him right," she said.

Syrah croaked his outrage. He leapt for Deli's nearest hand, hoping to hop onto the back of it, but she sat back a split second too early and pulled her hands away, and his leap continued much farther than he had intended. He soared to the edge of the wishing well. Half his body landed on the moss; the other half dangled into the chasm. He scrabbled for purchase, his blood coursing, his eyes rolling frantically upward to see if either Deli or Harrow had noticed him, but they were only looking at each other. One of his front feet slipped off the moss. For one terrifying second, he hung there from the knobby little toes of one front foot — then, with a gasping croak that nobody heard, his toes slipped free. He tumbled into the well.

"How's your pa doing?" he heard Harrow ask, and then darkness swallowed him. He fell, and he fell, and he never stopped falling. His heart beat so frantically that he knew it was close to popping, and his breath would not come at all. Where was the water? There had to be water. A geyser had pummeled him last time, so he knew it was down here somewhere, and any second he would smack it, and it would kill him. Given how far and how fast he was falling, the water's surface would be like stone.

But it wasn't. When he finally slipped into the water, it was painless. It enveloped him, warm and soft, and the voice of the well permeated his skin, filling his body and his brain.

What is your wish?

To be myself again, he thought desperately. *I wish to be myself.*

You are yourself, said the well.

My HUMAN self — please —

The water swirled around him. *Why should I help you?*

Because I'm trapped!

The well bubbled almost as though it was laughing. *Perhaps you deserve it.*

No I don't! Syrah thought, frustrated and frantic together. *I'm a good person!* He thought of all the times he had been nice to someone else. Giving gifts to his nieces and nephews. Bouncing on Jack to wake him up so their stuff wouldn't be stolen by bandits. Risking his escape plan to help Rapunzel when he hadn't trusted Cassis. Maybe he wasn't the best person in the world, but he was all right.

What do you want me to do? His thoughts were a rush. *I'll do it — I'll do anything —*

Lose yourself to be found, the well answered.

The water rose rapidly and Syrah rose with it, hurtling upward through the darkness until a pinpoint of light came into view. *What does that even mean?* he begged silently. *How can I lose myself? I'm already lost.*

The well lifted him to its surface and deposited him on the ground outside. *Transform to be transformed,* it replied, its voice fading away as the water retreated.

Wait! Syrah cried out soundlessly. *Wait, come back — my nana, is she alive? My sister Marsala, is she all right?*

But he had asked these questions too late. The well did not reply. Syrah slumped wetly on the moss, breathing hard.

Transform to be transformed. It wanted him to change.

But change *how?* What did it want? Something heroic? How was he supposed to manage that? It wasn't like he was capable of greatness. He could barely handle smallness.

This isn't fair, he thought angrily. *You're making this impossible.*

The well did not reply. The wood was utterly silent. So silent that Syrah became suddenly uncomfortable. He couldn't think why he was so anxious until he swiveled his eyes to take in his surroundings, and it struck him.

Deli and Harrow were gone. They had left him alone.

Syrah leapt into the tall grass that grew around the bottom of a nearby tree, and he cowered there, frightened and angry. He was supposed to transform himself into some perfect hero, and he was supposed to do it as a *frog* — and he was supposed to do it without getting killed in the process.

UNFAIR, he thought again. *A LITTLE HELP HERE?*

As if by magic — and perhaps it *was* by magic — footsteps approached. A shadow loomed over him.

"Glad I found you," said Harrow. "Wouldn't want to lose somebody's pet." He stuck out his black and glinting hand.

Syrah glared at his palm.

Thanks, he thought sarcastically in the well's direction. But riding with Harrow was better than being snapped up by a bird or having his legs gnawed off by a weasel. Resigned, Syrah hopped into the farmer's outstretched hand.

Just want to tell her. Pa's hiding something. Tired of keeping it to myself, shouldn't be a secret . . .

Harrow set Syrah on his shoulder and strode back toward the Thatch, a frown cutting deep into his glittering face. Syrah considered his profile, wondering about what he could have meant by a secret — and then a very satisfying idea struck him.

Maybe the Steelcuts were to blame for the Purge. Their oats were probably the poisonous ones. The Exalted Council would figure it out any day, and then the Steelcuts would get hauled off to prison and rot there for life.

Syrah let out a croak of vicious satisfaction, and then he shut his mouth and rolled his eyes back in the direction of the well. Could the wishing well hear his thoughts? It had heard them loud and clear when he'd been down there in that magic water. Maybe it couldn't anymore . . . But maybe it could. He had to assume that it could. Just in case. Syrah pressed his mouth shut in frustration.

You want me to be perfect, Wishing Well? Fine. I'll be perfect. I'll be nice and sweet just like Oat-head here — No, wait! I didn't mean that. Argh.

He had to find a way to *think* nicer. But it was hard being kind in the privacy of his own mind, where he had always been free to make fun of people all he wanted.

You'll see, he forced himself to think instead. *I can change. I WILL change. See? I'm doing it already. I am being a better person. Better, better, better . . .*

Harrow went around to the front of the Thatch and tipped his wide-brimmed hat to the gate guards, who waved him through. The housekeeper opened the door, looking a little rattled. She didn't move aside to let Harrow in.

"I have Walter's pet here," he said.

"You'll have to come back later," she replied, "the family is occupied —"

"It's *disrespectful!*" Roma Gourd cried out from upstairs. "It's unfair! You can't do this to him — to all of us —"

Harrow reached up for Syrah, but he had already leapt down to the floor and was bounding up the stairs, toward the racket. "Never mind — guess he knows where he's going," he heard Harrow say. "Funny little guy . . ."

A minute later, Syrah was in the family quarters, where he found a standoff. Roma stood at the open door of Calabaza's sickroom, facing down Luffa. Syrah stopped where he was to watch. The triplets too were spectating — Bradley's door was open just a crack and Syrah could see them all crowded there, listening.

Deli stood in the corridor beside her mother, speaking quietly. "Ma," she said. "Just hold on a minute. I'm sure we can figure —"

"Delicata, go to your room," said Luffa. "If your mother wants to fight her own battle for once, let her."

Roma watched her daughter go. When Deli's door closed, she seemed to feel how alone she was; she twisted her fingers fretfully. "Postpone," she said to Luffa. Her voice was trembling and high-pitched. "Nobody will blame you if you do. The cabinet will listen to you."

"Some members of the cabinet already share your opinion," said Luffa, "but the majority have voted to proceed with the election. We always said that Declaration Day would take place after the All-Tyme Championships. The ATC has concluded earlier than expected. Declaration Day is therefore tomorrow. Only those who publicly declare their candidacy at that time will be able to run for governor this term."

"But Calabaza can't declare anything!"

"I know he can't."

Luffa sounded so completely unconcerned that it made Syrah shudder. Didn't she care at all about what had happened to her son? Was she actually *glad* that he was sick? She must have been, if she was pushing to start the election before he could wake up.

Roma's pretty face contorted. "You're happy!" she cried. "You don't care if he dies as long as he's out of office!" she shouted. "You just want to control everything — you wish you'd never given up being queen, and you'll do anything to get your power back!"

Luffa snorted. "Roma," she said, "if I wished to be queen, I could retake my crown this very hour. Not a soul in this country would lift a hand to stop me. Be sensible for once in your life."

Roma made a catlike sound. "You're heartless," she said. "Cutting him out of the race while he's unconscious? How can you be so unfeeling? To your own *son*?"

Syrah couldn't help agreeing.

Luffa barely raised an eyebrow. "Anything else?" she said.

"Yes, as a matter of fact," said Roma, crossing her arms. "If a new governor moves into the Thatch, where will we live? If Calabaza loses his seat, we lose our home! Is that what you want? To throw the *children* out?"

"The children," said Luffa dryly, "will be fine. What you really want to know is where *you* will go, and the answer is this: You will stay in this house. It is Gourd property. I have long felt we ought to establish a new capitol building. The first leader of Yellow Country who is *not* a Gourd should have a new seat of command. You will not have to give up the mansion. You will not even have to give up much of the importance. You will always be the wife of a former governor, and you will always be connected with the Gourds. Do you feel entitled to more than that, or are we finished?"

Openmouthed, Roma gazed at Luffa for a moment. "Heartless," she repeated in barely a whisper. She went back into Calabaza's sickroom and slammed the door hard behind her.

Luffa went back downstairs, and Syrah pressed himself hard to the wall as she passed. The moment she was out of sight, Bradley exhaled. His door swung open wider as he released it and trudged back into his room. Syrah hopped after him and made his way to the windowsill, where Walter was standing, looking down at the drive.

"All because of porridge," Bradley said, with uncharacteristic quietness. He sank down on his bed. "He ate a few bites of porridge, and now he can't be governor."

"Pa barely even likes porridge," Tommy added. He sat on the floor at the foot of Bradley's bed and picked at a frayed bit of carpet.

"He didn't eat any," said Walter placidly. He was standing at the window, looking out at the drive. Behind him, his brothers exchanged a look, then shrugged and shook their heads.

Down on the driveway, carriages had arrived. Syrah recognized the people getting out. Tara Zu in her leather-rimmed glasses, Injera Teff wearing her baby in a sling, Clementine Pease flicking her valise open and arranging it into a stepladder so that she could get down from her carriage.

Bradley came over to see what Walter was looking at. "Just more meetings," he said, and walked away again. "Probably getting ready for Declaration Day tomorrow."

"Who do you think will run for governor?" asked Tommy mournfully.

"Anyone who does is a witch," said Bradley, flinging a pillow across the room with sudden violence. "Ma's right — it's disrespectful."

"It's like Grandmother Luffa doesn't even care," said Tommy.

"She *doesn't* care," said Bradley. "You know what they say. She sharpened her sword on the stone where her heart used to be, and when she cut that warlord's head off, she drank the blood right out of it."

"That's just a story," said Tommy uncertainly.

"Is it?" said Bradley. "She never washed that sword, you know.

She still sleeps with it on her wall, with the blood still all crusty on the blade. And you know where she sleeps is the same exact room where her whole family was beheaded. The floor is still red with their blood, and they rise up to haunt her every night —"

"You're stupid," said Tommy.

"Am I? Then why did Asti Huanui kiss me before we left Plenty?"

Syrah's croak of alarm was drowned out by Tommy's gasp. "She did not!" he cried. "You're lying. I'll write to Asti and ask her."

"Ask her what?" Bradley taunted. "Which one of us she likes better? Go ahead."

"Come on, Prince Frog," said Walter. "I'm hungry."

Syrah hopped onto Walter's shoulder and traveled with him downstairs, where he was surprised to see G. G. Floss standing in the foyer. She wore a crisp, cream-colored straw hat with a copper sash around the base, and she was balancing a large box in one arm while Physic Feverfew fussed over her other one. The Physic's usually severe gray topknot listed to one side — she had probably been watching over Calabaza all night.

"I'm telling you it's *fine*," Miss Floss was saying. "Don't worry yourself. I burn myself all the time, I'm awful. You'd think I just started making candy yesterday."

"This is a very serious burn," the Physic scolded. "It may even be infected. If I hadn't noticed the bandage, you would have gone home like this! Why didn't you come to me right away?"

"You're the Gourd family's Physic. It would be an imposition."

"Nonsense. If you promise you'll always make lemon buttercream truffles, then I promise I'll always bandage your burns."

Miss Floss laughed. "Fair enough," she said, and she nodded

toward Walter. "Would you take this box before I drop it?" she asked. "It's for your family — I'm so sorry about your father being ill. I'm sure it would be more useful if I brought actual food, but candy's all I'm good for, I'm afraid."

Walter rescued the large box from G. G.'s precarious hold, and he lifted the lid. Within was a garden of flowers, all of them white and golden and so beautifully arranged that Syrah could only stare. Daisies and lilies, starflowers and roses, tulips and sunflowers, each one incredibly lifelike. Syrah could hardly believe they were for eating.

Walter carefully lifted a white rose in his fingertips and smelled it. "Orange," he said.

"Very good," said Miss Floss. "Most people can't tell the diff — Ow!" She tried to pull her hand away from Physic Feverfew, but only succeeded in drawing more of the Hipocrath's attention.

"Is that *another* burn?" she demanded, seizing the purple fingertips of Miss Floss's other hand and yanking it toward her. She pushed up her sleeve. "Good morning, Exalted Nexus," she added, somewhat absently.

Miss Floss turned her head with a jerk. Nexus Burdock had just emerged from the back of the Thatch where the cabinet chamber was located. He stopped when he saw Miss Floss and came no closer, but watched as Physic Feverfew held one of her blue palms over Miss Floss's bandaged wrist.

"What happened?" said the Nexus.

"Burned herself," said Physic Feverfew. She withdrew her hand. "As I thought, it's infected. You'll have to come with me."

"Miss Floss," said the Nexus. "Wait. I owe you an apology. I shouldn't have told you the other day to mind your candy. You were only trying to help."

"Yes I was." Miss Floss's tone was aloof.

"I wonder if you'll help with something else," said Burdock, looking somewhat red. "When you're sufficiently healed, that is. Would you pay me a visit?"

"I'm terribly busy, Exalted Nexus."

"But it's about the election," said Burdock. "There's a candidate I hope you might be willing to endorse."

Miss Floss glanced back at him with more interest. "Perhaps I'll make a little time," she said, and she left the Thatch along with the Physic.

"What are those, Walter?" said Burdock, coming closer and peering into the candy box. "Exquisite," he said, his voice oddly grave. "Just like the real thing."

"Here," said Walter, handing him the box. "I don't like orange-flavored candy."

Walter headed to the dining room for lunch, leaving behind Burdock, who lifted a tiny, perfect starflower from the box and twirled it in his fingertips. It sparkled in the light. He set it back down, gave a brief sigh, and left the Thatch with the box under his arm.

Chapter Ten

*T*HAT night, while the Gourds slept, Syrah went around the house as he had done before. This time, however, he wasn't looking for ways to send messages. He knew now that it wouldn't matter. Only the well could help him — and the well wanted something from him. Something special. Something heroic.

What could he do that was good?

In the boys' rooms, he saw a hundred things he could have done if he were human-size. He could have put away Walter's messy clothes. He could have fixed Tommy's broken soldiers and horses. He could have told Bradley that the letter he'd started writing to Asti sounded pretty stupid and he ought to try again. It was not lost on him that, when he had been a human, he had never lifted a finger to assist with such things. It hadn't occurred to him to bother, although he realized now that it would have been incredibly easy.

As a frog, it was far more difficult.

He hopped up onto the boys' desks and pushed small things back into their places: quills, laces, bits of paper. Painstakingly, one by one, he carried Walter's marbles in his mouth and deposited them in the wooden dish that stood next to the marble racetrack. He got a little bit carried away at Tommy's war table, using his feet to push all the miniature soldiers and horses into marching formations and battle tableaux, and arranging the broken soldiers and horses to create scenes of devastation. He wasn't sure that this exactly counted as a good deed, but maybe Tommy would like it.

In Bradley's room, there was much less to do. Bradley was the most meticulous of the triplets. Syrah hopped up onto his desk again and reread the beginning of his letter to Asti.

You have probably heard that my pa is very sick, but don't worry, I'm still well. I am taking care of everyone here. Tommy does nothing but cry, of course. I never cry.

Syrah found a moth fluttering at the bedroom window, swallowed it, then hopped back up on Bradley's desk and regurgitated the half-disintegrated moth right in the middle of the letter. There. That letter wasn't going anywhere now — which was seriously nice of him. Bradley would only embarrass himself if he sent it.

He tried to get into Deli's room, but it was shut. So were Calabaza's and Luffa's. He saw something glinting at one edge of the long carpet that ran the length of the corridor, and when he investigated, he found that it was an earring, mostly hidden under the rug. A precious one, with a large, pale yellow teardrop gem hanging from a silver setting. It must have belonged to Roma. Syrah wondered how long it had been lost. He worked it out from under the carpet with his toes and pushed it out to the center of the carpet, where it could be discovered in the morning.

Inspired, he set off to peek under the edges of other carpets. There were probably lots of little lost objects in this house, and some of them would be easier to find as a frog than as a human.

For the rest of the night, Syrah hunted all over the top floor of the house, and by morning he had nudged and carried a variety of small things into the corridor. Three buttons, two of bone and one of copper, a tiny, scratched gold charm shaped like a teacup, a dog-eared playing card, a puzzle piece, and even a few coins. His greatest triumph of the night, however, was a silver thimble that he found in a dark corner, wedged deep down in a crack between two floorboards. He dug it out with his tongue, which was a disgusting task — the crack was full of ancient, musty grit; he felt like he was licking around inside a small tomb, and the thimble itself was tarnished and unpleasant to taste. But when he succeeded in prying it out, he was elated. He deposited it in the middle of his little pile of findings.

A small drop-leaf table stood snug against the wall between Deli's room and the now-empty bedroom that had once belonged to Christophen. Syrah settled down under this table, out of the way and mostly out of sight, and waited for the family to wake.

It was Deli who appeared first, though she did not come out of her room. She sneaked up the stairs, carrying a pack on her back just as she had yesterday morning, and carrying her shoes in one hand so that her footsteps would be softer. She approached her room silently — until she stepped barefoot upon the pile of objects Syrah had assembled. She shrieked in pain, hopped for a moment, then bent down to see what had hurt her.

"What the . . ." She crouched, set down her pack, and sifted through it. Her eyes flew wide. She lifted up her mother's earring. "This can't be the same one," she said.

At the far end of the corridor, Luffa's door opened, and she appeared in her dressing gown.

"You shouted," she said.

"Grandmother," said Deli, shooting to her feet. She moved sideways to block Luffa's view of her pack, but it was too late.

"Why are you dressed and packed?" Luffa demanded. "What have you been doing?"

Deli tried for a distraction. She held up the earring. "Somebody left a pile of stuff right outside my door," she said, her voice shaking a little. "I stepped on this — that's why I shouted. I think it's the earring my mother lost last year. There are lots of little lost things piled up here — but who found them and left them like this?"

Luffa looked halfway curious. She closed her door behind her and came to look down at the pile. "Like a little Skittish hoard," she murmured. "An imp must have been here."

"This one's engraved," Deli said, picking up the thimble. She rubbed her thumb over the tarnished top. "ACG . . ."

Luffa drew a sharp breath. "Hand me that," she whispered. Deli passed her the thimble at once, and Luffa gazed down at it, the muscles in her face working jerkily. "Aurantia Citrulina Gourd," she said. "This belonged to my mother."

Syrah's mouth sagged open.

"It must have lain hidden for a hundred years," Luffa whispered. Her voice was rough. "The Pink butchers melted everything down. But this survived." She closed her fist around the thimble. "Its return is a sign. Mama approves of my course. She forgives me. She sees —" Luffa faltered to a stop. "Excuse me." She went back to her room and closed the door behind her.

Deli swept the remaining lost items into her palm, took up her pack, and shut herself in her room. Syrah stayed where he was, staring down the hall at Grandmother Luffa's door. He had never seen the woman so emotional. Had that thimble really been stuck in that crack for a century? It had certainly tasted like it. . . . But that was amazing. And he'd been the one to find it. He couldn't believe that his hunt for lost bits and pieces had yielded such a treasure. He'd given back Luffa a piece of her childhood — a piece of her history. Of Yellow Country's history.

Yet he was still a frog. Apparently, finding thimbles wasn't good enough.

After lunch, he rode on Walter's shoulder out to the front lawn that sprawled before the Thatch, where an impressive crowd had gathered. Syrah thought it must have been several hundred people at least. There were only a few rows of seats at the front of the lawn; behind these, everyone else stood packed together. The back of the crowd extended all the way up the gently rising hill that led to the river, and more people were arriving all the time.

They were here for Declaration Day, Syrah realized, and he looked around with interest. Declaration Day happened only once every seven years, and since his own country held no elections, it was his best chance to see how it worked. Plus, this was the first Declaration Day when a Gourd wouldn't be running for the governor's seat. Anything could happen.

Walter took a seat in the front row, between Tommy and Bradley, and Roma sat beside them, looking elegant in her dark clothes and hat. She wore the pale yellow teardrop earrings that Syrah had restored to a pair, along with a bracelet of matching pale yellow stones. These she worried with her fingers, twisting the bracelet around and around her wrist as the crowd grew denser and louder behind her. She kept her eyes fixed on the flag of Yellow Country, which stood proudly in its bracket on the small stage that had been erected on the lawn. The stage was shaded by the grove of trees that lined the eastern edge of the lawn and traveled around toward the back of the Thatch. Unlike the pomegranate grove to the west where the Gourds buried their dead, every tree in this area was different.

When the bell tolled one, Clementine Pease came to the stage. She wore a long duster over simple work clothes and boots, and her short purple hair was combed back. Around her neck hung the emblem of Yellow: two golden sheaves of wheat, crossed. She set down her stepladder, climbed up to the podium, and lifted a speaking trumpet to her lips.

"People of Yellow Country," she said, and the crowd fell silent. "You are gathered here to witness history. But before we move ahead into our country's future, we must acknowledge our shared pain. Governor Calabaza has been taken very ill, just as so many of our good citizens have been taken very ill, by a sickness we do not yet understand. We know its source, but not how to cure its effects. As of our last count, fifty-six citizens of Yellow Country and twelve travelers from other nations have tragically lost their lives to this sickness."

Syrah listened, grim. Twelve travelers from other nations — were any of them his family? Surely if one of the Huanuis had died, someone at the Thatch would have mentioned it. They would have mourned. Wouldn't they?

"Many of the families of those we have lost are here with us today. In honor of their extraordinary strength, I ask you to set the grief of these families above your own grievances. Put aside your differences and be, today, a nation of strength and solidarity, and a people who support each other through loss. Let our every thought, our every word, be rooted in compassion for one another."

Roma sniffled and touched a handkerchief to her eye.

"Our minister of foreign affairs, Luffa Gourd," said Clementine, "reigned for thirty-six years as Queen of Yellow Country. She brought visionary change when she removed her crown and held the very first Declaration Day. For fourteen years, she served as governor, and since her retirement from that office, her son, Calabaza, has served in her place.

"Today is the eighth Declaration Day in our nation's history, and it is the first one in which no Gourd will declare candidacy. Today we leave our monarchy fully in the past as we take our first steps into a truly democratic future."

Anticipation thrilled through Syrah. Even if he didn't agree with Luffa's choices, he had to admit that this was exciting.

Others didn't seem so energetic. There was uneven applause and even some murmurs of dissent. Syrah looked around. The cabinet members sat in a row behind the Gourd family, several of them looking uneasy. In the row behind them, Syrah saw the Steelcuts. Huck looked exhausted; Harrow uncomfortable. G. G. Floss was also there, one of the few who applauded with enthusiasm.

"And so, if you're here to run, the time has come to stand and declare!" said Clementine. "Who'll go first?"

Behind Burdock, Huck Steelcut got to his feet. He made his way up to the stage carrying a seedling tree in a pot, which he set down beside the podium before picking up the speaking trumpet.

Syrah watched him carefully, thinking of what he had felt in Harrow's mind. Huck Steelcut had a secret, and whatever it was, if Harrow wasn't allowed to talk about it, then the Steelcuts surely didn't want the people of Yellow to know about it. *Was* it the Purge? Had Huck done it on purpose? But why would he do anything so awful, when it might be traced back to his farm?

Maybe he had done it to become governor.

Syrah let out a low, amazed croak. Of course. It was pretty convenient that this sickness had broken out right before the election — and it was *too* convenient that Calabaza had gotten sick. Especially if he hadn't eaten any porridge, which Walter thought he hadn't. Bradley and Tommy had dismissed Walter's comment, but Syrah thought he might be right. Had there been porridge on Calabaza's table at the ATC? Yes — and the bowl had been untouched.

Syrah remembered again that swinging lantern light in the carriage house. Huck Steelcut's lantern, maybe. Huck had been in Calabaza's box at the ATC, so he would've noticed that the governor hadn't eaten any porridge. He would've known that he had to feed Calabaza something else to make him sick. Like liver pâté sandwiches on oat bread. Syrah looked at the man who stood before them all on the stage, a silver cord shining around the brim of his hat and a silver S on his belt buckle, and he wondered.

Was he a murderer?

"My name is Huck Steelcut," he began. "And I declare my candidacy. But before I get into politics, I think we need to start with what's really on your minds this morning. A lot of you are wondering if my oats caused the Purge." He paused again and ran a weather-beaten hand through his salt-and-dark hair. "All I can tell you is that I've complied with Minister Pease's investigation, like every other oat farmer I know. We've surrendered sacks of our grain, and we're waiting for an answer. I pray to the ancestors that it wasn't my oats — but that's not to say I hope it was anyone else's. That's not a burden I'd wish on any farmer."

Huck doffed his hat and placed it on the podium. He shook his head.

"A lot of us are farmers here. We understand the difficulty of this situation better than government folks can. We carry a sacred duty. Every day, we wake before dawn, and we toil, and we strive to make sure that this nation remains a land of wholesome plenty. We are the ones who feed our people. We are the reason that Yellow Country stands strong. This sickness — this Purge — is an affront to everything we break our backs to protect: our people, our land, and our integrity."

"Hear, hear!" cried a voice in the back, and then several other voices rose in support. Syrah hopped up to the top of Walter's head to look back at the crowd, and saw that many people were now listening avidly, leaning forward, nodding their approval.

Huck gestured to his seedling pot.

"My offering today is an apple tree," he said, and then he added, "An apple nourishes. It can be dried or juiced, fried or baked. We can sell them whole, sell their cider, feed their cores to our stock. Every piece of what they are contributes in some way to our economy; nothing about them need go to waste. That's how we ought to see our farmers too. It's not just your labor that matters — it's your voices. You deserve a governor who'll listen to you. We've been governed a long time by people who know a lot about making rules, but not much else. Heck, we've got a law that forbids us from exploring gnomish magic that might make our farms more productive. How's that useful to anyone? Calabaza loves to say we ought to leave the magic to the magical, but if that magic can feed people, maybe we have a responsibility to investigate it."

This met with more shouts of approval, as well as some protest. Syrah heard snatches of "Finally!" and "Exactly what I've been saying!" along with "Not on *my* farm."

"But like I said," Huck continued, holding up a hand, "I'd listen to *you*. You ought to be the ones debating and deciding the future of farming — not some royal politician who's been holed up in a fancy house for decades, never getting his fingers dirty. It's high time for the hand that tills the soil to be the hand that steers the nation. Thank you."

The crowd made a wild noise of approval. Syrah was surprised. In spite of the Purge, Huck's message had sparked something in the audience. Syrah glanced at Luffa, whose face was immobile. It was impossible to tell what she felt.

Huck returned to his seat, and Clementine set down her stepladder and climbed up to the podium, speaking trumpet in hand. "Stand and declare," she said again. "Who's next?"

Nexus Burdock stood, and Syrah goggled in surprise. He wasn't the only one. A few people gasped. Luffa's eyebrows moved — barely, but it was there. Roma Gourd stretched out a trembling hand toward the Nexus, as if in appeal.

"But Nexus," she said weakly. "Calabaza — he's unconscious. He *trusts* you."

Burdock made his way forward, looking nauseated but determined. He grabbed a seedling tree from beside the stage and carried it up the steps to set it beside Huck's apple tree offering. When he reached the podium he picked up the speaking trumpet and closed his eyes. In a moment, it glowed golden, just as it had at the ATC, and when Burdock spoke, he did not have to raise his voice. He was calm and quiet but could easily be heard by every person present.

"Fig trees interest me," he said. "They're like children: full of potential, but frighteningly vulnerable. Ignore a fig tree, neglect it, and its life will be short. It will die and never give fruit. But if you accept the fig's fragility and give it your full attention as it grows, you will have a tree that lasts for centuries and bears fruit beyond compare." Burdock paused. He passed his light eyes over the crowd. "We are fragile," he said. "Vulnerable. Yet we are neglecting our weakness. Huck Steelcut accuses Calabaza of unfairly outlawing magical farming supports — which is true. But the whole truth is far more sinister."

Syrah felt a chill. He had debated with Burdock before, but this was real. This had stakes. And Burdock was good — he had the crowd's absolute attention. Their faces were uneasy. Fearful. People shifted in their seats and glanced at one another.

"Tell me," said Nexus Burdock. "Last year, when the jacks champion turned out to be the witch Envearia's child, what did we do?"

There was silence. No one moved or spoke.

Syrah wished he could have spoken. He had been there that day. He remembered exactly what they had done.

"We ran," said Burdock. "We *cowered*. Is that who we are?"

The question settled upon the silent crowd. Nobody stirred except Luffa, whose eyes narrowed. She studied Burdock as though she were seeing him for the first time.

"No, we are better," said Burdock quietly. "Nobler. We only ran away because we did not have a plan. Fear is natural — necessary for survival — but if we let it rule us, we are lost. We *must* have a plan. I have longed to take strong action against witches and other magical threats to our nation. I have petitioned Governor Calabaza countless times for his permission to use the full scope of my power to defend you all against such threats. But that permission has been denied me."

Luffa's expression remained watchful. Farther back in the crowd, G. G. Floss sat up straight, wearing a look of pleased surprise.

"Many of you will feel that one of the Exalted should not be governor," Burdock went on. "You will worry that it gives me too much power — and I understand your caution. But consider: As your Nexus, I can only give advice. When the governor asks for my thoughts, I share them. When the Exalted Council makes suggestions, I urge him to listen. But when he ignores me, there is nothing I can do."

Syrah couldn't nod, but he would have. What Burdock was saying made sense. Perfect sense.

"Some of you will think I'm disloyal for taking this opportunity to run for governor while Calabaza is unconscious," Burdock continued. "But I think you'll be angrier with him than with me when I tell you this: The Purge was preventable. No one had to die."

Instantly, the silence was broken, replaced by furious shouting. People stood. Demanded answers. Syrah looked around him, amazed. These people had been calm just minutes ago.

"For years, I have begged Calabaza to let me create a system of magical checks to ensure that the food we grow here in Yellow Country is safe for export and consumption — but *he has denied me.*"

The shouts became louder. People cursed. Someone in the back was sobbing.

"Make me your governor," said Burdock, his cheeks feverishly bright, "and I promise you that I will do more than make magic available to your farms — I will safeguard you. I will never let another Purge take our loved ones. I will never let another witch steal our children. I will use all the power my Exalted birth has granted me to make this nation safe. My name is Burdock, and I declare my candidacy."

The crowd roared with angry energy, and Syrah felt it too. Burdock was right. Calabaza had failed.

Maybe it was good that they were having an election — that the people had a chance to choose somebody new. The thought surprised Syrah, and he turned it over in his mind, curious. Was there something useful about a democracy after all? He wondered what his mother would say.

Burdock returned to his seat while Huck Steelcut appraised him in silence. Clementine moved to the podium again and climbed up on her stepladder. Her expression was difficult to read.

"Stand and declare," she said. "Is there another candidate who —"

Harrow Steelcut rose from his seat. His father gaped up at him. "Son," he said. "What are you doing?"

Harrow didn't answer. He stumbled away from his seat as though drunk, staggered a few meters, then he fell to his knees and vomited, white and unmistakable, as the crowd looked on in horror.

"NO!" Huck shouted, and ran to his son. Harrow collapsed in the white puddle, facedown. Huck rolled him over at once and wiped his face with a bare hand. "Son," he pleaded. "Harrow, honey, look at me. Open your eyes."

Harrow did, and they were black. "Mama," he rasped, and reached up for Huck's face. "Mama — where are you —" He turned his face, heaved, and vomited again.

Burdock hurried to them and crouched down on Harrow's other side. "Let's get him to a Physic," he said quietly. "I'll help you."

"How did this happen?" Huck cried. "He hasn't touched oats since the ATC —"

"What does this mean?" shouted a woman in the audience. "What did he eat?"

"It's *his* farm that did it!" cried a man. "It's Steelcut — he killed my mother —"

"Declaration Day is hereby suspended!" Clementine Pease had the speaking trumpet to her lips. "Go home, all of you, and wait for news. We will investigate —"

"You've investigated already!"

"You're doing nothing!"

"What are we supposed to do until then? Starve?"

"We will *investigate*," Clementine repeated. "As fast as we can. If you planned to stand and declare your candidacy today, send a message to the cabinet. It's time now to go on home and let us tend the sick."

But the people would not be appeased. Burdock had chosen the wrong time to rile up their fear and anger. Now they were bold with it.

"What about *our* sick? Is my son worth less than his?"

"We're not leaving without answers!"

"You want us gone, you drag us out!"

Clementine motioned to the governor's guards, who came forward and forced the angry crowd away from the stage. Soon, the only ones left were the Steelcuts, the Gourds, and the members of Yellow Country's cabinet.

"We need another emergency meeting," said Clementine. "Right now. Roma, take your children inside and send a carriage out here for Huck and Harrow."

Roma and the triplets departed at once, but Syrah hopped down from Walter's shoulder and onto a chair. He wasn't going anywhere.

Neither, it seemed, was Deli. She remained behind her grandmother, arms crossed tight. Her gaze was on Harrow.

"Somebody needs to get Physic Feverfew and tell her to hurry to Huck's," said Clementine.

"Me," said Deli instantly, and she shot off, running at top speed. Syrah watched her go, feeling sour.

Luffa also looked displeased as she watched Deli go.

"Burdock," said Clementine, "you help Huck with his boy, and then get Nexus Keene here, quick as he can make it."

"I don't want the Exalted Council on my farm," Huck rasped, staring down at Harrow, who was breathing heavily and perspiring so hard that his glittering skin made prisms in the beaded sweat.

"Mama," he moaned in misery, white drool running from the corner of his mouth. "Come back . . ."

"Huck, we have to." But Clementine sounded reluctant. "There's just no choice now —"

"I'll give him whatever he needs for his investigation," said Huck. "I'll hold nothing back, but that's my private property. You understand." He looked up at her, fervent. "Don't give him a writ to tear up my farm, I'm begging you."

Syrah studied him. Whatever his secret was, it was about to come out, and he was clearly terrified. More terrified about that than his son? Maybe he really *had* started the Purge. . . .

Though it didn't seem likely, now that Harrow had it too.

"The rest of you, inside," said Clementine. "We have to settle the matter of how to proceed with this election. Burdock, since you're a candidate, you're excused. Good, here's the carriage — let's get Harrow somewhere comfortable so he can fight this thing off." She crouched down beside Huck for a moment. "He's young and strong," she said quietly. "And he's not unconscious yet, which is the best possible sign. I'll come by tonight and talk with you before any writs are issued. You have my word on that."

Huck nodded. With Burdock's help, he lifted his son and carefully laid him in the carriage. Huck climbed in with him and pulled Harrow's sweating head into his lap.

On instinct, Syrah leapt onto the carriage wheel, then jumped over to the step, and bounced once more to get into the carriage itself. He barely made it before Burdock shut the door behind him. Whatever was happening on the Steelcut farm, he wanted to see it for himself. Maybe the Exalted Council needed a writ, but a frog didn't. He could investigate.

The carriage lurched to a start. Once Syrah got his balance, he hopped up onto the seat opposite Huck and Harrow, neither of whom noticed him. Harrow's eyes were dilated, and his mouth was moving, but no words came out. Sweat poured off him. Huck brushed a hand over his son's damp curls.

"Ancestors," he murmured. "Hear me now. My son's not involved, and he's too young to join you. Help him, please."

Involved in what? thought Syrah.

"Mama . . ." Harrow thrashed, and Huck held him tight as the carriage rumbled on toward Steelcut Farm.

CHAPTER ELEVEN

*T*HE Steelcuts' farmhouse looked like it had grown right out of the ground. It was tall and wide, cobbled from differently colored stones, and every stone was a different shape, yet they all seemed to fit together perfectly. Bright moss grew from between them, and large swaths of leafy greenery covered large sections of the walls. Flowering vines wrapped the whole roof as though in an embrace. A wide, covered porch surrounded the front and sides of the house, and a garden of bright sweet peas flourished along the porch roof. Thick, graceful lilac bushes grew along the outside of the porch, purple and willowy, providing perfume, privacy, and shade.

Syrah liked the place. It felt alive, like the wood where the well lay.

Huck carried Harrow into the house, and Syrah rode along by jumping onto Harrow's boot. He didn't want to touch the ground here; if the Purge had started in these fields, then there might be something wrong with the soil, and he didn't want to absorb any poison through his delicate skin.

The green, flowering farmhouse sure didn't show any signs of sickness, though. Everything was vivid and thriving.

Everything except Harrow.

Huck carried his son up the stairs and into a bedroom that was as green and flowering as the house itself. Syrah looked around, dazzled. Vines crawled up the walls and over the ceiling, creating a canopy of green cords and dangling blossoms. Huge ferns lined the walls, fanning tall and wide, their leaves thick and waxen, their flowers perfuming the air. It could barely be called a bedroom, except that there was a bed in it, but this bed was as overgrown with plant life as everything else. Thin, leafy branches wrapped the bedposts and the headboard, and the bed's canopy was a trellis full of blooming yellow starflowers. Even the desk and chair, though not covered in plants, were made of cobblestones like the walls of the house outside. Syrah had never seen an indoor space that was anything like it, and though it pained him a little, he couldn't help but admire it.

It was nice and warm in here too. There wasn't a stove or a fireplace in sight, yet it was as warm and humid in Harrow's room as it was back home on Balthasar. It felt amazing to Syrah, who hadn't experienced anything like his native climate in a very long time.

"They're coming to help you," Huck murmured, kneeling beside Harrow's bed once he had settled him into it. "Just hold on, son."

Syrah hopped from Harrow's boot onto the stone desk and sat there, trying to decide where he ought to go first. Huck Steelcut probably had an office of some kind, where he kept his information. Maybe he would find something there.

It was strange to think that he was able to explore where the Exalted Council themselves could not — he'd never thought of his frog form as useful before, but for spying, it was perfect.

A heavy knocking from downstairs brought Huck to his feet. "The Physic's here," he said, wiping sweat from Harrow's brow once more. "I'll be right back." He strode from the room and Syrah hopped after him. He watched from between the railings on the second floor as Huck descended the steps and opened the front door. But it was not a Physic who waited there.

The man who stood on the Steelcuts' porch was tall and striking. His dark hair was silver at the temples, his face lined and weathered but unquestionably handsome. He was dressed in long layers of dark leather and carried a black traveling bag. An Exalted amulet shone at his breast.

"Exalted Nexus Keene," said Huck, clearly taken aback. He bowed, but did not move out of the way. "I'm sorry, but I can't let you in."

"You must," said Nexus Keene. His voice was quiet, but firm. "I'm here to help your boy."

"And ransack my property."

"I will not venture farther than your son's sickroom. Not without a writ from Provisional Governor Pease. You have my word as an emissary of the Exalted Council."

"Emissary, huh?" Huck surveyed the Exalted Nexus. "From what I hear, you run the Council."

"Not officially," said Keene. "We work together."

"You're Nexus of Lilac, aren't you?"

"Yes."

"But just about every country in Tyme calls you when there's real trouble."

Keene acknowledged this with a nod. "One of the perils of doing your job well," he said, "is that people expect you to do it more often."

Huck still did not move. "You got here awful fast," he said. "How are you in Plenty one minute, and Cornucopia the next?"

"Magic is useful," said Keene. "I'd like to use it to help your son. Please let me."

Huck finally relented.

"Burdock told me this happened an hour ago?" asked the Nexus as they climbed the stairs.

"Yes, but it makes no sense," said Huck. "He wouldn't have eaten oats since the ATC."

"And you're certain he didn't eat any *at* the games?"

"No, I'm not certain . . . but wouldn't he have gotten sick by now?"

"That's exactly what I wonder."

They went into Harrow's room, and Syrah followed. He knew he ought to go and find Huck's office, but he had never seen Exalted Nexus Keene before, and he was impressed by the aura of power that seemed to radiate from the man. He knew that Keene had held him once, while he was hibernating. Rapunzel had found him frozen, thought him dead, and had brought him to the Exalted Council, where Keene had examined him and proclaimed him alive. Syrah had often wondered what heroic deeds and magic wonders he would have felt if he had only been conscious when Keene had held him in his palm. It was a shame he'd missed that adventure.

Keene looked briefly around the room, then pulled the stone chair to the head of the bed and sat down. He peered at Harrow.

"Unusual," he murmured. "I realize it's none of my business, but your son's appearance is unique." Keene glanced around the green and blooming room, which was also unique, though he did not say this. "Is he . . . is there magic involved?" he asked. "Who is his mother?"

"Harrow's adopted," said Huck. "I can't tell you his origins."

"Ah." Nexus Keene frowned. "A shame. It would help if I knew."

Huck said nothing.

The Nexus opened his traveling bag. Syrah saw boots inside it, and phials of different colors. The Nexus withdrew a small, bone-white compact that fit in his palm. He pressed a tiny button and it popped open to reveal a dark green powder.

"What's that?" said Huck.

"The only thing I've found so far that helps," said Keene. "Powdered Vangarden." He dipped his thumb into the powder, then smeared it on Harrow's temples and his throat. He put his hands out over Harrow, closed his eyes, and bent his head. His hands began to glow. Streams of light moved around them like a hundred quick fireflies, but cool blue and soft purple. The light made a humming sound.

When the Nexus withdrew his hands, nothing else happened.

"What now?" Huck demanded.

"Now we wait." Nexus Keene looked up at him. "I realize the timing is terrible," he said. "And I am truly sorry. But you should hear this now: We have traced the corrupt oats, and they all lead back to this farm."

Huck blew out a heavy breath. "There it is," he muttered, and he began to pace the room, back and forth. "There it is. I'm done for."

"Why do you say that?"

"No one'll trust my name or my crops after this," said Huck, with a hysterical laugh. "That's not clear to you?"

"No," said Keene. "We know only that the oats are corrupt. We don't know *why*. Surely it isn't your fault — and no one will imagine it is, now that your own son is sick. There must be a disease in the soil, a problem in the water, something beyond your control. Let me search your farm and find it, and we'll get your name cleared."

"I can't let you do that!"

"Why not?"

Huck put his head in his hands.

"Pa?" whispered Harrow suddenly.

Huck sat up with a gasp. "Harrow? You're awake?"

Harrow blinked his eyes and opened them. He looked up at Nexus Keene. "Who are you?" he mumbled.

"That was incredibly fast," said Keene. "No one else has woken up so quickly. And he realizes I'm a stranger, so he's in his right mind —"

Before Keene finished speaking, Harrow let out a high, keening sound and convulsed, weeping in pain. His tears were white. So was the sweat oozing from his pores. Syrah shut his mouth tight; the smell of moths was overwhelming.

"Harrow!" shouted Huck in terror. "Nexus, what is this?"

"I don't know," said Nexus Keene, his eyes narrow and curious as he watched Harrow jerk and writhe in agony. Huck tried to reach for his son, but the Nexus put out a hand to stop him. "Wait," he said. "Let him get it out."

"He's in pain!" said Huck furiously. "I can't just sit here —"

A scream ripped from Harrow's throat and he began to thrash as he had in the carriage. "Mama!" he shouted, and Syrah watched, horrified. He could not help but imagine his own sister in Harrow's place. Had she survived this awful thing?

"I've got you," said Huck, kneeling beside the bed. "I'm here, I've got you."

Harrow's body tensed horribly once more, his black, glittering skin filmed over in white tears and sweat — and then it all stopped, just as quickly as it had begun. He slumped and relaxed. His breathing became regular. He opened his eyes and looked up at his father. "Pa," he said weakly. "What's wrong? Did something happen? I feel . . . a little sick."

Huck wiped his eyes. "A little sick," he managed.

"And hungry," Harrow added. He glanced at Keene. "Who's this?" he said.

"That's Exalted Nexus Keene. He saved your life."

"Not exactly," said Keene. "Vangarden powder has needed several hours at least to have an effect on anyone else. Your body expelled the Purge with incredible efficiency, Harrow."

"The Purge!" Harrow shook his head in disbelief. "Did I have it?"

"You destroyed it. Something is at work in your blood, and if I can understand it, then I can help others." He withdrew from his traveling bag two empty phials and a sharp blade.

"You're not cutting into him," said Huck. "He's weak. Let him rest."

Harrow pushed himself to sit up. "You're saying you can use my blood to make a cure?"

"I can try," said Keene. "It would help if I understood more about your birth, but even without that knowledge, I can experiment."

Harrow glanced at his father, who gave him a warning look.

"Go ahead," said Harrow defiantly, turning back to Keene. He stuck out his arm. When Keene cut into him, he winced and sucked in a breath, but that was all. Syrah watched as Harrow's blood filled one small glass tube and then another.

"Did you eat oats at the ATC?" Keene asked him.

"I had that oatmeal cookie they were handing out at the gates," Harrow admitted. "When we found out oats were the problem, I was a little worried, but I figured if it hadn't made me sick already, then it wouldn't."

"Thank you," said Keene. He stowed the phials and held his fingers just above the incision in Harrow's arm. Light played about his fingertips, and Syrah watched in some amazement as Harrow's skin knitted together, stopping the flow of blood.

"Whoa." Harrow lifted his forearm to look at the small scar.

"I hope this will save lives," said Keene.

Another knock came from downstairs.

"That's the Physic," said Huck, getting up. "I guess I'll tell her to head on home."

"I'll tell her on my way out," said Keene, picking up his traveling bag. "I should get to work as quickly as possible." He paused before leaving and faced Huck. "I wish I didn't have to do it, but I'm going to send my colleagues to investigate this farm."

"Not without a writ you're not. I'll fight you on it."

"And I'll fight back. It's for the people of Tyme, Mr. Steelcut. Strange things are happening in many places — it isn't just the Purge. I have to understand what caused this, and soon, or it will only happen again."

When Keene was gone, Huck sank into the chair at the head of the bed.

"What are you hiding, Pa?" Harrow asked quietly. "I know there's something."

Huck looked down at his hands. "Thank you for not telling him about your mother," he said. "For a second, I thought you might."

"For a second I almost did," said Harrow. "I still might. If it can save people?"

"She asked us not to."

"I think she'd change her mind if she knew what was happening."

"She might already know."

"Or she might be dead," said Harrow angrily. "Why else would she stay away? She's never ignored me before. What if she *can't* come? What if Exalted Nexus Keene is right, and it's the land that's sick? Don't we owe it to her to find out?"

Huck stood. "You said you were hungry," he said. "I'll fix you lunch."

Once his father was gone, Harrow tried to get up from the bed, but he was too weak to manage it. He dropped back against his pillow with a grimace, while Syrah watched him, curious. Who was his mother? Huck had said he didn't know Harrow's origins, but clearly that was a lie.

Syrah hopped down from the desk and toward the door. Time to find out what was really going on here.

He searched through the farmhouse, going into open rooms and hopping around to see if there was anything useful. He found a guest room, two privies, a kitchen, a back room full of dirty boots and overalls that smelled of manure, and a small study lined with bookshelves stuffed with volumes on farming and plant life, *Edible Plants ~ An Illustrated Guide* among them.

Syrah paused before leaving the study, and his eyes traveled the faded lettering on the book. It was even more battered than Jack's mother's old copy, the leather scratched and faded with creases and breaks all along its spine.

Something was off, he thought suddenly. Something was wrong. The longer he looked at the book, the more he felt it: a vague sense of nameless unease. It was similar to the feeling he'd had as a boy, standing on the ship and crossing the Tranquil Sea to reach the mainland, and suddenly realizing that he had forgotten some important toy at home and could not go back to get it.

He was missing something. What was he missing? This was just like yesterday, with Calabaza's snack basket. . . .

That was it. The basket. Somehow, the book had reminded him of it. But why? Edible plants . . . The liver pâté sandwiches . . . There had been watercress in those sandwiches.

Watercress that was ever so faintly brown around the edges.

Juggetsbane. A toxic plant.

The details clicked into place in Syrah's brain, and he sat on the floor of the Steelcuts' study, gaping up at the bookshelves without really seeing them.

Somebody had poisoned Governor Calabaza. Somebody had fixed him juggetsbane and liver pâté sandwiches. Then that same somebody had gone out to the carriage house with a lantern, sneaked the basket into the carriage, and let everybody think that Calabaza had the Purge.

Syrah went cold all over. This was why Calabaza had gotten ill later than everybody else. Someone had taken advantage of the Purge to make it *look* like he was sick by accident, when really he'd been deliberately poisoned.

Maybe by someone who wanted to be governor.

Maybe by someone who didn't want *him* to be governor.

Syrah hopped out of the study, scarcely noticing where he went. His thoughts raced. Who could have done it? Luffa hadn't wanted Calabaza to run. Would she have poisoned her own child? Burdock hadn't wanted Calabaza to have another seven years as governor. Would he have poisoned him to stop it from happening? Huck Steelcut wanted to win the governor's seat. Was this how he had made sure he wouldn't have to run against a Gourd?

He heard two voices speaking low. He hopped closer to see who it was, but when he reached the end of the hall, he found a door that was shut tight. He stayed outside and listened.

". . . don't think it's wise," he heard Huck say.

"We can't let him run unopposed," a woman replied. Harrow's mother? No — the voice was familiar. Syrah concentrated, trying to place it, but a moment later, he didn't have to.

"I can't win, Clementine." Huck sighed. "You know the people won't support me now once they know for sure it was my oats. You've got to run instead."

"You sound like Luffa."

"Maybe she's right," said Huck. "Maybe you ought to be governor." He paused. "Keene as good as told me he's going to search this farm whether I like it or not."

"I don't have to give him a writ."

"Oh yes you do," said Huck. "If you don't, it'll look like you've got something to hide."

"Well don't I?"

"I'm the only one who knows that, and you know I'll keep quiet. You give Keene the writ, I take the fall, nobody ever knows you were involved. You can still run for governor, free and clear."

"No. We'll hide the evidence."

"How? Even if I could somehow harvest that whole field and ship it out to Pulsifer tonight, there would still be acres of windrows left behind. The Exalted will find their evidence."

"This doesn't make a lick of sense," said Clementine with sudden fierceness. "None of it. Twenty years we've been doing this — *twenty* — and all of a sudden, this Purge shows up? Why now? Why hasn't all of Tyme been vomiting white for years?"

"All I can think is that this new batch of seeds was rotten. The magic was wrong, maybe. They made a mistake."

Syrah listened hard, trying to follow. Huck and Clementine had been doing something in secret for twenty years? Something magical? And it had to do with the oats — with the seeds? And the seeds came from . . .

"Or they did this on purpose," said Clementine, her voice hard. "And if they did . . ."

"I can't imagine why they would."

"There are stories these days. Things going wrong. That fire in Quintessential, for a start."

Syrah's eyes bulged. Were they talking about Ubiquitous?

"Yeah." Huck was quiet. "You should go," he said. "It'll look bad if you stay too long. Give the Exalted Council their writ. Declare your candidacy."

"Get out of here, Huck."

Huck chuckled. "Run away?" he said. "Hide in the Violet Peaks?"

"Or Lilac. There are a lot of places a man of your means could go."

"I'll take my chances here."

"They'll put you in prison."

"Then that's where I'll go."

"But you've done nothing *wrong*."

"I say I have," said Huck quietly. "I thought I wasn't. My intentions were good. But if this is the outcome, then yes. I was wrong."

"Then I'm wrong too."

"I did the sowing," said Huck. "I'll do the reaping. But Clementine?"

"Yes?"

"Beat Burdock. I don't like him."

"I don't either. All right — I'll run. If you're sure."

"I'm sure."

There were clicking sounds, and a *snap!*, and then the door opened and Clementine Pease came out carrying her valise and looking determined. She didn't shut the door behind her, but strode past Syrah without noticing him and headed for the front of the house.

CHAPTER TWELVE

SYRAH took advantage of the open door to hop into the room. It was clearly an office, though more vibrant with vines and flowers than any office Syrah had ever seen. In one corner was a large picture window that looked out on endless golden fields of oats. Huck sat in front of this window at his desk, his heavy eyebrows furrowed. He picked up a pen and uncorked an ink bottle, then just as quickly corked it again and slapped the pen back down.

"Better check on the boy," he muttered, and he left the office.

Syrah wasted no time. He hopped onto Huck's chair, and then his desk. The paper in the middle of the desk was still blank — but no, there was ink on it. Bleeding through from the other side.

It wasn't blank. Huck must've turned it over when Clementine showed up. Syrah unfurled his tongue and tried to get it underneath the paper so that he could flip it, but he only succeeded in slicing his tongue on the edge. He winced and tasted blood.

He changed tactics. He planted his front feet on the letter and used his back legs to inch forward, scooting the paper toward the edge of the desk until it dangled more than halfway off. He took his feet off it and let it fall to the floor, hoping that, on its way down, it would somersault. For once, his hopes weren't dashed. The letter flipped in midair and landed writing-side up. It appeared to be only half-written — a few sentences, but no signature. There was an address, though.

> *Ubiquitous Productions*
> *c/o Pulsifer*
> *Venture, Republic of Brown*
>
> *Pulsifer,*
>
> *You've heard by now about our crisis. Exalted Nexus Keene says the sickness is linked to my oats, so don't expect another shipment from me anytime soon, or maybe ever. The Exalted Council plans to investigate my farm, so we should cut official communications now, but I need you to find a way to send word to me and answer some questions.*
>
> *Were the seeds you last supplied me different in some way? In all the years we've worked together, you've never done damage to my land, but now*

Huck had written no further. Syrah read the letter, and he read it again, and then he sat back on his hind legs and croaked, long and slow. The Steelcuts were doing secret business with Ubiquitous Productions. They were using Ubiquitous seeds and then sending them shipments of something.

But Governor Calabaza had outlawed magical farming. So Huck was a criminal — and Clementine Pease, the minister of agriculture, had known all about it. Twenty years, she'd said. So she was a criminal too.

Maybe she was the one who had poisoned Calabaza, to stop him from ever finding out about this. Maybe when the Purge broke out at the ATC, Clementine had realized that it was their fault, gotten desperate, and fed the governor a bunch of juggetsbane. Or maybe Huck had done it. They could even have worked together.

He had to figure out some way to get this letter back to the Thatch.

Syrah stuck his front feet on the paper and started pushing with his back legs to move it along. Slowly — torturously slowly — he moved the letter across the floor. He heard Huck's footsteps coming and tried to work faster, but there was no way he could get the letter out of the room before Huck got back.

He changed course and pushed the letter under a bookshelf that stood near the door, then squeezed into the small space under the shelf along with it.

Huck entered the office, went to his desk, and stared at the blank place where the letter had been. He rifled through a basket of papers, opened drawers and searched through them, and got down on the floor to look under the desk.

"Where in the White skies," he muttered, and he dumped out the basket of papers to check through it again.

A knock at the front door made him start. He hurried out, and Syrah squeezed back out from under the shelf, feeling bruised from being pressed. As quickly as he could — which was not quickly — he pulled the letter out and tried to lift a corner of it off the floor by sticking his moist toes to it and lifting them up. When he finally got one corner to stick to his toes, he snatched it in his mouth and started hopping. It was faster this way, pushing the letter in front of him by carrying it between his frog lips. He got out of the office and made his way toward the front of the house — then realized that Huck would be there. He had to go another way. Maybe there was an open window somewhere. Would he be able to hop up high enough, with the letter in his mouth, to get through a window?

He heard voices and panicked. For now, he just had to hide — it didn't matter where. He hopped through the nearest open door and found himself in the study, where he hid himself, along with the letter, underneath an easy chair. He could still hear the voices, but they were distant, drifting toward him from the front of the house.

"He's resting," he heard Huck say.

"But he's all right?"

Deli's voice. Deli was *here*. Her timing was perfect — if Syrah could just get the letter into her hands, he wouldn't have to figure out how to push it all the way to the Thatch.

"Go on home, Delicata." Huck's voice was gentle but firm. "He's had a rough day."

"Dee?" The rasping voice was Harrow's.

"Get back to bed," said Huck.

"I'm fine," Harrow replied, and then Syrah heard heavy, uneven footfalls on the stairs.

"Don't get up," said Deli, sounding fretful. "I just wanted to check if — I'll go —"

"Don't. Please."

"Harrow . . ." Huck's voice was pained.

"Pa, I'm fine. Dee, come on. Let's sit a minute. I need to —"

"Here, I've got you."

A moment later, Syrah watched from under the chair as Harrow's bare feet limped into the study, with Deli's boots beside them. The chair creaked over Syrah's head as Harrow settled into it.

"Thanks for coming to check on me," he said. "How's your pa?"

"Still unconscious. But I heard that maybe Nexus Keene can make a cure."

"He took my blood. He said he'd try. I hope it works."

"Me too."

The timing was perfect. Syrah tried to hop out from under the chair, but when he moved, the letter fell from his mouth. The moisture from his mouth had eaten through the corner of it. He flicked his tongue to get rid of the small wad of wet pulp that was left behind.

"I miss you," said Deli, so quietly that Syrah could barely hear her. He tried several times in succession to get the letter to stick to his toes again, but it wouldn't come up off the floor. Maybe because it was carpet in here — or maybe the carpet sucked the moisture out of his feet. He scowled in frustration.

"I miss you too. I'm glad you're here."

"I still have — feelings for you."

Syrah's heart gave a painful knock. She shouldn't have been saying this to Harrow — she should've been saying it to *him*.

"Dee," Harrow murmured.

"I always did," said Deli, and the words were tumbling out now, fast and shaky. Syrah didn't want to hear them, but he couldn't block them out. "I never stopped, but after the wedding — after the letter and the *Criers* and then what my grandmother said to me, I just thought I was better off staying by myself. And she's right, I'm selfish — look at me, telling you this now, when you're sick. What's wrong with me?"

You're not selfish, Syrah thought, trying to push the letter forward with his feet. It snagged on a bulging carpet loop and stuck.

"You're not selfish," said Harrow.

Syrah pushed harder, furious. *I said it first*, he thought. *And I knew her first. I know who she is, and I know it better than you. They all expect her to be perfect, and she practically is. Everything she does is for her family or her country or her team.*

It was true, he realized as he thought it. He had known for years how tough and loyal Deli was — but he had never valued her for it. He had thought she was boring for being so serious.

What had been wrong with him?

"Yes I am," said Deli bitterly. "You should be resting, and I know it, but when I saw you sick like that it scared me so bad — I couldn't stop thinking about how I kept pushing you away, when it wasn't your fault. That was selfish too."

"That was caution," said Harrow. "You got burned. You didn't want to get burned again. I get it."

Syrah pressed his mouth shut in frustration. He was the one who had burned her — but he was going to make it up to her. As soon as he was a man again, he would treat Deli like she deserved. She wouldn't need to go running back to Harrow. He turned around and tried to push the letter with his back feet.

"My grandmother saw us go out to the woods yesterday." Her voice was hard. "I knew she would. She always watches me. Today, after I ran and got the Physic for you, she told me I better not go losing my head again and writing love letters — that just because I'm a fool doesn't give me the right to make the whole country look foolish."

The letter finally budged. Now a corner of it was sticking out from underneath the chair. Syrah hopped out and started to drag it out the rest of the way, inch by excruciating inch. Neither Deli nor Harrow noticed him. Deli stood at the window, facing away from Harrow and hugging herself hard, just like she had that morning in the Thatch when Syrah had been thrown out. He paused in his efforts to gaze up at her. The sun outlined her profile, lighting her dark eyelashes, skimming the bridge of her nose and the stubborn thrust of her chin, making the curves of her mouth glow. He had kissed her once — and he'd made her cry with happiness. He could do it again.

If the well would just give him a *chance*.

"You're no fool," said Harrow, whose eyes were trained on her too. "If your grandmother can't see that, well, she's a hundred and four, and maybe her vision's not what it was."

"She told me to stay away from you."

"Are you going to?"

She hesitated, searching Harrow's face. Then she crossed the small room in two steps, bent down, and kissed him. Syrah croaked in protest, but nobody listened. Harrow pulled Deli into his lap.

"I don't want to hurt you," she gasped.

"Good," he mumbled, and kept kissing her.

"*RAWWWP.*"

The two of them broke apart and looked down. Syrah glared up at them, standing on the letter, which was now halfway out from under the chair. Plenty far enough for Deli to notice it, now that she wasn't busy kissing the wrong man.

"It's that frog," said Harrow slowly, his dark eyebrows drawing together. "The same one from your room."

"I seriously doubt it," said Deli, smiling a little, and then her eyes shifted just a bit to the right of him, and Syrah could tell that she was reading. Her eyes moved back and forth, and he quickly hopped off the letter so that he wouldn't hide any of the words. A moment later, she snatched up the letter from the floor. She was on her feet, and her smile was gone. Her fingers clutched the parchment as her expression changed from disbelief to outrage — to despair.

"What does this mean?" she demanded.

"What?" asked Harrow, looking perfectly confused. "I only read about two words."

Deli threw it into his lap, and Harrow skimmed it. He stiffened.

"This is my pa's business," he said. "Not ours."

"It *is* my business," said Deli, in a tone that reminded Syrah irresistibly of Luffa. "People have *died*. Ubiquitous seeds? Is that what he's using? To grow some kind of — illegal crops? Is that what he's shipping? Is that why the oats went bad? Is that why my father —"

"You're jumping to conclusions!" said Harrow hotly. "He wouldn't hurt anybody!"

Deli was silent for a long moment. Tears sprang into her eyes, and she fought them, turning away to hide her face. "Crop *rot*," she managed. "When will I learn? I am *done* —"

She ran from the study.

Harrow pushed himself to his feet. He could not follow quickly. He held on to walls and leaned on doorframes in an attempt to catch up to her, and Syrah followed on his bare heels.

"Dee, wait. Listen, please."

She left the farmhouse and slammed the door behind her without looking back.

YES, Syrah thought happily. *GOOD*.

Huck came out from his office at the sound of the slam and found Harrow leaning on the back of a chair in one hand and gripping the letter in the other. Syrah hopped under a side table to watch them.

"What *is* this?" Harrow shouted, holding the letter up in his fist.

Huck came to a halt. "That's where it was?" he said. "You took it?"

"Deli found it," said Harrow. "What *is* it?"

"Delicata took that letter? She was in my office? How?"

"It was on the study floor," said Harrow. "She never went into your office."

"But she read it. So they'll all know about it now, at the Thatch."

"What *is it*?" said Harrow for the third time. "Is it true? You plant Ubiquitous seeds? You're breaking the law. You're campaigning for governor, talking about how you want to listen to farmers and let them decide the future, but you're already here doing experiments that kill people —"

"You don't know what you're talking about."

"I guess not." Harrow crumpled the letter and threw it at his father, who caught it. "What am I supposed to say, when the Exalted Council gets here?" he demanded. "You want me to lie for you?"

"No, I'm going to tell them the truth," said Huck. "And until five minutes ago, part of the truth was that you never knew anything about this. That's all I want at this point, son. For you to be left out of it."

"Too late now."

Huck was quiet a minute. "Let me help you back to bed. You need to rest."

"I don't want your help."

Huck passed a weary hand across his brow. "I'll be in my office," he said eventually. "Shout if you need me."

He left the room, and so did Harrow, although more slowly. Syrah hopped out from underneath the table and looked around the room, wondering where he ought to go. Back to the Thatch? It was a long way to travel on his own — he'd likely be killed if he tried it. But if he could somehow get back to the Thatch and warn Deli that Clementine Pease was tied up in this Ubiquitous business just as much as Huck Steelcut, it might finally be enough to convince the wishing well that —

Syrah's thoughts broke off abruptly. A glass wall came down in front of him, not a centimeter from his eyes. He croaked in fear and tried to hop back, but there was glass behind him — glass on either side of him — glass above him too. He rolled his eyes frantically, looking for escape, but there was none. He was in a jar, trapped.

The jar flipped suddenly and Syrah tumbled down into the bottom of it with a groan of pain. He tried to leap up through the opening at the top, but he wasn't fast enough. It was already covered tight with a piece of linen, and black, glittering hands were moving fast, wrapping twine around the jar's mouth to hold the linen in place.

Harrow Steelcut lifted the jar up to his face and peered into it. Syrah met his gaze, shocked and terrified.

"All right, frog," said Harrow evenly. "Time to explain yourself."

CHAPTER THIRTEEN

$\mathcal{H}$ARROW carried the jar upstairs to his room, while Syrah's mind raced. Explain himself? Was Harrow serious? Did he understand?

Harrow shut his door and brought the jar to his desk. He pulled back the curtains, and afternoon sunlight poured through, illuminating the jar and warming it. Syrah squirmed, uncomfortable. If it got hot enough, he'd cook in this thing.

Harrow sat down to study him. Syrah stared back, breathing hard.

"I don't know many frogs who move letters around," Harrow said. "Fact is, I don't know any. Never met a frog who listened to directions or hopped up on people's shoulders like a tame pet either." He narrowed his eyes at Syrah. "So what are you, really?"

Syrah gave a long, amazed croak. Harrow *was* serious. He somehow understood that Syrah was not a frog. Harrow wasn't the first person he would've chosen to communicate with — in fact, he was pretty much the last — but the idea of communicating with anyone at all after fifteen months of being mostly ignored was so heady that he almost didn't care.

"I'll let you go," said Harrow. "Once you answer my questions. Let's see . . . how about one hop for yes, two hops for no. Sound good?"

For a split second, Syrah considered not hopping at all. Maybe if he just didn't answer, Harrow would give up and let him go.

But his hunger to be known as more than a frog by someone — anyone — outweighed his loathing.

He hopped once.

Harrow sat back, wide-eyed, and shoved both hands through his black curls, making them stick right up. "Skies above me, soil below," he whispered. "You *do* understand."

One hop. *Yeah. I understand. Your move, Oat Boy.*

"Did my mother send you?" Harrow asked him, leaning forward again.

Syrah hopped twice.

"Is . . . is she dead?"

Syrah didn't move. He had no idea. And as little as he liked Harrow, he wasn't about to lie to him about something this important.

"If you don't know," said Harrow, "hop three times."

Syrah did, and Harrow made a desperate noise. "Did the other fairies send you?" he asked.

Other fairies? Did that mean Harrow's mother was a fairy? Syrah gazed at the glinting golden flecks in his mesmerizing black skin, and he supposed that it made sense. His mother was a Yellow fairy — which was practically unheard of. They almost never showed themselves. Harrow must have been the only human born of a Yellow fairy in a hundred years — maybe even longer.

"Did they?" Harrow insisted. "Did her sisters send you?"

Syrah hesitated again. Should he say yes? If he said yes, maybe Harrow would think that he was magical and treat him with a little more respect.

Then again, if he said yes, maybe Harrow would never know who he really was.

Syrah hopped twice.

Harrow looked a bit crestfallen. "I hoped you were a sign," he said. "Bringing that letter about Ubiquitous — I thought you might be trying to show me why she can't answer me. But you have no idea where she is?"

Two hops. *Sorry, nope.*

"All right, well then — are you a magical creature?"

Syrah thought about it. He sort of was. But not in the way that Harrow meant. Two hops.

"So you must be a frog that somebody did magic on," said Harrow. "Did you used to be a regular frog, but then a Kisscrafter or somebody made you different?"

Two hops. *Nope again.*

Harrow looked afraid. "Did you used to be a person?"

Syrah shuddered with relief.

One. Single. Hop.

Harrow broke out in gooseflesh so bad that Syrah could see it. "Are you cursed?" he whispered.

Syrah hopped. *I'll say I am.*

Harrow shook his head in amazement. "Who were you?" he asked. "What happened?"

Syrah closed his eyes, so grateful that he could have cried. There was no way to answer those questions, but right now he didn't care. Somebody knew he was a person. Somebody cared enough to ask. It was enough to make him hate Harrow's stupid, glittering, Deli-kissing face just a tiny bit less.

Harrow leapt to his feet with sudden energy. "You're a person," he said. "Can you read? Can you spell?"

Yes. One hop.

"I'll write out the alphabet, and you can use it to spell out whatever you want me to know — how about that?"

Yes. YES. One hop.

"So if I let you out, you'll stay?" Harrow asked him. "You won't run for it?"

Hop for it, Syrah corrected mentally. He gave two hops for no.

Harrow ransacked his desk for parchment and ink, and he sat down to write out the letters. "Okay." He spread out four pieces of parchment. He had written the alphabet and the numbers, and they were spaced widely enough apart that Syrah could land on individual characters to make it clear what he was saying. Harrow untied the twine and removed the linen cap, and he tipped the jar sideways.

There was a knock at the door.

"Son?"

Syrah hopped into a potted fern and went still. Harrow swiftly stacked the parchment and flipped it over, then made his way to his bed and lay down. "Come in," he said.

Huck Steelcut entered with heavy, weary steps. Worry lines cut deep into his forehead. "As long as you know as much as you do," he said, "I want you to know something else."

Harrow waited.

"Those seeds from Ubiquitous — I've been planting them for nearly twenty years, with no issues at all. And it's true that it's a crime. I never got approval from Calabaza to introduce magic seeds into Yellow soil — but I had approval from someone more important.

Every one of those seeds was planted with your mother's knowledge and permission."

Harrow's face relaxed at once. "She *knew*?"

"She knew. I would never put anything in this ground that she didn't want there. I know you must blame me for her being gone, and maybe it is my fault, but she and I made the decision together, and I thought you ought to know."

Harrow seemed to consider this. "Why did you do it, though?" he said. "Money? Is this why our harvests are always three times better than anyone else's?"

Huck laughed, then caught himself and sobered. "No, that's all your mother's doing," he said. "And I'm not going to explain my motives." When Harrow looked like he was going to protest, Huck added: "It's not because I don't trust you. If you don't know the details, you'll have an easier time when they question you. And they're going to question you. Be ready."

Harrow didn't look entirely appeased. "What about when they question *you*?" he said. "What's going to happen?"

"I don't know."

"You should tell them about my mother. Tell them she approved."

"I respect her privacy. It's what she asked of me, and I won't break that trust without her permission. If she comes back, I'll ask her."

"Do you think she's alive?"

Huck looked out the window at the farm below. "I don't like to make guesses," he said. "She's strong and she knows the land, and she's got her magic . . . But maybe some poison in those seeds caused her harm. Or maybe she had to leave for reasons she didn't share."

"She wouldn't do that," said Harrow. "Not without telling me. Something's wrong."

Huck looked over at the tray on Harrow's bedside table, which was empty but for crumbs. "You polished off lunch," he said. "Still hungry? I'll fix you something else."

"No thanks. Not yet."

"Well, you let me know." Huck left the room and closed the door. Harrow hauled himself up out of bed, limped back to the desk, and looked around.

"Uh," he said. "Frog?"

Syrah made his way up to the desk, where he regarded Harrow critically.

Harrow looked abashed. "Guess you know some private stuff about me, huh?" he asked. "You probably know a lot of things about a lot of people."

One hop. *I certainly do.*

"Well then I hope you're not the kind who'd use somebody's secrets against them."

Syrah felt a stab of guilt. He was exactly that kind. He had used Deli's letter to hurt her as much as he could, and then he had done the same thing to Huck Steelcut today. He had brought Deli that letter about Ubiquitous — and why? Had it really been for the sake of Yellow Country, or had it mostly been because he didn't like Harrow and Deli together?

He wished he didn't know the answer.

"Who are you?" asked Harrow. "Can you tell me?"

Syrah surveyed the parchment and found the *S* — but he didn't hop to it.

If he said who he was, what would happen? Harrow would

have to tell somebody. He would make a report to the Thatch right away, and they'd tell his family, who would sail for Yellow at once. Everyone would focus on him. The *Criers*, the Gourds, the Huanuis — he would be Prince Syrah, Returned From the Dead. It was everything he'd wanted.

But now he wasn't sure. He was the only person in the world who knew that Governor Calabaza had been poisoned. As an anonymous frog, he could figure out who was responsible. He could go places that no one else could, and listen and spy without anybody knowing.

He hopped onto the parchment and sat on the *N*. He hopped to the *O*. Then the *T*.

NOT YET

He could not believe what he was saying. But his heart gave a funny throb that told him this was right.

Harrow frowned. "Don't you want my help?" he asked. "What about family? Friends? Don't you want to see them again?"

Syrah hopped once.

"Then tell me who you are."

He hopped twice.

"Why not?" said Harrow, looking at him with suspicion. "Are you a criminal? Or — hey, wait a minute. You dragged that letter out of my pa's office, and you made sure Dee saw it. Didn't you?"

Syrah didn't move.

"And you were in her room yesterday," Harrow continued. "She said she didn't take those *Criers* out, and I believe her — so *you* did that." He laughed, and the sound was a little bit wild. He sat back in his chair and braced his hands on the table. "*And* you followed us out there to that hole in the ground, which is right where she thinks — and you were making all that racket, like you wanted our attention, and now —"

Syrah held his breath. For the first time since becoming a frog, he genuinely did not want to be discovered, but it didn't matter. Harrow was about to get there.

Lose yourself to be found.

This was what the well had meant.

"I know who you are," said Harrow, his voice rough. *"I know who you are."*

He bent low over the desk and looked Syrah dead in his eyes.

"Your *Highness.*"

CHAPTER FOURTEEN

SYRAH was momentarily paralyzed. Somebody knew him, somebody finally knew exactly who he was. But the way Harrow was looking at him was terrifying.

He hopped twice to deny it. *No. I'm not him. You're wrong.*

"You are," said Harrow. "Prince Syrah of the Olive Isles." He laughed wildly again. "Great White skies. No wonder you've been all over Dee's life, following her, hanging out in her room —" He cut himself off. "Have you been hanging out in her *room* and watching her in *private?*"

Two hops. Two hops. Two hops again.

"Like I'd ever believe *you.*" Harrow pushed himself to his feet. "You gave her letter to the *Criers.* You humiliated her on purpose, you worthless piece of — and you wonder why she didn't want to kiss you? Yeah, I heard her turn you down. I was sitting right there."

Harrow was breathing hard, fists clenched. Syrah started hopping to the letters again.

I DIDNT MEAN —

Harrow snatched the parchment off his desk, flipping Syrah onto his back in the process. "Who cares what you meant?" He threw the parchment onto his bed. "I've thought a lot about what I'd say to you if you ever showed your face again," he said. "Now I just want you out."

He grabbed the jar. Syrah leapt to get away, but Harrow was too fast; the jar came down and he smacked into the glass. Harrow opened his window, still weak enough that he grunted with effort lifting the sash.

"I hope a hawk eats your guts," he said as he dumped Syrah out of his room and onto the porch roof.

Syrah tumbled into moss and sweet peas. Disoriented and in pain, he turned and tried to hop back up to the windowsill, but Harrow brought the sash down hard, shutting him out. Syrah hopped onto the outer sill. He put his gelatinous toes on the window, pleading with his eyes.

Don't leave me out here. I really will die. You know who I am — you can't do this to me —

Harrow jerked the curtain closed.

Syrah waited five minutes. Ten. Was Harrow really the kind of person who would leave a cursed prince all alone to fend for himself against predators? Because he seemed — much as Syrah hated to admit it — like a nicer person than that. Maybe when he calmed down, he'd change his mind.

He didn't. Syrah waited as long as he could, but after about half an hour, the sun began to set. If he didn't get down from here and find some cover, a hawk really would eat his guts.

Somehow, he had to get back to the Thatch. To Walter, who would protect him until he could figure out what was happening with Calabaza. He studied the landscape a moment. Not far away — a few hundred meters, maybe — a stream ran along the property, flowing toward the Ladle River, which in turn flowed toward the Thatch. That stream was his best bet.

He made his way down from the roof, hopping carefully along

the thick vines and sturdy leaves and large flowers that covered the house. It made sense to him now, the way the house seemed to bloom from the ground. If Harrow's mother was a Yellow fairy then she must be the one who did this. She had probably turned Harrow's bedroom into a garden too. She beautified their home, and she made their crops grow — Syrah thought he could guess why they didn't want anybody to know about her. People would be resentful of their good luck. Or they'd ask for favors for their own farms. And there would be a lot of talk in the town and in the *Criers* if anybody knew that Harrow was the offspring of a Yellow fairy, which was rarer than rare. Syrah wondered what it was like, having a fairy mother. It must have been all right, because Harrow was certainly upset about her being gone.

Maybe he could find her. He was a frog, and she was a fairy of the land — maybe he could somehow figure out where she was. Maybe he could even ask the wishing well.

The thought surprised Syrah. Harrow had dumped him outside to die; why would he do him any favors?

Because if you do, maybe he'll trust you and help you.

Syrah croaked his annoyance. Everybody wanted something.

When he reached the porch railing, he paused and surveyed the ripe oat fields that rolled away from the back of the house, high and golden. Those fields had Ubiquitous crops, and those were probably deadly to him, but he was going to have to hop down and take his chances.

He spied a massive, foot-size beetle toddling along at the base of the oat plants, its dark green wings folded. A Vangarden. The creatures only lived in Yellow Country, and they only came out to signal the harvest — if the soil was sick, they would surely avoid it. Syrah hopped off the Steelcuts' porch, unafraid of the Vangarden.

They ate nothing but roots. If there were snakes in this field, on the other hand . . .

He hopped quickly toward his destination, wondering how he would even begin to search for Harrow's mother. Maybe it was a stupid idea — he didn't know the first thing about Yellow fairies. He should probably just stick to figuring out who had tried to poison Calabaza.

As he hurried toward the stream, he became slowly aware of a strange vibration in his belly. Like humming. And the humming had a shape to it — a word that was being repeated over and over.

Frog frog frog frog.

Syrah stopped and looked around. The Vangarden was coming toward him, its carapace shining in the last rays of sunlight.

Frog frog frog frog.

Syrah watched it approach, unnerved. No animal had ever spoken to him before. Vangardens were magical, he supposed, but their only talent was knowing when things were ripe and chittering to let farmers know it was time for the harvest.

Come come come come.

The Vangarden stopped in front of him and bent its skinny little beetle legs to lower itself until its shell was flush with the ground. Syrah eyed it, not sure what it wanted him to do. Follow it somewhere?

On, said the vibration in his belly. *On on on.*

You want me to hop on you? Syrah thought, uncertain.

Yes yes yes yes. Carry carry carry.

The vibration was impatient. Annoyed, even. But there was nothing threatening or frightening about it.

Syrah hopped onto the Vangarden's back. *Where are you taking me?* he thought.

Message. The Vangarden's voice was no longer a vibration in the soil. Now that Syrah sat on its back, he could hear the creature speaking in his mind, like high, thin music. *Message message message.*

It carried him along the wide, gurgling stream that Syrah had seen before from the porch roof. It walked until darkness fell, then turned and cut a path through the oat fields. It turned again, and then again, making a jagged line toward its destination. Syrah lost all sense of where he was going. The moon rose, almost a perfect semi-circle, shining on the oats and lending them a silvery gleam.

Here here here.

The Vangarden had brought him all the way out beyond the fields to a place where no oats grew. They must have been over a league from the farmhouse now. They stood now on a large plot of flat, black soil. There was no protection here from the animals of the night, and Syrah kept fearful watch around and above him.

Off, said the Vangarden, stopping suddenly.

Syrah hopped off the beetle's shell and onto the soil, and he looked around, nonplussed. How was this a message?

Listen. Feel. Listen, feel.

Syrah listened, but heard only crickets and night birds. He felt, but mostly what he felt was warmth. The soil under his belly was unusually warm, actually. It radiated as though the sun were still shining on it, though the sun was long gone now.

Then he heard it. Breathing.

He tensed and rolled his eyes to check his surroundings for a fox or a raccoon, but except for the Vangarden, he was alone. Still, he definitely heard someone breathing. The sound was regular, slow, and deep. Like a person asleep.

Yes yes yes, said the Vangarden. *Sleep. She sleeps.*

Who slept?

Loess mother. Loess mother.

Was that Harrow's mother? Syrah realized in surprise that he already knew the answer. Dreamlike, disjointed thoughts drifted up from the soil beneath him, penetrating his skin and passing into him.

Poison inside me, in my soil, white cold. Vicious. Traitor. Sudden, no time. Seizing, twisting, helpless — sink down deep or die. Into the land, deep, deeper than poison. Sleep. Heal. How long? No telling.

Harrow. Harrow.

The soil under his belly ached, and Syrah understood.

She wanted to see her son, but she couldn't move.

Harrow's all right, thought Syrah. *He was sick too, but he recovered. He's going to be okay.*

He felt the land relax. A ribbon of wind licked across the patch of soil and twined around Syrah, tickling and cooling him.

I'll tell him you're alive, Syrah thought. *I'll tell him you're healing.*

The soil grew warmer; its energy flowed into Syrah, bright with gratitude. With tenderness. *Sleep now,* it said faintly, and its warmth ebbed. *Must sleep.*

The land went quiet.

The Vangarden lowered itself before him again.

Carry carry carry.

Syrah leapt onto the great beetle's back. It bore him away from the sleeping fairy and trundled back toward the Steelcut farmhouse, first taking paths through the fields, then following the stream. He rode along, lost in thought.

Traitor, the fairy had said. So it was true. The Ubiquitous seeds had poisoned her, and she hadn't been expecting it. After twenty years, she had trusted them. Just as Huck had. Why Ubiquitous Productions had done it, and whether they had even done it on purpose, Syrah had no idea. That was huge business, far beyond his ability to figure out. As for whether the poison oats had been fed to anyone deliberately . . .

He didn't think so. Huck Steelcut and Clementine Pease had both seemed genuinely shocked and grieved by the Purge. Neither of them had wanted this to happen.

But had they poisoned Calabaza with juggetsbane to keep him from finding out their secret?

Syrah found that he doubted it — at least in Huck's case. Huck was an honorable, reasonable man. The way he had spoken with Clementine, and the way he treated his son — he just didn't seem like a person who went around trying to assassinate governors.

But somebody had done it. Somebody had realized — and very quickly too — that all those people getting sick at the ATC was an opportunity, and they had moved fast to get Calabaza out of the way before the election.

Clementine Pease, perhaps, had done it. She was the minister of agriculture — she would know what juggetsbane could do. And she was going to run for governor now, instead of Huck. Maybe this had been her plan all along. She had known Huck for a long time — she might have counted on his honorable nature. She had expected that he would admit his own guilt while covering up hers — leaving her free to run for governor herself.

And then there was Burdock. The Nexus had drawn that red *X* through Calabaza's face — he had loathed the idea of another seven years under his governorship, and he was furious about Calabaza's policies on magic. He had taken advantage of Calabaza's unconsciousness to blame him for letting the Purge happen, turning the people of Yellow against him. Plus, Burdock was one of the Exalted; his magical training had probably taught him plenty about poisons and plants. And he had been staying at the Royal Governor's Inn right near the family — he could easily have walked out to that carriage house and planted a basket of food for Calabaza to eat.

But Burdock wouldn't do it. Syrah knew it in his guts. He had spent time with Burdock. Not enough time to know the man *well*, maybe, but enough time to know what kind of person he was. He played jokes on the triplets. He had taught Syrah to debate and offered him an apprenticeship. He wasn't full of himself, he wasn't quick to anger unless things were serious — and when they *were* serious, he wasn't afraid to take action. He had sent an international warning out about the Purge, even though it had made Yellow Country look bad, because he didn't want people to die.

It was Luffa, Syrah thought, who had really wanted Calabaza eliminated. He remembered the way she had treated him, that night in the carriage at the ATC. *"Run for governor, and I will come at you with everything I have. . . ."* She was the one who had pushed forward with Declaration Day, in spite of the fact that he was ill. And when she had seen her mother's lost thimble, what had she said? *"Mama approves of my course. She forgives me. . . ."*

What did Luffa need forgiveness for?

Syrah was so deep in contemplation that he forgot to think of danger. He didn't pay attention to the shadow that passed over him, or note the sudden shift in the breeze. By the time he saw the owl's talons, they were already open and outstretched in front of him, and he could not dodge.

The owl struck him. He fell from the Vangarden and lay on his back in the dirt, stunned, staring up at the tops of the moonlit oats as the stream babbled along beside him. He could not feel his heart or breath. He could not move.

The owl circled back and dropped, aiming for his belly with its beak. Its pitiless orange eyes glared from its masklike face, and Syrah realized that this was the last thing he would see. In a moment, he would be dead. He thought of his nana. Marsala. Rapunzel. The well. He thought of Governor Calabaza. He would never know who had poisoned him. Nobody would.

The instant before the owl stabbed him, the Vangarden blocked its path, opening its shining wings to shield Syrah. The owl slammed into the beetle instead and skewered it on its beak.

Go go . . . go . . . go . . .

The Vangarden's vibration died.

Horrified, Syrah tried to move. One of his feet was pinned down by the dead Vangarden, but the owl yanked it off of him, swinging its feathered head back and forth to shake the beetle's carcass from its beak. Syrah had only a moment.

He dove into the stream and swam down deep to avoid being eaten. His clear inner eyelids closed over his eyes, protecting them as he swam. He kicked his back legs hard to propel himself, swimming along with the current, moving as fast as he could. He did not stop kicking until he reached the Ladle River. The owl was far behind him now.

Syrah flowed westward with the river, toward the Gourds'

property. All around him there were minnows and small bugs, but he was still too upset to eat. He had only known the Vangarden for a few hours, but the creature had treated him like a friend. It had carried him and helped him — and then it had died for him. As a human, he had never thought of Vangardens as anything but oversize bugs.

As a human, he had never thought a lot of things.

He drifted along with the river until he reached the same dock where the triplets had come the other day to fish. He swam to the bank, but stayed on the rocks and waited, unwilling to make the rest of the journey alone. He didn't want any more adventures. He checked the sky and wondered what time it was. He had just decided that he could see the faint beginnings of morning light when he felt new vibrations in his belly. Running footsteps pounding along the riverbank, approaching the dock.

Deli. Running like somebody was after her. She finished her sprint at the dock and dropped her pack on the ground. Then she walked in a circle, hands on top of her head, sucking for air. After twenty seconds of this, she picked up her pack again, threw it over her shoulders, and sprinted off in the other direction.

Training. In the middle of the night. She really never stopped pushing.

When she came back and threw down her pack again, she also sat down in the dirt. "Done," she gasped, and dropped onto her back, breathing hard. Syrah wondered how long she'd been at it. Hours, probably, knowing her.

He eyed her equipment pack. If he could get into it, he could hitch a ride the rest of the way to the Thatch and not have to worry about any more close encounters. He hopped toward the pack, and onto it. It was buckled shut, but if she opened it to put something away, then maybe —

He froze. The sound of Deli's winded breathing had changed. She was still gasping for air, but it was different. Uneven.

She was crying.

Really crying, he realized after a moment. The kind of crying most people only did when they were children, or when they didn't think anybody was looking. She let out a sound of pure anguish and rolled onto her stomach, still sobbing.

He knew why. He could pretend he didn't, but he knew, and it cut him deep that she was crying over Harrow like this. Had she ever cried like this about *him*?

Maybe. Maybe two years ago, when he had laughed at her letter. Told her she was crazy. Said she wasn't pretty.

He wished he could go back and beat some sense into himself. But even if he could have gone back, he didn't think it would have mattered. The old Syrah would never have listened. He'd been a different person.

Deli sat up. She wiped her wet face with her hands, hiccuped, and then bent over and cried a little longer before she was really spent. When she got to her feet, she reached for her pack and snatched it off the ground without really looking at it. Syrah gripped one of the straps with all his strength and managed to stay on the pack even as she put it over her shoulders again.

She headed home at a brisk walk, sniffling every so often. By the time she reached the front door, she was composed.

Back in the dimly lit Thatch, Syrah drew a deep breath of relief. He had made it. In spite of Harrow's attempt to kill him, he was not dead. Deli carried him to her room and threw down the pack on the floor. He leapt for the open door before she could close it — she would probably undress after a workout like that, and he wasn't going to stay here and spy while she did. He definitely had *not* been lying to Harrow about that.

He intended to go to Walter's room, but stopped. At the far end of the family wing, Luffa's door was very slightly ajar. Light flickered within.

Syrah approached the door and peeked in. All the way across the bedroom, in front of a tall bookshelf, stood Luffa. She held a candlestick in one hand and searched through her books with the other.

Syrah tried to nose his way in. The door wasn't quite open enough for him to hop inside, but he was just able to wiggle through the crack. When he did, the door creaked open slightly farther, drawing Luffa's attention. She turned sharply away from the bookshelf she was searching, and walked to the door. Syrah quickly sidled along the inner wall of the room, staying in the darkness as Luffa opened the door wider and stepped out into the hall, holding out her candle to see who was there. After a moment, she stepped back into her room and firmly shut the door behind her before returning to the bookshelf.

While she searched, Syrah glanced around, morbidly curious. Bradley had said that the floorboards of Luffa's room were still soaked with her family's blood, but it was impossible to verify that claim in the gloom. Her fabled sword, however, hung in its scabbard beside the fireplace. Syrah studied the carvings on the scabbard, and he wondered. Luffa had saved her country once. She had beheaded a warlord and freed her people from what remained of the Pink Empire.

Only a person of great courage and fierce love for her nation could have done such a thing.

She was certainly capable of poisoning Calabaza, if she had thought it was the best thing for Yellow Country, but as he gazed at her sword, Syrah found himself wondering if she *would*. It just didn't seem like Luffa to sneak around putting juggetsbane in sandwiches. She was direct. Brave. Harsh and unpleasant, yes — but not devious. There was something cowardly about using poison, and Luffa was no coward.

Still, that wasn't proof she hadn't done it. Syrah swept his eyes around the room, hoping to find something noticeably suspicious. But the only thing he really noticed was that Luffa's room didn't look like it had ever belonged to a queen. The bed was just a simple platform with a mattress. The chair was just a wooden chair. There were almost no decorations or objects of great value about, except for a few pictures: a portrait of her family before they had been slaughtered, with a very small Luffa sleeping in her mother's arms; a small painting of herself at nineteen, straight-backed and solemn-faced at her coronation after the reclamation of Yellow Country — and beside this, a small portrait of Nana Cava at about the same age, staring out of the frame with those eyes that saw everything. Syrah gazed at her and wished that she could see him now.

I'm trying, Nana, he thought. *I'm paying attention to the election just like you wanted, and I'm going to figure out what happened to Calabaza. I'm doing my best for once. I really am.*

There was one other painting, wide and tall, taking up the better part of one wall, and the sight of it arrested Syrah. Balthasar. White shore, cobalt sky, turquoise water. The columns of the

Pavilions rising from the rock. Lush green vineyards rolling thickly away to the foot of Mount Olopua. Even in the dim light, the sight of his home was so beautiful that his longing overwhelmed him. Even if he never became a man again, he wanted to go home. The thought of slipping into the warm, embracing ocean, of basking on the rocks under his own hot island sun, of hearing familiar voices, smelling familiar smells . . . He didn't want to be a frog forever, but since the wishing well seemed to have given up on him, at least he could live out his frog days in the Olive Isles. And now that someone knew who he was, it was finally possible to make that happen. All he had to do was get back into Harrow's company, and he could find a way to tell everyone the truth. Within a week, he could be on a ship, sailing away across the Tranquil Sea.

But first, Calabaza.

Luffa huffed a short breath of annoyance and set down her candlestick atop a chest of drawers. She opened a small closet, took out a box of letters and papers, and put it on her bed to sort through it. Syrah wished he could see what was written on everything, but Luffa was standing several feet away, and the writing on the papers was too small. He could hop closer, but if he did, she might see him and decide to put him out.

She lifted a letter out of the box and paused, staring at its envelope, which had already been sliced open. She withdrew the letter and read it. "Cava," she said quietly, after a moment, and Syrah's heart hopped. Was that a letter from his nana?

Luffa set it on her desk and continued to search through the box. Syrah sneaked along behind her. Too curious to resist, he hopped up to her desk chair and then onto her desk to see what his nana had written. But Luffa had flipped the letter over; it lay on its front and there was not much written on the back. He read what little he could.

> I wish you would plant vines instead. The strong vines of Olive should grow around your home.
>> Be at peace, my sister, my heart. We shall see each other soon.

> Cava

"Ah," said Luffa, and Syrah looked up quickly to make sure she hadn't spotted him. She wasn't looking in his direction at all, but at a file marked *BURDOCK*. She took up her candlestick and headed for her door, and Syrah leapt down from the desk, keen to follow and find out what the file had in it.

Luffa made her way swiftly down the stairs and toward the front of the house. At the end of the great front hall, the door of the governor's office stood open. Light spilled through it. Syrah slipped through the door behind Luffa and hopped under a fancy chair that stood close to the wall.

Clementine Pease was already there, sitting in a throne-like chair behind an ornate desk in an office that didn't seem to belong to the Thatch. The whole room reminded him of his visits to Charming Palace — gilded furniture, mirrors, silver wall fixtures, and even a chandelier. It was the only room in the house that looked like it belonged to a king — but none of these things had been handed down from Yellow Country's old monarchs. The invaders from Pink had melted down all the Gourd family heirlooms except for a thimble, so Calabaza must have furnished the room this way. Clearly, he had enjoyed the idea of being royal governor.

Luffa shut the door with her foot, blew out her candle, and brought the papers to the desk where Clementine sat.

"It's all here," she said. "What little there is."

"Why did you bother collecting it in the first place?"

"Because the past matters," Luffa replied. "I've never liked the idea of having someone in this government whose past can't be traced."

"I don't want to throw his childhood in his face." The bags under Clementine's eyes were nearly as purple as her hair. "I just want to beat him."

His childhood. Syrah was immediately curious. Burdock was Exalted, and when the Exalted swore themselves to the Council, they took new names. Many of them left their previous identities behind. Did Luffa know something about who Burdock had been, as a boy? Syrah thought he could imagine it. Burdock had probably been something like the triplets. A bit of a troublemaker, but mostly smart and kind. Had he once played a prank that might make him look bad?

Had he done something worse?

"He played the crowd masterfully," said Luffa. "He is a very bright man. He will find a way to discredit you, and if you aren't prepared to turn it around on him, you'll suffer."

Clementine shifted in the seat she'd placed in the throne-like chair. "Luffa," she said. "I'm not the right candidate. Find someone else. I mean it."

"Don't be modest, Clementine. You're experienced, competent, and —"

"I know I am." Clementine pushed herself down from the chair and landed on her feet. She started to pace. "It's about Huck," she said. "About Ubiquitous."

Syrah waited, watching as Clementine paced back again behind the enormous desk. He could just see her purple hair over the top of it. Was she going to confess?

"Huck Steelcut made a terrible mistake," said Luffa. "I know that the two of you go back a long way, but this isn't a matter of friendship. Huck isn't getting back in this race. It's you against Burdock, and you need to prepare for debate."

Clementine ran a hand over the papers Luffa had brought down. "You said yourself these aren't even facts," she said. "Just rumors."

"His given name is a fact," said Luffa. "Confirmed by birth records. His parents' and younger sister's deaths are also facts."

"But his encounter with the Witch of the Woods is fiction?"

At the mention of the Witch of the Woods, Syrah's eyes bulged. That was the witch with the candy house — the one G. G. Floss had said was possibly killed by a starving young boy.

By Burdock, as a boy?

Syrah nearly croaked out loud. Could it be possible? He *was* Exalted. . . .

"Somebody killed her," said Luffa, shrugging. "Don't you find it curious that no one has ever claimed the honor of it?"

"So you think he has something to hide."

That was what Jack had said. Whoever had killed that witch must have something to hide, or else they would have taken credit for it. But what could Nexus Burdock have to hide?

There was a knock at the door. A messenger stepped into the room and bowed. "Madam Governor," he said, nodding to Luffa.

"Provisional Governor Pease. The Relay has a message from Exalted Nexus Keene."

Luffa and Clementine departed, and Syrah followed, hopping along the corridor. He paused when voices drifted in from outside one of the front windows.

"What are you doing here?" he heard Deli say flatly. "I don't want to talk to you —"

"I'm not trying to talk to you. I just — I have to *talk* to you —"

"Go home, Harrow."

Syrah leapt onto the windowsill. Deli and Harrow stood there in the pale morning light. Deli's eyes were puffy — it was impossible to miss that she'd been crying — but Harrow didn't seem to see it. He was sweating, and his eyes darted all over, as though searching for something. He adjusted his horse's reins in his hand, looking nervous and guilty and sick.

"I did something bad," he managed. "Real bad. I came to tell you —"

"You can tell the Exalted Council when they investigate."

"It's not *about* the farm, it's — last night, I —" He made a noise of anguish. "It's that frog."

You mean this frog? thought Syrah, enjoying Harrow's agony. He *should* feel guilty. He had very nearly murdered him.

Deli crossed her arms. "Frog?"

"The one from your room. You know the one — he took out those *Criers* and he followed us into the woods."

Deli stared at him. "He took out the *Criers*," she repeated. "Harrow, shouldn't you be home in bed?"

"I'm not sick!" he said. "I'm telling you, that frog — Skies, what if he's dead? What if he's dead and I killed him? I'd be an assassin, or —"

Deli looked genuinely worried now. She stepped up to Harrow

and touched his glittering brow with the back of her hand. "You're feverish," she said. "You sit right here. I think Physic Feverfew's upstairs, I'll get her —"

"No, please." Harrow dropped his horse's reins and grabbed her hands. "Listen. I'll tell you. And you'll believe me — you have to. That frog is —"

Syrah croaked loudly, and Harrow gasped. He looked back and forth, searching wildly, until he found him on the windowsill. "There he is," he cried, ecstatic. "Dee, look, he's —"

Syrah hopped twice, quickly. *Don't tell her who I am.*

Harrow trailed off. "He's . . . alive," he finished.

"Rawwp."

Deli pulled her hands out of Harrow's grip. "Walter was looking for him last night," she said, approaching the windowsill. "I'll take him upstairs."

But Harrow cut in front of her and put out his hand. Syrah leapt onto his arm, then up to his shoulder. He wanted to be with someone he could communicate with. Even if that person had thrown him out to die.

"Excuse me," said Deli. "He's not yours."

"I need to — uh — borrow him," said Harrow.

"*Borrow* him?"

"Yeah, for a — a thing. A thing I need to do."

Smooth, Syrah thought. *Liar of the year.*

"Right," Deli said, and her tone suggested that she was worried about the state of his brain. "Well. I'll tell Walter he's with you."

"Dee, wait. About yesterday —"

"You can stop right —"

"Please. Don't shut me out again. I had no idea what my pa

was doing. None. And if you know me at all, then you know I wouldn't lie."

Deli gazed at Harrow, and her expression was the same as it had been two summers ago, when Syrah had kissed her under that waterfall. Devastatingly serious. Full of longing. And so vulnerable — Syrah's breath stuck in his throat. Had she really looked at him like that? Why had he swum away? She was ready to give in; all Harrow had to do was take one step toward her and pull her close, and her resolve would crumble.

Syrah would have taken the step. Would have pulled her close.

Harrow stayed where he was and waited for her answer.

"I believe you," Deli finally said. "But I can't be with you. Leave me alone."

She went into the Thatch and shut them both out.

CHAPTER FIFTEEN

SYRAH and Harrow eyed each other.

"I opened the window," said Harrow after a moment. "You were already gone."

Syrah was silent.

"Who should I tell about you? I could take you to Nexus Burdock —"

Two hops.

"Then where?"

Yes-or-no questions, Oat Boy.

"Uh . . . do you want to go back to my house and use the letters to tell me what you want?"

One hop.

Harrow climbed onto his horse. "Should you stay on my shoulder?" he asked, and Syrah hopped twice; he wasn't sure that he could keep his footing once the horse started to gallop. Harrow carefully placed him in a saddlebag. There was a used handkerchief in it, which he pulled out and shoved in his pocket. "Sorry," he muttered. "This okay?"

Syrah croaked. It wasn't great, but it would do.

Harrow buckled the saddlebag shut. The horse started moving at a quick walk, and the saddlebag chugged with every step. Between the noisy, vibrating strikes of the horse's hooves against the dirt and the constant bouncing of the bag, Syrah was miserable for the next hour.

"Whoa, Jessie," he finally heard Harrow say, and then the saddlebag was open again, and Syrah hopped out onto his shoulder. Sunrise lit the Steelcut farmhouse, bathing its stones and vines and flowers in rose and gold light. Syrah wondered how long the beauty of the house would last, with Harrow's mother sleeping.

Harrow took him upstairs and spread out the parchment on his desk. Syrah hopped down. There were a lot of things he wanted to say, but shouting at Harrow one letter at a time seemed like more trouble than it was worth. He had to concentrate on what mattered. First things first.

LOESS

Harrow sank into his chair. "My mother," he said faintly. "How do you know — *what* do you know?"

ALIVE

"You said you didn't know if she was alive or dead!"

FOUND LAST NIGHT

Harrow breathed out. He put his face in his hands for a moment. "Thank you," he murmured. "Thank you." He looked up. "Where is she? Can I see her?"

Two hops. *TRAPPED DEEP UNDERGROUND SICK SLEEPING HEALING*

"So she did get poisoned. By the Ubiquitous seeds?"

One hop.

Harrow stood up. "I have to tell my pa," he said, but Syrah hopped twice, emphatic, and Harrow sank back down. "What is it?"

Syrah studied Harrow for a moment, and then he made his

decision. If he was going to figure things out, he needed help. He had to tell Harrow what he knew.

CALABAZA POISONED

"Yeah, he has the Purge —"

Two hops. JUGGETSBANE DELIBERATE

Harrow stared. "It wasn't our oats? But — wait, who would do that to Calabaza? Why?"

Syrah didn't know who, but he had a clear idea of why, and he swiftly hopped his answer.

ELECTION

"You better not be suggesting my pa." Harrow sat back in his chair, looking lost in thought. "Who else knows about this?"

JUST US

"How did you even find out?"

Syrah hopped. And he hopped. By the time he was done, he was sick of hopping and Harrow knew about the lantern in the carriage house and the basket with the sandwiches.

Harrow went for the door, while Syrah croaked indignantly and repeatedly. "I can't hide this," Harrow said. "The Exalted Council will think my pa did it. Our oats started the Purge — and he wanted to be governor, didn't he? They'll think it all connects. I have to warn him."

Syrah hopped twice, and twice again, frantic.

"And I've got to tell Dee," said Harrow. "She doesn't know her pa was poisoned on purpose, does she? I better tell everyone about you too. Your family needs to know you're alive."

Two firm hops.

"But *why*? Don't you want someone to help you?"

YOU HELP ME WE SOLVE

Harrow frowned. "You mean find out who poisoned Calabaza?"

One hop. *I SPY NO ONE NOTICE FROG*

"I did," Harrow pointed out.

CONGRATS OAT BOY

Harrow let out a peal of laughter. "Well, that is a first," he said. "Insulted by a frog prince." He hunkered down again in front of the desk and studied Syrah. "I guess it's true that you can pretty much go where you please."

HARD WITHOUT HELP

"I'll bet. Can't believe you've survived all this time."

NO THANKS TO YOU

Harrow rapped his fingers on the desk. "Shouldn't we try to break this curse that's on you?"

CANT

"You sure about that?"

Syrah was absolutely sure. Only the wishing well could break the curse, and it didn't seem to be in a big hurry to do it.

Harrow sat back in his chair, looking thoughtful. "I guess it's better if I *don't* tell Pa," he said, after a moment. "If he knows about the juggetsbane, he'll look guilty."

Syrah hopped.

"The thing is, though," Harrow went on, "I could have fed Calabaza those sandwiches. I walked Dee back to the inn after the Purge broke out. I had time to run out to the carriage house. You ever think of that?"

Syrah croaked. He had thought of it, but it didn't seem likely.

"You don't think it was me?"

Two hops. *No.*

"But you don't like me."

Syrah snorted a *ribbit*.

Harrow shrugged. "Then it's mutual," he said. "All right, if we're doing this, what's our next step?"

Syrah croaked in pleased surprise, and his chin swelled as he puffed up. It had been so long since anyone had really listened to him — and now Harrow, of all people, was going to let him direct.

PEASE LUFFA BURDOCK, he hopped. *SUSPECTS*

"My pa's not on that list?"

SHOULD HE BE

"Well no. I'm just surprised you don't think so. You saw that letter to Ubiquitous."

Syrah hopped twice. Huck Steelcut had planted bad seeds, but he hadn't done it on purpose. Syrah thought again of the way the man treated his son. Worrying over him, tending to him, speaking to him with respect and attentiveness, even when they argued. He tried to remember a single conversation with his own parents that had lasted more than a few seconds. A conversation where they had shared thoughts and questions, the way that Huck and Harrow did. He couldn't think of one. The only question they ever asked him was "Are you paying attention to your tutors?" — and then they rarely waited for an answer. They were busy, and Syrah was the youngest. He wasn't going to inherit the throne like Taurasi, or even stewardship of one of the islands, like his other older siblings. He was nobody important.

Maybe they didn't even miss him.

"Why do you suspect those three?" Harrow asked. "Did you see something?"

The answer to that question was long, and Syrah was suddenly very tired. He felt tacky all over instead of moist. He was getting dry.

WATER, he hopped.

"Huh? Oh, sure." Harrow left the room and returned with a wooden bowl of it. He held it toward Syrah, then suddenly retracted it, looking a little anxious. "It's from the basin in the washroom," he said apologetically. "It's still clean, but I guess if you're planning to drink it, I can run out to the well —"

But Syrah had long since learned not to be picky. He hopped down to the floor and tapped one front foot against the wooden board on which he sat. *Put it here.*

Harrow set down the bowl, and Syrah got into it with a croak of relief. So nice. He closed his eyes and slouched down until the water covered him completely, but he could not quite relax. Thoughts of his family needled at his mind. His parents, who mostly ignored him. His siblings, who treated him like he was just a stupid annoyance.

Well aren't you?

He had ruined Marsanne and Christophen's wedding. He hadn't even thought about how his revenge against Deli would affect them. He had mocked Marsala constantly, getting in her head whenever she tried to train for the ATC. Why had he done that? What kind of person did that?

If only he could know that she was all right. If Marsala was healthy, and if Nana Cava was alive, then he could still make it up to them. He could make it up to his whole family. As long as none of them had died in the Purge, he could still fix things.

And then it struck him there was someone he could ask.

He leapt out of the water and sprang up onto the desk. He hesitated to hop onto the parchment only because he was soaked.

"Something you want to tell me?" said Harrow, moving closer. He offered Syrah a rag to hop on so he could blot himself, and Syrah did so quickly. Then he made a frantic pattern on the parchment.

"I don't know what happened to her," said Harrow. "Wish I did. I'll check on her for you."

CHECK MY NANA TOO

Harrow froze. It took him a moment before he looked at Syrah, and when he did, there was pity in his eyes. Terrible, eloquent pity.

No. Syrah's heart throbbed, frantic. *No, never mind. I don't want to know.* As long as Harrow didn't say it out loud, it wasn't real. It wasn't true. *Don't tell me, don't tell me —*

"She died a year ago," Harrow said quietly. "A few weeks after the wedding."

Syrah did not breathe or move. He suddenly remembered how once, as a very young boy, he had nearly drowned. A wave had gripped him and he had gone under, tumbling until he was breathless and disoriented. The sea had turned him over and over again, relentless, until he thought he would never come up.

"I'm sorry," Harrow said, from what seemed to be a great distance away.

Syrah did not know what to do. His family was so large that he should probably have been used to death, but he wasn't. The Huanuis were healthy, long-lived. He had attended the funeral of a distant cousin or two, but not like this.

He could never tell his nana he was sorry.

He jumped down to the floor with a heavy thud, crawled back into the water bowl, and submerged. He didn't want to talk anymore.

Harrow picked up the bowl. He set it aside between two potted trees, where it was dim and smelled familiar. Plumeria flowers. The kind he had used to put in his nana's hair.

"I'll let you be," Harrow said, and left the room.

Syrah sat in the water bowl, wishing he could cry or run or scream, but he was trapped. Alone in the silence, with only the strength of his own mind to protect him, grief threatened to crush him. His nana was dead. The one person in his family who had seen him. Listened to him. The only one who had expected anything from him.

He had let her down.

He could still see the look in her eyes when she had sent him away from the Thatch. He could still hear her voice. *I was wrong about you. I thought you were more than you pretend to be. But you are not pretending.*

He could never show her. There was no fixing this. She had died thinking he was a disgrace.

When he could no longer stand the inside of his mind, he hopped out of the water bowl and went to Harrow's open window to feel the air on his skin. There were a few bugs crawling near the windowsill, but for once he was not hungry. He was surprised by how glad he was to hear the door open.

"How are you doing?" said Harrow.

Syrah hopped to the parchment. He sat there a moment, not sure what he was going to say until he started moving.

IM SORRY

It felt good to say it and mean it.

Harrow raised an eyebrow. "You owe that apology to Dee. Not me."

Syrah hopped once. He knew. But Harrow was the only one here, and he had to start somewhere.

Harrow appraised him. "Is that what got you cursed?" he asked. "Publishing that letter?"

Syrah thought about it. In truth, he wasn't sure why the well had done it, but he knew that his actions toward Deli hadn't helped him any. He hopped once.

"That's some penance," said Harrow. "Living your whole life as a frog. I'm not sure I could stand it."

His whole life as a frog. Syrah had never allowed himself to think it. He *had* to become a man again someday — that was what he had promised himself; that was what he had kept hanging on for. But maybe Harrow was right. Maybe this was it.

And maybe he deserved it.

NOT SO BAD, he hopped, trying to keep despair at bay. ANTS ARE TASTY

Harrow laughed. "Guess you haven't lost your sense of humor."

"Son!" shouted Huck Steelcut from downstairs. "They're coming."

Harrow ran from the room, then ran straight back. "Come on," he said, and, once Syrah was on his shoulder, he hurried down the stairs to stand with his father as a carriage approached their home. It bore the symbol of the Exalted Council: twelve angular shards arranged in a ring, each a different color, representing every nation in Tyme except Geguul.

"Go," said Huck. "Get out of here. I'll handle them."

"I want to help you."

"I'm not asking," said Huck. His weathered face was grim. "I'm telling. Get off the property. Find something to keep you busy. I don't want you here for this."

Harrow touched his father's shoulder. "All right," he said. "But Pa — she's alive."

Huck drew a sharp breath. "Your mother? She spoke to you?"

"Just trust me," said Harrow, with a glance at Syrah. "She's sick, but she's sleeping. Healing."

Huck seemed to gain strength from this information. He straightened up and squared his shoulders. "Go on now," he said. "Get out of here."

CHAPTER SIXTEEN

*H*ARROW cut out the back of the house and through the fields. Like the Vangarden, he traveled for a while along the stream that bordered the property, but he headed toward town instead of away from it.

"Guess I should've brought the alphabet with me," he said as he walked. "I don't know what you want me to do first. If you want to spy on Luffa or Minister Pease, our best bet is to head over to the Thatch, but once we get there, I'm not sure how I'll get in. Dee doesn't want me around, thanks to *you* —" He cast a hard look at Syrah. "So I'd have to come up with another reason to be there. Or, if you want to spy on Nexus Burdock . . ."

Syrah considered it. If he could poke around in the Nexus's house, maybe he could figure out if Burdock had actually killed the Witch of the Woods, or whether he was hiding anything. If he *was*, it might have nothing to do with Calabaza.

He hopped once.

Harrow whistled. "Spying on an Exalted Nexus," he said, with a shake of his head. "We have to be careful. I don't want to make things worse for my pa. I guess I could make up some excuse to visit him, and you could just slip inside once the door's open . . . but what business could I have bothering the Nexus? Maybe I could play like I'm checking in to see if Nexus Keene has had any luck with a cure."

Syrah hopped once in approval. That story would work perfectly.

Harrow turned north where the stream met the river and he walked along the riverbank. "I can't believe someone poisoned Governor Calabaza," he murmured. "It's sick. Luffa's cruel, but I don't know."

Cruel? Syrah wasn't sure he would have used that word. He hopped a couple of times, curious.

"You don't think so?" Harrow's tone was sharp. "You can't get a better grandchild than Delicata Gourd, but Luffa treats her like she's worse than useless. She has never given that girl one kind word, and after what you did with that letter, it got worse. She blames Dee for your nana's death."

Syrah croaked in astonishment. How was that Deli's fault?

"Luffa said she was weak to write that letter, and she caused the scandal with her foolishness. She said the whole thing broke your nana's heart and killed her."

But if anyone had done that, it was Syrah — and Nana Cava's heart was much too strong to be broken by a scandal. Luffa of all people should have known that. Cava had died of ripe old age, the *Criers* hadn't humiliated her to death — the idea was insulting.

Harrow was silent for a time, walking along, but Syrah could feel the tension in him, and could see his jaw working.

"You know what really gets me," he finally said. "Dee wrote *you* that letter. I don't think she's ever spilled her guts like that to anybody, but she did for you, and you didn't even —" He let out a long, angry breath. "She never wrote me anything like that," he muttered.

"Never said anything even close. You know what I'd give for — never mind. Just never mind. You've got to be the dumbest —" Harrow shut his mouth and made a muffled noise of fury.

Syrah was surprised. Harrow was jealous of him.

He wondered why that didn't make him happier.

For the next half hour, they trekked along in silence. "I wonder what they're doing to my pa," said Harrow quietly after a while. "Do you think they'll arrest him?"

Syrah hopped three times.

"Me either." He sighed. "I should've stayed with him."

Syrah hopped twice. It was better this way. They were free to explore and find things out — at least for a little while. Once the Exalted Council got their hands on Harrow, they'd want to keep him and question him. The idea made Syrah anxious; he had finally found someone he could communicate with, and he wasn't in a hurry to lose him.

They drew nearer to the center of Cornucopia, where the noise of a large crowd began to swell. They passed the big Ubiquitous store and Syrah thought of the last time he had been here, with Rapunzel and Jack. It seemed a lifetime ago. As they approached the park, a large yellow banner caught Syrah's eye. It hung in the window of the same shop where, months ago, Rapunzel had bought her wagon.

VOTE FOR BURDOCK
VOTE FOR THE FUTURE

There were lots of those banners around, Syrah realized, peering into other shop windows. Harrow took the bridge across the river, past the mills where the great wheels turned, and continued onto the main road into Market Park, which teemed with people. It was even more crowded than it had been during the jacks tournament last fall — or at least, he thought it was. His memory of that tournament was fuzzy. Along the green, Syrah counted a dozen or so food booths that also displayed Burdock banners. There were also lots of people wearing yellow fabric patches that read *VOTE BURDOCK* pinned to their shirts, and people wearing yellow sashes stood along the park's main paths handing small chocolate candies to everyone who passed.

"Progress is sweet," said a woman in a yellow sash as Harrow approached. "Burdock for governor!" Harrow refused the candy she offered, and Syrah didn't blame him. Last time Harrow had eaten something that someone had handed him in a crowd, he had ended up with the Purge.

They walked through the park, toward the same dais where Rapunzel had won the jacks contest. Here, the crowd thickened around them, forcing Harrow to slow his pace. G. G. Floss stood near the dais, beside a tall table covered in chocolates. A ribbon proclaiming *I STAND WITH BURDOCK* was tied around her hat, a shining copper *B* was embroidered on her butter-yellow sash, and equally bright copper bracelets glinted from her wrists. When she saw Harrow, she beckoned to him with her purple fingertips.

"You came!" she exclaimed. She sounded impressed. "I assumed you'd stay away, since — well. This can't be easy for you or your father."

"Everyone knows it was our oats, huh?" asked Harrow, glancing around. He shifted uneasily. "Was there some kind of announcement?"

"Big stories spread quickly." Miss Floss smiled sympathetically.

"I'm so glad you're here for the debate in spite of everything that's happening. It shows courage and strength of character."

"So, you're for Burdock?"

"Absolutely," said Miss Floss. "No contest." She held up a hand and wiggled her purple fingertips. "If there are going to be new laws about how magic and food work together, that's going to affect my business directly," she said. "Burdock understands magic. I can trust that he won't undermine the Copper Door. I can't say the same for his competitor."

"Who's running against him now?"

"Clementine Pease," said Miss Floss.

Harrow sucked a breath and glanced at Syrah, who thought he could guess what he was thinking. Now Harrow understood why Clementine was on Syrah's list of suspects. He hadn't had a chance to tell Harrow that she was running for governor, let alone that she had known all along about the Ubiquitous seeds.

"Exactly my reaction," said Miss Floss. "This is a woman who has been part of Calabaza's cabinet for over twenty years! We deserve someone new — someone who can lead this nation into the future. The Exalted Nexus and I haven't always seen eye to eye, but this isn't about personal feelings. It's about what's best for the country — and for business." Miss Floss spotted someone else. "Mr. Arusha!" she called out, and raised both hands to wave him over. Her copper bracelets gleamed. "Thank you so much for your help with the banners. Move up to the front if you can, they're going to start any second. . . ."

Harrow carried Syrah a little closer to the dais, but Syrah kept watching Miss Floss. What was she doing wearing bracelets? Just yesterday, Physic Feverfew had noticed infected burns on her wrists. Were they already healed?

"Want to stay for the debate?" Harrow asked.

Syrah hopped twice. This was the perfect time to go to the Thatch and spy — everyone was here in the park. He could get into the governor's office, or Luffa's room. He might even be able to get into Burdock's house.

"Just a couple minutes," said Harrow. "Come on, I'm curious."

Syrah hopped twice, irritated, but Harrow ignored him. He wove his way through the crowd till he was right up at the front of it — and now Syrah realized why he didn't want to go anywhere. Deli was there, seated on a platform that was raised on one side of the dais. She was dressed in formal clothes, and her posture was rigidly perfect, but her expression was exhausted. The triplets looked tired too, and even Roma did not look quite as beautifully arranged as usual. She had been staying up and looking after Calabaza, and it showed.

Two podiums waited on the dais, and Luffa stood between them. "People of Yellow Country," she said, and her strong voice carried. The field went silent at once. "Huck Steelcut is no longer a participant in this race."

There were shrieks of delight at this, as well as shouts of dismay. A few people booed.

"A new candidate has chosen to declare," said Luffa. "That candidate is Minister of Agriculture and Provisional Governor Clementine Pease. We are here today so that Minister Pease and Exalted Nexus Burdock can debate their views. They will conduct a civil conversation about their beliefs, here in public, where you can hear them. Nexus Burdock will begin."

Luffa returned to the Gourd family's platform as Burdock and Clementine approached their podiums. Clementine snapped open her stepladder and climbed onto it. Nexus Burdock shoved back his pale hair and looked out at the waiting crowd.

"Your support means the world to me," he began. "The banners you've sewn, the patches you're wearing — I never expected this. Together, we will build the future of Yellow Country: a nation that no longer fears magic."

The crowd shouted passionately. Parents raised their small children victoriously into the air.

"Never again will we run," said Burdock. "Never again will we cower. We will confront any threat that arises. We will insist on the highest standards of safety. We will heed the lessons of the Purge and ensure that nothing like it ever happens again." He pointed to Clementine. "Clementine Pease has an enormous advantage," he said. "She stands here today with the open support of Madam Governor Luffa Gourd, the savior of this nation and its former queen. She represents history. Tradition. She has served twenty years as our minister of agriculture — a vital role, and she has filled it well." He paused and allowed the field to grow absolutely quiet before asking: "Or has she?"

Clementine looked over at him, her dark eyes narrow and watchful.

"He's really good at this," murmured Harrow to Syrah, who hopped once. Luffa had said it herself. Nexus Burdock knew how to play a crowd.

"You have all heard by now that the source of the Purge is the Steelcut farm," said Burdock. Under Syrah's belly, Harrow's shoulder grew tense. "What you don't know is why it happened."

"No one knows why it happened," said Clementine. "The Exalted Council is investigating right now —"

"It's my turn to speak," Burdock cut in, and Clementine fell silent. "We have concrete evidence of wrongdoing on the Steelcut farm. Whether it is connected to the Purge is up to the Exalted Council to discover — but the wrongdoing did occur, and I think it's high time that all of you knew about it."

"We should leave," muttered Harrow, and he tried to step away from the dais, but there were people all around him. A quick exit was impossible without drawing everyone's attention. He pulled his hat down over his eyes and crossed his arms, trying to shrink from view.

"I think they ought to know a lot of things," said Clementine, taking hold of her podium. "About you, for instance."

It was Syrah's turn to tense. Was she going to say something about the Witch of the Woods? About Burdock's childhood?

"You'll get your turn," said Burdock. "And when you do, I'm sure the people would like you to explain how Huck Steelcut got away, for twenty years, with planting Ubiquitous seeds in Yellow soil and raising unregulated crops on that land."

The crowd exploded. Shouted questions and threats of vengeance rose in a violent chorus. Fists shook in the air; cowbells clanged; people chanted, "DOWN WITH STEELCUT!"

"Crop *rot*," Harrow breathed. In all the chaos, he tried once more to duck through the crowd and get away, but people were surging toward the dais, pressing in around him. He could hardly move.

"That information was confidential," said Clementine sharply, raising her speaking trumpet to have a hope of being heard over all the racket. "The investigation into Huck Steelcut's activities is ongoing. By sharing those details with the public, you have risked the integrity of that investigation and betrayed the cabinet."

"The public deserves the truth," Burdock replied instantly. "When I am their governor, I intend to report to them, not you."

This earned a cheer. But Syrah wasn't certain there was anything to cheer about. He stared at Nexus Burdock in surprise — and disappointment. He hadn't thought that the Nexus was the kind of person who would play dirty, but revealing confidential information had definitely been a dirty move. Yes, Burdock had once told the world about the Purge without first seeking permission — but that had been an emergency. People could have died. There was no emergency here, and nobody's life was at stake. Burdock just wanted to score points. He wanted to win, no matter what.

Syrah understood the feeling.

He also knew, without a doubt, that it was wrong.

"What about Exalted Nexus Keene?" Clementine demanded. "Won't you report to him? Won't you still be, first and foremost, a member of the Exalted Council?"

"The people of Yellow Country are my first responsibility," Burdock replied, looking out over his audience. "I was born Exalted, and I will always be Exalted, but as your governor, my full attention and loyalty will belong to you."

"How do we know you mean it?" said Clementine. "You swore a lifetime oath to the Exalted Council, didn't you? You dedicated your powers to their service to help the people of Tyme." Clementine paused briefly. "But you were a citizen of Yellow Country before that. Weren't you?"

Burdock's face went dead white. "How did Steelcut get away with it, Clementine?" he demanded, his voice dry. "You've been minister of agriculture the entire time he's been selling those crops back to Ubiquitous. And you noticed nothing? In twenty years?"

"You changed your name," said Clementine, ignoring the question. "As all Exalted do. You gave up your identity and chose the name Burdock. But if you're going to run for governor, if you're going to *belong* to us, as you say, then shouldn't we know who you really are?"

"I will tell you this," said Burdock, turning to the crowd. "Either Clementine Pease has been covering for Steelcut's misdeeds for two decades, or she is completely incompetent. Either she is lying to you, or she has been lied to —"

"Why don't you want us to know?" asked Clementine. "What is it you're trying to hide, Hans? Or do you prefer Mr. Rantott?"

Burdock's eyes flashed and his body heaved strangely. For a moment, Syrah thought that the Nexus might vomit. Hans Rantott. Was that his real name?

"Huck Steelcut's son is right here, Nexus!" cried a man in a yellow sash. He grabbed Harrow's shoulder so hard that he nearly shook Syrah right off of it. "He didn't have the Purge, look at him — he's fine!"

The angry crowd pressed in around Harrow, trapping him against the dais.

"You knew what was going on, didn't you?"

"You weren't really sick, you filthy liar!"

"My brother is dead! You killed him!"

Frantic, Syrah rolled his eyes to see if anyone was going to come to Harrow's aid. But Burdock still stood in shock, and though Clementine lifted her speaking trumpet and ordered the crowd to desist, nobody listened. The mob had its own mind now, and they wanted blood. Somebody had Harrow by the front of his shirt. Somebody else ripped his hat off him. Breathing hard, Harrow tried to scramble backward up onto the dais, but the large man who had first grabbed him now gripped him by both shoulders, forcing Syrah to jump up to the top of Harrow's head and hang on to his hair.

"Guards!" he heard Clementine cry.

The governor's guards fought their way toward Harrow, striking people when necessary and knocking them back.

"I'll kill you," said the big man who had Harrow's shoulders. He struggled to get free, but the big man's hands moved up to grip his throat. "You and your pa. I'll burn your rotten farm to the ground — you smug, mother-killing —"

A large, muddy rock sailed in from nowhere, barely missing Syrah as it whizzed past. It struck the big man square in the side of the head. He blinked — mud trickled down his cheek from his temple — and then he crumpled, unconscious. As he fell, the guards finally reached Harrow, who was trembling like he was freezing to death. A few of them dragged the large man away; the others made a protective semicircle between Harrow and the volatile crowd. Syrah gave a weak *ribbit* of relief.

"Who threw that rock?" one of the guards demanded. "Did anyone see?"

Nobody had. But Syrah's eye was drawn to the platform where the Gourd family sat. Roma looked dazed and horrified, but the triplets were staring at Deli, whose expression was fierce. She had mud on her fancy formal shoes, and her hands were dirty. She clasped them in her lap to hide them, and Syrah's stomach tightened.

"Are you injured?" one of the guards asked Harrow, handing his hat back to him. "Do you want us to escort you somewhere else?" When he didn't answer right away, Syrah hopped down to his shoulder again and nudged the side of his neck.

"Yeah," said Harrow faintly. "I'd like to leave now."

The guards shouldered their way through the dense crowd, protecting Harrow from injury, though they couldn't stop people jeering and throwing food at him. Harrow yanked his hat back down again and suffered the long walk out of Market Park, back to the other side of the river and out to the eastern edge of town, where the guards left him.

He walked back toward the farm in silence, slouched forward with his arms crossed over himself. Syrah waited for him to speak.

"They really mean it," he finally said as they drew near the stream that marked the Steelcut property. "They want to kill us."

Syrah didn't hop. He tried a sympathetic croak, but Harrow wasn't having it.

"This is your fault," he said. "Nobody would know about those seeds if not for you."

That wasn't entirely fair. The Exalted Council would have discovered the evidence during their investigation, and people would have found out eventually. But Syrah could not say this, so he merely hopped twice in protest.

Harrow turned and made his way through the oat fields, dragging his fingertips along the stalks as he walked. "I don't know what we're going to do," he said.

They approached the farmhouse, where there were now four carriages standing, all of them bearing the symbol of the Exalted Council. The front door of the farmhouse opened, and several people wearing amulets filed out of it. Two of them walked with Huck Steelcut between them. His hands were behind him, and a ribbon of magic light bound his wrists.

Harrow lurched as if to move toward his father, but Syrah hopped twice, then twice again, and then he leapt down to the ground and croaked, insistent. If Harrow went over there, he would get arrested too.

Harrow crouched down, hiding himself among the oats. "I can't hide from the Exalted," he whispered. "I'll just get in worse trouble if I do."

Syrah hopped away from the farmhouse and croaked again. He kept hopping, and Harrow followed him, staying low, until they came to the stream again, out of sight of the farmhouse. Here, Harrow dropped down and sat on the bank. He leaned forward over his knees and put his head in his hands.

"They really took him," he mumbled. Syrah hopped onto his boot. "I have to turn myself in. For my pa's sake."

Syrah hopped twice. *Bad idea.*

"You have a good reason why I shouldn't?"

One hop. *I have about twenty. Draw me an alphabet.*

Harrow almost seemed to hear this. He picked up a stick and started writing letters in the mud. Syrah began hopping to them, but it was useless; the moment he landed on a letter, he erased it.

"Come on," said Harrow, after several frustrating minutes of this. "There are blackberries across the stream. I'll crush them and write on a rock or something." He held out his hand, and Syrah hopped into it.

What are they going to do to Pa? I don't want to live here anymore — won't leave, because of my mother, but Skies, they hate us. Everyone hates us. Even Dee hates me now —

Syrah wished it were true.

She loves you, he thought bitterly. *She threw that rock for you.*

"She did?" said Harrow hopefully — and then he gasped and flipped his hand over, dropping Syrah into the dirt. He stared down at him, and Syrah gazed back, a little rattled but mostly just amazed. "I *heard* that," said Harrow. "I heard *you*. And you . . . did you hear *me*?"

Syrah's heart fluttered faster. Could he talk to Harrow, then? Really *talk* to him? Between his own magic, and Harrow's Yellow fairy blood, maybe he could. He bounced and bounced, wanting to be picked up so he could try it again. Harrow bent and held his hand out, then snatched it back.

"Have you been listening inside my head all this time?" he demanded.

Syrah hopped twice, and tried to get to his hand. Harrow kept it closed another moment, then uncurled his fingers and allowed Syrah into his palm.

I have to have my belly on your skin, he thought. *I only feel things clearly when people hold me in their hands. I've always been on your shoulder. I mostly try to avoid hands, because it's weird.*

Harrow shuddered. "It's real weird," he said. "I don't so much hear you as . . . feel you."

Great, thought Syrah. *Since you're the last person I want to have feeling me.*

Harrow snorted, and then his face fell. "Well, now what?" he said. "My pa's arrested, and they're going to be looking for me — we can't spy anywhere. I guess I could try sneaking to the Thatch, but —"

You can't sneak anywhere, Glitter.

"Glitter?" Harrow looked insulted.

Focus, Oat Boy. Clementine Pease knows about your father and Ubiquitous. She helped him all along.

"What!"

It was your father who told her to run for governor. He's covering for her and lying to the Exalted Council, saying she wasn't involved so she has a chance to get elected. I don't think she even wants to run — she just doesn't want Burdock to win. *So she didn't poison Calabaza so she could be governor, but she still might have done it so that he wouldn't find out what she and your father were up to.*

It was such a relief, such a sweet, intense relief to be able to say so much so quickly that Syrah couldn't help a croak of delight.

This is amazing except your hand is disgustingly sweaty.

"Uh, maybe that's because there's a wet frog in it."

Or maybe you're just one of those sweaty-handed guys. Deli probably wishes you'd wipe them off once in a while.

Ass, Harrow thought, and Syrah felt it. *At least I didn't get myself turned into a frog.*

True enough.

"Oh right." Harrow licked his lips. "I forgot you can hear that."

If it's not Clementine, it's Luffa or Burdock.

"What about Roma? She was in the carriage."

Why would Roma hurt him? She loves being the governor's wife. She hates to lose her status, and she was afraid that she was going to lose her home too, I heard her say so.

"My money's on Burdock. He was shady in that debate," said Harrow, frowning. "Why doesn't he want people to know his real name?"

I don't know. But he didn't want Calabaza to be governor — I know that for a fact. Plus he was at the Royal Governor's Inn, he could easily have put the basket in the carriage, and without Calabaza in the race, Burdock's probably going to be elected governor.

"You think he'll win?"

You saw how those people reacted. They love him. But I think Clementine Pease has more information about his past. We need to go and find out what it is.

"How?" said Harrow. "I can't get to the Thatch without being seen, you said it yourself."

What about Clementine's house? Do you know where she lives?

"Actually, yeah, and it's not far from here. But what if she won't help? What if she turns me in to the Exalted Council? Maybe I should tell her about the juggetsbane, so she understands —"

Don't. If she launches an investigation, Burdock will cover his tracks. We don't want him to know we're onto him.

"So what, then?" said Harrow. "I should show up at her house and expect her to tell me everything she knows about the Nexus?"

Tell her you know that she was in on it with your dad, but you'll keep quiet if she helps you.

"You want me to blackmail the minister of agriculture."

You're quick, Sweaty.

"You know, I've eaten frogs." Harrow stuck Syrah on his shoulder. "Lots of them. Let's go."

CHAPTER SEVENTEEN

CLEMENTINE Pease's cottage stood by itself at the far eastern edge of Cornucopia, surrounded by a garden that was prettier for being unkempt. Its roof and door were of typical height, but Syrah immediately noticed signs that someone of very short stature lived there. The doorknob was hung lower, the steps that led to the door were short enough for small legs to climb with ease, and the windows were closer to the ground than was usual. Harrow hurried toward the cottage, keeping his hat down, which Syrah wanted to tell him wasn't doing any good, given that his hands practically sparkled.

He knocked at the door. When Clementine opened it, her eyebrows arched. She stepped back at once to let him enter, peered outside, then shut the door and locked it.

"Is somebody after you?" she demanded. "Did those bullies follow you home from the debate?" She scowled. "Debate. Like that's what it was."

"The Exalted Council arrested my pa."

Clementine blew out a breath. She stuck one hand in her purple hair. "Did they question you too?"

"When I saw them there, I turned around and left."

"Ah."

"Please don't turn me in."

This is where you tell her that you know what she did, Syrah thought, but Harrow couldn't hear him, and he had a feeling that Harrow wouldn't be much use as a blackmailer anyway.

Clementine rubbed her head for a moment, then turned and beckoned for him to follow her. As they walked through the house, Syrah scanned his surroundings. There were potted plants in every corner, and chairs and tables slightly shorter than what he was used to seeing. Above the low sideboard in the dining room was a small, accurate portrait of Clementine with two younger people: a boy as short as she was, and a tall, round-figured girl. Her children, he supposed.

The papers stacked on top of the sideboard were far more interesting to him. He recognized them as the same ones that Luffa had given to her. Information on Burdock.

"Is Meyer still at the University of Orange?"

"He's a full professor now," Clementine answered, with unmistakable pride in her voice. "And Hesper's doing fine up in Bloomington. But you're not here for chitchat. You know you've got a frog on your shoulder, right?"

"Yep," said Harrow, pulling out a stool from under the sideboard. "He's tame."

Clementine looked interested, but didn't pursue it. She pulled out a chair with a raised seat and a short ladder between its legs, and she climbed up to sit across from him. "I'm not going to turn you in," she said, "but I can't hide you from the Council either. I'm in a tough spot as it is, with everything Burdock threw out there today." She studied Harrow briefly. "Was that the first time you'd heard about those Ubiquitous seeds?" she asked. "It must've been a shock to you. I'm sorry for what happened out there — the way they turned on you was vicious."

"I knew about the seeds, and I know you're in on it," said Harrow. "You knew about the Ubiquitous crops all along."

Clementine winced. "Huck told you?"

"I found out. But I'm not going to tell the Council."

That's the opposite of blackmail, thought Syrah. Irritated, he jumped to the pile of books and papers on the sideboard and started trying to dislodge some of them by pushing with his feet.

"I can't let you lie to them," said Clementine. "I've got enough on my conscience without that."

"I have to. If I tell them the truth now, they'll know my pa's been lying."

She clasped her hands in front of her. "We thought we were doing the right thing," she said. "I gave him permission to plant them because I knew Calabaza never would. And for a long time, it all worked fine. No one was hurt. No one was sick. We were feeding a lot of very poor people in places nowhere near as fortunate as Cornucopia."

"So that's why he did it."

"He didn't tell you that?" She snorted. "Leave it to him to hide the part where he's saving lives. I'm sorry he's going through this alone. I told him I'd give myself up."

"You can't. You have to beat Burdock."

"I'm not sure that's possible."

Harrow leaned forward. "You know things. About Burdock's past. Tell me what you know, and maybe I can help you."

"There's not much to tell," said Clementine. "Most of what I know is just speculation."

Syrah finally managed to push the top layer of papers off the pile. They drifted to the floor, and Harrow picked them up. "Hans Rantott, born in Arrowroot, twenty-first Orwhile, 1046, to Marzi and Radler Rantott," he read slowly. "Born in the caul, Exalted." He looked up. "This is Burdock?"

Clementine nodded. "His parents died when he was eight," she said. "Fever. It ripped through Plenty and the woods out there, and killed a lot of people, just like the Purge. He had one sibling — a younger sister. She was murdered by the Witch of the Woods."

Harrow made a noise of pity. "So it's not just the Purge he's mad about," he said.

"Calabaza was a very young governor then," said Clementine. "During his first two years in office, the Witch of the Woods was driven out of the Republic of Brown, and she moved into Arrowroot. She killed thirty children in Yellow Country, and he didn't lift a finger to stop her."

"Leave the magic to the magical."

"That's right. In truth, my heart goes out to Burdock. My own children were small around that time, and it was terrifying — everybody felt it. The families who lost children still feel it. Thirty years can't heal that. When that witch died, it felt like a curse was lifted from the whole country."

"And this?" Harrow asked, lifting the other paper he had taken from the floor. It was a *Town Crier* from the year 1056, and its headline stood out in bold, black letters: **WITCH OF THE WOODS SLAIN!** Syrah skimmed the article beneath it: a grisly account of what Exalted Nexus Keene had discovered inside the witch's candy home. The bones and hair of more than two dozen children, piled in filthy cages in the basement. Several more children were found totally intact but also dead, their bodies frozen in unnatural, doll-like shapes.

Just like the gingerbread children that G. G. Floss had shown them at the ATC. Syrah felt queasy at the thought, but he kept reading.

The witch herself was never found — after her death, the White claimed her physical body — but Keene believed that she had burned to death. He found her oven still lit and its door standing open, with one of her shoes outside it on the floor, as though it had fallen from her foot in a struggle. Just the way Miss Floss had described it.

Pushing the witch into her own oven. It was a bold move, Syrah thought, but a smart one. Possibly even the only strategy that would have worked. It would be impossible for a child, even an Exalted child, to attack a witch head-on and live. If she'd had even an instant's chance to react, she could have destroyed him. But if Burdock had surprised her from behind — pushed her in headfirst — he might have stood a chance at survival. And Burdock was smart. Strategic. Capable of playing dirty if that was what it took. He was the sort of person who *could* have done it.

True stories had a certain ring to them. Miss Floss had said that, and now Syrah thought he knew what she meant.

"It's hard to say whether there's any connection," said Clementine slowly. "Nobody knows for sure who killed that witch. But three days later, Hans Rantott went to the town hall in Plenty and reported his sister's death. After that, there's no record of him. He must have gone north to Lilac to train with the Exalted Council."

"You think *he* killed the Witch of the Woods?" Harrow checked the date on the *Crier*. "In 1056? He was only ten."

Clementine shrugged. "But he is Exalted. And if he was furious enough about his sister . . . it's not impossible."

Syrah tried to imagine a very young Burdock going into that ghastly house. Perhaps he had seen his sister's dead body. Perhaps the witch had tried to kill him too. What would an experience like that do to a person? Maybe it had warped his brain. Turned him into the kind of person who would put juggetsbane in Calabaza's sandwiches. After all, Calabaza had done nothing to stop the Witch of the Woods.

Maybe Burdock wanted more than to be governor. Maybe he wanted revenge.

"But why wouldn't he take credit?" said Harrow. "If he did kill that witch, then he's a hero. He should tell everyone it was him — they'd elect him in a minute."

Because he has something to hide, thought Syrah at once. *But what?*

Clementine smiled faintly and pointed to the pile of books. "Your frog is sitting on a possible explanation," she said. "The *Crier* from the very next day."

Syrah hopped down from the pile, and Clementine chuckled.

"He really is tame, isn't he?" she said. "It's like he understood me."

Harrow grabbed the *Crier* and held it up. The headline on the front side screamed **MORE HORRORS DISCOVERED IN WITCH'S LAIR.**

Syrah skimmed the page. Bodies in the attic, a necklace made of finger bones, a mostly empty treasure chest.

"Not that one," said Clementine. "Flip it over."

A sharp knock sounded at the front door.

Clementine got down from her seat. "Go out the back," she said, under her breath. "Hide in the garden shed. If it's the Exalted Council,

I'll pretend I didn't know you were there. Not that they'll believe me. Quick — I'll come and get you when whoever this is has gone."

She headed to the front door, and Syrah leapt to the table. Harrow picked him up at once.

Keep the Crier, Syrah thought.

Harrow stuck him on his shoulder, held on to the *Crier*, and made his way to the back door. They crossed the garden quickly, heading for the small shed, which stood beside a tiny brook. The brook moved at barely a trickle; weeds and water plants clogged its way. At first, Syrah only glanced at the weeds, but then he looked again, harder.

One of the plants looked just like watercress, except for faint brown edges on its leaves.

He began to bounce and croak. Harrow paused with his hand on the shed's door handle. He glanced at Syrah, then picked him off his shoulder and held him in his hand.

Juggetsbane. In the brook.

He felt Harrow's shock and the fear that surged through him as he shoved Syrah into his shirt pocket, then picked up his feet and ran, past the garden shed and away from Clementine's cottage, into the rolling farmland that lay beyond it. There was little cover out here, and few trees, but there were no people either. They met no one in the fields. Harrow kept running until he found a large oak, which he collapsed against, panting. Syrah hopped into his palm, annoyed.

I said it was juggetsbane, I didn't say she was chasing you with an ax.

"I just wanted to get out of there," Harrow managed.

Why? I could have gone back into the house and listened to see what she was up to. You could have asked her about the plant and pretended you thought it was watercress to see her reaction.

"She has juggetsbane in her yard and she wanted me to get in a shed! I think leaving was reasonable!"

We could have found out more. Now we can't go back. If Clementine's the culprit, she'll know something's up. You're miserable at this.

"Well sorry I'm not as good at sneaking around and lying as you are," Harrow retorted, shaking Syrah out of his hand so he could cross his arms. Syrah leapt up onto him and pushed against the hand he had tucked under his elbow. Harrow gave an exasperated sigh and let Syrah back into his palm.

"Juggetsbane roots make a really strong purple dye," said Harrow. "I forgot about that. She probably uses it for her hair. I wish I'd thought of that before —"

Just let me see that Crier.

Harrow spread the paper out on the ground, and Syrah searched for something that might be related to Burdock. He found it sandwiched between an article about an orphan girl who had become Plenty's youngest bakery apprentice and a recipe that promised perfectly balanced lemon curd.

THREE FOUND DEAD IN ARROWROOT FOREST

The story beneath the headline was brief. The bodies had been found in two separate homes. One was the cottage of Ava Cass and Holly Seaberry, an older couple who lived in a tiny glade. The two were discovered lying in their garden on a picnic blanket with mouths full of blue foam and what looked like a blueberry tart still unfinished between them. According to the story, the tart had been made from poisonous bluepeace berries, which were tragically easy to mistake for the real thing.

The third body belonged to woodcutter and recluse Grausam

Steppe, who lived in a hovel in the very deepest part of the woods. The report said that he had been dead a few days longer than the two women. He had choked to death on a morel mushroom.

A morel. Syrah remembered Rapunzel reading something about morels in *Edible Plants ~ An Illustrated Guide*, and he thought back now, trying to recall what he knew. Morel mushrooms looked like something else. He couldn't think of its name, but it was poisonous. It would steam silver if it was crumbled into hot liquid, swallowing a little bit would make it hard to breathe, and swallowing a lot would cause a person to suffocate. Grasuam Steppe might have looked like he choked, but really he would have stopped breathing from the poison.

One by one, the details clicked together with what Syrah already knew. He nudged Harrow's hand to be picked up.

Juggetsbane looks like watercress. Bluepeace look like blueberries. Morel mushrooms look like something too, I can't remember the name of it —

"Slumbercap," whispered Harrow. "Skies."

This is how he kills people. Plants that look like food.

It made him sick to think it of Nexus Burdock. But there was no denying it now.

"But an old couple and a poor woodcutter? Why would he do that?"

No idea. Maybe he likes killing. Or maybe they were in his way. Look at the front article again. Did it say something about an empty treasure chest in the witch's house?

Harrow flipped it over and nodded. "You think Burdock stole it for himself and killed those people because they tried to take it from him?"

I don't know.

"All right, that's it," said Harrow. "We have to tell somebody. Somebody who can move on Burdock fast, before he hides."

We can't. We have no proof.

"I have to. If I don't, and he does this again to somebody else, it'll be my fault."

They'll think you did it. How else could you know about the juggetsbane in Calabaza's basket?

"I know because you told me. So I'm going to have to tell them about you too."

No, not yet — I knew you were miserable at this —

"I'm telling Luffa Gourd," said Harrow, getting to his feet. "We're going to the Thatch."

No! If you go there, the Exalted Council will arrest you —

"Nice to know you care so much." Harrow patted Syrah on the head.

Stupid glittering oat-headed sweat monster —

"Love you too, little fella."

I will seriously kill you.

Harrow lifted Syrah to his shoulder. "You do that," he said, and he strode west toward the Thatch.

Chapter Eighteen

HARROW took a long path toward the governor's property, avoiding people as much as possible. He walked all the way around the north end of Cornucopia, then back to the river, where he walked west until he finally came to a small town that had its own bridge. He cut across the river and doubled back, staying near the woods. When he finally drew near to Cornucopia again, Syrah began to protest.

Two hops. Two hops. *Don't do this. Don't tell them. Let's finish this on our own.* But Harrow could not hear him and didn't bother to pick him up. He kept walking, determined, ignoring Syrah's insistent croaks.

By the time they reached the outer edges of the Gourds' property, it was dark, and Syrah was furious. He slammed himself against Harrow's neck to make himself clear. Harrow paused in the middle of a pumpkin patch and finally took Syrah off his shoulder to talk to him.

"I have to do what's right," he said. "If Burdock's really a murderer —"

Shut up! Somebody could hear you!

"Luffa will know what to do," Harrow went on. "She can get in touch with your family for you too. Don't you want to see them?"

Syrah did, very much.

"Then let's tell them you're alive."

I'll see them when this is done. We have to figure this out on our own. We're close to Burdock's house — take me there. Let me go inside and see what I can find.

Harrow said nothing, but as the moonlight played on his glittering face, Syrah could feel the turbulence in his mind. *I'm not comfortable with that. What if Burdock catches us — hurts us? Syrah's right, I'm miserable at this — I have to tell an adult —*

No you DON'T, thought Syrah angrily. *I won't play along. I'll pretend I'm just a regular frog, and they'll all think you're crazy.*

Harrow made a noise of frustration. *Selfish,* he thought.

But for once in his life, Syrah knew that he was doing the right thing.

Take me to Burdock's, he insisted. *That's where the proof will be. Look for an open window and let me loose, and I'll hop in and search. Then we can tell, all right?*

Harrow's acute discomfort permeated him. "This is the very last thing we're doing on our own," he said. "After this, we go to Luffa."

Fine.

The official residence of Yellow Country's Exalted Nexus sat just west of the Thatch, between the pumpkin fields and a watermelon patch. It was a house large enough for a family to be comfortable; the Nexus before Burdock had been married with several children. For a single man like Burdock, it was a huge amount of space.

"It's all dark," Harrow whispered as they approached. There didn't appear to be so much as a candle lit inside the house. "I don't think he's there. I'll check for an open window —"

Footsteps crunched toward them from the direction of the Thatch. Harrow gasped and dropped down behind a tree. Syrah hopped off his shoulder and out to where he could see what was happening.

Burdock was on his way home, carrying a lantern. It swung in the darkness, reminding Syrah of the carriage house at the Royal Governor's Inn. Fear skittered through him, and he retracted his eyeballs and swallowed hard. Maybe Harrow had been right. Maybe they shouldn't have come here alone to do this.

Another set of footsteps, quick and light, caught up with Burdock's.

"Where were you?" said a voice, and then its owner emerged into the pool of light cast by Burdock's lantern. "You said to come, but then you were gone. I don't exist at your convenience, no matter what you think."

G. G. Floss. She stood before Burdock, fists clenched.

"I was at the Thatch," said Burdock. "Keene arrived unexpectedly. He found a cure for the Purge — or at least, it was a cure in Plenty. It worked on everyone else in the Thatch, but for some strange reason it didn't work on Calabaza. He's still unconscious."

Miss Floss nervously pushed a strand of sandy hair behind her ear. "Why?"

"I think we both know that."

The corners of Miss Floss's mouth turned down. She looked away from him.

"Show me your wrists," said Burdock quietly.

"I'm not going to come out here every night —"

"Show me your wrists. Now."

Miss Floss pushed up her sleeves and held out her wrists, and her copper bracelets reflected the lantern light. They looked like shackles, Syrah thought. He hadn't noticed that before.

Burdock inspected them, turning her hands over. "Good," he murmured momentarily. "Hands up."

Miss Floss's hands rose into the air as though on strings.

"Hands down."

They dropped limply to her sides, and Syrah shivered, cold through. He had never seen anything so disturbing.

"You can't do this to me forever," she said, tearful.

"Yes I can," Burdock replied. "We both know that too."

"Physic Feverfew wants me to take them off. She says they'll stop my burns from healing."

"And what do you say if someone wants you to take them off?"

Miss Floss's eyes dimmed. When she spoke, her voice was wooden. "I will say 'No.'"

"Good." Burdock tilted his head. "Feverfew is pushy," he said. "What will you say if she tries to remove them?"

"I will say 'Stop. Leave them as they are.' Then I will run away and tell you."

"Perfect."

Miss Floss seemed to shake off the magic that had forced her to speak. Her face filled with rage. "I'll burn them off again," she spat. "I swear —"

A loud *snap!* caused Miss Floss to gasp. She looked over toward the tree where Harrow was hiding, and Syrah froze in terror. Harrow must have moved, he must have shifted and snapped a twig —

"Who's there?" Burdock called. His voice was hard. Cold. "Come out."

Don't do it, Syrah thought desperately, though Harrow could not hear him. *Let me handle this.* He bounced as high as he could and gave a mighty croak. He bounced again, closer to Burdock, and then he saw a small stick. He bounced onto it, deliberately causing another *snap!*, which badly stung his belly, but he kept croaking and bouncing, making his way closer to the lantern light until they could see him. G. G. jumped back as though frightened.

"It's only a frog," said Burdock, and he crouched, looking amused. "Nothing to fear, see?" He set down the lantern and put out his hand.

Apprehensive, but deeply curious, Syrah stepped into Burdock's palm.

The moment the Nexus touched him, the world vanished. He gasped as Burdock's thoughts overwhelmed him, vivid and real, different from any other mind he had encountered. He was trapped in a place that was filthy, low ceilinged and dim. It stank of human waste and decay. In his hands he held the bars of a cage, which he rattled, shouting hoarsely. His fingers bled. He had tried so many times to use his magic to destroy the cage or change it into something else, but every time he did so, it grew smaller. If he tried again, the bars might crush him. Bones and hair littered the floor around his feet. Sudden screams, raw and terrified, cut through the filth and darkness. The screams became shriller, crazed with terror, shredding what was left of his courage, making him scream in reply —

"Here," said Burdock mildly, setting Syrah at the edge of a very small pond near the house.

He sat in the mud, so distressed and disoriented that it took several long, shaking breaths before he was able to think. For a moment, in Burdock's palm, he had *been* Burdock. No — not Burdock. Hans Rantott. He had been Hans, a young boy, trapped in the nightmarish house of the Witch of the Woods, forced to listen to his own sister's murder.

But now, Hans Rantott was the murderer.

Syrah still had no proof. Maybe there was no proof. But his frog guts told him not to go into Burdock's house, no matter what. They had to get out of here.

"Come in," he heard Burdock say to Miss Floss. "Let's talk about the debate. About Clementine's little surprise attack."

"I'm going home."

"You're here. You might as well stay."

"Are you going to *make* me?" Miss Floss challenged.

"Fine, go, if that's what you want. Return tomorrow night."

"And if I don't?"

"You will."

Miss Floss turned and fled into the darkness. Burdock picked up his lantern again, and his light eyes shone eerily in the flickering orange light. He went into his house and shut the door.

Syrah hopped back to Harrow, who held out his hand. It was trembling, and his heart was beating so hard that Syrah could hear it.

Don't talk, he thought quickly. *Stay low and crawl as quietly as you can toward the woods. I'll ride on your back. If he hears anything and comes out, I'll bounce a lot and pretend it's me making noise again. Don't stand up until you're in the trees. Understand?*

Harrow nodded and began to crawl. His movements were nearly silent, but agonizingly slow. Syrah stayed on his back, anxiously watching Burdock's house grow smaller behind them until it was out of sight.

The moment Harrow had cover in the woods, he knelt up and took Syrah into his palm.

"We're going to the Copper Door," he said, and got to his feet.

We have to go to Luffa, Syrah replied. *You were right. He's insane. We need help.*

"I'm getting those cuffs off her wrists," said Harrow, walking so fast that he was practically jogging. His voice shook. "That poor woman. He's torturing her — we have to help her."

Didn't you hear me? I said you were right.

"No, *you* were right. We have proof now, just like you said."

Proof of what?

"That he victimizes people. Miss Floss must know something, or he wouldn't be doing this to her. We have to get those things off her and find out what it is."

What happened to this being the very last thing we did before going to Luffa?

"You heard him — Exalted Nexus Keene is at the Thatch. If I go there, he'll take me for questioning, and who knows how long he'll keep me? We have to do this now."

Harrow stowed Syrah on his shoulder and hurried toward town, moving at such a pace that Syrah thought they might even catch up with Miss Floss before they got to the Copper Door, but they did not run across her. At the center of town, the cobbled streets were full of moonlit mist that had rolled off the river. It was so late now that few people were out — Shepard's Alehouse was still open and noisy, but nearly all the other shops were closed.

Syrah flung himself into the fountain when they passed it, forcing Harrow to pick him back up.

Just hold on to me, all right? I can't talk to you up there.

"There's nothing to say."

Uh, yes there is. Her bracelets are magic. How do you plan to get them off?

This stymied Harrow for a moment, and Syrah heard his thoughts. *That's true. I don't know.*

See? Syrah shot back. *Let's go to the Thatch. Tell Luffa. Tell Exalted Nexus Keene, even. He can probably do something about it. We can't.*

"We're already here," said Harrow. "Plus which, Burdock told her not to let anybody take them off. Why would he bother to do that, if they can't be removed?"

He also told her to run away and tell him if someone tried it.

"I'll unlock them fast, and then she won't have to run."

I didn't see a clasp. They're solid metal.

"Then I'll cut them off her," said Harrow grimly, and he headed for the Copper Door.

The shop was closed and locked, and dark within. Inside the window glass, written prettily in piped frosting, were the words *PROGRESS IS SWEET! VOTE FOR BURDOCK!*

Harrow knocked, but no one came. A sign in the window directed deliveries to go around the back, so he went to the end of the row of shops and into a narrow alley, where he picked his way around barrels and over empty crates until he came to a door with a fancy *CD* painted on it. He pulled the delivery bell.

They soon heard movement inside, and then a voice. "Leave deliveries on the step."

"Miss Floss, it's Harrow Steelcut. Please let me in."

For a moment, the only reply was absolute silence. Then G. G. Floss opened the door. She looked ill and troubled, and not at all her usual stylish self. Her clothes were untucked, her sandy hair was in a loose, uneven tail, and she wore no shoes. She put her head out and looked both ways down the alley. No one else was there. She frowned and let Harrow in, then shut the door and locked it.

"I was getting ready for bed," she said. "I'm sorry to be so . . ." She glanced down at herself. "Barefoot," she finished, and chuckled.

"This isn't usually how I welcome guests. But guests don't usually show up at midnight, so you get what you get." She paused and checked Syrah. "Everyone loves frogs lately," she muttered, and then, "Why are you here?"

"It's about Burdock."

Syrah hopped twice. *No it isn't, remember? Don't tell her why you're here or she'll run.*

But Miss Floss had no idea what Harrow really meant. "I see," she said heavily. "The debate, and the way those people attacked you. It was dreadful, but it wasn't Burdock's fault —"

"No, I know. I just . . . do you have a pair of shears?"

Syrah groaned inwardly. Harrow was the worst.

"Shears?" Miss Floss raised an eyebrow. "Why?"

Harrow shifted. He scratched his head and set his hand on Syrah as though to pet him, and Syrah thought fast.

There's a tear in your boot and it's giving you a blister. You need to cut it off.

"There's a rip inside my boot," said Harrow. "A piece of leather came loose and it's giving me a blister. I just want to cut it off before I walk home."

"Oh." Miss Floss shrugged. "Sure, I have something you can use. Come on." She opened a door beside her and descended a long flight of narrow steps into a big, clean, well-lit workspace. Shelves lined the walls on either side of the door, full of platters that were piled with finished candies. Several wooden worktops were stationed around the room, all covered with different tools for candy making. Syrah saw molds, spatulas, rolling pins, cutting boards, and tiny whittling knives. There were colored dyes in dozens of little phials, and sugars of every color in copper-topped shakers. Above one of the tables,

Miss Floss had proudly framed a small article titled *PLENTY'S YOUNGEST APPRENTICE.*

But it was the next table that really caught Syrah's attention. On it stood a giant gingerbread house, half Miss Floss's size, even more spectacular than the one she had shown them at the ATC. It was a child's dream — with a chocolate chimney sticking out of a cloudlike meringue roof, nougat brick walls, pink sugar windows, and vanilla biscuit doors with gumdrop knobs. As a boy, Syrah would have longed to stick his fingers in the frosted front porch or snatch a shiny lollipop from the garden fence. Around the fence ran a stream that looked exactly like cool, flowing water. Beside this tempting house of sweets sat a smaller and much bleaker structure — a hovel made of black licorice and burned pastry. Outside it, a marzipan boy in ragged fondant clothing lay limp on the worktop.

"That house is amazing," said Harrow. "Curtains in the windows and everything. What are they even made of?"

"Very thin fruit leather," said Miss Floss. "It's all for the campaign. I'm going to do some storytelling tomorrow in the town square. You should come."

"Storytelling?"

"Clementine Pease wants people to think that Burdock is hiding his past, but that's not true. He has nothing to hide. He's a hero, in fact, and I'm going to make sure that everyone knows it." She went to one of the worktops and opened a drawer.

Maybe that was why Burdock was making her do things, Syrah thought. He wanted her to campaign for him. It made sense — G. G. Floss was influential. Lots of people would listen to her.

"It's warm down here," said Harrow, and Syrah agreed. He felt tacky and thirsty, and it was easy to see why. At the back of the room, shining like it had just been polished, stood a great copper oven, with an elegant CD etched into its copper door.

"How do you keep the candy from melting?"

"Magic," said Miss Floss, holding up a hand and wiggling her purple fingertips. Her copper cuff gleamed. "I can make candy do pretty much anything. Now, where did I put . . . Ah." She plucked a pair of kitchen shears from among other tools, and handed them to Harrow. "Those ought to work," she said.

"They, uh — they will. I think they will." He took a deep breath, and Syrah cringed, waiting to see what he would do. For a long moment, the answer was nothing. Harrow reached up to pet Syrah again, and Miss Floss watched him, frowning.

"Don't you need to fix your boot?" she asked.

I'll distract her, Syrah thought. *I'll mess with her stuff. When she tries to stop me, you take advantage and use the shears. Make it quick.*

"Okay," Harrow muttered. He moved closer to one of the work-tables and sat on a stool. He reached down as though to remove his boot, and Syrah leapt onto the table and headed for the sugar shakers. He banged into one, upsetting it. Yellow sugar scattered onto the worktop.

"Stop!" said Miss Floss. She reached for Syrah, then withdrew. "Ugh — I don't want to touch him. Harrow, would you please get your frog?"

"Yep." Harrow stood beside her, holding the shears open in his hand. Instead of reaching for Syrah he took Miss Floss by her finger-tips and pulled her wrist up in front of him. With a quick, sure movement, he slid the shears between the bracelet and her skin. He closed them hard, and they sliced through the metal. The first copper cuff fell to the floor.

Miss Floss's face went slack. "No," she said, in the flat, wooden voice she had used with Burdock earlier. She stared emptily down at the shining pink burn scars on her naked wrist. "No. Stop. Leave them as they are."

"I know you have to say that," said Harrow. "I know what he's doing to you. I'm here to help." He reached for her other hand, but her wrist, still shackled, swung away from him, forcing her to pivot and pulling her toward the stairs like a leash. She began to run just as Burdock had told her to, dragged by the cuff she still wore, until she grabbed the stair railing with her freed hand and held on tight.

"Stop," she said. "Leave them as they are." But she was crying. Her cuffed hand grabbed her free wrist and tried to rip it from the railing.

Harrow got behind her and reached around to grab her by the cuff. She made a sound of rage and fought him hard, yanking against his grip.

"Don't move," he shouted, holding up the shears. "Please, I don't want to cut you —"

Miss Floss grabbed her cuffed hand with her free one and tried to hold it against the wall to make it still. As she fought herself, she screamed the words again. "No — Stop — Leave them as they are —"

Now, Syrah thought frantically, wishing he could do anything to help Harrow finish it. *Cut it off now — you have to —*

Harrow pressed Miss Floss against the stairwell wall and pinned her forearm with his own, which was far stronger. With his other hand, he slid the shears into place and snapped them shut.

The second copper shackle dropped.

Miss Floss stumbled down the steps and sank onto the workroom floor, trembling. Tears stained her face. She stared in mingled horror and amazement at her burned, bare wrists.

Harrow knelt beside her, distraught. "I'm sorry," he said. "I'm so sorry, I wasn't trying to hurt you. Are you all right? Are you free?"

She nodded. "I'm free," she whispered. She turned to Harrow, and a smile broke across her face like the rising sun. "I'm *free*," she repeated, and she threw her arms around him. "Oh thank you," she said passionately. "Thank you."

Harrow returned her hug, though awkwardly. "It's all right," he said. "He can't hurt you."

Miss Floss laughed breathlessly and let him go. She sat back. "How did you *know?*" she said. "I thought nobody would know — nobody else ever realized."

"Somebody poisoned the governor," Harrow answered. "I thought it might be the Nexus. I was out there by his house tonight, and I saw him jerking you around like some kind of puppet."

"You were there," Miss Floss repeated, looking around until she found Syrah. "The frog," she said. "Of course — we thought that noise was the frog, but it was you, wasn't it?"

"Yes. I followed you here to help you if I could. I thought you might know for sure what the Nexus has done. I figured maybe that was why he put those things on your wrists."

Miss Floss got to her feet, nodding. "I do know what he's done," she said. "Oh, there's so much I can tell you about him. I knew him, you see. When he was Hans Rantott. I lived in the Arrowroot Forest, and I know everything — *everything*."

"Exalted Nexus Keene is at the Thatch," said Harrow. "I'll go there with you. We'll tell him what we know, and he can help us."

"Yes, I'm sure he can." Miss Floss went to the giant candy house and gently touched its chocolate chimney. "You freed me," she said. "I have to do something for you."

"No, don't worry about —"

"Please." She looked back over her shoulder at him. "Let me tell you what happened. I want to tell you now, before we go. Will you let me do that?"

Syrah hopped closer to them, eager to know what she had to say. He had gone to serious lengths to find out whether Burdock had poisoned Calabaza, and now he would finally get the answers.

"Of course," said Harrow. "Tell me."

She took a black apron from a hook on the wall, looped it over her head, and tied it shut. An embroidered copper oven glinted at its top. She took a handkerchief from her apron pocket and wiped her eyes, then smoothed back her sandy hair and retied it neatly in a tail. "I'm also going to make you the best cup of chocolate you ever had in your life," she said, squeezing Harrow's shoulder. "I'll just get the cream." She vanished down a corridor that branched from the room.

Harrow dropped into a chair by the oven, looking beat. He put out his hand for Syrah, who hopped into it. "We did it," he said. "I can't believe it."

Yeah . . .

But something was bothering Syrah. He couldn't quite say what, but he trusted the instinct. It was the same way he had felt about Calabaza's basket and the book of edible plants — that somewhere, he had missed an important detail. Something that mattered.

Harrow looked around the room. "Like what?" he said.

Syrah wasn't sure. He hopped down from Harrow's hand onto the floor, and as he swept his bulging eyes around the cellar, he had the feeling again. There was a clue in this room. Something out of place, perhaps. He eyed the severed copper cuffs on the floor. No, it wasn't those. . . . His gaze trailed along the giant gingerbread house and over the candy-making awards, then drifted to the framed article on the wall. *PLENTY'S YOUNGEST APPRENTICE*. That headline was familiar.

Miss Floss returned, carrying a tray laden with two jugs, a bowl of large chocolate pieces, a copper cup, and a copper shaker. She set down the tray and took a double boiler down from a hook on the wall.

"I have six awards just for hot chocolate," she said. "I don't even sell it in the shop — it's something I only make on very special occasions."

"I'm honored," said Harrow.

She filled the bottom pan with water from one of the jugs, broke chunks of heavy dark chocolate into the top, and set the whole thing on the copper oven's hearth. "What's happening with your father?" she asked, taking up a wooden spoon to stir the chocolate. "Does he know you came here to help me?"

"No. The Exalted Council arrested him." Harrow looked uncomfortable. "Honestly, they probably wanted to arrest me too, but they didn't find me. I'll have to turn myself in when we go back to the Thatch."

She stirred the cream into the double boiler; the smell of thick, dark chocolate wafted through the room. "Now, you said that Nexus Burdock poisoned the governor. Or at least that's what you think happened. Who else thinks so?"

Harrow opened his mouth and Syrah hopped twice. "Nobody," he said. "Did he do it? Did you see him? Is that why he put the cuffs on you?"

Miss Floss poured some of the cream off into a mixing bowl and took up a whisk. She began to beat the cream, light and fast, until she'd created peaks. "He didn't poison the governor," she said, and

Syrah looked up at her in surprise. "But that's not the whole story. The *real* story starts thirty years ago." She stirred sugar into the chocolate, slow and methodical in her movements. "Hans had no childhood," she said. "Nor did I. But we both made something of ourselves in spite of it. He was Exalted, of course, which helped. I apprenticed myself to a baker as a girl, and from there I went to a confectioner."

All at once, Syrah knew exactly where he'd seen that article. It was from one of the *Criers* they'd gotten from Clementine's house, he was sure of it. He leapt from Harrow's shoulder and bounced his way across the basement, onto the worktable closest to where the article hung, so that he could read the details.

It was the story of a little orphan girl who had emerged from the woods just a few days before the article had been published. She had been filthy and malnourished, and would give no name, but sought shelter with a local baker in exchange for work. A few days were all it had taken for the baker to realize that the girl was an artist in the kitchen, gifted beyond her years. A genius with a magic touch. In spite of her youth, he had offered her an apprenticeship.

Syrah's mind raced. If this article was about G. G. Floss, it meant that she had come out of the woods at almost the same time as Hans Rantott. Which meant that she had appeared in Plenty just after the death of the Witch of the Woods. And the deaths of Grausam Steppe, Ava Cass, and Holly Seaberry.

"While I was apprenticing," said G. G., "Hansel went north to train with the Exalted Council. But we never lost touch. We sent letters every week."

"Hansel?"

"My pet name for him. We were always very close, you see."

"Then why did he hurt you?"

"He thinks he knows best," said Miss Floss. "But my way is better."

She took the copper cup from the tray, poured liquid chocolate into it, and topped it off with whipped cream. She lifted the copper-topped shaker and tapped a generous shower of cinnamon onto the cream. A tendril of silver steam rose from the cup.

"For you." Miss Floss offered the cup to Harrow. "For everything you've done."

Syrah let out a long, slow croak.

Silver curl of steam. Slumbercap mushroom. A small amount would make it hard to breathe — a few swallows would paralyze Harrow's lungs —

"RAWWWWP!" cried Syrah, in terror. *Don't drink it, don't drink it —*

He leapt down from the worktable and bounced toward Harrow as fast as he could. He had to get to his hand — had to touch his skin and tell him.

"RAWWWWP!"

If only he could be a man again for one moment — if only he could say two words, then he could stop this, but there wasn't time. Harrow was already lifting the cup. Syrah's mind raced as he bounced nearer. Maybe he could knock the cup out of Harrow's hand — but if he did that, the liquid would slosh all over him. The slumbercap would kill him —

Harrow put the chocolate to his lips.

Syrah leapt to his knee, flinched for one moment, and then sprang as hard as he could toward the cup of poisoned chocolate, stretching out his front legs to bat it away from Harrow's mouth. He splatted against the boiling hot copper, scalding his belly, his chin, the undersides of his legs. He let out a ribbiting scream of agony.

"Hey!" shouted Harrow as he lost his grip. The cup went sideways. Hot liquid went everywhere. Syrah tumbled into a puddle of spilled chocolate, striking his head so hard that the room spun. For a moment he could not move. He sat there in the mess, dizzy, burning, terrified. Slumbercap seeped through his skin. His lungs would not expand. Panicked, he sucked for air as hard as he could, but it was like trying to breathe through wet cloth.

He struggled to move and barely managed to wriggle out of the puddle. His burned body flamed with pain. He regurgitated on reflex, vomiting up his entire stomach. It hurtled out of his mouth and hung there, inside out. He wiped it with his front legs to wash away the poison, though he knew it was no use; he hadn't eaten the slumbercap. He had absorbed it.

He swallowed his stomach, stumbled sideways, and grew still. Everything was getting dark. He felt Harrow's hands on him. Felt the fear in him.

"Your pet sure likes to knock things over, doesn't he?" he heard Miss Floss say. She laughed, but the sound was short. Uncomfortable. "I'll get you another cup."

"Hey," said Harrow urgently. His voice sounded far away. He shook Syrah a little. "You okay?"

Get out of here, Syrah thought, staring glassily up at him. *Get out, you've got to get out.* . . . He was sleepy. Terribly sleepy. He couldn't breathe, but at least he could not feel his burned skin anymore. And at least he had tried. Tried to do the right thing. Maybe Nana Cava had seen him from the Beyond. Maybe she was proud.

He could ask her soon. His eyes fell shut.

Then, just when he thought things could no worse, Syrah exploded.

CHAPTER NINETEEN

*T*HE explosion was brief — the length of a few seconds — but they were the longest seconds of his life. Every inch of his body was stretching, tearing — his eyes, his guts, his muscles screamed — and then the misery was over. He was on his belly on the floor, and now his body felt all wrong, huge and disjointed. His stomach was very far away. His back feet were on the other side of the room. His vision had narrowed; he could not roll his eyes to see what was behind him. He was enormous, bulky, heavy, and his skin was wet and burning all at once. But he could breathe in long, hard gasps if he tried hard enough. He sucked for air.

Miss Floss was screaming.

"He's with me!" he heard Harrow shout. "It's all right! It's Prince Syrah of the Olive Isles — he got turned into a frog, but now he's back. Get a Hipocrath, quick — and a blanket, get a blanket!"

Syrah heard Miss Floss run up the stairs. He tried to croak. He heard a groan.

A human groan.

"You're all right now," Harrow was saying to him. "I've got you." Syrah felt hands on his arms.

On his *arms*.

Tears sprang into his eyes. His upper arms were still on fire from where they'd struck the burning cup, but he didn't care. Harrow gripped him and hoisted him off the floor, pulling him up until Syrah was on his knees.

His knees. He looked down at them, and there they were. Knees. Human ones. He held up his hands, and when he saw his own fingers, a sob of joy tore from his throat.

"Here, take this." Harrow grabbed a long piece of yellow cloth from a basket under one of the worktables. It was a *VOTE BURDOCK* banner. He wrapped it around Syrah like a sarong and tucked it shut. "Can you walk?" he asked, crouching before him and offering his hands. Syrah grabbed on to them and used them to balance as he pulled himself to his feet. Tears of amazement coursed down his face. He was standing. He was human. Could he walk? He took a tentative step, still holding on to Harrow, and though he felt wobbly and off balance, he was able to put one foot in front of the other. He gave a victorious shout but barely made a sound. He sucked another long, thin breath.

He pulled his hands from Harrow's and stumbled to the tray. He picked up the shaker. "Slumbercap," he rasped. It was the first word he had spoken in nearly sixteen months.

Harrow gaped at him.

"Absorbed," Syrah managed, touching his stomach. "Through my skin."

"Can you breathe?"

Syrah sucked for air in a long, thin gasp, and held up two fingers, just barely apart.

"You knocked that cup out of my hand on purpose," said Harrow. His dark, sober eyes met Syrah's. "You saved my life."

Syrah pushed the shaker into Harrow's hand. "Evidence,"

he rasped, and Harrow shoved the shaker down into one of his pockets.

Footsteps thudded overhead.

"She doesn't know we know," Syrah whispered, and he dragged for another breath. "Let's get out of here — act normal."

Harrow looked anxiously at the stairs. "Right," he said.

They heard the door creak open at the top of the steps, followed by the jingling sounds of keys. A moment later, Miss Floss appeared, carrying a blanket in one hand and a pitcher in the other. A used rag stuck out of her apron pocket, and she wore gloves, which she had not before. She eyed Syrah suspiciously, but approached nonetheless and offered the blanket to him.

"Your Highness," she said.

Syrah was not about to touch anything that G. G. Floss gave him. Especially since she was wearing gloves — she was probably trying to protect herself from something she had done to poison the blanket in her hand. He hitched up the Burdock banner he wore. "All set," he wheezed. "Fits great."

She narrowed her light eyes. The corners of her mouth turned down.

"Uh — we've — got to go," said Harrow nervously, taking Syrah by the elbow. "Excuse us, but Prince Syrah needs to see the Physic."

"Of course," said Miss Floss. "It must feel very strange to be human again." She turned away from them and went about cleaning up the spilled chocolate.

Harrow headed up the stairs, and Syrah followed unsteadily. His balance was completely off; every time he set a foot on a higher step, he thought he would tip over backward. He finally leaned forward, put both hands on the steps, and crawled his way up. It was far easier.

"This is locked," said Harrow, when he tried the door. "And greasy," he added. He wiped his hand on his trousers. "Miss Floss?" he called.

She did not answer.

"Uh, Miss Floss?" said Harrow, louder. "We're locked in here."

Syrah's gut tightened, and not because of any poison. She had locked the door deliberately. He turned around and sat on the steps to peer down into the room but didn't see her there at all. He used the banister to haul himself back up to his feet. Breathing thinly, he made his way back to the bottom of the steps, with Harrow behind him.

"Where'd she go?" Harrow whispered.

Syrah pointed to the corridor where she had gone before to get the cream. A door marked *Storage* stood open.

Harrow strode toward it, but Syrah stayed where he was, weakened by the efforts he had made already. He leaned on a worktable, struggling to breathe. He just wanted one good breath. If he could inhale deeply, he knew he would feel truly restored. But every breath felt like he was drawing air through a straw that was pinched half-shut. His head pounded.

Just as he reached the corridor, Harrow tripped and stumbled a little. He stopped. Shook himself. "Whoa," he said. "That was awful strange."

"What?" Syrah managed.

"It felt like . . ." Harrow rubbed his chest. "Miss Floss?" he called. "Where are you?"

She emerged from the storage room, wiping her hands on her apron. Her gloves were gone, as was the used rag that had been in her pocket. "You're still here," she said, smiling. "I thought you were going."

"We're locked in."

"Yes, I guess you are." She moved a chair, dragging it until it faced the candy house. "Sit down, Harrow."

Harrow obeyed without protest, and Syrah tensed. Harrow was a bad liar, but he wasn't stupid — he wouldn't follow Miss Floss's directions now unless he had to. She was controlling him somehow — but how? She hadn't even touched him. She hadn't fed him anything either. Was there some kind of poison in the air? No, because if there were, it would affect her too. . . .

Miss Floss moved another chair into place. "Who saw you come here, Harrow?"

"No one." His voice was heavy. Wooden.

"Who knows you came?"

"No one."

Syrah glanced up the steps at the locked door. The doorknob glistened. G. G. Floss had put something on it, and whatever it was, it had drugged Harrow into obeying her.

"Who knows that Prince Syrah is here?"

"Only us."

"Very good. Now you sit here, Your Highness," she said, and she patted the second chair.

Syrah dragged for air, then stumbled to the chair beside Harrow's. He dropped into it, fighting for breath, and stared hollowly at the candy house. He had to make her believe that he was as drugged as Harrow. If she touched him with that greasy stuff, then they were both done for.

"Now, Prince Syrah, tell me. How long were you a frog?"

Syrah sucked for air. "Fifteen months," he managed, making his voice heavy like Harrow's. "Two weeks . . . Two days . . ."

"Not that you're counting," said Miss Floss. She sounded amused. "How in Tyme did you get turned into a frog in the first place? That's *got* to be a good story."

"I made . . . a wish," Syrah choked out. "I wished that Deli Gourd . . . would get what she deserved."

Miss Floss laughed in genuine delight. "And your nasty little wish backfired. A fairy heard it, perhaps? Now that *is* a good story — it's such a shame I'll never be able to tell it, I could create scenes that would truly do it justice. Unfortunately, it's about to have a very bad ending, so the world will never know what really happened to the Lost Prince of Olive. Just as they never knew what happened to the Witch of the Woods."

"What . . . happened." Harrow's voice was so dulled that his question lacked inflection, but that didn't seem to bother Miss Floss.

"I can tell you — and I will. It doesn't matter if you know. And I've wanted to tell this story for *so* long."

They had to get out of here, Syrah thought frantically. But how? Harrow would obey whatever Miss Floss told him to do, and Harrow was larger and taller than he was; Syrah was much too weak to drag him away, especially if he fought. And Miss Floss would fight him too. He might be able to fend her off, but he was very weak and could barely breathe, and she was stronger than she looked — she had given Harrow plenty of trouble when he'd tried to cut that bracelet off. There were knives in the room, and a fire poker — she could hurt Syrah badly, if she wanted to. Maybe even kill him. It would help if he could tie her up. He moved his eyes around the parts of the room that he could see without turning, searching furtively for something he could use, but he saw nothing even close to rope or twine.

Miss Floss walked around behind the worktable and stood between the candy house and the wretched hovel. "Once, there was an Exalted boy who grew up in the Arrowroot Forest," she said, and she lifted her purple fingertips. The marzipan boy who lay limp on the table stood up and faced them. "His name was Hans, but everyone called him Hansel. His parents were poor, but they loved him and cared for him and his sister, Gretel." She walked her fingertips through the air, and a marzipan girl walked out from behind the candy house. Her candy-floss hair was the color of sand, just like the boy's. They stood together, holding hands. "Hansel and Gretel were eight and six years old when their parents died of fever and they were orphaned. They went to their only living relative, a distant cousin named Grausam Steppe, a woodcutter who lived all alone, deep in the woods. He was not kind."

The two children walked toward the burned pastry hovel, and its black licorice door opened. No one emerged, but the marzipan children trembled and covered their faceless faces.

"He beat them," said Miss Floss quietly. "He inflicted unthinkable pain. Hans tried to stop him, but he was very young, and his magic was not strong enough. As punishment, Cousin Grausam beat his small sister unconscious."

The marzipan girl fell to the worktop and went still. The boy knelt over her, his back shaking as though with sobs.

"Hans never tried to stop him again. Instead, he made a plan to shield his sister from the worst. He showed Gretel how to cook for Cousin Grausam so that he would like her better. For many months, as long as she filled his stomach, he took out his temper on Hansel instead. She didn't want him to, but Hansel insisted it was the only way. And then one day, Cousin Grausam went too far."

The little marzipan boy removed his shirt. His body was covered in burns and lacerations. Syrah remembered. He had seen those scars on Burdock's body at the Royal Governor's Inn and assumed they were from magical training.

"Cousin Grausam was drunk," said Miss Floss. "He went after Gretel with a knife. Hansel was afraid and tried to get between them, so Cousin decided to teach Hans a lesson. He tied him up and burned him with a poker and cut him with the knife until he was almost dead. His screams were so frightful that Gretel ran away."

The little marzipan girl fled and hid behind the hovel, then emerged carrying a tiny basket woven from thin brown pastry and filled with small gray candies.

"She could not save him," said Miss Floss. "So instead, she went to a place in the woods that she knew, and she gathered mushrooms. She kept them in a basket until Hansel was awake. Once she was sure he would live, and he could walk again, she made Cousin Grausam a special supper. It looked just like his favorite. Mushrooms in gravy. Hansel didn't know what she had done until Cousin Grausam stopped breathing and died, and then Hansel was angry. He was afraid that Gretel would be jailed. They ran from Cousin Grausam's house and searched for shelter. They looked for many days, and became lost. They found little food or water."

The marzipan children approached the candy house.

"And then they found a dream, standing in the woods," said Miss Floss. "A beautiful house made all of candy, with a stream of cold, sweet water running around it. They drank from the stream, and ate from the house, and cried with relief. They knocked at the door and were let inside."

The boy knocked at the vanilla biscuit door, and it opened. He went in and his sister followed, clutching his hand.

"Alas for those poor children," Miss Floss whispered. "It was then they learned they knew nothing of horror."

"The Witch . . . of the Woods . . ." said Harrow, and though his voice was usually low and slow, now it dragged like dead weight. "Hansel . . . killed her."

"Hansel has never killed anyone," said Miss Floss, her voice suddenly sharp and bitter.

"Was it . . . Gretel?" Syrah wheezed, sucking for air.

Miss Floss laughed. "Poor Prince Syrah," she said. "You swallowed a little slumbercap, didn't you? You sound like you're choking to death." She came toward him and crouched before him. "To think, the missing prince of Olive, right here in my shop. Everyone thinks you're dead, you know. That makes things much neater for me."

She went to her copper oven and opened its door. She stoked the flames.

"No one will look for you," she said. "They stopped looking ages ago. But I'll have to be careful about your friend here." She ruffled Harrow's curls, then returned to the hearth. "Your father will try to find your body, won't he? If he's free to do so, that is. He might just wind up in Exalted prison for the rest of his life, which would be ideal. If not, then you'd better hope he doesn't try too hard to figure out what happened. People who poke around in my business don't last long."

"Leave . . . my pa . . . alone." Harrow's voice sounded stronger.

"You were almost clever," said Miss Floss. "You knew about the bracelets, but you didn't know what they were for, did you? If you had, you wouldn't be in this fix — with those cuffs on, I couldn't have done a thing to harm you. Never mind, though. It all worked out." She added chocolate to the pan and poured off some of the cream into her mixing bowl. She took up her whisk.

"Ava Cass . . ." Syrah rasped, trying to affect the same drugged tone as Harrow. "Holly Seaberry . . . Did they . . . poke around in your business?"

"Now, how would you know about Ava and Holly?" asked Miss Floss, whipping the cream with quick, confident turns of her wrist. "You've been busy reading old *Criers*. Who showed you those stories?"

"Clementine Pease," Harrow answered.

"Another one who needs a good serving of mushrooms and gravy," said Miss Floss. Her eyes were dangerous. "And she'll get them."

"You're her," Syrah rasped. He drew a ragged breath. "Gretel. G. G. . . . You never died. You killed . . . your uncle. And those women."

"*Two* nearly clever boys," said Gretel, looking at Syrah with interest. "I always heard you were a selfish little half-brained witch, but there's no denying you're brighter than people said. Not nearly as handsome, though. Everybody said you were handsome. I guess they just meant rich."

Syrah prickled in spite of himself. He focused on breathing. In. Out. Just enough air to keep him going. He watched Gretel's movements, waiting. If he couldn't tie her up, then he was going to have to do something else with her. He could push her into the oven — but he wasn't sure he had the stomach for that. Push her into the storage room, maybe. Lock her up. She had the keys, though. He would have to wrestle them away.

She poured cream into the pan, and sugar. She stirred for a

minute. "It's a little lumpy," she said apologetically. "This batch wouldn't win any awards. But there's no time to get it right." She poured hot chocolate into two cups, and Syrah tensed. He had an idea.

"Drink these," she said. "When you're dead, I'll just pop you both into the oven so there's no trace that you were ever here. That's how I killed the witch, you know. I was so young and so afraid, but I still tricked her into drinking the chocolate. She fought, once she realized she was suffocating. Fought like a donkey. Kicked me so hard she knocked out three of my milk teeth. And then, when I was still trying to push her through the oven door, the White came to get her and take her away."

She spooned whipped cream into the cups, and the copper oven on her apron glittered in the firelight. Copper Door, Syrah realized, his stomach turning. She had named her candy shop after those brutal events. She was totally unhinged.

"The White . . . can't come to Tyme," said Harrow.

"Not the Great White Fairy," Gretel agreed. "But a big shiny White light. It went right through my back, snatched the witch, and lifted her away. She was just a hunk of charcoal on top, with two hairy old legs sticking off. And then all the gingerbread children turned back into real children and fell on the floor, dead. And then I set Hansel free, and — Wait. Where's my shaker?" She set her hands on her hips and looked around for the slumbercap that Harrow had already tucked into his pocket. "I thought I left it right here."

She turned her back to search the nearest table, and Syrah moved as fast as his weakened state would allow. He stood, grabbed both cups of chocolate from the hearth, and when Gretel turned toward him again, he flung the scalding liquid right into her face. She screamed and clutched her eyes as Syrah grabbed for the pockets of her apron, trying to find the keys. Gretel kicked him with surprising force, and he stumbled back and fell to his knees. Gretel continued to moan, one hand over her face, but now her other hand was groping along the front of the hearth. When she found the poker, she gripped it like a sword. She swung it wildly, and nearly struck Harrow. She swung again.

"Harrow, duck!" Syrah gasped, and Harrow did as he was told, leaning forward just in time to avoid being smashed in the head.

"Harrow," Gretel cried. "Help me!"

Harrow rose from his chair. He lurched toward Syrah, raised his boot, and shoved it against Syrah's shoulder, knocking him to the floor.

"Harrow," Syrah managed in a rasp, "help *me!*"

Harrow obeyed. As Syrah struggled to kneel, Harrow swept Gretel's ankles with his foot, knocking her legs out from under her. She dropped to her knees hard, shouted in pain, and swung the poker. Syrah tried to jump out of the way, forgetting that he was no longer a frog and couldn't jump anywhere. The poker collided with his temple, and he fell sideways onto the floor, stunned. Gretel uncovered her eyes, which were red and squinting. She struck at him again, but this time she missed. The poker slammed against the wooden floor near Syrah's hand, and he grabbed the end of it in his fist. Gretel kept a tight hold, but he fought her for it.

"Harrow, get the pan!" she screeched. "Burn him!"

Panicked, Syrah finally wrenched the poker from Gretel's grip just as Harrow brought the hot copper boiler down on his foot. Syrah did not have enough air to scream. Momentarily blind with pain, he kicked against the agony, knocking the pan out of Harrow's hand. It flew at Gretel and struck her in the back of the neck before clattering to the floor. She made a noise of rage and picked up the pot by its handle.

"Harrow," Syrah managed, his voice barely audible. "Stop."

Harrow returned to his chair. Gretel launched herself at Syrah, armed with hot copper.

Syrah rolled onto his back, holding the poker like a lance, its sharp point angled toward Gretel, who had already flung her whole weight forward. She could not stop in time. She fell onto the poker, impaled on its point. Her eyes popped wide. Her mouth stretched in a scream, but she made no sound. She released the copper pan, which fell to the floor with a clang.

Syrah let go of the poker. Gretel thudded to the floor beside him, staring at him, her breath coming in shallow gasps.

"NO!" cried a familiar voice.

A wall of shining light appeared instantly between Syrah and Gretel.

"Hansel," Gretel whispered. Her eyes filled with tears.

Syrah pushed himself to his knees but could not stand; the bright light was a cage, and it held him where he was. He looked up to find Burdock standing over them both, stricken. The Nexus dropped to the ground beside his sister and touched the place between her ribs where the poker had gone through. Light played from his fingers, and she took a sudden, deep breath. The color came back to her face. Burdock pulled the poker free from the wound, and no blood seeped from it. Still, she did not move.

"What happened? Why did he do this?" Burdock took one of her hands and lifted it. "Where are your bracelets?" he whispered. "I came back to make sure you wouldn't really burn them off again —"

"Harrow cut them off," she choked, gazing up at him. "He knew things. He thought you poisoned Calabaza. I couldn't let him go."

Burdock's face crumpled. "No," he said, his voice breaking. "Not again."

"I told him not to cut them off," she cried. "I tried to run. It's not my fault."

"What did you do to Harrow?"

"I tried to give him slumbercap, but his frog stopped me."

"His . . ." Burdock's eyes moved to Syrah. "Your Highness," he breathed. "Syrah. Is it you?"

"Yeah," said Syrah, rubbing his chest and drawing a thin breath. "Hi."

"You're *here*?" Burdock let out a sound that was half laugh, half cry. He looked down at his sister. "Did you trap him? Keep him here all this time? But why?"

"It wasn't her," wheezed Syrah. "I was — a frog. Nobody knew."

"A frog," said Burdock, and understanding dawned in his eyes. "A *frog*. It was you out there tonight. It was you in my room at the ATC. It was you on Walter's shoulder — you've been everywhere. Seen everything."

"It doesn't matter," said Gretel, gazing up at her brother. "He can die. Everybody already thinks he's dead."

Burdock bent his head and made a low, keening sound.

"She drugged Harrow," Syrah managed. "Some kind of grease. He can't resist her."

Harrow moaned and closed his eyes. He looked like he was in pain.

"Is it killing him?" Syrah demanded.

"Servoil," Burdock murmured. "No, but if he touched it, he's extremely nauseated and he'll pass out soon. Gretel, where did you get it?"

"I stole it from your magic things," she said. "I was going to use it on you. To make you take the shackles off."

"They *protect* you."

"I know. I can't help it." Tears slipped from her eyes and ran down her temples. "I'm so tired," she said. "It's your turn now. You owe me. You made me kill the witch all by myself."

"No!" Burdock cried. "I tried, you *know* I tried, but I was a boy, I had no practice —"

"You could have killed Cousin Grausam."

Burdock pressed his mouth shut, gray-faced.

"You made *me* do it."

"I never made you —"

"You said you would protect me if anyone ever found out. You promised."

Burdock met her gaze.

"Kill them," Gretel urged, her voice growing fainter. "You have to. Put them in the oven so there's no trace." She breathed in and out. "You promised," she said, and then her head lolled to the side. Her eyes closed and her mouth went slack.

Burdock felt his sister's neck. "She's still alive," he murmured.

"Her tent at the ATC," Syrah said, and gasped for more air. "It was behind the carriage house. *She* poisoned Calabaza."

Burdock looked at him, pleading. "You have to understand," he said. "My sister is cursed. Witch magic — White magic — poisoned her when she was eight years old. It flooded her heart after she killed the Witch of the Woods. It twisted her. When she feels threatened, or believes I'm threatened, she can't stop herself. I gave her those bracelets to stop her hands. I did everything I could."

"You should have told someone."

Burdock laughed miserably. "Put my little sister in prison? After she saved my life twice?"

"She murdered your cousin."

"He deserved worse," said Burdock roughly. "You cannot imagine. Our parents loved us. When they died and our uncle took us as his wards — you cannot imagine."

Syrah was sure that he could not.

"He was a monster," said Burdock. "He had no human heart. Gretel was so small, and I did everything I could, but I was a child too, and I failed her. I have always failed her. I couldn't imprison her for what was not her fault."

"Ava Cass. Holly Seaberry."

Burdock made a noise of pain. "I know," he whispered. "I didn't realize what she was, what the White had done to her. We sought shelter with those women after we escaped the witch, and then Gretel thought they had to die. She was afraid they would find Cousin Grausam's body and know that one of us had killed him. After that, I sent her into town alone, with a new name. We had found money in the witch's house. Loads of it. I buried most of it where she could find it as she needed to, and I declared Gretel Rantott dead. Then I went north to Lilac, to the Exalted. As soon as I had enough training, I made the first bracelets."

"She got out of them. She poisoned the governor."

"Calabaza brought this on himself!" Burdock spat. "Every time he turned away from facing witches, every time he left his people unprotected in order to save himself — and his mother was no better! The great Luffa Gourd never vanquished the Witch of the Woods — a little child had to do it! My sister had to do it! And what did she get as thanks? White magic, burned through her heart! If only I could root it out of her — if only I could turn her back — I've tried so many times —"

Burdock put his hands over his face. Gretel lay before him, breathing shallowly.

"It's time to turn her in," said Syrah. "You have to."

Burdock lifted his head. His eyes were red with tears. "No I don't," he said, gesturing to the magic light that still encased Syrah. "Nobody knows you're alive."

Harrow moaned again, doubled over his knees, and dry-heaved.

"Harrow knows."

"Then I'll kill you both," said Burdock. "I'll tell everyone that you were never missing at all. You were hiding all year, on purpose, to take revenge on Harrow because Delicata Gourd hurt your feelings. Your ego couldn't bear the humiliation, the rejection — you went mad from it, and you spent a year plotting to kill him. When I found you, I tried to stop you, but it was too late — and then you attacked me. I tried not to kill you, but you were vicious. You left me no choice."

Syrah stared at him. He sucked a breath. "No one would believe that!"

Burdock gave a rough laugh. "You were never very self-aware. People don't think much of you, Your Highness. They'd believe me. It would be easy."

Syrah tried to push against the magic bars that held him, but it was hopeless. He could not move. "Don't," he begged. "You're not a murderer. You take care of your sister — you help Yellow Country — that's who you are."

"An appeal to my sense of ethics," said Burdock, nodding. "Not a bad strategy. But you forget: I've been lying for thirty years. This would just be one more lie — and I would have the comfort of knowing that, for once, I had protected Gretel instead of the other way around. My conscience would barely feel it."

"I want to see my family."

"I don't care what you want," said Burdock. "I'm sorry for your parents, but the truth is they've gotten over the worst of their grief already. It's not as though you were a favorite."

Syrah drew a ragged, painful breath. "Fine, I'm worthless," he said, "but Harrow isn't. He should live."

"He's a decent young man," Burdock agreed. "But if you're asking me to choose between his life and my sister's . . ."

"Nobody has to die."

Magic light flickered around Burdock's fingers. "I wish that were true."

"Maybe it is. You don't know, because you've never tried to save her."

Burdock fixed Syrah with a deadly look. "You know nothing," he said.

"You haven't told Keene about her," said Syrah, as quickly as his breath would let him. "You haven't asked the Council for help. For all you know, they *can* save Gretel, but you're too much of a coward to find out."

Burdock flinched. A hit. Syrah kept talking, though his lungs burned and his head grew light. It pounded from the lack of air.

"She always has to do the hard things," he said, blinking hard to stay conscious. "She freed you from your cousin. She freed you from the witch." He gasped and pushed on. "Now you're the Nexus of Yellow, and you're running for governor — and she's in shackles, suffering. Is that how you want her to live her whole life?"

"No." It was a whisper.

"Then *tell* someone."

"But if they can't help her —"

"You'll know you tried. And no one else will get hurt."

Burdock shook his head. The light that weaved in patterns around his fingers intensified.

"If you're going to kill me," Syrah said, his voice ragged, "just tell me first. Is my sister alive?"

Burdock stared at him. "Your sister."

"Marsala. I saw her at the ATC. She had the Purge and I don't . . . I don't know if . . ."

Please don't let her be dead.

"Keene developed a cure," said Burdock faintly. "Marsala made a full recovery."

Tears sprang into Syrah's eyes. "Good. That's — really good. Thank you."

All the energy went out of Burdock's face. His hands dropped to his sides, and the light around his fingers flickered out. The magic cage that held Syrah vanished. The moment he was free, he tried to push himself to stand. He had to get out of here before Burdock changed his mind.

"Forgive me," said Burdock softly, but he wasn't talking to Syrah. He picked up his sister's hand and held it. "It's for you. I love you."

Syrah staggered toward Harrow, who was still doubled over, clutching his stomach. Syrah took him by the elbows and helped him stand. Neither of them had much strength, but they leaned on each other and hobbled slowly toward the stairs.

"I'll wait here," said Burdock quietly behind them.

Syrah didn't answer. He needed all his breath and energy to hoist himself up the narrow steps. He just wanted to get out.

Shoulder to shoulder with Harrow, he stumbled through the front entrance of the Copper Door and limped slowly into the dark town square. At once, people on horseback caught sight of them and drew near. They surrounded Syrah and Harrow, holding up torches. One woman dismounted, wearing Exalted vestments. Her amulet rested heavily against the front of her cloak.

"I am Exalted Aravinda," she announced. Her vibrant voice rang out in the quiet square, and her eyes shone like a cat's. "By description, this must be Harrow Steelcut. Did you think you could run from the Exalted Council, Harrow?"

Harrow didn't answer, but moaned again and doubled over. He vomited on Syrah's bare feet.

Syrah barely cared. He had been through far worse. "Slumbercap," he said, pointing to himself, and then he gestured to Harrow and sucked a breath. "Servoil."

Exalted Aravinda raised a black eyebrow. "Servoil is forbidden," she said. "How did he get it?"

"Burdock," Syrah managed. "Cellar of the Copper Door. With his sister. She's a murderer. And she poisoned the governor." He inhaled deeply. "You're welcome."

Aravinda's eyes glittered as they swept over Syrah, still dressed in nothing but a banner. "And *you* are?"

"Prince Syrah of the Olive Isles," he rasped, attempting to bow with a flourish just as Harrow passed out cold. His full weight slumped against Syrah, who didn't have the strength to hold him up. He fell to his knees, taking Harrow down with him. "Please take us to a Hipocrath."

Chapter Twenty

*T*HREE days. He had been a man again for three days, and every moment he was grateful. He would never stop being grateful.

The Exalted Council separated him from Harrow. They took Syrah immediately into their care and made him more comfortable than he could remember being in a long, long time. He stayed in a luxurious tent, where he slept in a bed and had pillows again. Magical professionals tended to his every need; Kisscrafter healers soothed his burns and stitched his wounds, while a Hipocrath coaxed the slumbercap out of his system. He ate and drank like a prince again. Everything was perfect, except that he was isolated from outside contact and did not know when he would be allowed to see anyone. The only people allowed to visit were members of the Council and professors from the University of Orange who wanted to study the effects of the strange magic that had imprisoned him in the body of a frog for so long. They poked and prodded and bandaged and salved him, leaving not an inch uninvestigated. They found scars from all the times he'd torn his thin skin, puncture wounds from the places he'd been bitten and clawed at, bruises and small fractures from having slammed against things and having things slammed against him. Every time they found something new, he was invited to tell the story of how it had happened, and they listened to him avidly, asking questions, taking notes, and always congratulating him on his wits and courage.

It was strange getting so much attention from so many important adults. They seemed to think he was special. He didn't quite know what to do with it.

The only thing he didn't tell them about his life as a frog was that he had been able to hear people's thoughts through his belly. It didn't seem right for anybody else to know that. Those moments had been private. He had given away somebody's secrets once; he wasn't making that mistake again.

On the third morning, he asked for a pen and paper. He knew what he had to write, but it was harder than he had expected. Setting things down in words made the truth so obvious that he felt stupid and small for having taken so long to come around to it.

But he owed Deli a letter. A good one. And he wasn't leaving anything out, no matter how painful.

He had just signed his name when Exalted Aravinda arrived, sat beside his bed, and subjected him to the least pleasant experience of his three-day stay: an interrogation that went on for hours. She pressed him for every detail he knew about the juggetsbane poisoning, and she demanded information about the conversations he had overheard as a frog, trying to assess whether he was privy to any sensitive information that he should not have possessed. He was honest in his replies, but Aravinda was not satisfied.

"You were the one who brought the Steelcuts' relationship with Ubiquitous to the government's attention," she said. "How did you know about it?"

"I found a letter," said Syrah. "I told you."

"That letter has since been hidden or destroyed," said Aravinda, studying him closely with her light green cat's eyes. "As has all other correspondence between Huck Steelcut and Ubiquitous Productions. It should have been brought back here as evidence."

"I was a frog," said Syrah. "No thumbs, no pockets . . ."

Aravinda pursed her lips. "If you knew the stakes, you wouldn't be so flippant."

"Why, what's wrong?" asked Syrah, sitting forward. "Is it Ubiquitous?"

But this, Aravinda would not answer. She left the tent, and when the flap opened again, Syrah sat back against his pillows, amazed.

"Exalted Nexus Keene," he said. "I'm honored."

"Your Highness. The honor is mine." Keene sat in the chair where Aravinda had just been. He looked troubled. "I need to understand something," he said. "As a frog, you traveled quite some time with Rapunzel. Is that right?"

"Yes," said Syrah. "Thanks, by the way, for telling Rapunzel I was hibernating. If you hadn't, she might have buried me alive."

"Aha." Keene looked gratified. "That was you, of course it was. Now it makes sense."

"What does?"

"When I first held you, I thought I felt the touch of magic, but it faded quickly — almost as though it didn't want to be felt or found."

"The well didn't want anyone knowing who I was."

"Yes, so say the reports from my colleagues. A fascinating aspect of your journey — and a frustrating one, I have no doubt. But that's not what I'm here to discuss. When Rapunzel defeated Envearia, were you there?"

Syrah shook his head. It was on the tip of his tongue to tell Keene that Rapunzel hadn't defeated anybody — Rapunzel *hated* when people treated her like a witch slayer — but Keene continued before he could speak.

"A shame," he said. "Then perhaps you can help me understand Gretel Rantott instead."

Syrah grimaced at the sound of her name. "Sure," he said. "I'll try."

"As you know, she was touched by the White," said Keene. "But that's impossible — or should be, without making a witch's bargain." He pushed back his silvering hair. "The White should not be able to make physical contact with Tyme," he said. His gaze was urgent. Worried. There was even sweat on Keene's brow, and the sight of it made Syrah prickle with fear. How bad did something have to be to unnerve the most famously courageous and powerful mortal in Tyme? Was it related to what Aravinda had said about the stakes? What *were* the stakes? They couldn't be in danger from the Great White Fairy . . . could they?

"What can you tell me?" Keene pressed. "Did she explain?"

"Not really. Gretel said that when she was putting the witch in the oven, she got about halfway through when a white light came down. She said it went through her back and took the witch's body. That's all I know."

Keene nodded tensely. "That is consistent with Burdock's story," he said. "Which helps me somewhat."

"Can't you ask Gretel?"

"She remains unconscious," said Keene. "That fire poker went right into her heart. We are attempting to revive her so that we can try to help her heal from the White sickness, but it may not be in anyone's power to do either."

Into her heart. Syrah felt almost guilty for doing it. She had left him no choice, but still, the story of her life was such a terrible one that he mostly just felt sorry for her — which was easier now that she wasn't trying to kill him.

"I thank you," said Keene, standing. "And I commend your bravery."

"I didn't really have a choice."

"Survival is a ruthless and effective teacher," said Keene. "You discover your deepest strength when you have no choice. Be glad of it. There is nothing more powerful than knowing what you are capable of."

After Keene's visit, Syrah was declared fit enough to leave the Exalted Council's camp, though he was cautioned not to exercise strenuously for at least a week. He dressed in the clothes the Exalted had given him. They were tailored and handsome, fit for a prince, but they could have given him a grain sack with neck and armholes, and he would have been happy. He had his body back.

It was different, though, his body.

He checked the mirror they had left for him, and his stomach gave a funny squeeze, like it did every time he saw his new reflection. His hair was still long and wavy, and his skin was still as brown and tanned as it had been when he had last left Balthasar, but his lean, firm belly was gone, replaced by a round, frog-like gut, and the angles of his jawline were hidden by a froggy sort of double chin. He knew it shouldn't bother him. He ought to be free from petty vanity after everything he'd suffered. He guessed some flaws were harder to shake than others.

The Exalted had set up camp on the north side of the river, not far from Harrow's house. A carriage had him there in fifteen minutes, and he marveled at the ease and speed of it. To be able to climb into a carriage and say where he wanted to go — it was such luxury, but he had never once appreciated it. How had he never appreciated it?

When the front door of the farmhouse opened, Syrah was almost knocked off his feet by the force of Huck Steelcut's hug.

"You saved my boy," the man said hoarsely. He released Syrah, who stepped back, baffled and embarrassed. "Harrow told me what you did," Huck said, wiping his eyes. "I owe you my life."

Syrah had no idea what to say.

"He's upstairs with Delicata," Huck went on. "You go on and say hello."

Deli. Syrah felt for the letter in his pocket and he suddenly felt clammy.

"You're not arrested?" he asked Huck, stalling a bit.

"The cabinet acquitted me," said Huck. "Nexus Keene pushed for it. He said I'm not to blame for the Purge any more than the girl who cracked that acorn in the Jacquard factory was responsible for that fire. It's Ubiquitous that's the problem." Huck crossed his arms. "I don't know as I agree," he said. "I knew I was breaking the law. But I'm not going to throw myself in prison."

"What about the election?" Syrah asked.

"If you can believe it, I'm still going to run," said Huck. "In fact, I'm on my way to the Thatch this minute. Go on, now. Harrow will be glad to see you."

Huck left the house, and Syrah climbed the stairs. It seemed to take longer now than it had when he was a frog. His feet were heavy with dread. He knocked at Harrow's door.

"It's me," he said. "Syrah."

"Come in!"

Syrah pushed the door open. Harrow lay against his pillows, glittering. Deli sat in a chair beside him, her expression impassive. Her eyes were on Syrah, but he couldn't detect a trace of emotion in her face. She had never looked so much like her grandmother.

"Prince Syrah of the Olive Isles," said Harrow warmly. "Sorry I threw up on your feet."

"And burned me. And threw me out a window. I should have you beheaded."

"Ha-ha."

"You don't know if I'm joking. For all you know, I'm a miserable tyrant."

"Maybe you used to be," said Harrow. "Now you're not so bad."

"Not so *bad*? I took poison for you, Glitter."

Deli's mouth twitched.

"So you're still sick, huh?" Syrah asked.

"That stuff was brutal," said Harrow. "They said the nausea doesn't usually last this long, but coming right after the Purge, I can't seem to shake it."

"But you will."

"Yeah. I will."

Syrah came to stand beside him. He put a hand on Harrow's shoulder. "Thank you," he said. "For figuring out who I was and for going along with my plan."

"It was a terrible plan. It wasn't even a plan."

"But it worked."

"Barely."

"We're alive," said Syrah. "And I'm human. I'm going to call that a win." He glanced at Deli. "Delicata Aurantia," he said. "Good to see you. How's your father?"

Her expression clouded. The crease between her brows went deep. "Now that they know what's really wrong with him, Physic Feverfew was able to wake him," she said. "But it's bad. He's not himself. I guess he might never be again." She paused. "Thank you," she said, sounding pained. "I'm glad you figured out what really happened."

"Not just me. Give some credit to my friend here."

Harrow looked at him in surprise. "Your what now?"

Syrah shrugged. "My friend," he said. "I hope."

Harrow seemed to consider this. "A royal friend," he said at last. "That could work."

"I'm an eighth child," said Syrah. "The perks aren't great. No private island or anything."

"Well then, never mind."

The two boys grinned at each other. Deli gazed from Harrow to Syrah, apparently at a loss.

"By the way," said Syrah. "You should know, your boy here can't lie to save his life. Literally, he will die."

Harrow yanked the pillow out from behind his head and threw it at Syrah's face as hard as he could, which was pretty hard. Syrah caught it, laughing madly.

It was so, so good to be a man again.

"I'd better get home," said Deli, rising. She reached a hand toward Harrow's shoulder, caught herself, pulled back before touching him. "Feel better," she said distantly.

The way Harrow gazed up at her, Syrah was pretty certain that his friend was not going to feel any better as long as Deli kept a big, frosty wall between them.

That wall was his fault. He had damaged her trust. He owed it to her to at least try to repair it.

Syrah had faced his share of hardship. But this part was going to be the hardest.

"I'll go with you," he said to Deli. "If that's okay."

"Uh . . ." Deli looked uncomfortable. "I guess."

Syrah whacked Harrow with the pillow, then handed it back. "I'll come back soon, all right?" he said. "Try to stop puking." He followed Deli down the stairs and out of the farmhouse.

"I walked," she said. "I wanted some air."

"And some time away from home?"

She didn't answer, but the crease between her brows deepened.

"You can ride with me if you want."

She got into the carriage with him. For a while, they sat in silence. Syrah took the letter out of his pocket and looked down at it, his stomach churning. Suddenly everything he'd written seemed small and stupid.

"What's that?"

"I don't know," said Syrah. "Nothing."

"It's got my name on it."

"Yeah." He handed it to her, cringing. "It's not an apology," he said. "I don't think there's an apology I could make that would fix what I did."

"No." She turned it over in her hands. "So what is it then?"

"It's a confession."

"Confession?"

"Just read it."

Deli opened the letter and unfolded it. "'I, Syrah Huanui, Prince of the Olive Isles, hereby declare that I am guilty of the following crimes.'"

"You don't have to read it out *loud*."

"'Number one,'" said Deli, "'I deliberately played with your feelings. I kissed you to tease you and mess with your head, and then I made fun of your looks and treated you like you were nothing. I did it because I thought I could get away with it, and because I thought it was funny, and because I thought I was better than you. It was cruel. I was wrong. You deserved better.'" She glanced at him, then kept on reading, her voice strong and calm. "'Number two. I took your private, personal writing and I gave it to that scribe at the wedding. I did it to hurt you, because you rejected me. It was vicious. I have no excuse. You deserved better.'"

Deli paused. Her jaw worked back and forth for a moment.

"'Number three. I made fun of you for being serious without understanding anything about your life. But now I've seen you with your family. I see what they expect from you, and how your grandmother treats you. I had no idea how much pressure you were under. I was wrong to judge you. You deserved better. Number four.'" Her voice hardened and her dark eyes turned sharp as knives. "'I confess to thinking you're beautiful and amazing, and I realize now I'm the dumbest thing alive for not liking you back when I had the chance —'"

She stopped abruptly, folded the letter back up, and shoved it into the envelope.

"There's more," said Syrah, his heart beating hard.

"I'm done." Deli shoved the letter at him.

"Keep it. Publish it in the *Criers*. Hang it in the town square."

"It would teach you," she replied.

They rode on in silence. Syrah wished there were something he could do, something he could say that would prove to her that he meant every word of that letter, that he was truly sorry and would take it all back if he could. But there was no getting an egg back in the shell. She was never going to feel that way about him again. Some things, once lost, could never be earned back.

He studied her profile. The tiny moles on her right cheek were shaped almost exactly like a heart. How had he never seen that before? Just one more thing he had noticed too late.

But Harrow had noticed — Syrah would have bet his life on it. Harrow, he was certain, had seen Deli's worth right away. He had appreciated her. And he had never tried to hurt her on purpose.

Syrah had to work hard to get the words going. They were jagged, at first. Painful. He had to force them out.

"You know, your boyfriend almost murdered me when he found out who I was," he managed. "He stood up for you."

Deli was quiet a moment. "We're just friends," she said.

"Is that right? Because I saw you throw a rock at someone's head for him, and I saw the way you kissed him the other day too. Real *friendly*."

"Shut up, Syrah."

"He's a good one, Deli. Maybe even good enough for you." Syrah paused and gathered his strength. He had flung himself against that boiling-hot cup for Harrow, and it had nearly killed him, but in some ways, doing this burned more. "He loves you," he said. "And you love him. Who cares what your grandmother thinks?"

"You still think you know everything," she muttered. "You haven't changed at all."

"You don't think?" He paused. "You were right, by the way."

"Be specific."

"That hole in the ground, out in the woods. That was where I disappeared, just like you thought. I don't know what it is — a fairy, or something else — but I know you were telling the truth when we were kids. You did fall in there, and it lifted you out. It must have thought you deserved to be saved. Me . . ." He gave a brief laugh. "Not so much."

Deli held his gaze a moment. "You were really a frog. All that time."

"I most certainly was."

"What will you do now?"

Syrah was quiet. "I guess I'm going to figure that out," he said. "I can't go back to the way things were." He tried to imagine it. Showing up at Marsala's practice just to laugh at her. Chasing Deli down just to reject her. He didn't think he knew how to do that anymore.

"I meant, are you going back to Balthasar," she said, smiling a little.

"Oh. Yes — soon."

"Your family will be glad to see you."

Would they? It hurt his heart to wonder. He rubbed his chest.

"You should join the launchball team," said Deli after a moment.

Syrah's heart gave another painful beat. She sounded like his nana. "Why?" he asked.

"Because it would be nice to have some real competition next time around."

"I'm not fit for that," he said, gesturing to his new frog gut. "Not anymore."

"Please. I could train you up in three months flat."

"*Train* me? You want to kick me back into shape?"

"Kicking sounds good." Deli eyed him. "If you want, I'll write up a schedule for you, same as the one I follow. It'll get you fit for try-outs. But you have to do everything I tell you. You have to work *hard*. No skipping, no cutting corners. Otherwise it's a waste of my time."

Syrah considered for a moment. "It *would* be pretty fun to beat you at the next ATC."

"Keep dreaming."

"And launchball training won't be nearly as hard as being a frog was . . ."

"You could not be more wrong."

Syrah laughed. "Fine," he said. "I'll do it."

"Good." She raised her voice. "Stop the carriage," she called to the driver, and then turned to Syrah. "Get out and run the rest of the way to the Thatch."

"What?" Syrah cried. "I can't start *now*. I was laid up in bed until this morning! I've barely been human again for three days, and they told me not to exercise yet because of the slumbercap . . ." At the look Deli gave him, he trailed off.

"Excuses, huh?" She crossed her arms. "Forget it. I knew you couldn't —"

"No, I can." Syrah jumped down from the carriage. "I'll run. You go back to Harrow's."

Deli hesitated. "My mother —" she began, but Syrah cut her off.

"I'll tell her you're going to be late. She can handle being on her own for a while."

"She really can't."

"Then I'll help her," said Syrah. "I'll get the boys off her hands, I promise. You go."

Deli sat back. "Okay," she said. "But you better *run*."

Syrah took off and didn't look back. Running was much harder than he remembered — he was tired inside of thirty seconds, and he could barely hear the carriage horses' hooves over the sound of his own labored breathing. Soon enough, he couldn't hear the horses at all. Deli had gone back to Harrow. He tried not to think about how happy they were going to be, making up and getting back together.

Instead, he focused on home. Balthasar. White sand, clear water, warm sun. His room. His family. Launchball, even. He couldn't wait to see the look on Marsala's face when he showed up for team tryouts. Maybe he could leave for the coast tomorrow and be on a ship the day after that.

Nana Cava's room was going to be so empty.

He reached the river and jogged into Market Park, then continued along the riverbank, toward the Thatch. He passed a Vangarden chittering its cheerful song of ripeness at the edge of a melon patch, and he paused. Behind the giant beetle, nearly hidden in the twisting vines, a pair of eyes gleamed.

Syrah strode toward the eyes. "Tsst," he hissed sharply. "Shoo. Get out of here." An orange cat — the very same one that had tried to kill Syrah not long ago — leapt out of its hiding place, meowing angrily at being discovered and deprived of its lunch. It bounded away toward the barns, and Syrah crouched beside the Vangarden.

"You had a brave friend," he said, reaching out his hand to it. "I'm sorry that he died."

The Vangarden stepped forward and tickled his fingers with its antennae. He ran a gentle hand over its smooth carapace, stood, and jogged on. When he came close to the docks, he saw the triplets there, fishing. Or at least, Walter was fishing. Bradley and Tommy appeared to be trying to shove each other into the river.

"There he is!" Tommy gasped. "We can ask him right now."

"Fine, but I'm right!"

Bradley and Tommy rushed Syrah, nearly knocking him down. He held out his hands, laughing. "Whoa there," he said. "What's the question?"

"Was it you who went down Bradley's shirt at the Capital Championships last year?" Tommy demanded. "Were you that same frog?"

"You weren't," said Bradley. "There's no way you were."

"Sorry, Bradley," said Syrah, and Tommy whooped in ecstasy.

"I *told* you!" he crowed. "I told you it was him! You owe me five thorns, or else I get to push you in the river with your clothes on."

"I'm not paying you anything," said Bradley bitterly.

"Then stand on that rock."

Bradley sighed, but stood where he was told. Tommy shoved him hard, sending him into the water with a splash. He crawled back up onto the rocks, drenched.

"I knew you were Rapunzel's frog," said Walter mildly, pulling a fish from his hook and recasting his line.

"What was it like?" asked Tommy. "Did you eat bugs?"

"Of course he didn't eat *bugs*," said Bradley, and he looked so furious and wet that Syrah didn't have the heart to contradict him. "You must've been able to jump pretty high, though."

"That is true."

"It sounds fun," said Tommy. "I'd like to be a frog."

"I can't believe you didn't get anybody to notice who you really were," said Bradley. "It took you fifteen months? You should've spelled out your name in the dirt or something."

"Good point," said Syrah dryly.

"When will you go back to Balthasar?" asked Walter.

"As soon as I can get on a boat," said Syrah. "You'll all come for the Crush this fall, right?"

The boys eyed each other.

"I don't know," said Bradley. "It isn't the same with our families anymore."

"When Nana Cava died, we all went for the funeral," Tommy added. "But we didn't go back for the Crush. And then your family didn't come for the Turning this year."

"Grandmother is too sad," said Walter. "She wants her sister back."

They were all quiet at this.

"Where are all those people going?" Syrah asked momentarily, pointing to the carriages that were filing toward the Thatch. There were dozens of them, and more pulling up all the time.

"The public assembly," said Bradley.

"For the election," said Tommy. "Grandmother Luffa says we still have to have one."

So that was why Huck had been on his way to the Thatch.

"I'd like to see that," Syrah said, but the triplets protested that he had to stay with them and answer their frog questions. "I'll tell you what. If you stay here and fish until supper, I'll eat with you and tell you everything."

They gladly agreed to this arrangement, and Syrah jogged up toward the Thatch, wheezing. His lungs really weren't fully healed — that much hadn't been an excuse — and by the time he reached the house, he was too winded to do anything but walk. He went around the outside of the Thatch until he reached the atrium that connected to the cabinet chamber. The place was packed;

every bench was full and every inch of standing room occupied. Syrah stayed just outside, under the trees that had been planted for Luffa's parents and siblings. He couldn't see much from here, but he could hear Clementine's voice.

"Yes, I knew about the Ubiquitous seeds," she was admitting. "I sanctioned Huck's experiment. The Purge was my doing as much as his, and it would be wrong of me to hold that back. If we're going ahead with this election, then I don't want to win because I was a liar. That's not how we want to start this country's new age of democracy. If the truth disqualifies me, so be it."

"If I'm not disqualified, you're not." The voice was Huck's. "The field is even now. The people can choose their governor based on whose positions they agree with, instead of basing their votes on who did or didn't cause the Purge."

"We want Burdock!" cried a voice, and this single cry quickly became a chant. "BURDOCK! BURDOCK! BURDOCK!"

Syrah listened, sickened and amazed. The story of Hansel and Gretel Rantott had been on the front of the *Criers* for three days. These people knew that Burdock had lied to protect his sister even when she had murdered innocent women and poisoned their governor. How could they want him in charge of the country?

"He hasn't done anything wrong!" shouted a man. "He knows better than anyone the dangers of magic — look at his childhood!"

"He escaped the Witch of the Woods!"

The shouts of support continued until Syrah couldn't stand to listen to them anymore. He stepped away from the atrium, angry, and walked through the ancestral grove until the shouts became too distant to understand. This couldn't be what Luffa had wanted, when she had laid down her crown and given her people the vote.

"Syrah."

He turned, startled, to see Luffa standing at the edge of the grove, looking out over the same pumpkin field where the wedding had taken place, nearly sixteen months ago.

"Grandmother Luffa. I thought you'd be in the assembly."

"I have to keep my distance."

"Why?"

"Because the election was about to collapse," she said. "They were calling for me to step in as provisional governor."

"And this time, you want the country to find its way without you. But what if it doesn't?"

Grandmother Luffa studied him for a long moment. "It will."

"I'm not so sure," said Syrah. "Clementine just admitted she knew about the Ubiquitous seeds. Now all the people are calling for Burdock. They want *him* to be governor."

"Who is to say they are wrong?"

Syrah was shocked. "You think they should elect him?"

"No. But Clementine and Huck both chose to conduct a secret experiment, and the people bore the devastating consequences."

"They never meant to hurt anyone."

"They made their decision without the people's knowledge or support. If the people now feel that they've been done a disservice, they should have the right to elect someone else, even if I disagree. Especially if I disagree." She looked out on the fields again. "You were a frog," she said. "It must have been difficult."

"Not as difficult as beheading a warlord," he replied. "You weren't much older than me, were you?"

"I was eighteen."

"That's pretty amazing for eighteen. Leading an army, ruling a country — all I had to do was hop around for a while."

"I had no idea what I was doing," Luffa answered. "But history has no patience for nuance. One day, they will tell your story, and they will get it wrong."

"Do people get your story wrong?"

Luffa started walking, away from the grove and out through the field. Syrah followed. "Cava wants me to plant vines for her," she said, and she turned back to look at the grove. Syrah stood with her and looked where she pointed. "I think perhaps there."

"Too much shade. Vines need full sun."

"Ah." She studied the back of the Thatch. "It will be the first time anything has been planted here for someone who is not a Gourd."

"Sure she is," said Syrah. "Just like you're a Huanui."

Luffa was silent. Her jaw worked slightly, just as Deli's had in the carriage, and suddenly Syrah felt his own grief swell up from the depths of him, surprising him with its strength.

"I didn't get to go to my nana's funeral," he said. His head suddenly felt like it was stuffed with wool. His ears rang; his eyes were stinging wet. "When you plant those vines," he managed, and then he had to stop and gather himself. "Maybe you'll let me help," he finally mumbled.

She was silent.

"I let her down," he said. "I let you all down, and I'm so sorry. I wish I could tell her I'm sorry."

"She knows," said Luffa quietly. "She sees you."

"You think?"

"The Beyond is like a window at night. Standing inside the lit house and looking out into the darkness, one can see nothing. But from outside in the darkness, everything within is bright." Luffa paused. "She slew the warlord. Not I."

Syrah gaped. "Nana Cava?"

"You knew her. You know it is possible."

Syrah found that he could easily imagine it. He nodded.

"Stories take the shapes they take. My people believed what they needed to believe."

"And it didn't bother my nana?"

"Not at all. She encouraged it."

"What did she think, when you gave up your crown to make Yellow a democracy?"

Luffa chuckled. "Oh, she called me a fool. I told her that *she* was the fool. We stopped speaking for a while, and then she wrote and told me that while she did not understand my choice, she still admired my bravery. She possessed courage of the blood, she said, but I possessed courage of the spirit. She was . . . a singular creature."

They stood together quietly for some time, Syrah contemplating all this.

"You know," he said, after a while. "Delicata's pretty singular."

Luffa narrowed her dark eyes.

"And she's not responsible for my nana's death."

"Stop right there."

"All she wants," said Syrah, determined, "is for you to tell her she's enough. And she *is* enough — she's more than enough, and you know it. She's killing herself to make you proud, but if you don't give her a kind word, and soon, she's going to start hating you — and you're going to lose the only other person around here who's anywhere near as tough as my nana was."

Luffa regarded him for a long moment in silence before she snorted and turned away. She stalked back to the Thatch, leaving him there. But Syrah thought he recognized the tone of that snort, and he felt sure that she had listened.

Alone, he wandered away from the Thatch. At first he didn't mean to take a long walk; he was just appreciating the twilight, and the feeling of his own feet beneath him. He passed through the pumpkin patches and out beyond the fields, until he was at the edge of the woods. Even at dusk, with little light, the greenness from within those woods shone, beckoning to him.

He went in. The cover of trees was so dense that the deeper he went into the wood, the darker it ought to have become, but everything growing here seemed to possess its own light. It really was magic, this place — Syrah could actually feel the cool tingle of its strange power seeping into him like water through a frog's skin. Thick moss glowed faintly beneath him and ran like a river ahead, marking the path and muffling his footsteps as he traveled through the green and silent grove. He knew where he was going.

When he reached the wishing well, he knelt beside it.

It was as deep as ever, and as dark. Syrah looked down into that darkness and wondered what it was that lived there, and why it did the things it did. He couldn't be the only person who had come here and made a foolish wish. Did the well curse everyone who tried? He felt sure that it did not. Why had it chosen him, then — and how had it known him so well? Was it a fairy? Some other creature of the Shattering? There was no way to tell. He supposed he could have wished for the answer, but if his wish went wrong, he might wind up a frog again. Or worse. No, it was better not to fool with wishing wells.

He reached out a hand and dragged it along the inner rim of the well, where the soil was damp and black. The tingling of magic became a vibration, buzzing in his hand like a living thing. It was strong, that energy — but warm. Accepting. It did not want to repel him. He left his hand where it was, touching that soft soil, and he wondered what he would wish now, if he were brave enough to make wishes. He could wish for Yellow Country to get the governor it needed. He could wish for Calabaza to get well. Or for a chance to say good-bye to his nana.

Syrah closed his eyes. He couldn't see Nana Cava again, but he could still become the man she would have wanted him to be. He could make her proud in the Beyond. He could make himself proud.

The soil grew warm beneath his hand. For a fleeting moment, Syrah felt a hand take his own and press it gently, as if to give him strength. Then it was gone, leaving him with a full heart and a sense that he was ready.

"Thank you," he said. And, in spite of everything, he meant it.

EPILOGUE

*I*T had been nearly sixteen months since his disappearance when Prince Syrah stepped off a ship and onto the shore of Balthasar, where his family was waiting. His parents cried and held him. His sisters and brothers welcomed him. They brought him back to the Pavilions, where the Huanuis had gathered from across the islands to welcome him home with food and music and revelry by torchlight.

His place at the long family table, however, had not changed. He was still at the children's end, mostly surrounded by nieces and nephews, so far from his parents that he had no idea what they were discussing with his older siblings.

"I'm glad you're back," said Asti, who sat beside him looking like the young future queen she was. Syrah was startled by the change in his little niece, who was not so little anymore. "How are the triplets?"

"How is Bradley, you mean?" said Syrah, raising an eyebrow. "I heard he kissed you."

"He *tried* to kiss me," she replied. "I prefer Walter. He doesn't say stupid things."

Laughter drifted from the head of the table, where his mother the queen was very much enjoying something that Crown Prince

Taurasi the Perfect had just said. Syrah felt a stab of jealousy. He wished he were part of it.

Maybe he ought to go up there. Sit down with them. Make himself part of it.

He got up, feeling strangely nervous, and went toward his parents. Halfway to his destination, he was stopped by Deli's older brother Christophen, who stood up to greet him, holding a tiny triplet in either arm.

"Congratulations," said Syrah.

"Thanks," said Christophen, who looked exhausted. "Deli just Relayed. She said my pa is doing fine, and I shouldn't come home. Then Ma Relayed and told me she needs me to get on the next ship and help her take care of him, but . . ." He looked down at his babies. "I'm kind of busy," he said. "How was he, when you saw him? Do you think I should head home? Be honest."

"I think you should stay here," said Syrah. "He's not dying."

"She said he wakes up every day thinking it's the day before they left for the ATC."

"It's true," said Syrah. "His mind isn't right anymore — I'm sorry. But he's healthy otherwise. You could probably visit in six months or a year and things would be about the same. He's walking again, a little bit, and he's eating. He's pretty cheerful, actually. He thinks he's governor, and your mother won't let anybody tell him otherwise."

"So he has no idea who won the election."

"Wait — did they publish the results?" said Syrah eagerly. "Who won?"

"I thought you would have heard."

"No, I just got off the boat — who's governor?"

"Nexus Burdock."

The news hit Syrah like a stone in the gut. "That's a mistake," he said. "A big one."

"Technically he didn't commit any crime," said Christophen. "He was a child when he hid his sister from the law, and after thirty years he can't be punished for that."

"I had to talk him out of murdering me and Harrow Steelcut," said Syrah angrily. "But since he didn't actually *do* it, I guess he's still governor material."

"This is why I'm for the monarchy," said his sister Marsanne, looking up from the triplet she was nursing. "Less mess. You know what you're getting."

"What about Clementine Pease?" asked Syrah. "Is she still minister of agriculture, at least?"

"No, Governor Nexus dismissed her and appointed someone else."

Syrah slapped his forehead in frustration. "Luffa never should have pushed for that election so fast."

Christophen looked taken aback. "Have some respect," he said.

"I have great respect," said Syrah. "That doesn't mean I can't think she's wrong."

"And having the election was wrong?"

"She held Declaration Day too soon. She wanted your father out of the race, so she forced things ahead before people had a chance to recover from the Purge. They voted out of fear. They see Burdock as a protector — he's not, but now Yellow is stuck with him. What reason did he even give for getting rid of Clementine?"

"Her ties to Ubiquitous," Christophen replied.

"There are good reasons to be distrustful of Ubiquitous these days," said Marsanne sagely. "Yesterday, the Governor Nexus permanently banned all Ubiquitous products in Yellow Country. The Blue Kingdom did the same."

"Banned them!" said Syrah in surprise.

"Did they really?" said his older brother Carnelian, leaning across the table to get in on the conversation. "That's huge news."

"It was in the *Criers* this morning," said his sister Barbera, who sat near the head of the table. "And I'm personally against it. People use those acorns for help with all sorts of things. You can't just take away something that people rely on — not unless you have a plan to replace it."

"Those acorns are killing people," said Bianca, beside her. "Children died in that Purge. If one of them had been yours, you would feel differently."

"I agree," said Carnelian. "Sometimes, a situation is so urgent that it demands a swift decision, plan or not."

"Exalted Nexus Keene is urging all governments to ban those acorns," said Queen Claret. "Ubiquitous magic is causing widespread chaos. First that terrible fire in Quintessential, then poison in the soil of Cornucopia, and now there are signs that animals are being affected."

"Animals?" said Syrah, surprised. He hadn't heard about this. "Where?"

"Certain violent creatures of Crimson have been seen outside their usual territories," said his mother. "There are reports that dangerous animals all over Tyme are growing in number, as well as rumors of strange, unidentified beasts coming out of the Impassable Swamps."

Maybe this was what Exalted Aravinda had meant when she had talked about the stakes.

"What about here?" Syrah demanded.

"We haven't seen any trouble," said his father. "The benefits of being an ocean away from the mainland are many. But we are seriously considering Nexus Keene's advice. The best way to protect our people may be to rid the islands of Ubiquitous now, before we see negative effects — not after."

Syrah frowned. "Maybe," he said. "But we should do our own investigation. I can tell you from experience that 'Governor Nexus' Burdock, or whatever he's calling himself, is nobody to follow."

"What about the Blue Kingdom?" said Bianca.

"King Clement is weak," said his mother, waving a dismissive hand. "I don't trust him."

"Exactly," said Syrah. "We should handle this our own way. Did Burdock even ask the people if this was what they wanted, or did he just issue a ban?"

"He issued a ban," said Bianca. "He's protecting his people — whether they want those acorns or not, it's still the right thing to do."

"I don't know about that," said Syrah, thinking of his conversation with Luffa. "People want a voice. If Burdock makes a move like that without their consent and support, it will come back to burn him."

His eldest brother, Crown Prince Taurasi the Perfect, had set down his goblet and was staring at him. "Listen to you, little brother," he said. "Paying attention to world government and current events? I never thought I'd see the day."

"Wait until I'm one of your advisors," Syrah replied. "Then you'll be really surprised."

His older siblings chuckled tolerantly, making Syrah bristle. Taurasi smirked. "We'll see," he said, and though Syrah longed to shoot back that he *would* see, he knew better than to say anything else just yet. He would have to do things, get involved, show them he meant it. It was going to take time.

Nearly sixteen months as a frog had taught him plenty.

◆   ◆   ◆

One week later, he sat on the roof of the Pavilions, perched on a wide, white parapet, a spyglass in his hand, watching the Tranquil Sea and waiting. When the ship he was waiting for came into view, he nearly jumped in the ocean and swam out to meet it. Instead, he got up and ran, racing down the stairs and across the Pavilions at top speed. He shimmied behind the waterfalls and, out of habit, stopped under the plumeria tree. If Nana Cava had been alive, he would have picked a flower for her.

He plucked one anyway and twirled the blossom in his fingertips — and then he smiled. He knew someone whose hair he could tuck it into. Nana Cava would have liked her. She was brave as anything.

Syrah ran the rest of the way to the docks and reached them, panting. When the ship finally pulled into port, two people disembarked who made Syrah's heart leap. The boy was short, with dark hair and bright eyes, and the girl was tall, with fair hair that hung to her waist, rippling in the sea breeze and glinting in the sun.

"Rapunzel," Syrah said warmly, when she approached him. He reached out his hands to her, but she did not take them. She gazed at him, unspeaking.

"You're really him?" she said. "Prince Frog?"

Syrah nodded.

"Then . . . he's never coming back. He's really gone for good."

Syrah looked to Jack for help.

"He's literally right in front of you," said Jack. "He's just not a frog anymore."

Rapunzel studied Syrah for another minute. "I'm glad you're a person again, of course, if that's what you want to be, Prince Frog." She stopped. "I mean, Prince Syrah." She stopped again and looked at Jack. "Wait, do I have to say 'Your Highness'?"

"Never," said Syrah. "Look, I know it'll take some getting used to. But I feel like we're friends already — I know so much about you."

"I can't believe you were with us all that time," said Jack. "You heard everything we said — saw everything we did."

"Everything," Syrah agreed. "Every single thing." He grinned in a way that made pink patches flare in Jack's cheeks.

"I've really missed you," said Rapunzel.

"I've missed you too." Syrah tucked the plumeria flower behind Rapunzel's ear. "Welcome to Balthasar," he said. "Come on, I have something for you."

He took the two of them to a little inlet a few leagues down the shore, where a sailboat stood waiting. He had spent most of the week getting it ready for them.

"It's for you," said Syrah. "Both of you. So you can have adventures at sea."

"Are you serious?" said Jack, delighted. "This is amazing."

Rapunzel said nothing. She looked anxiously from the small boat to the big blue ocean, and Syrah knew what she was thinking.

"You took care of me," he said. "You didn't know who I was, but you were always kind — we'll just pretend the part where you almost froze me to death never happened," he said, when Rapunzel looked suddenly guilty. "Let me help you with this. Let me teach you to swim." He held out his hand.

Tentatively, Rapunzel put hers into it. "But I'm scared," she whispered.

He squeezed her fingers. "You've done scarier things."

She seemed heartened by this. "That's true. All right — teach me."

Before the day was out, she had taken her first strokes. Soon after, Syrah was able to coax her onto the sailboat. Inside of a month, she was handling the sails herself, confidently steering around the southern tip of the island and back again. They were nearing the Pavilion docks when Syrah heard a hoarse shout.

"Looking semi-fit, Syrah!"

It was Deli. She stood on the launchball practice platform, tossing the golden ball up into the air and catching it again in rhythm. Syrah motioned for Rapunzel to turn the boat around.

"I thought you weren't coming until tomorrow," he said when they got close enough.

"Grandmother Luffa missed the islands. Said she couldn't wait another day."

Syrah completely understood. "When did you get here?"

"An hour ago. Harrow's at the Pavilions, and he's pretty excited to see you. I cannot for the *life* of me figure out why."

"And you're out here practicing?" he teased, tutting at her. "It's not even the season yet."

"Champions only have one season."

Syrah grinned. "Challenge accepted," he said. "Let's do some training."

Deli set her ball down in a basket. "You have to *earn* the right to train with me."

"By?"

"Beating me. In this race. Go!" She dove into the water and took off.

"Where are we even racing to?" Syrah shouted after her, but she wasn't about to stop. He jumped off the boat and started swimming toward his home, with Rapunzel and Jack cheering behind him.

For a while, he raced as fast as he could go, feeling the beautiful stretch in his arms as they cut through the water, feeling the beautiful burn in his legs as they kicked. Then, lost in the ecstasy of it, he forgot about winning, and Deli, and everything in the world except how good it felt to be right where he was. He rolled onto his back to float in the warm sea, and he gazed up at the blue sky, his heart full to bursting, laughing simply because he could.

ACKNOWLEDGMENTS

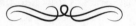

This book exists because of
Ruth Virkus
Nick Thomas
Cheryl Klein
Kristin Brown
Devin Smither
Ben Layne
David Carpman
Kathy MacMillan
Melissa Anelli
Gerry and Mike Morrison
Malcolm and Elinor
Reign
my students
and coffee.

ABOUT THE AUTHOR

Megan Morrison is a middle-school teacher and a writer. She cofounded the Harry Potter fan fiction site the Sugar Quill, and has been developing the world of Tyme since 2003. She lives near Seattle, Washington, with her family. Please visit her website at meganmorrison.net and follow her on Twitter at @megtyme.

This book was edited by Cheryl Klein and Nick Thomas and designed by Baily Crawford. The production was supervised by Melissa Schirmer. The text was set in Adobe Jenson, with display type set in Bitstream Arrus BT. The book was printed and bound at LSC Communications in Crawfordsville, Indiana. The manufacturing was supervised by Angelique Browne.